A Haven for Her Heart

Books by Susan Anne Mason

COURAGE TO DREAM

Irish Meadows
A Worthy Heart
Love's Faithful Promise

A Most Noble Heir

CANADIAN CROSSINGS

The Best of Intentions
The Highest of Hopes
The Brightest of Dreams

REDEMPTION'S LIGHT

A Haven for Her Heart

❖ Redemption's Light · 1 ❖

A Haven for Her Heart

Susan Anne Mason

BETHANYHOUSE
a division of Baker Publishing Group
Minneapolis, Minnesota

© 2020 by Susan A. Mason

Published by Bethany House Publishers
11400 Hampshire Avenue South
Bloomington, Minnesota 55438
www.bethanyhouse.com

Bethany House Publishers is a division of
Baker Publishing Group, Grand Rapids, Michigan

Printed in the United States of America

ISBN 978-0-7642-3519-1 (paper)
ISBN 978-0-7642-3780-5 (casebound)

Scripture quotations are from the New Revised Standard Version of the Bible, copyright © 1989 National Council of the Churches of Christ in the United States of America. Used by permission. All rights reserved.

This is a work of historical reconstruction; the appearances of certain historical figures are therefore inevitable. All other characters, however, are products of the author's imagination, and any resemblance to actual persons, living or dead, is coincidental.

Cover design by Koechel Peterson & Associates, Inc., Minneapolis, Minnesota/Jon God-fredson

Author is represented by Natasha Kern Literary Agency.

20   21   22   23   24   25   26   7   6   5   4   3   2   1

In memory of Velma Demerson,
whose real-life story of incarceration
at the Mercer Reformatory for Women
inspired Olivia's journey.

A Note from the Author

Dear Reader Friends,

Writing a book about a maternity home has been on my mind for quite some time. When I originally wrote *A Most Noble Heir*, I'd envisioned a sequel to Nolan and Hannah's story, featuring Hannah's younger sister, Molly, who would open a maternity home—or a home for wayward girls—in Victorian England. However, that book never materialized, and the idea sat on the back burner for quite a while.

Then, while brainstorming a new series for Bethany House, the idea came up again. Right around this time, I read a disturbing story in the paper about a woman named Velma Demerson, who was arrested in Toronto in the 1930s for being pregnant and unmarried. I kept the newspaper clipping about the harrowing details of her life, and it occurred to me that Olivia Rosetti, my heroine for the first book in the REDEMPTION'S LIGHT series, would need a compelling reason to open such a facility. Velma's story provided the inspiration for that.

In the meantime, I learned that Velma had written a book entitled *Incorrigible* about her experience in the Andrew Mercer Reformatory for Women (or "the Mercer," for short), and

I ordered a copy. It was not an easy book to read at times. The horrors she endured were beyond description, but it captured me so thoroughly that I decided to use her experience as a catalyst for my heroine.

I wanted you to know this before you read Olivia's story, which is a little grittier than the usual books I've written. But the horrors that Olivia goes through really happened to Velma and to many other incarcerated women. Eventually, the Mercer Reformatory was closed down, but not until 1969—thirty years after Velma's stay there. It's hard to imagine such atrocities occurring so recently in our history.

In her later years, Velma gained the courage to sue the Ontario government for her mistreatment. She continued campaigning for an apology and seeking restitution for all women who had been incarcerated under the same law that had imprisoned her, right up until she passed away in 2019 at the age of ninety-eight.

That being said, I hope you enjoy Olivia's journey—how her search for respectability and healing leads her to help other women and how Darius teaches her the value of unconditional love while mirroring God's love for each one of us. (Of course, Darius's journey is not without a few bumps of its own!)

Until next time, my profound appreciation for your support and encouragement!

Susan

*I have swept away your transgressions
like a cloud, and your sins like mist;
return to me, for I have redeemed you.*

Isaiah 44:22

Prologue

Toronto, Ontario, Canada
November 1939

Olivia Rosetti turned up the volume on the radio in the empty parlor. Thankfully, her parents had gone out to a church meeting tonight, giving her the rare gift of a few hours alone. With her older brother out for the evening as well, she could listen to the radio on her own for as long as she wished, without Leo and Papà arguing, and Leo getting so angry that he'd snap the machine off. Ever since Leo had failed the army physical due to a heart murmur, he hated all reports of the war. Especially since their brother Tony, one year younger than Leo, had passed all the tests and was headed overseas. Her youngest brother, Salvatore, safely cocooned at the seminary, was likely oblivious to the fact that the world was embroiled in conflict.

Olivia twisted the dial until the static lessened and the deep voice of the broadcaster boomed through. Surely there would be news of the war at the top of the hour. Not that it would give her any details of her fiancé Rory's fate. Or Tony's. But listening to reports of the Canadian troops and their whereabouts helped her feel closer to both of them. In those moments, she could picture Rory in his uniform aboard the deck of a ship, heading to Britain to fight for freedom from Hitler's tyranny.

Oh, Rory, why did you have to join the war so soon? If you'd known about my situation, would it have stopped you from going?

She ran a hand over the slight swell of her abdomen, a sick sense of dread rising through her. Last night, with no options left, she'd finally divulged her secret to her mother, who, despite Olivia's protests, had immediately told her father. As expected, Enrico Rosetti had not taken the news well at all.

Olivia's hand instinctively went to her cheek, still tender from her father's blow.

"Did you ever consider how your sins would affect the family? That it could jeopardize your brother's calling?" he'd shouted, eyes wild. *"Taking up with an Irishman was bad enough, but this? You are a disgrace to the Rosetti name."*

Only her mother's tearful pleas had stopped Papà's tirade, half in English, half in Italian. Then, with a last curse word, he'd slammed out of their apartment over the store and stomped down the stairs, off to drown his sorrows with his comrades. Olivia prayed he hadn't told them the reason why he was drinking that night.

Static from the radio crackled over the room. Olivia fiddled with the tuner, attempting to get a clearer signal.

"Eight people were killed and sixty-two injured in Munich last night in a failed attempt to assassinate Adolf Hitler. The German leader, who had been speaking only moments before the bomb went off, was unharmed."

She twisted her fingers together at the mere mention of the dictator's name. Would the war have ended if the assassin had been successful? She breathed a prayer for forgiveness for wishing such a thing. Yet it seemed this one man continued to wreak havoc on the entire world, and she couldn't really blame someone for trying to eliminate him.

On some level, Olivia was proud of Rory for wanting to defend his country against such a despot. But on the other hand, she wished he hadn't been quite so patriotic. Quite so willing to leave her behind.

A loud knock sounded on the door. Olivia's heart began to race. Who would be coming here at this hour? Everyone in the neighborhood knew the store was closed, and most of her parents' friends would be at the church hall. Leo was at the local tavern playing pool with his friends and wouldn't be home until the wee hours.

She clutched the threadbare arm of the chair, a shiver of foreboding racing through her. "Who is it?"

"Toronto Police. Open the door, please."

The police? What did they want? Had someone been in an accident?

Heart in her throat, Olivia smoothed her hair and removed her apron, draping it over the armchair. Taking a deep breath, she crossed the room and opened the door.

A large man in uniform stood on the landing. "Are you Miss Olivia Rosetti?"

"Y-yes."

A flicker of emotion passed over his granite features. "I'm here to inform you that you are under arrest."

"Arrest? For what?" Her hand flew to her throat. Was this a joke? There had to be some sort of mistake.

"You are charged under the Female Refuges Act with being incorrigible. I'm afraid you're going to have to come with me."

"What does that mean? I don't understand. . . ." Her legs trembled so hard beneath her pleated skirt that she grasped the hall table for support.

A glimmer of sympathy shone in the man's eyes. "Your father has taken out a warrant against you. He claims that you are unmarried, under the age of twenty-one, and . . ." He hesitated, his gaze sweeping her slender form. ". . . with child."

Heat flooded her face, but she held her head high. "That may be undesirable, but surely it's not a crime."

"I'm afraid it is. Granted, it's not a law I've had to enforce very often, but when a complaint is made, we must act."

Her mind spun, still unable to grasp what the officer was telling her. "My fiancé left for the war, otherwise we would already be married." A tiny but desperate fib. "As soon as he comes back, we'll . . ." She trailed off at the immovable set to the man's jaw.

"I'll give you a minute to get ready. Then I have to take you down to the police station."

April 1941

Freedom. Open spaces without any horrid, confining bars. Olivia had craved this luxury for almost eighteen months, yet now that she was finally released from prison, the reality fell far short of what she'd imagined.

Her blue plaid work dress and navy cardigan hung loose, offering little warmth against the chilly spring air as she trudged along King Street, carrying her near-empty handbag. With each block she traveled, her sense of panic increased.

Freedom, it turned out, came with a whole new set of problems, proving she wasn't really free at all.

Instead, she was homeless, penniless, and friendless. Where could she go? Did she dare darken her parents' doorstep? Without even enough money for bus fare, it could take an hour to reach her family's store on foot. If she did, and she was able to get her mother alone, would Mamma help her? Or would obedience to Papà keep her from aiding her only daughter?

Olivia's steps faltered. Unused to walking for so long at a time, her feet screamed in protest. Blisters burned on her toes and heels. Her shoulders sagged forward, as if unwilling to bear the burden of her problems. But with little choice, she forced herself to plod on.

Just when she thought she couldn't continue, a familiar street sign appeared above her. *Kensington Avenue.* A few blocks farther west and she'd reach Rosetti's Market. Her stomach growled and curled in on itself, the gruel she'd eaten for her last meal at the Mercer Reformatory long since burned off. The little extra weight she'd put on during her pregnancy had been stripped away by long hours of laboring at the sewing machines in the reformatory factory. That, along with the meager food rations, had left her much thinner than before her incarceration.

Olivia approached the storefront with caution, her steps slowing as conflicting emotions swirled within her. How she'd dreamt of this moment every day during her confinement, of returning to the sights and sounds of the store. The vision of Mamma in her apron at the front counter, laughing at the chatter of the Italian ladies as they chose their vegetables. The smell of overripe fruit on sale at the front aisle. The clang of the cash register opening and closing. She'd missed everything about her home, her mother most of all. In a family of men, she and Mamma were kindred spirits, always sharing a secret smile, a knowing wink.

But a nagging worry dimmed the excitement of Olivia's homecoming. Would Papà allow her to come back? Surely she'd paid for her sins and had earned admittance back into the family. But deep down, part of her railed against asking for aid from the man who'd caused her suffering in the first place.

Forgiveness, preached so easily from the tongue of the prison chaplain, sat hard on her unwilling spirit.

But if humility granted her a place to lay her head while awaiting Rory's return, then she would swallow her pride and bide her time. Once this dreadful war was over and her fiancé came home, maybe then she could put the past eighteen months of misery behind her. Her hand rested on her flat abdomen, and the perpetual ache in her chest intensified. Would that even be possible after all she'd lost?

A lone figure stepped out onto the sidewalk beside the crates of apples and oranges and began to sweep the dirt from the entrance.

Mamma!

Her heart leapt at the sight of her mother's kerchief and apron, head bent in concentration on her task. Unbidden tears burned Olivia's eyes. How she'd missed Mamma's comforting touch while she was locked away these many months, treated worse than a caged animal in a laboratory. How she'd longed for her mother's love, her words of encouragement, her home-cooked food that cured every ill or worry.

Olivia's steps quickened, a smile tugging her lips upward. "Mamma," she cried, emotion strangling her voice.

Her mother looked up. The broom dropped to the ground as she rushed toward Olivia and clasped her in a tight embrace.

"Oh, *mia preziosa ragazza.*"

The whispered words of endearment washed over her soul like a balm. After kissing Olivia's cheeks, her mother wiped her eyes with her apron.

"You are too thin," Mamma clucked as she held her by the shoulders. "You need to eat."

As if in answer, Olivia's stomach growled. She laughed at her mother's raised eyebrows.

"I am hungry, Mamma. Is there anything left from the noon meal?"

"*Sì.* There's some soup and—" Mamma stopped, a sudden frown wrinkling her brow. "We must not let your father find you here. Come around to the back."

Olivia straightened, her gut giving a painful lurch. So Papà had not forgiven her, just as she'd suspected.

Mamma grabbed her arm, and they slipped like thieves down the side alley to the rear entrance into the storeroom. Bypassing the storage bins, they climbed the narrow staircase up to their apartment. Mamma moved swiftly into the kitchen, opening the icebox to remove a large cast-iron pot. Olivia's mouth watered just thinking of the delicious meal it might contain. Minestrone soup, perhaps?

A large loaf of bread sat on the cutting board on the counter. Olivia hesitated, then hunger overcame her reticence, and she reached for the knife to cut a thick slab. After slathering on a layer of butter, she took a large bite. Never had anything tasted so good.

Mamma ladled the soup into a bowl. "It's cool now, but it will fill your belly."

"Cold is fine, Mamma."

Olivia pulled out a chair at the table, the same green tablecloth she remembered still in place. She gulped down several spoonfuls of the soup, relishing the burst of flavors she'd almost forgotten existed. Prison fare had been bland at best. She swallowed, glancing around her old home. It seemed like forever since she'd been here, yet nothing had changed. The same worn sofa and armchair. The same radio on the rickety table in the corner.

Down the narrow hall, all appeared unchanged as well. The door to their parents' room was closed as usual. Neither she nor her brothers ever dared venture in there without an invitation. The door to Leo's room sat slightly ajar. And her door, the first one visible, was also closed. Would Mamma have left Olivia's room exactly as it had been before she'd been banished?

"I do not think he will allow you to return." Her mother's soft voice was filled with regret. Sorrow clouded her dark eyes, now etched with many more worry lines than two years ago.

Before this horrible war had started.

Before Olivia had made the worst mistake of her life.

"I want to come home, Mamma. What can I do to make it so?"

Mamma shook her head and turned away to return the soup pot to the icebox.

Footsteps stomped on the stairs. "Rosina? *Sei qui?*"

The spoon in Olivia's hand trembled, spilling liquid onto the tablecloth.

Her mother sent her a panicked look. "Go to your room. I will talk to him."

Olivia stood and headed toward the bedroom, her instinct to run quickening her pulse. But then she stopped. "No. I will face my father. I will not hide."

"Olivia, please." Mamma's eyes went wide, darting to the stairs.

A second later, Papà appeared in the doorway. The moment he spied Olivia, he came to a halt, the rag rug skidding beneath his feet. The color drained from his face, and, for an instant, Olivia thought she saw a flicker of happiness flash in his eyes.

She took a tentative step toward him. "Papà."

He held up a hand, his features hardening, and turned furious eyes on Mamma. "How dare you defy me and bring her here?" he said in Italian. Papà only used English when absolutely necessary.

"Enrico. *Per favore . . .*" Mamma cowered behind the table.

Why had Olivia never realized what a tyrant her father was? How he bullied everyone into submission? Outrage sparked her courage, and she stepped forward, shoulders squared. "It's not Mamma's fault. Don't be mad at her."

His dark brows formed a solid line over his eyes. He crossed his arms, his stance combative.

Her legs shook, from fear or fury she couldn't tell, yet she didn't retreat. Ugly words, accusatory words, circled her brain, but before she said something she couldn't take back, she worked to rein in her emotions. Despite what he'd done to her, despite how he treated her mother, Olivia had to be smart. She needed a place to live. Needed to be with Mamma again. And somewhere underneath her anger and pain, she still loved her father. She had to try to mend the rift in their relationship. Taking a deep breath, she made a deliberate attempt to humble her attitude. "Papà, I've come to ask for your forgiveness. And to see if I can please come home."

Several seconds ticked by, then her father grunted. "*Il bambino*?"

Olivia's muscles seized with a spasm of grief, now as familiar to her as breathing. Clenching her hands into fists, she held her head high. "They took him from me, as you knew they would. They put him up for adoption."

Her mother gasped. Her father remained silent.

"*Un ragazzino*?" Mamma's sorrowful whisper sliced through Olivia's stoic calm.

Her throat closed up, and she could only nod. Yes, a little boy. Her son, Matteo, whom she got to hold for only a few precious minutes before he was ripped from her arms.

Her father shook his head. The coldness in his eyes sent a shiver down Olivia's spine. "We no longer have a daughter. You are not welcome here." He turned to point a finger at Mamma. "Rosina, you are needed in the store." Without a backward glance, he disappeared down the staircase.

Tears slid down Mamma's cheeks. "I'm sorry, *cara*."

Olivia's lips trembled. Part of her wished her mother would stand up to Papà. Tell him that Olivia was their daughter and that of course they would forgive her. But Mamma couldn't risk the wrath of Enrico Rosetti being turned on her.

"I'll just get some of my clothes, then." Swallowing hard to hold back the tears that begged for release, Olivia went down the hall to her room and pushed open the creaky door. Her jaw dropped. The room had been stripped bare, with nothing but the bed in the middle, leaving it more sterile than her cell at the reformatory had been. All her photos, her bulletin board with her awards from school, all gone.

She rushed to open the closet. Only barren wire hangers swung there. She turned to see her mother wringing her hands in the doorway. "Mamma, where are my things?"

"He . . . he got rid of them."

"He what?"

Olivia scrambled to the scarred wooden dresser, yanking open drawer after drawer. Every one empty. Her lips quivered. All her clothes, her mementos from childhood, and—most importantly—all Rory's gifts to her, gone. Her mind struggled to remember what treasures she'd hidden there. The book of poetry where Rory had inscribed words of love, the dried rose pressed between the pages, and the silver locket he'd given her for her eighteenth birthday. She sank onto the soft mattress, grief fresh in her throat.

"I managed to save a few things." Mamma reached under the bed and drew out a cloth bag. She undid the drawstring and revealed a few pieces of clothing and a battered cigar box. Then she drew the string tight again. "You can look at them later. I must go." She pushed the bag into Olivia's arms.

"Mamma, did Rory send any letters here from the army?" She yearned for any word of him. Proof that he was still alive and that he missed her as much as she missed him.

It had been hard enough not having any member of her family visit her for the past eighteen months. But not receiving any word from Rory had been sheer torture. She had no idea if her letters had reached him, if he even knew she'd been pregnant, or that she'd given birth to their son. In her dreams, she'd imagined Rory leaving the war to come to her rescue. But she'd never heard a single word from him.

Her mother looked away. "Oh, *cara*."

"Papà destroyed those too?" Why was her father so cruel? But then again, he'd always despised Rory, "a filthy Irishman" he called him, and likely blamed him for leading his daughter astray.

"*Mi dispiace*."

"Why are you sorry? It wasn't your doing." Bitterness coated Olivia's tongue. Her mind whirled with the unfairness of all that had happened to her. If God was out there, He was certainly exacting His punishment. "I'll just have to wait for Rory to come home, then. Papà can't keep us from being together."

Mamma shook her head, tears glittering in her eyes. "Oh, Olivia. He isn't coming home."

Olivia's heart slowed to a dull throb in her chest. "Of course he is. As soon as this ridiculous war is over." Or maybe sooner. She'd even prayed that he would be injured, just a little, enough to warrant them sending him home to recuperate. Was that selfish of her? Her fingers tightened on the drawstring.

"No, *cara mia*. Rory . . ." She hesitated. "Rory *è morto*."

Olivia's head jerked up so fast she bit her tongue. "Dead? No. That's not possible."

Her mother's face crumpled. "*Sì, cara.* Eileen came to the store to tell us. They got a telegram three months ago."

"She came here?" Olivia heard her own voice echo in the empty room. If his sister had come to the store, then it must be true.

Her hands shook, her heart shriveling in her chest as the ache spread outward and the horrible words sank in. Mamma would have no reason to lie. No cause to deceive her. But how had Olivia not known? Surely if she and Rory were soul mates, she would have felt his absence from this earth.

The distance she'd felt from Rory since he left to join the war now widened into an unending chasm, one that could never be crossed. She'd clung to their unborn child as the one tangible bond connecting them, but when the authorities had torn baby Matteo from her arms, Olivia's hope had wavered.

Once Rory is home and I'm with him again, she'd told herself, *all will be back to normal. We will overcome this loss together.*

Now that would never happen.

A keening wail escaped her throat as she bent forward over her knees. "No. No. He can't be gone. They made a mistake. He's coming back to me."

Mamma laid a hand on her back. "Mi dispiace," she said again. "May God have mercy on you both."

———— ❧ ————

Ruth Bennington stood on the sidewalk in front of St. Olaf's Church and simply stared at the beauty of the building before her. As usual, the beckoning lights from within penetrated the inky dusk, seeming to reach out and draw her inside. With a weary sigh, she climbed the stairs leading to the front door, grasped the metal handle, and let herself into the vestibule. The calming scent of candlewax and sulfur greeted her.

"Well, Lord. Will tonight be any different? Or will you see fit to grant my request at last?"

Ruth moved farther into the sanctuary until she came to her usual pew. She made the sign of the cross and sat down on the hard bench, relishing the feel of the unyielding wood beneath her.

On the altar in front of her, two tiny flames flickered. Even in the dim interior, Ruth could make out the stained-glass windows and the paintings of the saints that adorned the pale walls.

How long had she been coming to this place to worship? Forty years? Maybe closer to fifty. Ever since she and Henry had moved to Toronto as newlyweds. A soft smile curved her lips. They'd been so young back then, so naïve, with no idea where life would take them or when their roads would diverge.

Almost involuntarily, her eyes moved to the plaque under the window nearest her. *In memory of Henry Ward Bennington. Gone from us too soon. From his loving wife, Ruth.*

A lone tear wound its way down her cheek.

It's time, Lord. Not that I can tell you how to manage things. But I've been alone for years now. I'm tired. I want to see my Henry again.

With a gloved finger, she wiped the moisture from her face and began her prayer ritual. If she were fortunate and tonight was indeed the night God chose to grant her request, she'd make sure she was ready.

Two hours later, Ruth hauled her stiff frame up from the seat, disappointment her usual companion. God had not let the life seep from her while she prayed. If only she could muster the courage, she'd do the deed herself, but images of hellfire and damnation kept her feet firmly rooted to this earth.

"Thy will be done," she whispered, as she did every night when leaving the church.

The depressing prospect of returning home alone made her bones ache. At least when Henry had first passed away, she'd had her grandson, Thomas, living with her, so the mausoleum of a house hadn't felt so empty. But since the boy had moved out two years ago after they'd quarreled, Ruth had done nothing but pray for her own death. A prayer that maddeningly had gone unanswered.

She shuffled past the pews, almost too weary to lift her feet. If she hadn't paused for a brief moment at the last row, she likely wouldn't have heard the soft moan that drifted through the air. Ruth froze, straining her ears. Had she imagined the sound?

A second later, a slight movement caught her attention. She swiveled, peering down at a huddled figure lying on the bench. Long dark hair spilled over the woman's face, obscuring her features. She shuddered and moaned again.

Was she ill?

Ruth glanced around the empty building, a shiver of nerves rushing through her. Maybe the woman wasn't in her right mind. Maybe she had some contagious disease.

Or maybe, like Ruth, she'd come here to pray for death.

Ruth gathered her courage and approached her. "Hello? Are you in need of help?"

The woman moved, swiping her hair from her face as she attempted to sit up. "*Sì, per favore.*" She was hardly more than a girl. But her eyes were glassy and her cheeks feverishly red.

Ruth took a step back. "Are you ill? Can I call someone for you?"

The girl leaned back against the pew, head lolling. "No one to call."

No one? How could that be? Such a lovely young thing. Or she would be when she was cleaned up. "Where do you live, dear?"

The girl shook her head. "Nowhere."

Ruth straightened. She may have led a somewhat sheltered life, but she knew when someone was in trouble, and this girl was hanging on by a thread. "Wait here. I'll be right back."

She rushed out of the church, a new energy to her step. Tonight the pastor would earn every penny of his meager paycheck and leave his warm bed to give them a ride to her house.

2

Olivia awoke slowly, certain she must be dreaming. Never had she felt such a soft mattress, one that smelled of lilac and lavender. Maybe she'd died and gone to heaven. If so, she didn't want to open her eyes. She'd just float into eternity on this cloud of comfort.

Firm fingers touched her wrist, staying there for a time before moving to her forehead.

Mamma. Taking her temperature as she did when Olivia was young.

She fought to force her heavy lids open. Only for Mamma would she give up heaven.

She blinked, trying to focus on the figure in front of her.

"How is she, Doctor?" a strange woman asked.

Not Mamma.

"Her fever is coming down. The medicine must be starting to work."

A vest with silver buttons was the only thing Olivia could seem to focus on. She squinted, and the face of a man came into view.

"Hello, young lady. Nice to see you awake."

"Where am I?" Definitely not in her jail cell and definitely not at home. Nor was she in the church where she last remembered being.

"You're in my home" came the female voice. "I'm Ruth Bennington. And this is my physician, Dr. Henshaw."

Olivia's gaze shifted from the surprisingly young man to a tall, slender woman behind him. Her gray hair was pinned up, her eyes gleamed with intelligence, and she wore an air of authority. Enough authority to make Olivia tremble beneath the quilt. She'd met women like this at the reformatory and had learned to stay out of their way. Because once someone in charge noticed you, there was nothing but pain.

"It's all right, dear," the woman said. "I found you in St. Olaf's Church, almost delirious. Reverend Dixon and I brought you here, and I called Dr. Henshaw."

The man smiled. "You've been here two days, and I think you've finally turned the corner." He reached for the stethoscope he wore around his neck. "If you'll permit me, I'd like to listen to your heart again."

Olivia's breath caught in her chest, alarm spurting through her.

"I'll give you some privacy." Mrs. Bennington turned to leave the room.

"No!" Olivia clenched the covers and pulled them higher, the image of the reformatory's medical clinic springing to mind. Once that door closed and you were alone, unspeakable things occurred.

The older woman turned back, eyebrows raised. "I promise you're in capable hands with Dr. Henshaw."

"And believe me, Mrs. Bennington doesn't say that about everyone." The doctor winked at Olivia.

"Please stay." The words came out so softly she doubted the woman had heard.

But Mrs. Bennington nodded. "Very well. I'll sit over here in the corner."

Olivia's hand relaxed, releasing the covers, but she eyed the doctor warily. He was under thirty, she estimated, and quite nice-looking with neatly trimmed brown hair and kind eyes.

The doctor gave her a small smile, then listened to her heart, looked into her eyes, ears, and mouth, and finally sat back with a satisfied expression. "I believe the infection is almost gone. For now, drink plenty of fluids and take the medication I left with Mrs. Bennington." He rose and picked up his bag. "I'll be back tomorrow to see how you're doing. I predict a huge improvement in the next twenty-four hours."

Olivia's lips cracked as she tried to smile. Perhaps she had misjudged the man. "Thank you."

"You're most welcome. Good day, ladies."

Mrs. Bennington rose from her chair. "Thank you again, Doctor. I appreciate your diligence."

"I can show myself out." He gave a slight bow and left the room.

Olivia released a long breath, and rather than face the woman's curious regard, she took in her surroundings. The room was enormous, bigger than her parents' kitchen and parlor combined. Red flocked wallpaper graced the walls, and an ornate mirror sat above a dark wood vanity. On the far right was a large fireplace, where a fire burned in the grate. Overhead, a chandelier with little crystals shimmered, catching the glow from the embers.

"I hope you'll be comfortable here," Mrs. Bennington said. "My room is right down the hall if you need anything."

Olivia nodded, still struggling to comprehend how this stranger had brought her into her home.

"Can you tell me your name?" Mrs. Bennington's bright blue eyes stared at Olivia expectantly.

"Olivia Rosetti," she said.

"Olivia. A pretty name for a pretty girl." Mrs. Bennington smiled softly. "Are you hungry or thirsty, dear?"

Olivia's first thought was to refuse, so used to going without. But her parched throat and cracked lips begged for moisture. "Thirsty."

The woman's features relaxed. "I'll have some tea and water

brought up immediately. And maybe a bit of chicken broth, if the cook has any handy. You rest and don't worry about a thing."

At the door, the woman paused and looked back over her shoulder. "I don't know what circumstances brought you to the church, but you're welcome to stay here for as long as you need. No questions asked."

Olivia pressed her lips together. Moisture built behind her lids and she blinked hard. Her throat worked, but no words would come, so she simply nodded, hoping the woman would understand her gratitude.

Seemingly satisfied, Mrs. Bennington left the room.

Dr. Henshaw returned the next day to check on Olivia. True to his prediction, she had experienced a fair improvement in her health. She was able to sit up in bed and had taken some toast and tea.

This time, Olivia allowed the doctor to conduct his examination without Mrs. Bennington in the room. The man's gentleness and caring attitude inspired Olivia's trust. She studied him as he opened his bag to retrieve his instruments. He had hair the color of the chestnuts sold in Papà's store and a mouth that rested in a natural smile. His hazel eyes held warmth and concern, unlike the cold, empty stare of the Mercer's female physician.

Once Dr. Henshaw had taken her temperature and listened to her heart and lungs, he looped his stethoscope around his neck and pulled a chair closer to the bed. When he sat down and pinned her with a serious gaze, Olivia's heart began to thump heavily in her chest.

"Miss Rosetti, I'd like to speak frankly if I may." His tone, though professional, vibrated with concern.

Olivia gripped the blankets. Had he found something else wrong with her? What if the rumors at Mercer were true and the tests they had performed on her weren't really tests at all? That might account for her contracting this mysterious infection. She glanced at the doctor, attempting to gauge his demeanor, but his handsome features gave nothing away.

Anxiety fluttered in her lungs. "Is the infection back?"

"It seems under control for now," he said carefully. "But what I wasn't able to determine was the source of the infection." He paused. "Have you been around anyone who's been ill? A family member? Someone in the workplace?"

Heat crawled up Olivia's neck. Images of several Mercer inmates flew to mind before she could steel herself against them. The persistent hacking coughs that many of the women endured. The rumors of other, nastier infections that some inmates carried. Could she have contracted something life-threatening from them?

"Miss Rosetti?"

She bit her lip. He would need to know her background in order to help her. "I was recently released from the Mercer Reformatory for Women. It . . . wasn't a very sanitary place."

His eyes widened, but his expression remained calm. "I see. May I ask how long you were there?"

"Almost eighteen months. I got out early for good behavior." Ironic when she was deemed *incorrigible*.

"Was this the only time you were ill while there?"

If only she could crawl beneath the bed and hide. Ignore his inquiries that would only lead to more questions she had no desire to answer.

She shook her head. "I developed an infection after . . ."

"After?" Dr. Henshaw prompted gently.

She lifted her chin and gave him a defiant stare. Bitterness coated the back of her mouth. Let him judge her if he dared. "After the birth of my son. They refused to let me nurse and took him away."

"You gave birth in prison?"

"In the hospital. I stayed there for several days before they brought me back to the reformatory. Without my son." Her body began to shake, recalling the grief that had left her debilitated for weeks and the phantom pain of the child no longer in her womb.

"That is most unfortunate, Miss Rosetti. I'm sorry you had to go through that."

Olivia couldn't respond, his sympathy suddenly too much to bear. No one except Mamma had shown her the smallest morsel of compassion.

They sat in silence for several seconds, until he cleared his throat. "Other than that, were you healthy? No further complications from the pregnancy?"

"No."

The doctor folded his hands on his lap. "I don't know quite how to say this, but I feel I must ask."

Her stomach tightened, as though expecting a blow. She waited, hardly daring to breathe.

"Were you . . . mistreated in the reformatory?"

All the air left Olivia's lungs. Mistreated? If only he knew the half of it. The truth begged to be said, but she had no idea how to phrase the words.

"By the other inmates?" he asked. "By the authorities?"

She shook her head. Not in denial of his inquiry, but to let him know she couldn't talk about the atrocities that had occurred. Could never speak of them to anyone.

"I know this is a delicate topic," he continued, "but I would be remiss to ignore the warning signs."

What signs? What had he seen? She curled her arms around her body in a protective manner, trying to shield herself.

Dr. Henshaw removed the stethoscope from his neck and placed it in his bag. "While you were unconscious, I had to conduct an exam to try and ascertain the cause of your condition."

Heat scorched Olivia's cheeks, visions of the prison infirmary clouding her mind. The horrid metal bed with the stirrups. The

31

tray of heinous-looking instruments. The soulless eyes of the doctor. Her lips quivered, and she pressed her hands into fists. But no words would come out.

"There are indications from the numerous needle marks and what appear to be random incisions around your . . . private parts," he said gently, "that you might have been the victim of some unorthodox surgical procedures." He leaned forward, his forehead wrinkled. "Did someone violate you, Miss Rosetti?"

A sob broke free from her aching throat, unleashing a hot flood of tears. She crumpled back against the pillow, her eyes squeezed shut as every indignity she'd worked so hard to suppress came back in a rush. The leather straps pinning her down, the horrific injections, the slice of the scalpel with nothing to numb the pain, followed by burning chemical treatments. Returning to her cell to suffer alone, praying for death to claim her.

Olivia rocked back and forth on the bed. How could the officials allow the prison doctor to perform such despicable acts? A female doctor, at that. One who should have had compassion for other women. Why hadn't anyone in charge tried to stop her?

"It's all right, dear." A soothing female voice finally broke through Olivia's anguish. "You're safe now. No one is going to hurt you again."

When at last the storm of tears was spent, Olivia opened her eyes. Mrs. Bennington sat beside her on the bed, while Dr. Henshaw hovered by the dresser. The distress on his face made Olivia wonder if perhaps he hadn't had a chance to impart his bad news after all.

"Am I dying?" she croaked out.

The doctor came forward, his expression grim. "No, Miss Rosetti. You are not dying. I promise you that."

Mrs. Bennington handed her a handkerchief, sending Dr. Henshaw a pointed look. "I think our patient needs to rest now, Doctor. Could you come back tomorrow when she's feeling stronger?"

"Certainly, Mrs. Bennington." He reached for his bag, then

turned to Olivia. "You've been through a terrible ordeal, Miss Rosetti. Whoever did this should be horsewhipped and jailed for what they've done." A muscle in his jaw ticked, but he made a visible effort to control his emotions. "If you ever wish to talk about it, or if you have questions, please know that I am at your service."

Darius Reed sat on the side of the bed, sinking into the soft mattress, a picture book in hand. "Were you a good girl for your grandmother today, Mouse?"

Big brown eyes stared up at him. Eyes so much like her mother's. "Yes, Daddy. I'm always good."

"So, you deserve a bedtime story, then?"

"I deserve two—no, three—stories." She held up her fingers. "I was extra good today."

"I see." Darius's lips twitched at his daughter's negotiating tactics. Maybe he'd make a businesswoman out of her when she grew up, and she'd follow in her father's footsteps. "What made you extra good?"

She grinned, hugging a ragged teddy bear to her chest. "I helped *Pappoú* in the garden."

Darius winced. His father insisted that Sofia call him by the Greek name—not Grandpa or Granddad or Pops, as Darius would prefer—stubbornly refusing Darius's attempt to become more Canadian.

"I'm sure he appreciated your help." Darius settled a pillow at his back and flipped open the book. "Ready?"

Sofia nodded and popped a thumb in her mouth, her head resting on Darius's shoulder.

Warmth filtered through his chest. These were the best moments of his day. Coming home to his tousled-haired daughter, receiving her neck-strangling hugs, drinking in the sweet scent from her recent bubble bath, seeing those eyes light up with that smile just for him—these were the things that made every hour of sweat and stress worthwhile. The long hours at the office were a sacrifice he was willing to make in order to give Sofia the best life possible.

It still chafed his pride that he'd had to move in with his parents following his wife's death, but in the aftermath of such tragedy, he'd come to rely on their love and support to help ease his and Sofia's grief. They were the only family Sofia had left, the only ones he trusted to care for his daughter. But the drawback of accepting their help was that his daughter was picking up too many Greek words and customs for his liking.

One day soon, once Sofia was in school, they'd get their own place and he would weed out the Greek traditions as deftly as his father weeded the garden.

Darius set his jaw. His daughter would be accepted as a full Canadian as was her birthright. No cultural sneers or prejudice would ever taint her the way they'd tainted him.

The way they'd destroyed her mother.

"Why didn't you come home for dinner, Daddy?" Sofia shifted to peer up at him. "*Yiayiá* cries sometimes. I think she misses you too."

Darius pressed his lips together. How did a four-year-old turn guilt into an art form? "Grandma cries over lots of things. Like burning the stew."

That elicited a giggle. "She does. Yesterday she dropped a cup, and she cried when she was cleaning it up. I told her big girls don't cry, but she didn't like that."

"No, she would think that rude. You must respect your elders, remember?"

Sofia's eyes went wide. "I know, but sometimes things just pop out of my mouth."

Darius bit the inside of his cheek to keep from laughing. His little girl had that right. The words she said sometimes . . . He sighed and snuggled in closer. "Which story will we read first?"

"The princess one."

Of course. He turned the ragged pages and then began to read, thanking God for the precious gift of his daughter, the source of joy that motivated his every waking moment, his every breath.

Don't worry, Selene. Our baby will have the best of this world. She will never suffer the way you did.

3

our days later, Olivia finally felt strong enough to venture out of her room. She'd found the drawstring bag Mamma had given her on the tufted bench at the foot of the bed and had plucked out a blouse and skirt, horribly wrinkled but at least clean. For the past few days, Mrs. Bennington—or Ruth, as she insisted Olivia call her—had helped her to the lavatory down the hall, and now Olivia knew her way. The modern convenience of a large claw-foot tub, porcelain sink, and flush toilet had apparently been added several years ago in an attempt to modernize the house for Ruth's grandson, who lived with her at the time. Only one of many stories the widow had entertained Olivia with while she recuperated.

After freshening up, Olivia used the hairbrush she found in her room to tidy her hair and, with no hairpins available, simply braided the tresses into a thick plait, tying it with a string pulled from the hem of her blouse. Before she put her bag away, she reached inside to assure herself that the knitted blanket she'd put there—the one tangible reminder of her son—was safe. Bringing the wool to her nose, she inhaled the faint baby scent that still had the power to rip the air from her lungs. Then, with a shaky breath, she tucked it back inside. She didn't care if she lost everything she owned as long as she still had that blanket.

Her nerves now steadier, she made her way down the wide staircase to the main level. Though she felt uneasy wandering around a house that wasn't hers, she couldn't resist lingering in the foyer to admire the beautiful woodwork. Carved arches marked each doorway in the hall. The staircase railing and ornate newel posts were themselves works of art. Countless paintings graced the walls, a mixture of landscapes and portraits. Ruth must be an avid art collector, or perhaps her late husband had been the connoisseur.

"There you are, my dear. How wonderful to see you up and about." Ruth appeared in the hallway. Tall and elegant in a simple gray dress and pearls, she reminded Olivia of royalty.

"I'm still weak, but overall much improved. Thanks to you and Dr. Henshaw."

Ruth came forward to take Olivia's arm. "I planned on having breakfast in the sunroom. So much more cheerful than the stuffy dining room."

Olivia murmured some sort of agreement, unsure what a sunroom or the dining room looked like.

"I'm glad you're able to join me. My cook has prepared some lovely hotcakes. Served with butter and maple syrup, there's no better treat in the morning."

They had reached the end of the hall and entered a room that took Olivia's breath away. Floor-to-ceiling windows surrounded the space, flooding the area with sunlight. A round table and chairs sat in the center of the room, while several seating areas flanked the surrounding windows. Plants and flowers overflowed everywhere, almost like a gardener's greenhouse.

"It's beautiful," she whispered.

"I knew you'd like it. Come and sit. Would you like coffee or tea? Or perhaps orange juice?"

"Coffee, please." She took a seat, noting the covered platters in the middle of the table, the gold-edged plates, real silver utensils, and white linen napkins. She folded her hands in her lap. Nothing about this seemed right. She didn't belong in such a fancy place. She should be back in the cramped apartment over the grocery store that smelled of spices and cured meats.

"Is anything wrong, Olivia?" Ruth was staring at her, a frown marring her high forehead.

"You've been so kind to me, and I don't wish to—"

A woman in a black-and-white uniform came in. "Are you ready, ma'am?"

Ruth's attention shifted. "Yes, Anna. You may serve us."

The maid proceeded to lift the lids from the platters. An enticing aroma filled the air as she served the fluffy pancakes and poured maple syrup from a glass jug. Then she filled the cups with coffee from a silver urn and quietly left the room.

"Why don't we eat first," Ruth said as she laid her napkin on her lap, "and later we can have a long-overdue conversation."

Olivia nodded, shoving her anxieties aside for the moment and succumbing to the pure pleasure of eating. For the first time in over two years, she actually savored her food, lingering over each bite.

After breakfast, Ruth poured them more coffee and they went to sit on one of the sofas with a view of a lovely back garden.

Ruth set her cup on a side table and settled back against the cushions. "Now then, why don't you tell me what's on your mind?"

Olivia glanced at the older woman. Ruth had been so kind, yet if she knew she'd offered shelter to a recently incarcerated woman, Olivia was sure she'd order her out of her house immediately. "I don't know how I can ever repay you for all you've done," she said quietly.

"No payment is necessary. I was happy to help."

"But you don't know anything about me."

Ruth held up a hand. "My dear girl, I don't need to know what unfortunate circumstance brought you to St. Olaf's that night. One day, I hope you might trust me enough to tell me the whole story. In the meantime, let me tell you what brought *me* to that

38

church." She lifted her chin. "I've been going there almost every night for years, begging God to take my life."

Olivia jerked so hard that coffee sloshed onto the saucer. "Why would you do that? You have everything you could possibly want."

"It might seem that way, but trust me, all the money in the world doesn't make up for being alone. Losing my husband. Being estranged from my family. Having many acquaintances but few real friends." A flash of emotion passed over her features. "Almost every night, I go to that church and pray for hours, yet every time, God sees fit to deny my request. Then one night, as I prepared to leave and wallow in my misery once more, I came upon a young girl in need of help. And so I acted." Ruth shook her head. "This might sound fanciful, but I believe you were an answer to my prayers. Instead of taking my life, God gave me a reason to live."

The coffee churned in Olivia's stomach. This was too much. She could not be Ruth's reason to live, not when her own life was in shambles. "I don't believe that," she said. "And you shouldn't either." She pushed up from her seat. "I have to go." She headed blindly down the hall toward the entrance.

"Olivia, wait." Ruth caught up to her at the foot of the staircase. "Let's finish our conversation, and then if you wish to leave, I won't stop you."

Olivia gripped the railing, indecision pulling at her.

"You said you didn't know how to repay me. If you tell me what brought you here, I'll consider us even." Ruth's features, though firm, radiated sincerity.

Olivia closed her eyes, then opened them on a sigh. Perhaps it would be best to get it all out in the open. And once she'd spilled her secrets, Ruth would be the one who wanted Olivia to leave. "All right. But I'm warning you, it's not a pretty story."

"And that's when you found me in the church." After Olivia finished her confession, her eyes burned with unshed tears, and her chest felt hollow from reliving some of her worst moments. She inhaled and risked a glance at Ruth's face.

The woman's lips were pursed, and the lines around her eyes appeared deeper. A moment of silence passed, then Ruth rose and walked to the wall of windows. The morning sun spattered the room with light—a direct contrast to the gloomy mood inside.

Olivia's stomach twisted into knots. Just as she'd feared, her angel of mercy had lost all respect for her. How could she not? Even her own parents would have nothing to do with her.

Olivia stood and straightened her spine. It was clear there was no one she could rely on except herself. She would have to forge her own way in the world.

Alone.

"I'll get my things and be on my way," she said. "Thank you again for your hospitality."

Ruth turned around. Tears streaked her wrinkled cheeks and anguish darkened her eyes. "Please stay a moment longer. I have something I'd like to tell you. Something I've never told anyone except my dear husband, God rest his soul." Her thin lips quivered.

Olivia raised a hand to her throat. She'd expected anger and disgust, not tears. She returned to the sofa and waited while Ruth took her seat.

The older woman removed a handkerchief from her pocket and wiped her cheeks. "First, let me say how sorry I am for everything you've been through. No woman should ever have to experience such demoralization. It's reprehensible."

Olivia's chest tightened. "Thank you for saying that."

Ruth nodded, her gaze direct. "I can empathize with your tale because I went through something similar in my youth, though my experience was nowhere near as horrific as yours." She drew in a shaky breath. "I too had a child out of wedlock. And like you, my child was taken from me."

Olivia's jaw dropped. This poised, confident woman had been

through an illegitimate pregnancy? Olivia could only imagine how difficult it would have been for Ruth fifty years earlier. Yet she had obviously survived and gone on to lead a good life.

Perhaps there was hope for Olivia too.

"Like you," Ruth continued, "my family disowned me. It wasn't until I met my husband that I truly began to feel whole again. Henry overlooked my past and loved me unconditionally. Which is why, since he died, I haven't felt quite anchored to this world." A look of sorrow passed over her features. "My heart remains with Henry, wherever he is."

Olivia winced at an unexpected wave of grief for Rory. She would never have the chance to build such a long-lasting relationship with him. How much harder would it have been to lose him after forty years? "What did you do after the baby?" she asked.

"I was fortunate to have a great-aunt who took me in. She lived in Montreal and spoke more French than English, but we managed to get along. I worked for her husband in his printing shop, which is where I met Henry."

"How did you end up in Toronto?"

"Henry's family was here, and he wanted to move back. He decided to open his own print shop, which did very well." She fingered the necklace at her throat. "Eventually we were blessed with a son and, for the most part, led a happy life. Still, there always remained a void within me that never went away."

Olivia pressed a hand to her chest. "Your first child."

Ruth nodded. "Not a day goes by that I don't wonder what became of her. All I could ever do was trust her to the Lord and pray she had a happy life too."

Olivia held back the bitter words that sprang to her tongue. How could Ruth trust God? Where was He when these babies were snatched from their mothers' arms?

"It saddens me greatly," Ruth went on, "that as a society we still haven't learned from our mistakes. That young women and children are treated with such callousness."

"Or worse." Olivia hadn't told Ruth the entirety of her horrific experience in the reformatory. Certain details were better left unsaid.

Ruth blinked in the sunlight, seeming to collect herself. "Have you considered trying to find out what happened to your son?"

"There's no point." Olivia gripped her fingers together until her bones ached. "The Children's Aid worker made it clear that I wasn't entitled to any information about Matteo. That I no longer had any rights to my son." She closed her eyes against the shaft of pain in her chest. Would the agony of those words ever lessen?

"That's so unfair." Ruth reached over to pat her arm. "Am I correct in assuming you have nowhere to go now? Or is there someone who will take you in as my aunt did for me?"

Another wave of hopelessness threatened to engulf her, but Olivia pushed it back. "There's no one. That's why I was in the church, working up the nerve to approach the minister for help."

Ruth pulled herself up tall, her regal bearing returning. "Then you would be doing me a great favor if you would consider staying here with me. At least until you figure out your next move."

Olivia exhaled slowly. Conflicting emotions warred within her. Would it hurt to stay a few more days until she could secure some type of work? The idea of being a live-in maid for someone like Ruth had filtered through her thoughts. That way she'd have a place to sleep, food to eat, and a modicum of respectability—as long as any potential employer never learned of her past. "I would appreciate staying a little longer. Just until I can find a way to support myself."

"Wonderful."

Ruth's eyes brightened in a way that solidified Olivia's fears about being Ruth's *raison d'être*. That was more responsibility than she could bear in her current fragile state.

"I don't wish to sound ungrateful," Olivia said, "but you need to understand that I cannot be your salvation. You must find your own reason to live."

Ruth only gave her an enigmatic smile.

Olivia set her jaw, her stubborn streak rearing its head. After being abused both physically and mentally these many months, she was tired of trying to live up to other people's expectations. Tired of letting everyone down when she failed to meet them.

From now on, she would worry only about herself, at least until she could safely put one foot in front of the other again.

4

arius entered the auto repair shop, his nose wrinkling at the overpowering odor of grease and motor oil. He pulled his briefcase tighter to his side, loath to get any dirt on the new leather or on his good clothes.

A black sedan sat in the first bay, its hood raised. Darius strode around to the front bumper. Denim-clad legs and worn work boots stuck out from under the chassis, and the clank of tools echoed in the garage.

"Hello, Papá."

The noise ceased, and the rest of his father's torso appeared, followed by a face blackened with sweat and grime. "Darius. What brings you by?" He pulled himself to his feet and reached for a rag, dragging it over his face. His unruly dark hair stood up in tufts, his overalls frayed and stained.

Darius's gaze dropped to the perpetual black under his father's fingernails, and his gut tightened. "I needed to speak to you without Mamá around."

The smile faded from his father's weathered features. "That doesn't sound good."

Best to just get it out. "I want you to stop teaching Sofia Greek words. She's going to start school in the fall, and I won't have the other kids making fun of her."

As expected, his father's face hardened. "My granddaughter will learn Greek. She will learn her family's traditions."

"No, she won't. She will fit in with the other children in her class and give them no cause for bullying." Memories of his own school days, ones he fought to keep buried, burst to the surface. The taunts of the other boys. The constant humiliation. The frequent beatings. "Sofia is Canadian, and she will act like a Canadian."

"Canadian is good. But she is also Greek. She will learn of her heritage." His father wiped off his wrench with vicious strokes.

"How can you say that after what happened to Selene? Do you want Sofia to suffer a similar fate?" Darius's fingers tightened into fists at the mere mention of the hatred that had incited violence against Selene and her parents. Every time he thought of someone deliberately setting fire to their family restaurant, of Selene and his in-laws perishing in such a horrific way, outrage burned through him, hotter than any flame.

His father turned his back to rifle through his toolbox. The rigid set of his shoulders told Darius he was not ready to concede defeat.

"Isn't that why you changed our last name?" Darius pressed. "To make us sound more Canadian? To avoid the persecution you experienced when you first came to this country?"

He whirled around, dark eyes blazing. "You throw my actions back in my face? Is this how a son respects his father?"

Darius closed his eyes, counted to ten, and opened them. "That's not why I brought it up. I only want to remind you of the hardships you faced—we faced." He softened his voice. "I know you want a better life for Sofia."

Papá tossed the rag down, not meeting Darius's gaze.

Darius let out a breath. "What about a compromise? Once she's old enough to understand when to use Greek and when not to, you can teach her our customs. Until then, I'm asking you to respect my wishes."

Several seconds passed in silence. At last his father nodded. "Tell your mother I will be working late." He stuck his head under the hood and started to tighten the oil cap.

Regret settled like a stone in Darius's gut as he left. He didn't want to hurt his father, but if it meant protecting Sofia, he had no choice.

Twenty minutes later, Darius walked into his parents' house. Mamá and Sofia would be happy he was home early tonight. They could eat dinner together and maybe go for a walk afterward.

In the kitchen, he found his mother at the stove, stirring a steaming pot.

He bent to kiss her cheek, then opened the icebox to grab a bottle of milk. Whistling, he took a glass from the cupboard and filled it up.

"How was your day?" he asked before he gulped down half the glass in one long swallow.

"Fine. Sofia helped me with the laundry. Wore herself out, poor thing. She's having a nap."

"Wow. She must have worked hard." He laughed. His four-year-old had long outgrown her afternoon nap and usually protested loudly if one was suggested.

Mamá put a lid on the pot, then turned around, wiping her hands on her striped apron. Hurt shone in her eyes. "She told me today that she wants a new mother."

His heart pinched. "Oh, Mamá. She didn't mean anything by that. She adores spending time with you."

"Yes, but I'm still her yiayiá, not her mother." She pulled out a chair and sank down onto it. "Perhaps it's time, Darius. Time to find a good Greek girl and start over. Make a new home for Sofia with brothers and sisters."

Darius wiped the milk from his upper lip, his gut clenching. "I don't want a Greek wife, Mamá." After losing Selene at the hand of lawless thugs, he'd vowed never to experience that type of pain again and to shield his daughter from the hatred that had killed her mother. He rose and placed his glass in the enamel sink. Perhaps the time had come to tell his family about Meredith. He leaned a hip against the counter and crossed his arms. "I need to tell you something, Mamá. I've been seeing someone for a while now. She comes from a good family here in Toronto."

His mother's eyes narrowed. "Is she Greek?"

Darius held back an exasperated groan. "No, she's Canadian, of British descent, I believe. Her name is Meredith Cheeseman."

"Cheeseman?" Mamá snorted. "Does her family make cheese?"

Despite his frustration, Darius chuckled. "They don't make cheese. Her father is a business associate of mine."

Mamá shook her head. With a great sigh, she heaved herself up from the chair. "Cheeseman. What kind of name is that?" She muttered something in Greek and resumed her position at the stove.

Darius pushed away from the counter, reining in the urge to defend himself. His mother just needed time to become accustomed to the idea. Best to leave her be for the moment. He trudged up the narrow staircase to Sofia's room and peeked inside. She lay curled on her bed, the princess book tucked under one arm.

Darius walked over and quietly pulled the quilt up to her chin. "One day you'll have a new mother, Mouse. One who will love you as much as I do. I promise."

The door slammed shut behind her. Olivia absorbed the vibration that shuddered through the air before setting off down the sidewalk. Another job interview, another rejection. The meetings always started off well, but as soon as Olivia tried to fabricate an explanation about where she'd been for the past year and a half, the interviewers picked up on her evasiveness and promptly showed her the door.

She'd been living with Ruth for two weeks now, and with each day that passed, her hope of obtaining a job dimmed. It looked like she would have to swallow her pride and ask for Ruth's help. With the woman's many connections in the city, surely she could find someone willing to hire her. At this point, any type of work would do, no matter how menial.

Olivia attempted to shake off her gloomy mood. The next stop of the day—a visit with her friends at the reformatory—would require putting on a brave front. As much as it might pain her to do so, Joannie and Mabel deserved a visitor filled with hope, not one who looked like she was facing the gallows.

With renewed determination, Olivia continued down King Street. The fact that her interview had been mere blocks from the reformatory had spurred her to keep her promise to visit the friends she'd left behind. In particular, Olivia worried about Joannie, who had always looked so frail, despite her pregnancy. Her due date had passed, so it was entirely possible that she'd had her baby by now.

At the corner of King Street and Jefferson Avenue, Olivia's feet slowed to a stop. A bus whizzed by, creating a gust of wind that fluttered her skirt about her knees. Up ahead, the Mercer Reformatory occupied most of the block. Her stomach tightened at the sight of the tall brick building with its menacing turrets that towered above the rooftop. Legions of iron spikes created a high fence surrounding the prison, their ominous shadows increasing the dread building within her.

How could she go back into that chamber of torture? What if they said there'd been a mistake, that she'd have to serve the rest of her sentence after all?

She gulped in several deep breaths, willing her nerves to settle, yet her legs continued to balk at her efforts to move forward.

"They can't force me to stay," she said aloud. "I can walk out the door any time I choose."

Hiking her purse higher onto her shoulder, she entered the gate and started up the walkway toward the entrance, attempting to ignore the ghoulish memories that haunted her. The same hollowness she'd felt the day she arrived sat in the pit of her stomach. She recalled the stern matron standing on the steps to supervise the intake process, her disapproval evident in her perpetual scowl. Now, Olivia entered the vast entry hall on shaking legs, once again feeling as insignificant as an ant. Yet as frightened as she'd been then, nothing could have prepared her for the horrors that had awaited her.

Olivia's heart beat too rapidly in her chest. With a quick prayer for courage, she headed to the front office, where she paused to check her reflection in the window. She'd taken great pains with her appearance today, dressing in the new suit Ruth had insisted on buying her for her job search. She'd wanted to look professional for the interview as well as for any of the Mercer staff she might encounter. Prove to them that she was not the incorrigible young woman they'd proclaimed her to be.

Plus, she wanted to give Joannie and Mabel hope.

Hope that one day they too would be able to return to a normal life.

Olivia followed a matron, one who thankfully didn't seem to recognize her, to the visitors' area. Since she'd never had any visitors, she'd never been in this room before. Not even Mamma had come to see her in the eighteen months she'd been imprisoned. Now she looked around, noticing the several metal tables and uncomfortable-looking chairs. A guard hovered by the door to the hallway. Today must be a slow day, as only one other woman occupied the area. Olivia chose a seat on the opposite side of the room, clasping her clammy hands on the table and willing her heart to quit racing in her chest.

A few minutes later, Joannie appeared. Her face lit up when she saw Olivia, and she rushed over to the table. Since hugging or touching of any type was forbidden, Olivia settled for giving the girl a big smile. One that faltered when she took in Joannie's appearance.

Her limp brown hair was pulled back from her face in a long tail. The basketball-sized bump that had once protruded in front of her was gone, and the prison uniform now swallowed her thin frame, making her appear even younger than her seventeen years.

The chair legs scraped the floor as she sat down. "You came. I didn't think you would."

"I promised, didn't I?" Olivia fought to keep her expression pleasant. "How are you? I see you've had your baby."

Joannie nodded. "A little girl."

Olivia wet her dry lips. "Is she here with you?" Some of the women who gave birth while incarcerated were allowed to bring their babies back from the hospital and keep them in the make-shift nursery on the third floor. But others, like Olivia, weren't so lucky. She had no idea what criteria was required to be allowed to keep one's baby and had never dared to ask. She did know that anyone as young as Joannie usually had her child taken to the Infants' Home, since the authorities deemed them incapable of providing for a baby.

Sorrow flitted across the girl's face. "A lady from Children's Aid came and took her away."

Visions of the tall, slender woman who'd come to see Olivia in the hospital came to mind. "Mrs. Linder?"

"Yes."

"She took my baby too." Spasms shot through Olivia's chest. Having to return to this horrid place without her baby had been one of the worst days of her life.

Joannie's lips trembled. "She said my little girl would have a better life with people who could give her a real family." A tear slid down her face.

Olivia closed her eyes briefly. "I'm so sorry, Joannie." Most of the women here had no way of knowing where their babies ended up or how they fared. It was all so unfair. "I'm sure your baby will be just fine."

Joannie nodded, wiping the back of her hand across her eyes. "I hope so."

After a few somber seconds, Olivia attempted to lift the mood. "Where's Mabel? I thought she'd be here too, or would they not allow you both to visit at the same time?" Maybe Mabel was working her shift in the factory and was unable to get away. It seemed strange for Olivia to think of the world inside the prison continuing without her. The drudgery of work every day, the silent meals in the dining room where talking was forbidden, the precious minutes allowed outdoors.

More tears flooded Joannie's eyes. "Mabel's gone." The strangled words were barely audible.

"Gone? Did they grant her an early release too?" A cold feeling opened up in Olivia's stomach. "I thought she had another six months to go."

Joannie shook her head. "S-she's dead."

Olivia gasped, jerking back on the hard plastic seat. She held a trembling hand to her lips as images of the plump blond girl with laughing eyes sprang to mind. Of all the people Olivia had met here, Mabel was the last one she'd ever worried about succumbing to illness. "How? What happened?"

"They won't say. Rumors are going around that she had some sort of venereal disease."

Phantom pain shot through Olivia's body, the words conjuring up the tortures that took place in that medical room. Had they done something worse to Mabel? Had their so-called treatments caused the girl's death? Mabel had been only nineteen and had given birth just after Olivia had come to the reformatory. Still, Mabel had never lost her cheery disposition, always quick to tell a joke or offer a sympathetic ear. She'd been looking forward to starting her life over at the end of her sentence. Now all her dreams had ended before they'd begun.

Olivia's jaw muscles tightened as she fought back tears. Crying solved nothing, especially not in here. With every rapid blink, anger seeped through her body until her limbs shook. "It's not right what they're doing here," she said in a low voice so the guard couldn't hear. "We don't belong in a place like this. Yes, we made mistakes, but we still deserve somewhere safe to go. Somewhere we wouldn't have to worry about people hurting us or taking our babies."

Joannie swiped at her red nose with the sleeve of her uniform. "I wish a place like that existed."

Staring into the girl's tearstained face, something fierce came alive inside Olivia. Something stronger and more intense than her anger. Olivia had escaped this house of horrors, but the women still caged within these walls continued to suffer. These women needed somewhere else to go. A place where people understood what they were going through and treated them with kindness. But how would one begin to bring about such a change?

With great effort, she focused back on Joannie. "When is your release date again?"

"September twenty-fifth."

"Where will you go? Have you had any word from your family?"

Joannie shook her head, a strand of hair falling across her cheek. "They don't want anything to do with me. I don't know what I'm going to do."

In spite of the rules, Olivia reached over and squeezed Joannie's fingers. "Don't worry. I'll have somewhere for you to stay by then. In the meantime . . ." Olivia dug in her purse and pulled out a scrap of paper and a pencil and quickly scratched down some information. "Here's the telephone number where I'm staying. If you need me, just call." She swallowed. "I'll try to come back for another visit soon."

"Thanks. It will give me something to look forward to." Joannie's eyes seemed huge in her thin face.

Olivia rose and went around to pull the girl into a tight hug. "Don't lose hope. Things will get better, I promise."

A frowning guard came toward them. "No touching the prisoner."

Olivia stepped back but did not apologize. "Say hello to the others for me. And tell them not to give up. Time will pass quicker than you think."

She brushed past the guard on her way out into the corridor. Though every cell in her body urged her to flee this place, her conscience would not allow her to take the cowardly way out. Instead, she marched to the front office.

The startled receptionist snapped to attention as Olivia entered. "Can I help you, miss?"

"No, thank you. I know the way." Before the woman could stop her, Olivia strode to the inner office door and entered without knocking.

Mrs. Pollack looked up, a scowl marring her plain features. "What is the meaning of this?"

Olivia's hands shook, but she stood her ground. "I need to speak with you."

"You have some nerve barging in here like—"

"After everything I went through in this place, you owe me this much."

The woman's face blanched, though she held Olivia's gaze with a steely glare of her own. "You have two minutes to say your piece and leave. Or I'll call the authorities."

As the woman intended, the words sent chills through Olivia's limbs. She lifted her chin. "I want to know the truth about Mabel Stravinski's death."

Mrs. Pollack's mouth hardened. The loud ticking of a clock on the beige wall seemed to taunt Olivia. She used to stare at the same industrial clock across from her cell when seconds passed like hours. Back then, time meant nothing, but now the ticking reminded her of the days she'd lost and would never recover.

At last, the woman released a breath. "Mabel was being treated for the advanced stages of venereal disease. During treatment, she suffered a massive seizure, and Dr. Guest was unable to re-vive her."

Olivia stared. "Did you call an ambulance? Get her to a hos-pital?"

"There wasn't time. It all happened too fast." She spoke with no emotion, as if Mabel's life meant nothing. "I'm sorry. I know this must have come as a shock."

Rage pulsed through Olivia, shooting pain through her tem-ples. "Don't pretend you're not aware of what goes on in that clinic and the horrors that woman puts us through. How can you allow her to get away with it?"

"Dr. Guest is a well-respected physician. I will not allow you to malign her reputa—"

Olivia slammed her palm down on the desk, causing papers to scatter. "Have you heard the screams coming from her exami-nation room? Have you ever once visited the isolation chamber where I was kept for over a month? That dirty, disgusting room with only rusty bedsprings to lie on when I was writhing in pain for days?"

A spark of fear leapt in the woman's pale eyes.

Olivia gave a harsh laugh. "No, of course not. You wouldn't want to witness what goes on behind those doors, because then you might have to actually do something about it." She straight-ened and drew in a ragged breath. "How can you live with your-self for allowing such atrocities to happen? I hold all of you here equally responsible for Mabel's death." She glared at her for another second, then whirled around and strode out into the reception area.

"Miss Rosetti. Wait."

But Olivia had borne all she could take for one day. She slammed out the main doors and didn't look back.

5

After getting off the bus, Olivia walked the remaining blocks to Ruth's house, her mind still spinning. As the buildings passed in a blur, her anger lessened, and her focus turned to solutions. It was too late for dear Mabel but not for other girls who might find themselves in trouble. If they had somewhere to turn before being arrested for vagrancy, or for being unmarried and pregnant like Olivia, or for resorting to criminal activities to feed themselves, perhaps their futures wouldn't look so bleak.

For the first time since her own arrest, the oppression weighing on her spirit lifted, and a new energy infused her. Though her relationship with God hadn't been the best lately, this sudden sense of purpose seemed to be a sign from above, showing her what she needed to do.

If only she had a clue how to begin.

As she approached Ruth's property, Dr. Henshaw stepped out of an auto parked by the curb. He smiled when he saw her. "Miss Rosetti. What good timing. I was just coming to see you."

Olivia frowned. She'd been declared cured, her health restored. Why, then, was he here? "Good afternoon, Doctor. Are you this diligent with all your patients?" Her words held a ring of challenge.

"Only ones who deserve my extra diligence." His hazel eyes twinkled.

"I can assure you I am in perfect health. You needn't waste your time." Though her tone was teasing, she kept her gaze steady. The man was charming in his own way; however, Olivia feared he might harbor hopes of a more personal relationship, one she was not interested in pursuing.

Not with any man.

They had reached Ruth's front door, and he opened it for her, stepping aside to let her enter.

"I don't consider a visit with you wasting my time." He removed his hat. "The reason I'm here, though, has more to do with your emotional well-being than your physical health."

Olivia set her purse on the hall table, then motioned the doctor into the parlor. "Has Ruth been telling tales behind my back?" she asked as they took a seat, trying not to take umbrage at his insinuation that she might be mentally unsound.

A reddish hue infused his cheeks. "Mrs. Bennington may have mentioned her concern over your inability to secure employment and how it might be affecting you."

"I will admit it's disheartening, though not unexpected. I have no real experience other than working in my parents' store." She moved an embroidered pillow out of her way. "And I have no explanation as to what I've been doing for the past eighteen months."

"I can see how that might make obtaining a job difficult."

"Difficult? Try impossible."

His expression softened. "Are you sure you're doing all right? It would be natural to suffer an emotional setback after all you've been through."

"I'm fine, Dr. Henshaw." Olivia gritted her teeth, regretting once again all that he had discerned about her experience at the reformatory.

"There's no shame in—"

"I'm fine." Olivia clasped her hands together. "I wish you and Ruth would stop treating me like I might shatter at any moment."

His shoulders visibly stiffened. "Forgive me. I only wished to offer my assistance should you need it." He rose from the armchair. "I'll leave you in peace."

Heat burned Olivia's cheeks. The man had been nothing but kind, and she'd practically snapped his head off. She followed him into the hall. "I'm sorry, Doctor. You didn't deserve that."

He stopped by the front door, then slowly turned to give her a tight smile. "It's all right. I realize you must be very frustrated."

"That doesn't excuse my rudeness." She took a step toward him. "Actually, I could use your advice about something if you have a minute."

"Certainly." His eyes brightened as he followed her back into the parlor.

"You may not know the answer to this," she said after they had resumed their seats. "In fact, you may think I've lost my mind."

He smiled. "I'm sure I won't."

How could she begin to explain her idea when the very thought made her tremble? She'd planned to talk to Ruth first, but as a physician, Dr. Henshaw might be the better person to begin with. She squared her shoulders and plunged ahead. "I need to know what might be involved in opening a maternity home."

He stared at her for a second, brows raised. "A maternity home?"

"That's right." She lifted her chin. "It occurred to me that the city is lacking in resources for women who find themselves in trouble. They need a safe place to go. Somewhere they feel understood and cared for."

"By trouble, I assume you mean a pregnancy out of wedlock?"

"For the most part, yes." Not every woman in the reformatory had been pregnant, but each one had a sad tale to tell. "It occurred to me that this could be a way to create something positive from my ordeal."

He pursed his lips, studying her. "Opening such a home would be a huge undertaking."

"I realize that." Her calm tone belied the riot of nerves shooting through her body. "Would I require a permit from the city?"

"Not necessarily. Especially if you intend it to be a private maternity home. A publicly funded facility would be subject to many more regulations."

Olivia leaned back against the sofa cushions. "But there must be some sort of rules governing a private home. Inspections? Limits on the number of residents?"

Yet the Mercer was a government-run organization, and as far as she knew, there were no inspectors keeping tabs on what went on within those walls.

"You might be right. I could look into the matter if you wish." Interest lit his features.

"I'd appreciate that. Thank you." Inquiries from a respected physician would likely hold more weight than those from a woman recently released from prison. "What would the next step be?"

He stroked his chin. "Well, the first thing you would need is a site for your venture. I suppose the best bet would be to rent a property for that purpose."

"Right." The daunting prospect of finding real estate in the city—much less being able to afford it—threatened to overwhelm her, but Olivia shoved her misgivings aside. "How would one go about finding such a property? Would I require a real estate agent?"

"There's no need for that." The firm voice rang out from the doorway.

Olivia swiveled to see Ruth staring at them, her eyes brighter than her blue cardigan. "Why would you need to rent a property when we have the perfect location right here?"

Olivia gaped at her. "Ruth, I never meant to imply . . ." Surely she wasn't offering her own home for such a purpose.

Ruth came in and perched on the arm of the sofa. "I used to think about turning this place into a boardinghouse or a small inn, but I do believe a maternity home would be the perfect idea." She trilled out a delighted laugh. "What do you say, Olivia? Do you think we could be partners in this endeavor?"

Olivia's mind spun with too many thoughts at once. "This is all very sudden. I only came up with the idea this afternoon. Are you sure, Ruth?"

"Olivia makes a valid point." Dr. Henshaw rose, a frown creasing his brow. "I think you should take more time to consider the ramifications before you make any big decisions."

Ruth only laughed again and waved a hand. "At my age, time is a luxury I can ill afford. And for the first time in years, I'd have a purpose again. No, I don't need another minute to think about it. But I would appreciate you looking into the legalities for us, Doctor."

He blinked, looking as bemused as Olivia felt. "Very well, as long as you promise not to rush into anything before you hear from me."

"Certainly, though it couldn't hurt to talk to my architect about some possible renovations."

Olivia could scarcely believe that Ruth would offer her home for a project of this magnitude. Yet what better property could she find on her own?

And who better to have on board? A woman who had experienced the shame of an unexpected pregnancy but who now held a place of prestige and respect in society. Her connections could turn out to be most advantageous in getting this project off the ground. It must be a sign that this was God's intention all along.

Ruth turned to Olivia. "I think we'll make an excellent team, my dear. Don't you?"

Olivia smiled as a tiny bud of hope unfurled within her. "I do believe we just might."

6

Two months later

Seated in the dining room one week after the successful opening of Bennington Place Maternity Home, Olivia sipped her coffee and took a moment to reflect on the whirlwind mixture of highs and lows that had taken place over the past two months.

One of the highs, of course, was the realization of her dream, the opening of the maternity home. It had been a day to remember, with a fancy ribbon-cutting ceremony and refreshments for the select group of invitees who had attended.

Not long afterward, however, Olivia had experienced one of her worst lows on the occasion of Matteo's first birthday. She spent most of the day crying, reliving every moment of the precious time with her newborn son, and the heartbreak of having to relinquish him to the Children's Aid worker. She couldn't help but wonder where he was now. Had his new family thrown him a party? Bought him presents?

In the midst of Olivia's melancholy, Ruth had been wonderful. She had instructed their cook to bake a small cake in the boy's honor, and after dinner that night, Ruth had placed a candle on top of the cake, and the two had celebrated Matteo's special day.

Remembering her son that way had helped Olivia feel closer to him and eased the raw ache in her heart just a little.

With a sigh, Olivia shook off the sad memories and looked across the table at Ruth. Gratitude filled her heart. Gratitude and . . . affection for the woman who had accepted a stranger into her home without judgment or condemnation.

Olivia might not have wanted to be Ruth's salvation, but Ruth had definitely turned out to be hers. She'd saved Olivia from the ashes of destruction and breathed new life into her soul, giving her the opportunity to turn her hardships into something that could benefit others.

"I still can't believe Bennington Place has become a reality," Olivia said. "And that we already have two residents."

Since their official opening one week ago, two women had found their way to them: Margaret, a young girl of eighteen, and Patricia, a woman in her mid-twenties.

"I know. And it's only the beginning." Ruth reached over to squeeze Olivia's hand. "I've been rattling around this old house by myself for years now. Despite several offers to buy the property, I just couldn't let it go." She smiled, her gaze scanning the dining room's velvet wallpaper. "Perhaps I was meant to put the house to good use and allow its loving walls to shelter those in need." She pressed her lips together. "I think Henry would have agreed that Bennington Place is a fine idea."

"I'm sure he would."

Over the past weeks, Olivia had discovered that Ruth Bennington was a force to be reckoned with once she put her mind to something. She'd jumped right into making renovations to the house, hiring a contractor to add a new bathroom and reconfigure the layout of the bedrooms to make more room for potential residents. They now had six guest quarters with two beds each to start, plus a nice suite for Olivia. Still, it had involved a large outlay of money—one she hoped Ruth wouldn't regret should the venture not go as planned. But the dear lady had assured her it was a risk she was willing to take.

"By the way, I've heard back from Dr. Henshaw," Ruth said, stirring sugar into her coffee. "He's agreed to be our doctor on call and is willing to offer his services for a small fee."

"That's wonderful. I know he'll treat the women with kindness." *Just like he treated me.* "But will he have time with working at the hospital as well as seeing his private patients?"

"He'll make time. Mark Henshaw is a remarkable young man. Not only is he raising his younger brother, he also volunteers his services to those living in the Ward."

"That *is* impressive." Olivia knew the area well. Her parents thanked God every day that they hadn't ended up in those slums like so many other immigrants.

"Of course," Ruth continued, "we also need to find a reputable midwife. And hopefully our upcoming fundraiser will bring in a group of benefactors to help cover our operating costs. Speaking of which . . ." Ruth pushed the morning paper across the table with a broad smile. "We made the front page of *The Daily Star*." She pointed to an article underneath the latest war news.

A photo of Bennington Place accompanied a caption that read *Local Widow Opens Private Maternity Home in the Heart of the City.*

Ruth beamed. "The reporter promised the story would be visible, but front and center? How marvelous! Think of how many people will learn about us now."

Nerves skittered up Olivia's spine at the thought of the extensive publicity their new venture would receive. It had taken every ounce of Ruth's persuasion to ensure the reporter didn't use the term *unwed mothers* in the headline, which might have garnered a negative reaction from the community. They certainly didn't need that as they strived to get their project off the ground.

Olivia scanned the printed words beneath the photo, anxious not to find any mention of her name. She let out a relieved breath. As promised, she was only referred to as Mrs. Bennington's partner. Olivia didn't want anyone to associate Ruth's name with a woman who'd been arrested and incarcerated at the Mercer Reformatory.

Ruth rose to clear the breakfast dishes from the table. "I do wish you would take more credit for our venture," she said, as though reading Olivia's thoughts. "After all, this is your vision more than mine. All I did was provide the location."

Olivia stood and refolded the newspaper. "You did much more than that. Not only did you provide the capital for the renovations, but you also opened your home and your heart to me. I don't know where I'd be without you." She blinked hard as she pulled Ruth into a hug.

"You're the one who saved me, Olivia dear."

"Then for that, I'm grateful. You have too much life in you to give up."

Ruth laughed. "God willing, I'll have enough energy to see this project through."

"You better." Olivia grinned. "Because I can't do all this by myself."

Darius entered his office on the eighth floor of the downtown building and set his briefcase on top of the mahogany desk. As he did every day, he inhaled the smell of leather and ink and let out a satisfied sigh. This was what he'd been working so hard for. This beautiful office with its view of the city signified he was well on his way to the bright future he'd envisioned for himself and Sofia.

"Any idea what's got the boss all worked up?"

Darius turned to see his colleague Kevin Caldwell in the doorway. His blond hair was more disheveled than usual, as though he'd been running his hands through it.

"No, I've been out most of the morning." Darius crossed his arms. "What's going on?"

"I swear there's steam coming out of Walcott's office."

"Maybe I should schedule another meeting off-site." Darius grinned. Their boss's temper was nothing new. Each employee learned to deal with it in their own way. As the newest member of the Walcott team, Kevin had not yet found a coping method. Darius slapped the man on the shoulder. "Don't worry. Whatever the problem, it will likely blow over by tomorrow."

A door slammed down the hall. "Reed. My office. Now!"

Darius winced. "Then again, tomorrow is a long way off. Wish me luck."

"You got it, pal." Kevin poked his head around the door, looked left and right, then scurried off.

Darius braced himself as he approached the boss's office and knocked on the door.

"Come in." The familiar bellow allowed his nerves to ease. If Darius had committed some grievous error, the command to enter would have been laced with profanity.

"Is there a problem, sir?"

The older man turned toward him. "You tell me." He slid a newspaper across the polished surface of his desk.

Darius moved forward to pick it up. After the first glance at the war headlines, he couldn't determine what had Walcott so hot under the collar, but then the photo of a house caught his attention.

"The Bennington property."

Mr. Walcott scowled. "How long have I been trying to get Widow Bennington to sell to me?"

"Years?"

"More than I care to count." Mr. Walcott slapped a palm to the desktop. "And now this 'young woman' they mention in the article has convinced her to open a maternity home. Of all the harebrained—"

Darius glanced at the man's reddened complexion and frowned. "Come on, sir. It's not worth having a heart attack over." Lately, with the man's burgeoning waistline and his fiery temper, Darius feared for his superior's health.

"What would make a woman pushing seventy want to play nursemaid to a bunch of pregnant women?" Mr. Walcott paced the area behind his desk. "She should be sitting in a rocking chair on a porch somewhere, knitting or playing bridge." He smashed a fist into his palm. "None of this makes a lick of sense."

Darius had to concede the man made a valid point. Still, getting upset enough to turn his face that shade of purple was a bit excessive. "Why don't we sit down? Let's put our heads together and see what other options we have."

Walcott pierced him with a hard stare. "You think we still have options?"

"Of course we do. The Bennington mansion isn't the only viable property in town. We can find another space worth purchasing."

"I don't want another property. That estate is in the perfect location. Think of the building complex we could put up there. I've had the blueprints for Walcott Towers in the vault for years, waiting for the Bennington property to open up." Walcott rubbed his chin, a determined look coming over his features. "But you're right, Reed. We still have options."

Darius's stomach began to churn. He knew that look, and it usually meant trouble.

"You are going to use your charms to convince Ruth Bennington that this maternity home is a terrible idea and that she should sell her house to us. With what I'm willing to pay her, she could open three homes in another part of town."

Darius bit back an immediate rebuttal. What his boss said was true. If Mrs. Bennington sold to Walcott Industries, she would get top dollar and could easily open a more modern facility somewhere outside the heart of the city, which would make more sense for that type of establishment. How did the caption under the photo phrase it? *A home for underprivileged women.*

Darius held back a snort of disgust. He wasn't an idiot. This so-called maternity home was meant to harbor morally corrupt women whose foolish life choices had landed them in trouble of their own making. Wouldn't they rather be hidden away on the outskirts of town?

He skimmed the rest of the article. *Black-tie event. $25 a plate fundraiser. Investors welcome. Proceeds will be donated to Bennington Place.*

So Mrs. Bennington was looking for financial aid. That meant the whole enterprise could be on shaky ground.

"Did you read the entire article?" Darius asked.

"Of course I did. Why?"

"It sounds like the lady needs more capital and without it, she might not be able to stay in operation long." Darius raised a brow. "We could use the black-tie event as an opportunity to warn any potential backers away from this venture."

"Hmm. Good point." Walcott plopped back onto his leather chair and rubbed his goatee, a sure sign that the cogs were turning. "Get yourself a tuxedo, boy. You and I are going to this shindig. Between the two of us, we should be able to persuade anyone foolhardy enough to attend not to waste their money."

Darius kept his expression even, masking his dismay at having to attend another tedious affair, not to mention having to find suitable attire, since his usual good suit wouldn't do for this event. Plus, it would mean another night he'd have to disappoint Sofia.

"In the meantime, I want you to pay the widow a visit. Get a feel for what's really going on there and make a case for why she should consider selling. Use those persuasion skills you've picked up on our dime."

Darius forced his lips into a smile, though it felt more like a grimace. Mr. Walcott took every opportunity he could to remind him that Walcott Industries was paying for the business courses he took on Saturday mornings—courses he needed to eventually earn his degree, which would hopefully merit a large raise, or maybe even a promotion. "Fine. I'll call and arrange—"

"Don't call. She'll only refuse to see you. Go over unannounced. You're much more likely to get in that way."

Darius nodded. "Fine. I'll go first thing tomorrow."

He tugged his tie loose as he left the room. Arguing with a stubborn old widow would likely be a colossal waste of time, but if it kept the boss happy, then Darius would consider it a win.

7

The next morning, Olivia whipped the eggs into a frenzy in the ceramic mixing bowl, then poured them onto the hot skillet. It was the cook's day off, and Olivia didn't mind stepping in to fill Mrs. Neale's shoes. In fact, she rather enjoyed it.

From the open kitchen window, the melodious sounds of the birds cheered her soul. Mornings were her favorite time of day, when everything seemed new and fresh, untainted by the events to come. She loved to sip her coffee as she helped in the kitchen and watch the sun rise over the hedges in the backyard, the stillness of the early hours creating a cocoon that suspended reality for a brief interval.

It was a time when Olivia could pretend that the tragedies in her life hadn't happened and that she was still a young girl full of hope for the future. Not the jaded twenty-two-year-old she'd become.

The eggs sizzled and hissed, reminding her to stir them before they burned. Margaret and Patricia didn't need their breakfast ruined, especially since Olivia was still trying to make a good impression on them.

Margaret sometimes seemed restless, unsure whether to stay

or go. But Olivia hoped that with an outpouring of kindness, she and Ruth could convince her to stay.

She spooned the eggs onto a platter and turned off the heat. Glancing at the clock, she calculated the time remaining for the biscuits. Five more minutes should be perfect. Then she'd make tea for Margaret, who didn't like her brew too strong. For Patricia, who preferred coffee, a fresh pot sat on the stovetop, filling the kitchen with a delectable aroma. Olivia had missed her favorite morning beverage while at the reformatory, where she'd been lucky to receive some lukewarm tea. Amazing how such small luxuries could be taken for granted.

The sound of chimes from the doorbell rang through the house. Olivia startled. Who would be coming here at this early hour? Her head snapped up. Maybe another woman in need had read about their home in the paper.

With fresh eagerness, Olivia hurried down the long hallway toward the front of the house, a fervent prayer on her lips. *Lord, help me to be a welcoming face to whomever you've brought to us.*

Putting on her best smile, Olivia opened the door. Her expression turned to a frown as she took in the dark-haired man on the porch. "Can I help you?"

The man scanned her from head to toe in one quick glance. Then his vivid blue eyes focused on her with an intensity that made her squirm.

"Um . . . yes," he said. "That is, good morning. I'm looking for Mrs. Bennington."

Olivia regarded the man's pinstriped suit and the fedora perched at a jaunty angle over his forehead and stood more firmly in the door's opening. "I'm afraid she's not up yet. May I tell her who came by?" Hopefully he'd get her insinuation that it was much too early to be calling on anyone.

He chuckled. "Forgive me for arriving unannounced at this hour. But the matter I wish to discuss couldn't wait. My name is Darius Reed. And I'd like to—"

"Olivia? Who's at the door?" Ruth's voice echoed from the hall behind her.

Olivia's heart sank. Now she'd never get rid of him. Reluctantly, she opened the door wider. "A man named Mr. Reed. He wants to speak to you about something important. Or so he claims." She speared the man with the glare she learned from Mamma when dealing with annoying customers.

The stranger only smiled. "Mrs. Bennington? My name is Darius Reed. I'd like to talk to you about . . . your new venture here."

Olivia's gaze narrowed. Something about that statement rang false.

Ruth stared at him, sizing him up, then nodded. "Very well, Mr. Reed. Join me for coffee?"

"I'd love to, ma'am." He removed his hat and stepped inside.

Ruth turned. "Oh, forgive my manners. This is my partner, Miss Olivia Rosetti."

"A pleasure to meet you, Miss Rosetti." He gave a slight bow, his eyes twinkling.

Obviously he expected her to be impressed, but she refused to be taken in by false charms. "Excuse me," she said. "I have something in the oven." Turning on her heel, she retreated down the hall to the kitchen.

Wisps of black smoke escaped from around the stove's cast-iron door. *No!* Their uninvited guest had made her burn the biscuits. Grabbing a tea towel, she opened the door and waved away a wall of smoke, then grabbed the tray and set it on the stovetop with a sigh. All that remained were small blobs of charcoal. Definitely not edible. Everyone would have to settle for toast to go with the now-cold eggs. That and the leftover muffins from yesterday would have to do.

"Can I do anything to help?" A tentative voice came from the doorway.

Olivia swiped a hand across her forehead and looked up to see Margaret standing by the counter. Only eighteen years old,

70

the girl seemed afraid of her own shadow. Olivia had yet to get her to open up about the circumstances that had brought her to Bennington Place, but she was patient. She'd wait until Margaret was ready to talk.

"How are you at making toast?"

The girl smiled. "I can manage without burning it."

She handed the girl a knife to slice the loaf of bread. "Great. Because this morning I can't say the same."

Darius sipped the delicious brew and set his cup aside. "Best coffee I've had in ages," he said to Mrs. Bennington, who was seated on the sofa across from him.

"All thanks to Olivia. She has a secret ingredient I've yet to get her to reveal." The woman chuckled with obvious affection.

"A woman of many talents, I take it. Are you two related?" Darius had been astonished by the beautiful young woman who'd greeted him at the door. So much so that the speech he'd practiced on the way over had flown from his mind. Those big brown eyes under finely arched brows had mesmerized him, as did the upsweep of dark hair that accentuated those high cheekbones, those full lips . . .

Mrs. Bennington's brows rose. "Do we look like we're related?"

Heat crept up his neck. How did he answer that without insulting someone? Miss Rosetti definitely favored what he assumed was an Italian heritage, judging by her last name, whereas Mrs. Bennington couldn't look more British. "It's possible."

"True. But no. We're friends and now business partners." She calmly set her cup on the coffee table. "What exactly would you like to know about our maternity home?" Her shrewd gaze landed on him without blinking.

"Well, for starters, I wanted to know what made you decide to start such a venture." He didn't add *at your age*, but she seemed intelligent enough to grasp his implication.

"I have my reasons. Personal ones that I need not disclose to you." Her eyes narrowed. "May I ask what firm you represent? And what interest they have in our facility?"

He could lie. Pretend he was here as a potential investor. But lies didn't sit well with Darius. If he expected his daughter to tell the truth, how could he do any less? He pulled a business card from his suit pocket. "I'm with Walcott Industries, ma'am. And I'm here to make you a proposition, one that could benefit you greatly and allow you to open two or more such maternity homes."

The woman's mouth turned down. "I highly doubt that, Mr. Reed, given the price of real estate in Toronto these days."

He leaned forward, elbows on his knees. "That's my point. If you moved your operation outside the city limits, you'd get a lot more property for your dollar. You could afford two houses easily with the profits you'd make from selling this place."

A crash sounded in the hallway. Darius's gaze swung to the doorway, where Miss Rosetti stared down at a platter of baked goods that were now scattered on the floor.

He jumped up and rushed to assist her.

Miss Rosetti looked past him. "Ruth, you're not thinking of selling the house, are you?"

The older woman rose. "No, my dear. I most certainly am not." She shot Darius a glare. "I was just about to inform Mr. Reed of that fact."

He helped the younger woman scoop up what looked like blueberry muffins and heaped them on the platter, which had fortunately stayed intact.

"Please join us, Miss Rosetti," he said. "I believe this conversation concerns you as well." Perhaps she would see the merit of his offer once she learned all the details.

She set the plate on a side table and took a seat next to Mrs. Bennington.

Darius hesitated, gathering his thoughts before crossing the room. "I'm here on behalf of Walcott Industries to make you the following offer." Reaching into his interior jacket pocket, he withdrew the papers that Mr. Walcott had drawn up. He placed them on the table in front of the women, then resumed his seat to wait while they read the short piece.

Miss Rosetti put a hand over her mouth, her eyes wide.

Mrs. Bennington, on the other hand, remained expressionless. A few seconds later, she straightened. "It's a generous offer, there's no denying that. Much more than the last time Mr. Walcott tried to entice me to sell. But you can tell your boss that my answer remains the same." With one finger, she slid the paper across the table. "I respectfully decline."

Miss Rosetti's shoulders sagged in obvious relief.

"But why would you turn down that kind of money?" Darius couldn't fathom her reluctance. She'd never get a better price for her property.

"This home belonged to my late husband and to his parents before him. It holds far too many memories for me to let it go." Mrs. Bennington got regally to her feet. "I'm sorry you've wasted your time, Mr. Reed. Now if you'll excuse us, we must get on with our day."

His mind scrambled for something to make her change her mind. "Mrs. Bennington, if you'd just reconsider—"

"You heard her." Miss Rosetti moved up beside the widow, color flooding her cheeks. "She said no."

Interesting. It appeared the younger woman had taken on the role of protector. Not that Mrs. Bennington needed anyone to defend her. Which begged the question: What exactly was the relationship between these two?

"Good day, Mr. Reed." Mrs. Bennington's words were polite, but the look she gave him was pure steel.

Darius knew when to cut his losses. "It was a pleasure meeting both of you." He gave a slight bow and left the room.

As he walked back to his car, his stomach sank. Mr. Walcott

wouldn't be happy at his lack of progress. Apparently Darius's charms weren't as effective as his boss had imagined.

Still, there was more than one way to achieve their desired outcome.

Darius's thoughts turned to the black-tie event. Though he hated to give up an evening with Sofia, he had no choice. He needed to get to the bottom of this strange alliance, and by doing so, perhaps he could figure out a way to break it.

8

Olivia frowned at her reflection in Ruth's full-length mirror, unable to recognize the glamorous-looking woman in the periwinkle gown who stared back. Except for the same brown eyes, she could see nothing recognizable about herself.

Ruth had insisted on lending Olivia a dress from her own closet, and since the two shared a similar build, the only alteration required was a shortened hem. Ruth's maid had quickly completed that task yesterday, and now the dress fit Olivia like it had been made for her. Yet that did nothing to alleviate her mounting anxiety.

Her scowl deepened. "Do I really have to go with you? I'm sure you'd do much better on your own."

Ruth stood beside her, the picture of elegance in a long silver gown and what looked like real diamonds sparkling at her neck. "Nonsense. You look spectacular."

That was the problem. Olivia didn't want to look spectacular. She'd always downplayed her looks, never wishing to draw undue attention to herself. Rory had been the only man she'd ever wanted to notice her, and he'd appreciated her natural look. Now, in this dress, with the borrowed pearl earrings and necklace, and her hair swept up in a cascade of curls, she'd never looked so dazzling. However, unlike Cinderella, Olivia wasn't sure she liked the sensation. It felt far too much like she was pretending to be someone she was not.

And though she might look the part of a society woman, she was in no way equipped to handle conversations with the hard-nosed businessmen Ruth planned to solicit financial support from.

Peering into the mirror, Ruth patted her hair. "One glimpse of you, my dear, and everyone will want to meet the woman who has inspired me to make such a bold move."

Alarm forced the air from Olivia's lungs. "You're not going to tell them—"

"Heavens no. I'd never do that. Your story is yours alone to share, or not, as you see fit."

"But how will we explain my involvement? People are already suspicious of our friendship." The skepticism in Mr. Reed's blue eyes came immediately to mind.

"I have it all worked out. I'll make an official statement at the beginning of the gala explaining how we met at church and how I offered you a place to stay during a transitional phase in your life. Our friendship grew from there, and we discovered a mutual passion for helping women in trouble, which led to the creation of Bennington Place. That should ward off most questions."

Olivia shook her head. "They won't accept that explanation. I know it."

Ruth took her firmly by the shoulders. "We have nothing to hide, Olivia. You must believe that in order to make everyone else believe it. If you cower in a corner like a frightened mouse, people will assume you're withholding something."

"But I am! My pregnancy. My incarceration. Either one could damage your reputation if word ever got out." Her hands shook as she pulled on elbow-length white gloves. "Maybe I should stay in the background as one of your employees hired to work in the home. No one would question that."

Ruth frowned. "You are much more than a mere employee."

Olivia's gaze dropped to the carpet. "I don't deserve to be." She certainly hadn't provided anything other than some opinions on how the house might run. No money. No property. No expertise— other than knowing how it felt to be alone and afraid . . .

"Olivia, look at me."

She raised her head, her eyes meeting Ruth's in the mirror.

"You are a child of God, just like everyone else in this world. We all make mistakes, and we are all worthy of redemption."

Olivia shook her head. It wasn't God she was worried about. It was the judgment of those morally superior types who would be in attendance tonight, looking for some juicy gossip.

"Believe me, all the people coming to this gala have made their share of mistakes too." Ruth tipped up her chin. "Repeat after me: They are no better than me."

"They are no better than me," Olivia whispered.

"With a little more conviction, please."

Olivia's lips twitched. "They are no better than me." Her voice came out louder this time.

"That's more like it." Ruth gave her a quick squeeze. "If you get in over your head with anyone, make an excuse to come and find me. I promise you will get through this, and it will be worth it when the donations start flooding in."

Olivia gave a reluctant nod and took a last look at herself. If only she could believe Ruth's claim, then maybe the nerves pinching her abdomen would subside long enough for her to draw a full breath.

Darius tugged at his overly tight bow tie as he entered the posh lobby of the Royal York Hotel. There were a thousand things he'd rather be doing tonight than attending this fundraiser. Even plucking chicken feathers for his mother sounded more fun than mingling with a bunch of rich socialites.

From time to time, his job required that he attend these types of events, and every time he had to grit his teeth and remind himself that it was only one unpleasant aspect of his career. In truth, Darius didn't really want to fit in with people who were more concerned with appearances than with establishing honest relationships.

The one thing that made this evening almost bearable was the fact that Miss Rosetti might be in attendance. Something about the woman aroused his curiosity. Her obvious youth seemed at odds with her serious demeanor as well as the world of pain that had radiated from her eyes. Yet there was a simplicity to her he'd found charming. She'd been wearing a plain skirt and blouse when they met, her dark hair in a tidy braid down her back. Even without a hint of cosmetics to enhance her features, her riveting brown eyes and heart-shaped face had captured his attention.

That she intrigued him took him by surprise, since she was the exact opposite of Meredith Cheeseman, the woman he'd been dating for several weeks now. What that said about him he didn't care to examine.

"Darius, there you are." Mr. Walcott crossed the carpeted lobby toward him, looking very polished in his black tuxedo. "I'd begun to think you weren't coming."

Darius shrugged off his unsettling thoughts to focus on the task at hand. "I'm here." *Begrudgingly*. He pasted on a smile. "Shall we get this over with?"

Mr. Walcott frowned, taking the cigar from between his lips. "Try to show a bit more enthusiasm, and remember what's at stake here. We need to warn off as many investors as possible." He led Darius to the wide staircase and started up, a trail of smoke drifting after him. "For the life of me, I don't understand how Mrs. Bennington expects to make money on this enterprise."

"I don't believe making a profit is her principal aim."

"Then that's her first mistake. One we will take full advantage of." He steered Darius toward the open conference room doors. "Who would want to invest in a business that doesn't intend to make a profit?"

"A philanthropist?" Darius peered inside the room, dismayed to see so many people milling about. He'd thought it might be a small affair.

Mr. Walcott ignored Darius's remark and headed inside. "Good thing there's a crowd," he said. "We won't be as visible. The less obvious we are, the better, if you get my drift."

"I understand. Subtlety is my middle name."

Walcott snorted, then blew out a smoke ring. "Ah, I see my first target. A. J. Worthington. You start on the other side of the room, and we'll meet up later to compare notes."

Once his boss had left his side, Darius blew out a relieved breath. *Overbearing* was almost an understatement when it came to Vincent Walcott. Darius preferred to handle matters with less bluster and more finesse.

He moved into the crowd, the strains of a three-person orchestra barely audible over the hum of conversation. Nodding to people as he went, he scanned the guests for any familiar faces. None, however, stood out. When he stopped at the bar to order a glass of ginger ale, someone slapped him on the shoulder.

"Mr. Reed, I didn't expect to see you here." Frederick Conboy, the mayor of Toronto, squeezed in beside him at the counter and ordered a scotch and soda.

Darius had only met the man once. The fact that he remembered Darius's name was more than impressive.

Conboy tugged his striped vest. "Are you here on business, or is this a personal invite?"

Darius calculated his response. What better opportunity could he have to feel out the mayor about the unseemliness of the Bennington project? This man's disapproval could potentially render the whole venture null and void.

"Business, sir. My employer is very much opposed to this

maternity home. He feels it would be a hindrance to the commerce in the area."

"I never thought of it as a hindrance." The mayor studied him. "Though it did cross my mind that the enterprise might be a little out of place in that area of town." He accepted the drink from the bartender and threw a few bills into the tip jar. "Mrs. Bennington argued that it was an ideal location with the right visibility for the women who would require their services."

"But what type of people will the facility attract?" Darius leaned toward him. "And will it undermine the neighboring businesses?"

The mayor pursed his lips. "You make a good point. I haven't made up my mind whether to endorse the home or not. I'll have to consider the businesses directly involved and get the owners' opinions on the matter." He clapped Darius's shoulder again. "Nice talking to you, Mr. Reed. Enjoy your evening."

"You too, sir."

Darius let out a relieved breath, then gulped down some of his ginger ale. Mr. Walcott would be happy to hear that the mayor hadn't yet decided to support the home. At the very least, Darius hoped he'd succeeded in planting some seeds of doubt.

The crowds in front of him parted, and a flash of blue caught his eye. An elegantly dressed woman stood with her back to him, talking to Mrs. Bennington. Darius moved through the group toward them. Who was the widow trying to coerce now? Some wealthy businessman's wife?

As he got closer, Mrs. Bennington stepped away to speak to someone else, and the woman in blue turned.

Darius's jaw dropped. It couldn't be . . .

The woman's eyes met his, and she instantly stiffened, her expression turning hostile. Then she ducked her chin and pushed through the crowd in the opposite direction.

Darius blinked. What happened to the simple young woman he'd met the other day? This woman wore a flowing blue gown and long white gloves. Her hair was styled in an elaborate fashion on top of her head, with some loose curls left to frame her face. But what really disturbed him was the bright red lipstick that made her painted lips stand out a mile away.

His shoulder muscles cinched. It seemed his initial impression of Miss Rosetti had been dead wrong. She was no better than a lot of the conniving women he knew, those who used their looks to lure men for their own purposes. Resentment burned through Darius's system, spurring his feet to move. He would make sure she didn't use her charms to take anyone for a sucker.

With renewed energy, he pushed through the crowd until he spied the flash of blue again. He slowed as he approached, realizing she was standing very close to a man in a brown suit.

But it wasn't just any man. It was Elliott Peterson, one of Walcott Industries' most influential, albeit obnoxious, clients.

Darius's lip curled. He should interrupt and save the sorry lout from the woman's wiles. It couldn't hurt to have the man in his debt.

Peterson leaned down and whispered something in Miss Rosetti's ear.

"How dare you!" She jerked away from him, but Peterson grabbed her arm.

"Come now, Miss Rosetti. You don't think I'd simply give my money away without some type of . . . reward?"

Disgust coursed through Darius's blood as he imagined what the man must have insinuated. No matter what he'd assumed about her intentions, Miss Rosetti didn't deserve to be treated in such a manner.

Darius stepped forward and held out his hand. "Mr. Peterson! I never would have pegged you for a philanthropist, especially not for a project of this nature."

The man's florid face turned thunderous, but he released his grip on Miss Rosetti to shake Darius's hand. "My financial dealings outside of Walcott Industries are none of your concern, Mr. Reed."

Darius ignored the implied threat. "I'm sure you'd like Mrs.

Bennington's input on any discussion involving the home. Shall I call her over?" He gave the man a steely stare, issuing a challenge of his own.

"Stay out of this, Reed. Or I'll tell Walcott you're interfering where you don't belong." The sour scent of whiskey washed over Darius's face.

Miss Rosetti used the distraction to back away several paces.

"I'm sure you don't wish to cause a scene," Darius said smoothly. "Especially with Mayor Conboy here tonight. It wouldn't do to make a bad impression."

Peterson growled his displeasure but immediately scanned the room, then gave a stiff nod. "We'll continue our discussion at a later date, Miss Rosetti. Right now, I see someone I need to speak to." With that, the man strutted off.

Darius turned back to the ashen woman. "It's a shame how some people can't hold their liquor," he quipped, hoping to lighten the situation. However, his poor attempt at humor fell flat when she didn't smile or thank him for his help.

"Excuse me, I need some air," she said stiffly. Without a backward glance, she headed toward the exit.

He blinked. The woman's whole body had been shaking. Had Mr. Peterson threatened her?

Darius quickly followed her out of the room into the hallway.

She paused by the staircase railing, pulled a handkerchief from her purse, then swiped it across her mouth, leaving a bright streak of red on the white cloth.

"Miss Rosetti, is there anything I can do for you?"

Her head flew up, and for a brief second, raw vulnerability flashed over her features. Tears trembled on her lower lashes, but she dabbed them away. "No, thank you. I'll be fine."

Darius took a cautious step forward. "I don't know what that man said, but he obviously upset you."

She pressed her lips into a thin line, shoving away from the railing to head down the stairs.

He hesitated only a moment before following her again. In her distraught condition, she might be prey for some other unscrupulous type. He would just keep an eye out and make sure no one else bothered her.

Olivia walked straight through the hotel lobby and out the front door, where she gulped in the cool night air.

She'd predicted this evening would turn out badly, and she hadn't been wrong. Dressing in this outrageous outfit had given everyone at the gala the wrong impression. Maybe other women could pull off this bold appearance, but all Olivia could hear was her father's voice. *"A woman who wears lipstick is nothing but una prostituta."*

The man who'd accosted her certainly thought she had loose morals, and likely he wasn't the only one making errant assumptions.

She paced the sidewalk in front of the hotel. If she had any idea how to get back to Ruth's house, she would start walking right now, despite her uncomfortable shoes. But she hadn't paid much attention to the route the taxi driver had taken. Nor did she have the cab fare to get a ride home.

She'd have to go back inside and tell Ruth she wanted to leave. However, the thought of disappointing the woman grated on Olivia's already taut nerves.

"Miss Rosetti?" a man said behind her.

A man whose voice was now becoming annoyingly familiar.

"Per l'amor del cielo." She whirled to face Mr. Reed. "Why are you following me?"

His lips twitched. "Did you just curse at me in Italian?"

Heat bled into her face. "Why? Are you Italian?" Though he had light olive skin similar to hers, his hair was darker, almost black, and his brilliant blue eyes were unlike any of her relatives'.

His grin broke free this time, dimples appearing in his cheeks.

"No, I'm not, but I do understand enough of the language to know when I've annoyed someone."

She huffed out a breath. "You didn't answer my question, Mr. Reed. Why did you follow me?"

And why do you look so handsome in that tuxedo? Olivia purposely kept her gaze trained on the traffic in front of them. She needed to guard her thoughts and her words around this one. He saw too much with those sharp eyes.

His dark brows drew together. "I sensed that man upset you more than you let on. I wanted to make sure you were all right."

The fact that his eyes drew hers like a magnet only increased her frustration. "I'm fine, now that I'm away from him." However, the man's vile words echoed in her mind, and she shuddered.

"You're cold. Here. Take this."

Before she could protest, Mr. Reed had removed his suit jacket and draped it over her shoulders. Warmth enveloped her, along with the spicy scent of his aftershave.

"Would you like to go back inside? Or perhaps I can see you home?"

While part of her wanted to take him up on his offer, the other part didn't quite trust him. It was too much of a coincidence that he was attending their fundraiser when only the other day he'd been trying to convince Ruth to sell her house. And just now he'd tried to dissuade Mr. Peterson from supporting their venture. She squared her shoulders. "Why are you here tonight, Mr. Reed? To discourage anyone who might wish to invest in our home?"

The light left his eyes, and his gaze shifted to the sidewalk. He seemed to debate his answer before releasing a long breath. "It's not a crime to make sure potential investors have all the facts. I'm merely bringing their attention to the concerns of the business owners in the area." He gave an unapologetic shrug, the wind flapping his white shirtsleeves.

She frowned. "What concerns?"

He shifted from one foot to the other. "To be honest, Miss

Rosetti, there's a fear that your home might attract some . . . undesirable types. Ones who might hinder clients from frequenting the businesses in the neighborhood."

He seemed to be talking in riddles. "What sort of undesirable types?"

A flush moved into his cheeks. "I don't like to say the word in front of a lady."

She frowned. "You mean streetwalkers?"

He nodded.

"That's the most narrow-minded, judgmental—" She inhaled sharply in an attempt to gain control of her emotions. "We intend to run a very respectable establishment, Mr. Reed, no matter who frequents our doorstep. We will provide women in need with a place of refuge, no matter their circumstances, until they're back on their feet with a plan for their future."

"Are you speaking from experience?" he asked softly.

She froze, every muscle tensing. Had he been looking into her background? Trying to find something to use against them? She fought to keep her expression neutral as she recalled the answers Ruth had made her practice. "As you no doubt heard Mrs. Bennington explain, I . . . fell on hard times recently, and Ruth was kind enough to offer me a place to stay."

He studied her, his blue eyes darkening. "So you decided to extend her kindness to other troubled women?"

She couldn't tell if he was mocking her or was genuinely interested. "In a manner of speaking, yes. We both have our own reasons for wanting to do this. Reasons that don't concern you." She turned on her heel and headed toward the hotel entrance.

"Miss Rosetti, wait. I didn't mean to pry. I'm honestly trying to understand what's behind this venture." His long strides brought him up beside her.

Once inside the lobby, she came to a halt. Then she removed his jacket and handed it back to him. "If you really want to know what we're all about, Mr. Reed, I challenge you to leave your preconceived notions behind and come see our operation with an open mind. Perhaps you'll learn something if you do."

He stood, staring, an expression of admiration creeping over his face.

A surge of power rushed through her. For once, she'd stood up for something she believed in, and amazingly enough, someone had actually listened.

"And when you report back to your employer, Mr. Reed, I hope you'll make him understand once and for all that Bennington Place is not for sale."

9

arius walked through the reception area of Walcott Industries, heading directly toward his office. The meeting with a potential client had not gone the way he'd envisioned at all. He'd thought he had the deal for a property on Bay Street wrapped up, but now the owner seemed to be wavering. Darius sensed that someone else might be making a more lucrative offer. Unless he could figure out who his competition was and what they were proposing, he wouldn't know how to make the proper counteroffer.

On top of that disappointment, his conversation with Miss Rosetti from two nights ago had left him strangely unsettled. Her insinuation that he had some sort of misguided bias against the maternity home grated on him.

"If you really want to know what we're all about, I challenge you to leave your preconceived notions behind and come see our operation with an open mind. Perhaps you'll learn something if you do."

He snorted. Why did her low opinion of him rankle so much?

Scowling, he shoved the key into his office door. With a bit more force than necessary, he tossed his briefcase on the desktop. The only good thing about today was that Mr. Walcott was out for the afternoon. Darius's report on the Bay Street property could wait until tomorrow.

A familiar laugh echoed down the hallway, breaking through his thoughts. Darius froze, his shoulders instantly tensing.

What was Meredith doing here? He searched his memory for some plans they might have made but couldn't recall anything.

He headed toward Kevin's office, where the sound of voices coming from the open door made him pause.

"Why, Mr. Caldwell, I think you've missed your calling in life." Meredith's laughter tinkled out. "You should be on stage as an entertainer."

Kevin's throaty chuckle followed. "You're too kind, Miss Cheeseman. I'm happy I could keep you amused while you wait. Though if I were Darius, I'd never leave such a lovely woman alone for long."

Darius peered around the doorway. Meredith was seated on the corner of Kevin's desk, beaming a smile at him. In her matching yellow dress and hat, she resembled a living ray of sunshine. Kevin stared up at her with a besotted look on his face, oblivious to Darius's presence.

What was he up to? Kevin knew Darius was courting Meredith. So why would he home in on Darius's territory?

A prickle of irritation itched the back of his neck, but he schooled his features into a pleasant expression before entering the room. "I thought I heard a familiar voice. Meredith, you didn't tell me you were dropping by today."

Her eyes went wide as she jumped to her feet. "Darius, there you are."

Kevin shoved his seat back and rose, a deep flush invading his cheeks.

"I was about to give up on you." Meredith smoothed her dress. "Mr. Caldwell was kind enough to keep me company until you returned."

"So I see." Darius shot Kevin a look. "Thank you, Kevin. I believe I can take it from here."

The man had the grace to look sheepish. "Yes, sir. It was a pleasure, Miss Cheeseman."

"Likewise. I hope to see you again, Mr. Caldwell." With a flick of her sleek blond curls, Meredith sailed out the door.

Darius followed her into his office. "To what do I owe this unexpected visit, Meredith?"

Her poise seemingly back in place, she graced him with a coquettish smile as she came over to straighten his lapel, a tiny gesture that hinted at an intimacy Darius found reassuring. Maybe he'd misinterpreted the flirting between her and Kevin. Then again, flirting seemed to be as natural as breathing to Meredith.

"I came to invite you to dinner tonight. Mama and Daddy insist." She pouted. "You always have an excuse, but—"

"I'd love to come to dinner."

Her brows arched. "You would?"

"It happens I have a free evening."

The Cheesemans usually dined later than his own family. If he left the office soon, he could spend a couple of hours with Sofia before heading out. Then he wouldn't have to feel guilty for another night away from his daughter.

"Wonderful." Meredith clapped her hands together, her attractive features brightening. "We'll expect you at seven, then."

"Seven it is."

She reached up on her tiptoes and kissed his cheek. The floral scent of her perfume enveloped him like a promise. "I'll see you then, darling. And don't be late. Daddy abhors tardiness."

Satisfaction spread through Darius's chest as he watched her walk away. Meredith was beautiful and sophisticated, a true Toronto blue blood—exactly the type of woman he hoped to marry one day. With the prominent Cheeseman family behind them, Sofia would be accepted into all the right social circles—ones Darius could only dream of—guaranteeing his daughter the bright future she deserved.

Perhaps if things between him and Meredith continued to

blossom, he could give Sofia a new mother sooner than anticipated and get her away from her grandparents' influence before his little girl became too ethnic for her own good.

"Has any of the fundraising money started to come in yet?" Olivia asked Ruth as they washed the supper dishes. Two days had passed since the gala and they hadn't spoken at any length about the event.

"As a matter of fact, I received a few donations today." Ruth placed a newly dried teacup in the cupboard. Though they had a cook to prepare the main meals and a maid to help with many other household chores, Ruth and Olivia often helped tidy the kitchen in the evenings. "I do wish we could have pinned the mayor down for an endorsement. I'm certain that once he gives us his backing, the floodgates will open and even more money will start pouring in."

"Is there a reason why he's hesitating?"

"I presume he's waiting to see which way the wind blows, politically speaking. He wouldn't want to alienate any potential voters."

Olivia scrubbed a pot with a brush. She'd never paid much attention to politics. Whenever Papà talked about it with her brothers, she usually tuned them out. But now that Olivia was starting her own nonprofit venture, she should probably learn as much as she could about the way the city operated.

"Excuse me, Mrs. Bennington. There's someone at the door." Margaret appeared in the kitchen doorway. "It's a woman, and she asked for you."

"Thank you, Margaret." Ruth hastily dried her hands. "Olivia, you'd better come too in case it's a potential new guest."

"Yes, of course."

Ruth had started calling the women who stayed at Bennington Place *guests*, a lovely term that made Olivia think of a cozy hotel or inn.

She followed Ruth down the hallway to the front entrance, where a young woman stood, suitcase in hand. Her loose-fitting dress did a poor job of concealing her expanded girth.

"Good evening. I'm Ruth Bennington. And this is Olivia Rosetti."

"Hello." The woman bit her lip, anxiety radiating from her. "I'm Nancy Holmes."

"Nice to meet you, Nancy. Won't you come into the parlor so we can chat in comfort?"

The woman followed them into the front room, where they took seats around the coffee table. Miss Holmes set her suitcase beside her chair and clutched her hands on her lap. Red-rimmed eyes darted nervously around the room.

"Would you care for something to drink?" Olivia asked. "Tea or lemonade?"

"No, thank you."

Olivia longed to give her a hug and tell her everything would be all right. But she didn't dare yet, not until the woman felt more comfortable.

"I read about your home in the newspaper," Miss Holmes blurted out. "And I'd like to know how much it costs to stay here. I don't have much money, but I could pay something."

"We don't require compensation," Ruth said in a soothing voice. "All we ask of the women staying here is that they help with the chores in any way they can."

Miss Holmes blinked. "Oh, I see."

She looked to be in her mid-twenties with plain features, her light-brown hair pinned back in a bun. Her gaze continued to bounce around the room.

Olivia slid closer on the sofa. "How far along are you, Miss Holmes?"

The woman's gaze darted to Olivia's face, then away. "Almost five months. And please call me Nancy."

"What about the baby's father?" Ruth asked.

Nancy's features hardened. "He wants nothing to do with me. He doesn't believe the baby is his."

Not an uncommon occurrence as Olivia was discovering. "I'm so sorry. But please know that you're more than welcome to stay here if that's what you decide."

Nancy's whole frame slumped. "I have nowhere else to go. My father just returned from an extended business trip and told me I had to leave."

"I know what that's like, believe me." Olivia's throat tightened as she forced away memories of her own father's reaction. "You don't have to worry, Nancy. You have a safe place with us." Olivia's chest warmed as it always did when she said those words. Words she only wished she could have heard.

"Thank you so much. You have no idea how much that means." Nancy's voice broke.

"Have you eaten dinner?" Ruth asked.

The girl shook her head. "I've been sitting in the park for hours trying to figure out what to do."

"Then I'll heat a plate for you while Olivia gets you settled in." Ruth rose from her seat. "Welcome to Bennington Place, Nancy. I hope you'll soon feel right at home."

Seated at the Cheesemans' dining room table, Darius sipped from his water glass while discreetly studying the room. A magnificent room at that, with vaulted ceilings and an ornate chandelier hanging over the long mahogany table. Crystal, china, and silver graced the long expanse, with several vases of fresh flowers spaced evenly along the way.

This was exactly the type of house Darius envisioned owning one day. Classy and elegant. Not filled with mismatched furniture and worn carpets.

"It's good to finally have a chance to speak with you, Mr. Reed." Meredith's mother, a tall, stylish woman with the same coloring as her daughter, pierced him with a shrewd gaze. "Meredith has told us wonderful things about you. And of course my husband knows you from your business dealings."

"I'm honored to meet you too, ma'am." Darius set down his glass and shifted slightly on the plush chair.

"So, tell us a little about yourself. How long have you lived in Toronto?"

"All my life. My parents moved here before I was born."

"Ah. And what does your family do?"

With effort, Darius held the woman's gaze and did his best not to flinch, picturing his father's grease-stained overalls and perpetually dirty fingernails. *A mechanic's lot in life*, Papá always said. "My father owns his own business. My mother looks after my daughter while I'm at work and takes care of the family." Had Meredith told her parents that he had a daughter? He ran a finger under his collar.

"What type of business is your father in?" Mr. Cheeseman picked up his fork. "Property management like yourself?"

"No, sir." Darius hesitated. "He owns an auto repair shop."

Mr. Cheeseman's hand stilled for a moment before he continued to cut his steak. "I imagine business must be brisk now that so many people have cars."

"Very much so." Darius picked up his water and took a sip.

"You should see Darius's office at Walcott Industries, Mama," Meredith jumped in. "It overlooks the whole downtown."

"How did you end up working for Mr. Walcott?" Mrs. Cheeseman peered at him over her wine glass.

Darius tried not to squirm as he swallowed his last bite of steak. This felt more like a job interview than a friendly dinner. "I started in the mail room and worked my way up while taking business courses."

"Impressive. Are you still studying?" Mr. Cheeseman asked.

"Yes, sir. I take a course at the university on Saturday mornings. It will take a while to earn my degree, but I will eventually do it."

"I admire a young man with ambition." Mr. Cheeseman pointed a fork at him. "Judging by our dealings with your company, I know you'll go far there."

"That's my plan, sir."

"I understand you live with your parents at present." Mrs. Cheeseman made it sound as though it were a sin not to have a place of his own.

"A temporary arrangement, so my mother can watch Sofia while I work."

Why did Darius feel the purpose of this whole meal was for Mr. Cheeseman to convince his wife that Darius was worthy of their daughter? And why did he feel that he was failing most miserably?

Meredith pushed away from the table. "Darling, I'd love to show you Mama's gardens out back before we have dessert." She held out a hand to him.

"Good idea." Mr. Cheeseman beamed. "It's a lovely summer evening. And Marion's roses are something to behold. We'll have coffee and cake in the parlor when you're ready."

Ignoring Mrs. Cheeseman's disgruntled look, Darius followed Meredith through the house to a rear door that led to the garden.

Once outside, Darius exhaled a long breath, grateful for the reprieve. What an incredible yard. Slightly outside the downtown core, this neighborhood allowed for larger expanses of lawn and beautiful landscaping. He had no doubt that despite Mr. Cheeseman giving his wife credit for the amazing floral display, a hired gardener was most likely responsible for its manicured upkeep.

Meredith took his arm as they made their way along the flagstone path. "I'm sorry for all Mama's questions," she said. "I know Daddy will have a word with her while we're out here. Hopefully she'll be more hospitable when we return."

"That's all right." Darius smiled down at her. "It's only natural to want to know more about the man who's dating her daughter."

A gleam of interest lit her features. "And this is only natural too." Without warning, she tugged him behind a tall cedar tree and kissed him smack on the lips. His pulse immediately thudded to life, but he quickly pulled away from her.

What was she thinking? Her parents could be watching from any window.

Meredith's blue eyes swirled with a mixture of hurt and embarrassment. "Darius, don't you find me attractive?"

"Of course. You're a beautiful woman, Meredith."

"Then why haven't you tried to kiss me? We've been dating for a while now, and all you've done is kiss my cheek."

Why hadn't he? The answer to that was complicated. Residual loyalty to Selene perhaps, combined with indecision as to how serious he was about their relationship. He didn't want to give Meredith any false impressions until he was certain about their future. "I guess I was taking things slowly."

"What if I don't want to go slowly?" She peeked up through her long lashes. "What if I'd like to go much faster?"

Darius blinked at her bold declaration, his collar suddenly seeming too tight again.

"I'm twenty-one, Darius, and my parents are serious about me making a good match." She gave a shrug. "I'm afraid if you don't make your intentions known soon, Daddy will marry me off to one of his other acquaintances."

Darius frowned. "Why the rush?"

Meredith hesitated, then sighed. "It's because of my sister. Sissy's turning eighteen in a few months, and Mama is planning her debut."

"Debut?"

"Her coming out to society. Introducing her to all the eligible men."

"Oh." He still didn't see the problem.

"As the oldest daughter, I'm supposed to be married, or at least engaged, by then. Otherwise it's an embarrassment to me and my family."

"That's . . ." *Ridiculous*. But he couldn't say that without offending her. "I don't know what to say. Our traditions don't include such a ceremony."

She clutched his arm. "If you care about me at all, won't you consider asking Daddy for my hand? I . . . admire you very much, Darius. You're the one I want for a husband." She pulled his face close and kissed him again.

This time he let himself explore the sensations that washed over him. The softness of her lips, the brush of her fingers over his cheek, the way her lush figure felt in his arms. It had been a long time since he'd held a woman, and the feelings rushed back in an explosion of need.

Before things got too heated, he pulled back and attempted to get his heart rate under control. There was definite chemistry between them, which boded well for a future together. Really, what was he waiting for?

The answer hit him square in the chest. *Sofia*.

"I'd like you to get to know my daughter first, Meredith. After all, if we marry, you'll play a big part in Sofia's life."

Meredith's lips turned up. "I'd love to. She seems like such a sweet child. It will be an honor to be her stepmother."

She was saying and doing all the right things. So why were silent alarm bells ringing in his head?

"Very well. I'll speak to your father this evening and make my intentions known. If your parents agree, we can be engaged before your sister's party."

She gave a little squeal and clapped her hands. "I'm so happy, Darius. I promise I'll make you a good wife." Then she paused, her lashes fluttering. "Would you mind if we make it official tonight? It would mean the world to me."

He stared at her, trying to decipher her true motive. If he'd sensed the least bit of smugness or conceit in her request, he would have refused outright. But the hint of vulnerability in her eyes crumbled his reserve. "I suppose a few more weeks won't change anything." He took her hand. "Meredith, will you be my wife and Sofia's stepmother?"

Actual tears formed in her eyes. "Yes, Darius. I would love to."

Because she expected it, he pulled her close and kissed her again. A seal of the promise he'd just made to her.

Then, forcing away any lingering doubts, he smiled down at her. This upcoming marriage would secure his future and, most importantly, Sofia's. His daughter would go to the best schools and enjoy every opportunity in life. Darius would never have to worry that she might be exposed to the type of prejudice that he and Selene had suffered. Prejudice that had ultimately caused Selene's death.

He gazed up at the clear skies overhead, his thoughts turning to his late wife. *I hope you approve, Selene. We'll never have to worry about our little one again.*

10

Olivia and Margaret strolled along the sidewalk, heading back to the house. Even though it was still early in the day, the heat had already started to climb. It would be hot and sticky by the afternoon. All the more reason Olivia tried to take her walks in the coolness of the morning.

Olivia scanned the buildings as they walked. It was a lovely neighborhood, right on the border of the commercial district, with residences on the other side. The only thing that marred the street was the empty lot to the left of Bennington Place. Ruth told her that someone had bought her former neighbor's place some years back and had torn the house down, but nothing had been done since. She imagined the new owner must have run into financial difficulties and couldn't afford to rebuild. A shame for such a nice property to sit idle.

Perhaps if the maternity home did well enough to warrant expansion, one day they might be in a position to purchase the lot and build there themselves.

Just another one of her daydreams.

Olivia smiled as she walked, breathing in the fragrant air. She enjoyed her daily outings and did her best to get the residents to join her, knowing how beneficial exercise would be for their pregnancy. Even in the reformatory, the inmates had been encouraged to walk the perimeter of the yard during their thirty minutes of daily activity. That half hour was the only time they'd had any semblance of freedom, when they could speak to one another without worry of censure. Her thoughts flew to Joannie with a pang of guilt. Olivia hadn't been back to see her since she'd learned the awful news about Mabel. She really needed to make time to go back and visit, to remind her friend that she wasn't alone.

"I think Patricia is starting to feel better," Margaret said as they turned a corner. "Her appetite has certainly improved."

"I noticed that too." Olivia glanced over at her companion. Margaret had started to blossom herself, coming out of her shell more around Olivia and Ruth. The fact that she would even venture out in public was a huge achievement in Olivia's opinion.

"How about Nancy?" she asked, taking advantage of Margaret's willingness to talk. "Has she opened up to any of you?"

"Not really. She keeps to herself mostly, but she'll come around in time. Like I did." Margaret gave a shy smile that brightened her eyes. With the morning sun illuminating her clear skin and freckles, she appeared even younger than her eighteen years.

A wave of affection rose in Olivia's chest as she wound her arm through Margaret's. "I'm glad you feel comfortable with us. That was one of our main goals in starting Bennington Place. We want our residents to truly feel at home."

"You're doing a wonderful job of that."

Shouting from up ahead drew Olivia's attention. Across the street, their neighbor Mr. Simmons stood on the curb, gesturing toward a woman pacing in front of Ruth's gate. Olivia quickened her steps toward them, while Margaret hung back.

"We don't want your kind around here," Mr. Simmons shouted. "Go back where you belong."

The woman came to a stop, gripping the bag in her hand. She was dressed in a red skirt and long black jacket, an outfit much too warm for the weather. A mixture of emotions played over her heavily made-up features, and she looked ready to bolt.

"Can I help you?" Olivia asked as she approached. A glance at the woman's waistline told Olivia that the woman was definitely expecting.

"No, thank you." She retreated a few steps.

Olivia slowly came closer, noting that Margaret had already moved past them and headed inside, leaving the gate open behind her.

"I told you this would happen," Mr. Simmons continued to rant. "First lousy immigrants, now women of ill repute."

Olivia whirled to face the obnoxious man. She'd put up with his snide remarks before, but she would not allow him to harass anyone else. "That's enough, Mr. Simmons. You need to mind your own business."

"This neighborhood is my business, and I don't appreciate a bunch of loose women living here."

Blood thundered in Olivia's ears. How dare he talk to them like that? Using all her self-control, she bit back a string of Italian insults, knowing that stooping to his level would only fuel his hatred. Instead, she turned her back on the horrible man.

"I'm terribly sorry about that," she said to the woman. "My name is Olivia Rosetti. I help run the maternity home. Would you like to come in for a cup of tea?"

The hardness in the woman's dark eyes eased a bit. She pursed her painted red lips and shook her head. "I do not know. Maybe dis was not a good idea." Her words were laced with a distinct French-Canadian accent.

"Please don't allow that rude man to sway you. Come inside and see what the residence is like. If you don't care for it, all it will cost is a few minutes of your time."

Indecision played across the woman's features.

Olivia took the opportunity to look over her shoulder, relieved to note that the old man had trudged back onto his porch.

"All right," the woman finally said. "I will take that cup of tea."

"Wonderful." Olivia led her up to the front door. "Please come in."

Because Margaret and some of the other residents were in the parlor, Olivia ushered the woman to the sunroom, where they could have more privacy. Ruth was out at an appointment, or Olivia would have invited her to join them. She asked the woman to have a seat and then went to the kitchen to see about the tea.

On her way back, Olivia hesitated in the hall, sensing the need for caution with the woman inside. She'd seen several prostitutes while at the Mercer, and though none of the other inmates were allowed to interact with them, Olivia knew enough to recognize a woman in that profession. Mr. Simmons's accusation might very well be true. The thought gave Olivia pause, but this woman deserved the same consideration as any other potential resident.

Lord, please help me to treat her fairly, without judgment, and to do what's best for her and her child.

On an exhale, Olivia summoned up her friendliest expression and entered the room. "Mrs. Neale will bring our tea in a moment." She took a seat on the sofa, silently blessing the warming rays that made the room so cheerful. "May I ask your name?"

The woman sat rigidly on her chair. "Cherise." She lifted her chin as if to challenge Olivia to say anything about it.

"What a lovely name." Olivia smiled and folded her hands in her lap. "How can we help you, Cherise?"

A beat of silence ensued while the woman seemed to consider her words. "As you probably noticed, I am having a baby in about two or three months."

"And you need a place to stay until then?"

"Yes." The terse reply accompanied a hard stare. "But I need to know what would be expected if I come here."

Cherise's tough exterior didn't fool Olivia. The woman's trembling hands hinted at the fear beneath her bravado.

"Nothing would be expected other than helping with a few chores where you're able."

Cherise rolled her eyes. "What about going to church and atoning for my sins?"

Olivia kept her tone even. "We're always happy if our residents choose to attend services with us, but it's not a requirement. There's no judgment here, Cherise. Our goal at Bennington Place is to keep you healthy, ensure a safe delivery for your child, and assist you in making decisions for the future. In other words, we're here to support you in any way we can."

Cherise frowned. "You are so young. How can you know about such matters?"

Olivia considered her answer, then decided honesty was the best policy. "I may be young, but I was once in your shoes. My family disowned me, and if Ruth hadn't taken me in, I don't know where I would be today." She withheld the part about being incarcerated. Olivia chose to share her experience at the reformatory only with people she trusted absolutely.

One perfectly lined brow rose. "You have a baby?"

Olivia sucked in a breath. The mere mention of Matteo still had the power to shatter her.

Just then Mrs. Neale arrived with the tea. Glad for the distraction, Olivia thanked her and rose to pour the drinks, amazed that her hands remained steady.

Once Cherise had taken a few sips of her tea, Olivia felt ready to continue the conversation. "You asked about my baby," she said. "I was forced to give my son up for adoption. Something I wouldn't wish on anyone." She held Cherise's gaze. "I believe every mother should have the right to decide whether or not she will keep her child. It's one of the reasons Ruth and I started Bennington Place."

"*Je comprends.* I see." Cherise set her cup aside. "To be fair, you should know what I do for a living."

Olivia held up a hand. "We only need to know if you are in any danger. Or if your profession might bring danger here."

"I do not think so. I worked as long as I could until I could no longer hide my condition. Then my . . . boss threw me out. He will not try to find me."

"Do you have any family?" Olivia asked gently.

"*Non*." Her mouth flattened into a hard red line.

There was a story there, Olivia was certain.

"Very well. Would you like to see our rooms?"

Cherise hesitated. "How many other women are here?"

"We have three so far. You will be the fourth."

"Will I have to share a room?"

"For now, no. Eventually when we get more residents, you might have to."

Relief eased the tension in her face. "And you do not require payment?"

"No." Olivia smiled. "We only ask that you are respectful of everyone else and do your part to keep the house clean."

"The others, they will not object to someone of my . . . profession being here?"

Olivia wished she could answer with any degree of certainty. But so far, the women had been very accepting of each other without being nosy about one another's backgrounds.

"Everyone here has a story, Cherise. Some girls are open about their circumstances, some are not. We have a policy that none of our guests are to treat one another disrespectfully. So, unless you wish to tell them, they can only speculate." She paused to soften her voice. "Though it might not hurt to wash off a little of your makeup."

The woman's shoulders stiffened, but she nodded. "I can do that."

"Good." Olivia rose. "Let's get you settled upstairs. Welcome to Bennington Place, Cherise."

11

Olivia sat at the big oak desk in the office she now shared with Ruth and pored over the figures in front of her. For once she was grateful for her experience in keeping her parents' books at the store, which allowed her to understand the intricacies of expenses versus income. The trouble was, she also knew when things weren't going well. Biting her lip, she redid her calculations, then huffed out a loud breath.

In the red again.

Wincing, she recalled her optimistic words to Mr. Reed at the gala about not requiring their venture to make a profit. But they at least needed to break even. Somehow they would have to find a way to obtain more donations, or else drastically reduce their expenses. Maybe tonight she and Ruth could find time to sit down and go over each item, line by line.

The doorbell chimed. Olivia waited to see if one of the girls would answer.

Most of the women were too nervous to answer the door, in case it was someone they didn't wish to see, like an angry partner or family member. Remaining invisible was a top priority for most of them, which was something Olivia wanted to work toward changing. No matter their circumstances, they were all children of God, deserving of compassion and forgiveness.

A second bell sounded.

It could be another woman in need of shelter. The thought of missing a potential resident spurred Olivia forward as she headed down the hall and opened the door.

Darius Reed stood on the stoop, a grin on his handsome face. "Good afternoon, Miss Rosetti. I've come to take you up on your challenge."

She bit back her annoyance and schooled her features into a cool mask. "What challenge is that?"

"Don't tell me you've forgotten already?" He stepped inside onto the mat. "As I recall, you encouraged me to set aside my preconceived notions and view your enterprise with an open mind." He doffed his hat. "So here I am."

Oh no. What had she gotten herself into? Olivia never dreamt he would take her literally. She studied him for a moment, frowning. "You could have telephoned first."

"And you could have said no."

She bit her lip. All the residents were upstairs at the moment. She supposed it wouldn't hurt to try and make Mr. Reed understand their goal in starting Bennington Place. Perhaps then he'd stop his campaign to discourage potential investors and to convince Ruth to sell. "Since you're here, I guess I could show you around the main level."

"Sounds like a good place to start." He hung his hat on a hook in the front hall.

Olivia gestured to the door on the right. "You've seen the parlor. This is our main gathering area. We have tea here in the evenings and listen to the radio or do needlework. Some of us are knitting socks for the soldiers." It seemed everyone knew someone away at war.

Mr. Reed's presence filled the room as he scanned the interior. "Very nice. Did you help decorate?" He ran a finger over the wooden mantel.

"No. This is the original décor. All we did was add some more seating and a few side tables."

He turned the full force of his blue eyes on her. "Did Mrs. Bennington have to make many renovations? I heard about some construction work going on before the official opening."

Olivia tensed. Was he fishing for information to use against them? "We had a bit of work done upstairs." She clasped her hands in front of her as she walked the perimeter of the room. "Ruth added a second, larger bathroom and reconfigured the bedrooms to accommodate more residents."

"I see."

"And she updated the kitchen as well." Olivia bit her lip to curb the tendency to ramble. Why did this man make her nervous?

"I'd love to see that."

Olivia frowned. Could his reason for feigning interest in the renovations be to ascertain the property's new worth? "Let's move to the dining room next. The kitchen is at the back of the house."

"I shall defer to the expertise of my tour guide." A teasing note rang in his voice.

She glanced over to find his eyes brimming with amusement.

With an annoyed huff, she led the way down the hall to the dining room. "This room hasn't changed either, except that Ruth added a larger table and more chairs. One day, we hope to have a full house that can include up to twelve residents."

He looked around the room, his gaze moving from the sideboard to the pictures adorning the walls. "Tell me more about your goal in opening this home, Miss Rosetti."

"Very well." She rested her hand on a chair back and paused to search for the right words, wanting to provide enough information to satisfy his curiosity without revealing too many personal details. "We want to offer women in crisis a safe haven where they can stay until they're able to get back on their feet."

"Pregnant women in particular, I presume, since it's a maternity home."

She lifted her chin. "Yes, but we wouldn't turn away any woman in need of shelter. There's a definite lack of this sort of resource in the city."

His dark brows rose. "Not really. Toronto has several maternity homes that I'm aware of."

"True, but those are mostly religion-based—not that I have anything against religion," she added hastily when he frowned. "However, some women prefer a nondenominational residence. Our aim at Bennington Place is to provide a welcoming atmosphere, one that enables women to determine the best course for their future and their child's."

"You sound as though you're speaking from experience." Mr. Reed's blue eyes drilled into her.

Olivia gripped the chair, her heart racing, but somehow she managed to hold his gaze without wavering. "I have witnessed some very sad cases, Mr. Reed, and have become passionate about injustice toward the underprivileged in our society. Women and children in particular." She gestured to the door. "Shall we continue the tour?"

He waited a beat before nodding. "After you."

They exited the room and moved toward the rear of the house, where a narrow corridor branched off to the right.

Mr. Reed peered down the hall. "Where does that lead?"

"To the library that now serves as our office. Beyond that room is a storage closet, a sunroom, and the stairs to the basement."

"I do appreciate a good library. Do you mind?" He started toward the office.

Olivia struggled for an appropriate response. Yes, she did mind, since their private financial records lay open on the desk with various receipts and invoices strewn about. Instead of answering, she rushed ahead and entered the room before him. "It's a bit of a mess in here. I was right in the middle of some bookkeeping when you arrived." Smoothly, she slid over to the desk and closed the ledger, then straightened the papers into a pile.

"Don't tell me you're a bookkeeper as well?" Again he seemed to be teasing her. He came closer, his woodsy scent surrounding her.

"I know how to keep a business ledger, if that's what you mean."

"A woman of many talents, it seems." He winked and then wandered over to peruse the bookcases.

Her nerves continued to spin in the presence of this man who elicited a contradictory mixture of annoyance and admiration. While his attention was elsewhere, she took the opportunity to study him, noting the fine cut of his suit, the starched white shirt and crisp necktie. His dark hair was meticulously styled off his forehead, highlighting his well-shaped brows and thick lashes. He reminded her a little of Clark Gable from the movie posters she'd seen. Her mouth pinched. He was far too good-looking for his own good. Probably guilty of breaking hearts all over the city.

As he reached out to examine one of the volumes, Olivia glanced at his hand, noting the absence of a wedding band. How had a handsome, successful man like Darius Reed escaped marriage? Come to think of it, how had he escaped going to war? He was of the right age and seemingly fit. So why was he still here when good men like Rory sacrificed their very lives to serve their country?

Irritation snapped through her. "Why are you not off fighting in the war, Mr. Reed, like all the other respectable men?"

His hand stilled before he replaced the book and slowly turned. When he did, no trace of amusement remained. "Believe me, if I'd had no responsibilities, I would have signed up immediately."

She raised a brow, waiting for more of an explanation.

His blue eyes turned hard. "My wife died just before the start of the war, and my young daughter needed me. I was not about to have her lose both her parents." He shoved his hands into his pockets, his mouth flattening into a grim line.

Heat scorched Olivia's cheeks. "I'm sorry. I had no idea. . . ." She trailed off, certain nothing she could say would make up for her insensitivity. "Forgive me. I sometimes blurt things out without thinking."

Mr. Reed shook his head. "No need to apologize. It's a question I get asked quite often, and I'll admit I'm a bit touchy about the subject." His face relaxed into a smile. "Now, what's next on our tour?"

Darius stood in the massive kitchen beside a double-sized range and whistled. "What my mother wouldn't give for a stove like this."

"Impressive, isn't it? We figured we'd need a large oven to feed the number of residents we expect." Miss Rosetti gestured to the high kitchen cabinets. "These cupboards were already here, so we had more than enough storage for the extra dishes and cookware."

He crossed the pristine linoleum floor, obviously recently installed, toward a white cabinet in the corner with a metal handle. He ran a reverent hand over the smooth surface. "Is this a refrigerator?"

Miss Rosetti grinned. "It is. Ruth splurged on this, mostly to impress the cook, I think, though I will admit it's very convenient. The salesman told us that soon every household will have one." She laughed, her eyes brightening. For a brief moment, the guarded look left her features, and she seemed almost relaxed.

"It makes our little icebox at home look rather outdated." His lips twitched into a smile.

"Where do you live, Mr. Reed?" She leaned against the counter near the sink.

He almost said "the Greek quarter" but caught himself in time. "Near Danforth Avenue. I'm staying with my parents right now so my mother can watch Sofia while I work."

"Sofia. What a beautiful name." Miss Rosetti's whole face softened. "I imagine she's the light of your life."

Darius nodded, his throat tightening. "She's my whole world. The reason for everything I do."

She stepped closer. "Then she's lucky to have a father like you. Not every child is so fortunate."

Darius stared into her deep brown eyes, mesmerized by the churn of emotion he saw there. Sorrow, regret, and perhaps a touch of admiration? What secrets did their depths hold?

She lowered her gaze, as though suspecting she'd revealed too much, and the sweep of her lashes brushed her cheeks.

"What about your family?" he asked, hoping she might open up about herself. "Do they live nearby?"

He regretted his words immediately when her whole demeanor changed. Visible anguish washed over her features before her expression hardened.

"They live on the other side of town. Not far from the Jewish Market," she said.

"Ah, one of my mother's favorite places to shop when she gets the chance. Does your family own a business there?" His heart beat a quick rhythm in his chest. He risked alienating her altogether with his barrage of questions, yet he couldn't seem to help himself. He wanted to know so much more about this mysterious woman.

"Not in the market itself, but a few blocks away." She scooted by him to open the refrigerator and removed a glass pitcher. "May I offer you something to drink?"

"No, thank you. I'm fine."

The obvious ploy to change the subject led him to suspect all was not right between Miss Rosetti and her family. He recalled Mrs. Bennington saying at the gala that Miss Rosetti had fallen on hard times or some such expression. "I take it you're not on good terms with your family."

Her head whipped up. "That is none of your business, Mr. Reed." Her frosty tone matched the icy pitcher in her hand. She glared at him before taking a glass from an upper shelf and filling it with the chilled water.

Darius ran a hand over his jaw. *Terrific*. Just when she was becoming more at ease around him, he'd overstepped the invisible boundary once again.

"It's a bad habit of mine, asking too many questions," he said ruefully. "Especially when I sense a mystery in the making." He gave her his best smile, one that usually got him what he wanted. In this case, another smile.

But her lips remained pressed into an unforgiving line as she returned the pitcher to the refrigerator.

Darius searched for a way to get the conversation back on track. At this rate, she'd show him to the door, and he certainly wasn't ready to leave yet. Before he could come up with an idea, the clatter of rapid footsteps sounded.

"Olivia! I need your help." A frantic female voice came from the hall. "There's a flood in the bathroom. What should I do?"

Miss Rosetti whirled around and darted out of the room.

Darius followed right on her heels.

A pregnant woman stood at the base of the stairs, her blouse and skirt showing dark wet patches. Damp strands of hair lay plastered against her cheeks.

"Margaret, what happened?" Miss Rosetti rushed up the staircase, the girl right behind her.

"I don't know," Margaret said. "I was washing my hands and the next thing I knew water started spraying everywhere."

"In the new bathroom?" Miss Rosetti asked over her shoulder.

"Yes. I tried to stop it, but it was too much."

"Oh dear. Ruth will be devastated." Miss Rosetti increased her pace and took a sharp right turn at the next level.

Partway down the corridor, they entered a room. One of the women shrieked.

Darius dashed inside, dismayed to find the tiled floor covered in over an inch of water. A stream spewed forth from the curved pipe below the sink.

Already soaked, Miss Rosetti opened a closet door, grabbed a stack of towels, and began to throw them onto the floor.

"Allow me." Darius pulled a towel from her arms. Squinting against the spray, he bent to wrap the cloth around the leaking joint. Once the flow stopped, he tied the ends into a knot. "That should hold it for a little while. Long enough to get a plumber here, hopefully. A bucket underneath would be helpful too, if you have one." He wiped the moisture from his face.

"Thank you. That's a great help." Miss Rosetti then turned to the distraught pregnant girl. "Margaret, go and get some dry clothes on. Mr. Reed and I will handle the situation."

"I'm so sorry." Margaret looked close to tears.

Miss Rosetti put her arm around the girl's shoulders. "It's not your fault," she said in a soothing voice. "Maybe the plumber didn't tighten the joint properly when he installed the sink. Or maybe a crack developed. I'm sure he'll fix the problem in no time." She smiled at her. "After you change, would you mind putting the kettle on for tea? I think we'll need a cup once we finish here."

Margaret nodded, looking decidedly relieved. "Right away."

Once the girl had left, Darius gave Miss Rosetti an admiring glance. "You handled that very adeptly."

One side of her lips tipped upward. "I learned that trick in my parents' store. If a customer complained about the peaches not being ripe enough, I moved them on to the plums." She wiped her hands on the waist of her skirt, then pushed a long strand of hair off her forehead. "I'll get a bucket, and I'd better call the plumber before Ruth gets back and sees this disaster." She hesitated, a hand on the doorframe. "You don't have to stay, Mr. Reed. You've done more than enough already."

He looked down at his sodden pants and shoes and shrugged. "A little more water won't matter at this point. I'll start drying up in here while we wait for the repairman."

"That's very kind of you." She gave him a smile that held so much gratitude he felt his chest expand.

"There are more towels in the bathroom down the hall if you need them," she said. "I'll bring a mop with the bucket when I return."

A second later, she was gone.

Darius stared at the door long after her footsteps had faded down the hall. Then he turned his attention to the soggy pile of towels on the floor and the makeshift tourniquet he'd rigged around the pipe.

If he hadn't intervened, a great deal more damage would have occurred. The water might have soaked through to the ceiling of the room below them. That type of damage could risk them failing an inspection, perhaps even forcing the home to close down. If he just loosened that towel, no one would be the wiser. . . .

He clenched his molars together. Though Mr. Walcott would have no qualms doing just that, Darius was not that kind of man. He would never purposely cause harm to someone or their property.

Grabbing a stack of fresh towels, he began to soak up the water from the floor, the vision of Miss Rosetti's warm regard spurring him on to finish the task.

For another one of those smiles, he would do just about anything.

12

Ten minutes later, Olivia climbed the stairs to the second floor, the string mop clutched under her arm. Mr. Reed had certainly surprised her with the way he'd jumped in and stopped the flood before irreparable damage had been done.

Very gallant. And very unexpected.

Perhaps she'd misjudged the man, thinking he'd had an ulterior motive in coming to see the home. If he wanted their venture to fail, he certainly wouldn't have rushed to their rescue like that.

She paused to collect her emotions before entering the bathroom, determined to give the man the benefit of the doubt.

Mr. Reed stood over the claw-foot tub, wringing out a dripping towel, his shirtsleeves rolled up past the elbow. He turned as she came into the room. "I tied another towel around the pipe for good measure. Once you run the mop over the floor, it should be good as new."

"Thank you." She peered under the sink, relieved to see no more water for the moment. "The plumber should be here in about twenty minutes. He sounded quite upset that this had happened."

"As well he should." Mr. Reed draped the towel over the side of the tub. "Do you have a clothesline out back where I can hang these to dry?"

"I'll do that, Mr. Reed. You needn't bother."

114

"It's no bother. And won't you please call me Darius? Mr. Reed sounds far too formal."

She swallowed. Formal might be a much safer idea. But she didn't wish to be rude. "Very well. And you may call me Olivia."

"Olivia." The word sounded almost lyrical on his lips. "Such a beautiful name."

She bent over the mop to hide her blush and avoid getting lost in the power of his gaze. Concentrating on her task, she pushed the strings into the tight corners, making sure to soak up every last bit of moisture.

When she spun around to place the wet mop in the tub, her foot slipped on the damp floor. She gave a cry, her heart pounding as her arms flailed.

A warm hand grabbed her around the waist and yanked her upright.

She gasped and gripped Darius's shirtfront. Without her meaning to, her eyes fixated on his chest where a dark sprig of hair was visible above the opened top button of his shirt. She swallowed hard and attempted to move out of his arms, only to find her footing still precarious.

"Careful. Those tiles can be slippery." His breath stirred the wispy hair at her ear.

Before she could react, he lifted her into his arms and carried her out to the hallway, where he set her feet carefully on the carpeted floor. Even then, he didn't release her right away, smiling down into her eyes.

Her face felt overwarm, and a hum of electricity raced through her body. She blinked and took a step away. "Th-thank you," she managed, all too aware of his arm still firmly around her. "I'm all right now."

He watched her with such intensity that heat flooded her system. For her own good, she needed to put some space between her and this unsettling man. "I . . . I'll take those wet towels down to the clothesline."

He only grinned. "I can carry them. Just show me the way."

She held back a sigh. It seemed she wasn't going to get rid of him quite so easily.

Darius placed a wooden peg on the clothesline and scanned the long row of colorful towels flapping in the breeze. Since when had the simple act of hanging laundry become so pleasurable? It certainly wasn't this enjoyable helping his mother with the chore.

He shot a look at Olivia, her cheeks flushed, biting her lip as she pinned the last corner of her towel, and the answer became clear. After holding her in his arms for a few brief seconds, he'd had to fight the sudden urge to kiss her. And now it seemed he would do any chore, no matter how trivial, just to extend his time with her.

He gave himself a mental shake, rolled down his still-damp shirtsleeves, and buttoned them. He had no right thinking about Olivia Rosetti that way. He was an engaged man and could not afford this unexpected attraction. Not only was it a conflict of interest to his boss's goals, but it was disrespectful to Meredith as well.

Mr. Cheeseman had been ecstatic the night they'd announced their intention to marry. His wife, however, was far less enthusiastic. No matter. Darius was certain he and Sofia would win the woman over before the wedding, which he hoped would take place before the start of the school year, so he and Meredith could take Sofia to her first day of kindergarten as a family.

He glanced once more at Olivia. He had to stop mooning over her like a lovestruck youth and focus on his priorities—his career, his daughter, and his wife-to-be.

Nothing else mattered.

As soon as the plumber came and Darius made sure the man honored his commitment to fix the leak, he would take his leave. And tomorrow he would find a new way to fulfill Mr. Walcott's mandate.

Olivia lifted the empty wicker laundry basket. "Would you care for a cup of coffee, Mr. Reed? I mean, Darius." Her cheeks grew pinker, making her even more attractive.

Not that he was noticing.

"Coffee would be nice. Thank you."

Darius followed her through the back door into the kitchen.

"Oh good. Margaret made both tea and coffee, so we won't even have to wait." Olivia set the basket on the floor, marched over to the stove, and lifted the coffeepot. "Cream and sugar?"

"Black is fine."

She poured the dark liquid into a ceramic mug and handed it to him. Her fingers brushed his as he took it. She snatched her hand away and turned back to the sink. She fiddled with the taps, then seemed to stand frozen while the water continued to run.

Setting his cup on the table, he reached around her to turn it off. "I don't think we need another flood today." He chuckled, hoping to put her at ease. But he realized his mistake straightaway as her intoxicating floral scent invaded his senses.

She backed away from the counter. Snatching a towel from a hook, she made a show of drying her hands.

Had he made her uncomfortable? Or was she as affected by him as he was by her?

While he contemplated what to say next, the doorbell rang.

"That's probably the plumber," she said. "Excuse me."

Darius expelled a long breath. He needed to get a grip on himself and gain control of his emotions.

At the rumble of voices in the hall, he made his way to the front entrance.

A man stood smiling down at Olivia, admiration evident on his face.

Darius recognized the man immediately. "Dr. Henshaw? What are you doing here?"

The physician's head snapped up. "Mr. Reed. This is an unexpected surprise."

Olivia frowned, looking between the two men.

"I'm here to check on a patient." Dr. Henshaw's gaze took in Darius's somewhat disheveled appearance. "What are you doing here?"

He shrugged. "Learning more about the maternity home and inadvertently helping with a leaky pipe."

Dr. Henshaw laughed. "I'm sure there's more to that story." He turned to Olivia. "Miss Holmes is expecting me. May I go up?"

"Certainly, Doctor."

"Good to see you, Mr. Reed. Give my best to your parents. And don't forget Sofia's next checkup."

"I won't."

As the physician toted his bag up the stairs, Darius could feel the weight of Olivia's stare.

"Is Dr. Henshaw your family physician?" she asked.

"He's Sofia's doctor. But whenever he comes to the house, my mother insists on feeding him a meal." Darius laughed.

"My mother does the same thing with our doctor." Olivia's features relaxed, the suspicion leaving her eyes. "Dr. Henshaw has agreed to be the physician on call for our home. He's a very kind person." A soft smile flitted across her lips.

Darius stiffened. Did Olivia have feelings for the man? A strange flicker of unease tightened his chest, and instantly he bit back the unwelcome sensation. It was none of his business whom the woman cared for.

A knock at the front door provided a well-needed distraction. "Looks like the plumber is here at last," he said brightly.

And just in the nick of time. The sooner he got away from Olivia's captivating presence, the sooner he could clear his head and come up with a way to obtain this property for Mr. Walcott.

Then he'd never have to be tempted by the lovely Miss Rosetti again.

13

The next day, as Darius mulled over his dilemma regarding the Bennington house, the leaky pipe brought to mind the perfect idea. He would arrange for a surprise inspection of the entire Bennington property—from the peaks of the lofty roof to the bowels of the musty basement. Judging by the age of the house, something would likely fail such an intense examination.

Darius could call in an anonymous tip to the government agency, and with any luck, the inspector would find enough wrong with the building to halt operations and maybe even force a closure of the home. Mrs. Bennington would then be much more likely to accept Mr. Walcott's offer. Walcott would get his property, and Darius would get his raise and maybe even a promotion.

But what would that do to Olivia's dream?

Darius forced the thought away. Everything would work out. The women would merely purchase a new property, one better suited for more residents, and Olivia's mission would continue at a different location.

When all was said and done, everyone would win.

Before guilt could get the better of him, he lifted the telephone receiver and placed the call.

Moments after he hung up, the clock on his wall sounded out ten chimes. Darius straightened his tie, grabbed his notebook, and made his way to Mr. Walcott's office. His boss detested anyone being late for a scheduled meeting.

After a quick knock, Darius entered the room.

Mr. Walcott looked up, tight lines pinching the edge of his mouth. "Have a seat. I hope you have some good news for me today. I could use some."

"Is anything wrong, sir?"

"I'm afraid so. We're on the verge of losing one of our best clients. Elliott Peterson says he doesn't think he can work with us any longer, that our lofty principles aren't in keeping with his." He peered at Darius, rolling an unlit cigar between his fingers. "You don't know anything about this, do you?"

Darius shifted on his chair, his stomach diving to his shoes. He swallowed. "I had a bit of an altercation with him at the Bennington fundraiser. He was making lewd suggestions to Miss Rosetti, and I had to step in." But that was weeks ago. Why was the man making waves now? Darius squared his shoulders. "To be honest, sir, Peterson seems to have the morals of a swine."

Walcott glared at him. "As long as his money continues to flow into our bank account, I don't give two hoots about the state of Peterson's morals."

Darius pressed his lips together to keep from arguing. It was becoming harder and harder to reconcile his Christian way of life with the reality of the business world, where people like Mr. Walcott seemed willing to go to any lengths for personal gain.

"Let's hope this blows over in a few days," his boss said. "In the meantime, tell me about the Bay Street property."

In his most professional manner, Darius explained the setback there. "But I still think we can win this one if I keep after them."

Walcott shook his head, his jowls quivering. "In light of the Peterson affair, we'd better hold off on making another offer until we get a better idea of what he's going to do. I need to determine how much available capital we'll have coming in."

"That sounds prudent."

"And where do we stand on the Bennington property?"

Darius leaned forward in his seat. "I've arranged for a surprise inspection by the city in the hopes they'll find something to shut the place down."

"That's it?" Walcott whipped the unlit cigar from his lips. "You'll have to be more proactive than that. Find a way to stop this maternity home nonsense and make selling the house the widow's only option."

"Sir, you of all people know how stubborn Mrs. Bennington can be. Bullying doesn't work or she would have given in to you by now. Let me continue this my way." At least then Darius would have a small measure of control over how Walcott Industries handled the women. He feared that if his boss had his way, things could get ugly.

Walcott heaved out a breath. "Fine. I'll leave it up to you for now. But once I'm certain Peterson won't pull his business, we'll have to redouble our efforts." He pointed his cigar at Darius. "Start thinking about another angle in case this inspection idea doesn't pan out. It goes without saying that your job could depend on it."

Olivia pulled the black netting over her face and stepped inside the vestibule of St. Michael's Cathedral. Her heart pounded, and her palms were slick with perspiration beneath her gloves. Just standing in this holy place brought back waves of shame and guilt, reminding her how far she'd fallen from the innocent girl who used to attend here.

The solemn strains of organ music drifted out from the interior of the church. With the ordination of six new priests today, the building was filled almost to capacity. Olivia peered through the open door to catch a glimpse of their family pew halfway down the aisle. Mamma's lace mantilla was visible beside her father's dark suit jacket, their heads bent in prayer. Her brother Leo sat on the other side of her mother. Olivia's heart squeezed, sending spasms of pain through her chest. Tony must still be away at war, but she should be with her family to celebrate Salvatore's ordination. However, as the proverbial black sheep, she knew she would not be welcome.

She wondered what explanation her parents had given Sal as to why his sister wasn't here for his special day. Or, for that matter, where she'd been for almost two years. Had they told him of her disgrace or would he simply think she didn't care?

Oh, Sal, I hope you know I'd be there if I could. If only Papà would allow it.

Olivia moved quietly through the dimly lit church. She might not be able to sit with her family, but she could at least watch from the back as Sal was ordained. She hurried to an open seat in a rear pew, one on the aisle in case she needed to make a quick exit.

The ceremony had already started, the liturgy in Latin booming out over the cavernous space, the cloying smell of incense hovering in the air. After several minutes passed with no one recognizing her or questioning why she was sitting at the back of the cathedral, she allowed herself to relax and let the familiar prayers flow over her.

She stayed until Sal had been ordained, then slipped out the rear door. She found a spot by some bushes where she could watch the procession exit, hoping for a closer glimpse of her brother in all his finery. Papà would have his Kodak camera ready to capture photos of this momentous occasion, the day his son became a priest. For an Italian Catholic family, there was no greater honor.

Several minutes later, the enormous double doors opened and the officiants filed out, followed by the six newly ordained men. Olivia scanned the group for her brother's face, the one she'd cherished since childhood. Unlike Leo and Tony, whose sole purpose seemed to be to torment her, Sal was the brother who always looked out for her and intervened when Leo and Tony's teasing turned mean-spirited.

Dear Sal. How she'd missed him since he'd entered the seminary. Tears misted her vision, and she hastily blinked them away. She would not allow anything to spoil one second of her brother's finest moment. There would be time for grieving later.

At last she spotted him, the second to last to emerge. His wide grin showed off his straight white teeth, and his dark eyes reflected a joy Olivia could only envy. The clergy formed a line to greet the congregants as they emerged, a bit of a breeze fluttering their robes.

If only Olivia dared to approach them to give her brother a kiss of congratulations. But Mamma, Papà, and Leo would be out soon, and she wouldn't create a scene that would ruin Sal's triumphant day.

As more well-wishers gathered round, Olivia dared to venture closer, drawn in by the exuberant greetings, the laughter and tears of the proud family members. For a brief second, Sal looked in her direction, and her heart jumped into her throat. Did he see her? Would he acknowledge her?

She lifted a gloved hand in silent greeting. The smile froze on his face, his eyes changing from joyous to sympathetic. He gave the barest of nods in her direction before the person in line claimed his attention.

Her father appeared next. Olivia shrank back into the shadows, but still, some force compelled her to keep watching. Papà wrapped Sal in a bear hug, practically lifting him off the ground. Then he took out a handkerchief and mopped his eyes.

"You made me so proud today, my son," he said in Italian.

Mamma elbowed Papà out of the way so she could kiss Sal's cheeks, then Leo came forward to offer a handshake. Sal said something that made all three of them laugh out loud.

Olivia's shoulders drooped under the weight of her sorrow.

It was torture watching her family and not being able to join in their happiness. She pressed gloved fingers to her lips to keep a sob from escaping.

Was this how her life would be from now on? Relegated to the shadows, stealing glimpses of her family from afar? Would anything change if she ever made something of herself and achieved respectability once again? Would her parents then be able to forgive her and welcome her back into their hearts?

Her gaze fell to the ground. If that ever happened, it wouldn't be anytime soon. She lifted her eyes for one last glimpse of Sal in his vestments, then, with a heavy heart, turned and walked away.

Olivia arrived back at Ruth's to find the house in an uproar. Three of the residents were huddled in the front sitting room, chattering like nervous magpies—a highly unusual activity for the women, who usually remained sedate.

Had one of the residents gone into labor? She mentally ran through each of the women. No one was really near their expected delivery date. So, what could it be?

Olivia skirted by the parlor, intent on making a bracing cup of tea before finding out the cause of the drama. But in the kitchen, she found Mrs. Neale in a tizzy as well. The cook's brown hair had escaped her cap, which sat askew on her head. She muttered to herself as she pulled pots and pans from a lower cupboard.

"Mrs. Neale?" Olivia halted in the doorway. "Is something wrong?" *Please let it not be another leaky pipe.* She scanned the floor for any evidence of water, but everything seemed dry.

"You could say that. An inspector from the city turned up. Here to conduct a surprise inspection, or so he claims."

Olivia frowned. "But we had an inspection done before our official opening. Why would they need to do another one so soon?"

"I haven't a clue. You'd best ask Mrs. Bennington."

"Where is the man now?"

"In the basement. He wants me to clear out these cupboards because he's coming here next."

"Try not to worry, Mrs. Neale. I know you keep an immaculate kitchen."

Olivia headed down the back corridor to the basement stairs. Her emotions still raw, she purposely channeled her sorrow into anger to give her courage.

Picking her way carefully down the stone stairs, she entered the musty basement, cool air wafting around her. "Hello," she called. "Are you down here?"

"Over by the water heater," a male voice answered.

If she had any idea where the water heater was, that statement might have been useful. She headed across the dirt floor in the direction of the voice, ducking to avoid cobwebs, and finally spotted a light in the far corner.

"I'm Miss Rosetti, the co-directress." She pulled herself up to her full height as she approached a man dressed in dark overalls, a cap covering his head.

"Barney Cameron, city inspector." He held out his badge for her to see.

"May I ask what brought about this visit? A full inspection was done before we opened."

"We had an anonymous complaint. Probably a neighbor. Said there were some serious plumbing issues and possibly rats in the cellar."

"Rats? That's absurd." Olivia scanned the dark floor, resisting the urge to climb on one of the boxes against the wall just in case.

Mr. Cameron crouched down and aimed his flashlight at the corner. "Not really. There are fresh droppings here."

Goose bumps broke out over her skin. "Well, I'm sure we're not the only house with this issue. Can't you set a few traps to take care of the problem?"

The man shoved a pencil behind one ear. "That's not my job,

miss." He rose and went to write something on a clipboard. "I think I'm finished down here. Let's head up to the next level."

Seated in her wing chair in the parlor, Ruth did her best to quell her annoyance and maintain an air of calm. The inspector had been here for hours and was still poking around in her attic. It had been years since she'd ventured into that space. She could barely remember what items she had stored up there.

What rankled her most about the situation, however, was the fact that someone had phoned in a complaint to the city about them. It had to be Mr. Simmons from across the street, since Ruth couldn't imagine anyone else having a concern about their home. He had made his displeasure known as soon as he'd read the article in the newspaper.

"Should we delay dinner until the inspector's gone?" Olivia entered the room, her question breaking into Ruth's musings.

Ruth looked at her watch. "I believe that's wise, unless the man's bent on staying the entire evening." She shook her head. "I simply don't understand why anyone would have called in a complaint. It doesn't make sense."

Olivia took a seat on the sofa. "Mr. Cameron mentioned the plumbing issue," she said slowly. "Yet no one knew about the leak except the residents, the staff, and . . ." A frown wrinkled her brow.

Ruth sighed. "Mr. Reed. He was here at the time, wasn't he?" She hated to think the pleasant young man could be behind this setback. Still, a charming exterior sometimes hid a devious heart. And he did work for the loathsome Mr. Walcott.

"But Darius seemed so kind." Olivia leaned forward, her eyes troubled. "He jumped in to contain the leak and then helped me hang up the wet towels."

"Darius, is it?" Ruth gave her a long look.

Patches of red appeared in Olivia's cheeks. "Why would Mr.

Reed go to all that trouble and then turn around and report us to the city?"

"I can think of one reason. Vincent Walcott."

"But what would his boss gain from another inspection?"

Ruth rose and smoothed her skirt. "Mr. Walcott will go to any length to get what he wants. He likely hopes that the building will fail the exam, and the inspector will force a closure of the home. Mr. Walcott probably imagines that I would then be disheartened enough to sell him my house." She squared her shoulders. "That will never happen. I'd sell to anyone but him if I had to."

A throat cleared behind them. "Mrs. Bennington?"

Ruth turned to see the inspector in the doorway, cap in his hand. "Yes, Mr. Cameron. Have you finished?"

"For now. I will have to return tomorrow with a longer ladder to reach the highest point on the roof."

Ruth gave him her best imperious stare. "The next time you plan a surprise inspection, Mr. Cameron, I suggest you come more prepared."

The man literally squirmed under her disapproval. "If I'd known what I was getting into, I would have," he muttered.

Ruth chose to ignore his comment. "What happens when you're finished?" she asked. "Will I be privy to what you report back to the city?"

"Yes, ma'am. I will discuss my findings with you when I'm done. I'll let you know any issues I discovered and the steps needed to pass the next inspection."

Ruth expelled a loud breath. "Very well, Mr. Cameron. I suppose that's fair, though I don't appreciate how this all came about. You must know that we just had an inspection before our home opened."

He shrugged. "That may be true, but if a complaint is made, we have no choice but to follow up."

"I think I should be allowed to know the person responsible for this. Was it Mr. Simmons across the road?"

The man's expression became guarded. "Even if I knew, I'm not at liberty to say."

Olivia appeared at her elbow. "What happens if we fail the inspection, Mr. Cameron?"

He lifted one shoulder. "Unless it's something insurmountable that necessitates the immediate closure of the house, you'll be given the opportunity to make the necessary changes in order to pass another inspection."

"How extensive do you think that might be?" Olivia blinked at him with wide eyes.

The man's face became flushed under Olivia's keen attention. "Well, Miss Rosetti, I'm not supposed to divulge anything until the report is complete, but so far the issues I've found appear quite minor. As long as the roof is in decent shape, you should have no problem making the repairs."

Olivia smiled. "That's a relief. Thank you, Mr. Cameron." She gave Ruth a subtle wink.

It seemed the old saying was true. You could catch more flies with honey rather than vinegar. Perhaps Ruth could take a lesson from her petite partner.

14

Olivia strained her neck to look up at the skyscraper in front of her. Though she'd seen many tall buildings downtown before, she'd never actually been in one. But today she intended to confront Mr. Reed at his office and find out exactly what he was up to.

Had his interest in learning more about the home and his gallantry helping with the leak all been a ruse? Or had it been his boss's underhanded tactics to call in a complaint without telling him?

On the way up in the elevator, Olivia gave herself a stern talking-to. No matter how handsome she found Mr. Reed, no matter how kind or sincere he seemed, she knew better than to let herself be swayed. The residents at the home were her priority, and she would make sure that Walcott Industries knew that she and Ruth would not be trifled with.

The elevator doors opened, and she stepped out into a modern-looking reception area.

"Hello," she greeted a well-groomed receptionist. "I'd like to speak with Mr. Reed, please."

The woman smiled. "Do you have an appointment?"

"No. But I'm sure if you tell him Miss Rosetti is here, he'll see me."

"One moment, miss." The woman headed down the hall.

Seconds later, she returned. "Mr. Reed says to go on in. Third door up ahead."

"Thank you." Olivia pulled herself up tall and headed for the office, heels tapping the tiles as she walked.

As she reached the door, Darius appeared in the opening, buttoning his suit jacket.

He smiled. "Olivia. To what do I owe this unexpected pleasure?"

She drew in a breath and braced herself against the lure of those enticing dimples. "I need a word with you in private, if you don't mind."

"Of course. Come in."

She entered an immaculate room dominated by a large desk. Framed artwork decorated the walls, while picture windows overlooked the cityscape below.

She took a seat in one of the guest chairs.

"I hope the plumber was able to fix the leak after I left." Darius resumed his place behind the desk.

"He was. And he didn't charge us for his time, seeing that he had failed to secure the pipe correctly in the first place."

"That's good news." He leaned forward on his desk. "So, what brings you by Walcott Industries?"

Steeling herself against his appeal, she gave him a serious stare. "I need to ask you a question, and I'd like an honest answer."

His dark brows rose, but he nodded. "Go ahead."

She squeezed her hands around the handle of her purse. "Did you call in a complaint to the city in order to initiate an inspection of our home?"

His features froze. Then a tiny muscle in his jaw ticked. "Yes." His gaze slid to the desktop, his expression pained.

Her back stiffened against the chair as disappointment shot through her. "Why would you do such a thing? You knew what caused the leak. There was no need to involve the city." She pressed her lips firmly together to keep them from betraying her. How could he have been so helpful at the time, only to use their misfortune against them?

Yet why was she surprised? Had anyone in her life ever acted in her best interest?

No, they'd all done whatever they wanted, no matter how it affected her. Rory had left for the war, despite her repeated pleas to stay. Then, in her time of greatest need, her father had banished her, and her mother had sided with him. Not one person had ever put her needs first.

Why would Darius Reed be any different?

"I know it's no excuse," he said, "but my boss has assigned me the task of getting Mrs. Bennington to sell her house at any cost. I was trying to find the least . . . harmful way to go about that." He gave a sheepish shrug. "I figured if the home failed an inspection, Mrs. Bennington might accept Mr. Walcott's generous offer and open a facility somewhere else."

Olivia drew in a shaky breath. "Did you ever once consider how that would affect the women living at Bennington Place? How upsetting it would be for everyone?"

He hung his head. "No, I didn't."

"Not only that, you pretended to be interested in the home when you were actually there as a spy. You lied to me—to all of us." She rose on unsteady legs, attempting to corral her anger. "Bennington Place might be just a building to you, Mr. Reed, but to the women who live there, it's their sanctuary. Their place of refuge when they have nowhere else to go. How could you be so cruel?" Despite her best efforts, her chin quivered. She blinked hastily and headed to the door. With her hand on the knob, she turned. "We will pass the inspection, Mr. Reed. And we will stay open."

She marched out into the hallway, almost crashing into an attractive blond woman coming toward her.

"Olivia, wait." Darius's voice sounded behind her. "Please let me make it up to you."

She rounded on him. "You can do that by leaving us alone."

He came to an abrupt halt. His mouth opened, but no words came out.

Olivia jabbed the elevator button, relieved when the doors opened in front of her. She entered and quickly hit the button for the ground floor. When she looked up, all she saw was the anguish on Darius Reed's face as the doors slid closed.

Darius punched his fist into the wall beside the elevators, self-loathing seeping through his pores. The hurt on Olivia's face ripped through his insides like a blade.

She was right. He hadn't been honest in his intentions, feigning interest in the home in order to find something he could possibly use to achieve his goal. He'd never fully considered the ramifications of shutting down the operation. He was only worried about obtaining the property for Walcott Industries and how that would benefit him.

He rubbed a hand over his face. How utterly selfish could he be?

"Darius? What on earth was that about?"

Meredith? In all the confusion, he hadn't even noticed her. With supreme effort, he pushed back all the negative emotions and pasted on a neutral expression. "I'm sorry, Meredith. I didn't see you there." He walked over to kiss her cheek.

But she scowled at him. "Who was that woman? And why did she tell you to leave her alone?"

Stress beat a pounding refrain through his temple. "It's a business matter. Nothing to worry about." He took her by the elbow to guide her back to his office, away from the curious gazes of the receptionist and other staff members who'd come out to see what the commotion was about.

The tight press of her lips told him he would have to work hard to restore her good mood.

"That didn't sound like a business problem," she said as he

closed his door. She crossed her arms, her forehead pinched. "It seemed personal to me."

Darius released a breath. "Miss Rosetti is upset because Walcott Industries is trying to buy her property." Not entirely accurate, but close enough. "Please ignore that unpleasant episode and tell me why you're here."

Mistrust still vibrating from her, Meredith perched on the edge of the chair Olivia had just vacated. Her mouth was pressed into a hard line, and her foot tapped an agitated refrain on the tiled floor.

He could almost see her working to tamp down her suspicion.

At last, she gave a stiff smile. "Actually, I came to see if we could take Sofia on an outing tonight. Now that we're engaged, I thought she should get to know me before the wedding."

"The wedding?" Darius struggled to focus on the change in topic, his emotions still reeling from his encounter with Olivia.

Meredith's thin brows rose. "Weddings generally follow engagements, Darius. And I don't see why we should put it off."

Surprised, he studied her. He'd thought he'd have to work hard to get her to agree to a quick wedding. "Is this still about beating your sister to the punch? Or is there another reason for your hurry?"

Her lashes fluttered down. "It is about Sissy. Once she has her debut, all my family's attention will be focused on her. Call me vain, but I'd like to get married before she steals my spotlight."

Though Darius suspected there might be more to it than that, he couldn't deny that Meredith's desire for a short engagement could work well with his plan to be married before the fall. He came around to lean against the desk. "I'm glad you feel that way," he said. "I was hoping to get married before Sofia starts school in September, so she'll have a mother and a father like the other children in her class."

Meredith's expression turned thoughtful. "Were you thinking the end of August, then?"

"Yes. Could you be ready that soon?"

He couldn't help but recall his wedding to Selene—her home-made dress, her flowers from the garden, the small reception in the church basement. Meredith would never settle for anything so ordinary. But a big society wedding could take months of preparations.

She tilted her head, the brim of her jaunty red hat dipping over one eye. "What would you say if I wanted to get married sooner?"

"Sooner?" *Wow*. He hadn't expected that. "I suppose it could be arranged."

She entwined her fingers with his. "How about the beginning of August?"

His mouth fell open. "That's only a few weeks away."

She laughed and got to her feet, looping her hands around his neck. "I know it sounds crazy, but I'm just so eager to be your wife. I don't want to wait a moment longer." Then without warning, she planted her lips on his.

Her passionate embrace overruled any trace of unease that had arisen at her surprising declaration. Could it be as simple as that? She loved him and wanted to start sharing his life as soon as possible?

A door slamming in the outer office brought Darius's attention crashing back to his surroundings and the fact that this was highly inappropriate behavior for the workplace. He gently set her away from him with a smile. "You have a point. There's not much difference between the beginning of August or the end. It would give us more time to settle in as a family."

She clapped her hands. "Thank you, Darius. I can hardly wait to tell Daddy. He'll be thrilled."

"I hope so." He got to his feet, more than a little bemused by the whirlwind events. "Why don't we take Sofia out for some ice cream tonight?" That way, Meredith wouldn't have to deal with his mother's scrutiny just yet. Because once Mamá learned he intended to marry this girl, she'd be all over Meredith like honey on baklava.

"That sounds like fun." She kissed his cheek. "I'd better let you get back to work." With a wave, she sashayed out of his office.

Darius raked a hand over his jaw and sank onto his chair, unable to fully comprehend everything that had just happened.

In a matter of weeks, he would be getting married again. Yet, the enormity of that news paled in comparison to his regret over the hurt he'd caused Olivia. With a loud exhale, he picked up his pen and tapped it on his blotter. Somehow he needed to find a way to make it up to her and earn her forgiveness.

He couldn't bear to be another reason for the pain he always saw in her eyes.

15

Olivia twirled a pencil in her hand as she watched Ruth pore over the ledger.

Seated behind the desk, her reading glasses perched on her nose, Ruth shook her head. "This doesn't look good, does it?"

"I'm afraid not. And now with Mr. Cameron's report saying we need major repairs to the roof, I don't see how we'll be able to come up with that large sum on top of all our other expenses." Olivia gave Ruth a searching look, praying that maybe the widow had another bank account with a large balance, enough to tide them over until this bad spell had passed. She still couldn't figure out how the problem with the roof had been missed on the first inspection, unless Mr. Cameron had been more thorough than the initial inspector.

Ruth removed her glasses and rubbed the bridge of her nose. "I suppose I could go back to the bank, but I doubt that will help. When I got the funds to cover the renovations, the manager was already apprehensive about loaning me the money. I hate to have to approach him again so soon."

Olivia's lungs deflated. She hadn't realized that Ruth had already borrowed money for the remodeling. What were they going to do now?

"This is all my fault." Olivia got up to pace the room. "If I hadn't dragged you into this, you wouldn't be in this mess." Not only was the home at risk of closing, which would put the residents out on the streets, but Ruth could potentially be forced to sell the house that had been in the Bennington family for years. Would Walcott succeed in gaining the property after all?

"Olivia, please don't despair. As a famous American general once said, 'I have only begun to fight.'" Ruth gave a tight smile. "We need to collect some of the money promised by our donors and perhaps target a few new ones." She tapped a pencil to her lips. "Let me make some phone calls and see what I can come up with."

Olivia nodded. "All right. I'll work on more ways to reduce our expenses." Thankfully they'd already purchased the supplies for the nursery, including several bassinets, baby clothing, and diapers. "Do you think we should tell the residents about this?"

"Not just yet. We don't want them to worry unnecessarily."

"What about the midwife? When will she need to be paid?"

Ruth had managed to secure a local woman named Mrs. Dinglemire, who had many years of experience. They had paid a retainer to engage her services, but she had yet to meet with the residents individually, and some were getting fairly close to their due dates.

"We have a few more weeks until then," Ruth said. "And even so, we should be able to pay her salary. It's the bigger outlay of cash for the roof that concerns me."

The doorbell rang.

Please, no more bad news. Olivia didn't think she could take one more setback. "I'll get it."

Still consumed by their financial woes, Olivia opened the door. Her mood deteriorated even more at the sight of the man on the doorstep.

"What do you want, Mr. Reed?" she said in her iciest tone.

He pulled off his hat and held it to his chest, a pleading expression in his eyes. "I want to apologize again, Miss Rosetti. Won't you allow me to explain?"

She hesitated, hating that even after everything he'd done, she still had a hard time saying no to the man. "Very well. You have five minutes."

"Thank you. You're more than gracious." He stepped inside and, without waiting for an invitation, moved straight into the parlor.

She ground her molars together and followed him. "I don't see what more there is to discuss. You want this house, and we aren't selling. No matter what manner of tricks you come up with."

He had the grace to look ashamed. "I do feel terrible about what I did. And about how it must seem like I was deceiving you."

"Seem like?" Olivia swept across the carpet. "You were spying on us, Mr. Reed, for your own selfish purposes, trying to find something to use against us."

"I guess in the back of my mind I hoped I might discover something that would aid my cause. But I honestly did want to learn more about your facility, and the more I learned, the more I came to admire what you're doing here." He shook his head. "What you said yesterday made me see how horribly selfish I've been not even considering the women who live here. I assumed Mrs. Bennington would sell this house and buy another, not taking into account the huge disruption to everyone's lives."

"I'm glad you realize that now." Olivia crossed her arms. "Margaret and Patricia are nearing their due dates. That kind of stress could bring on early labor." Perhaps if the man knew the women's names, he would think of them as real people. "And Nancy, Cherise, and Jenny are just getting used to us."

Jenny, an extremely introverted girl, was the latest to arrive. Olivia suspected she may have been abused. She was only recently starting to let down her guard and join them for meals.

He hung his head. "I apologize again. Is there anything I can do to make it up to you?"

The man seemed sincere, but she didn't fully trust him.

"I don't suppose you know a good roofer? One who accepts payment in installments?"

His dark brows shot together. "What happened to the roof?"

"The city inspector found a problem, and in order to pass the next inspection, we need some extensive repairs."

He frowned. "I can ask around. Maybe one of my father's clients might know an outfit."

She inclined her chin. "That would be appreciated."

"Is there anything else I can do?" He moved closer.

Close enough for her to see the silver flecks in his eyes. She'd be a fool to be taken in by him again. "No, thank you. I think you've done quite enough for the time being."

Darius hated the mistrust evident in Olivia's beautiful brown eyes. Hated that his impulsive action in bringing about the inspection had led to such dire consequences.

But wasn't that what he'd hoped would happen?

He must seem like the biggest hypocrite imaginable—helping her with the leak one minute and complaining to the city about possible violations the next.

"Thank you for hearing me out," he said as he put on his hat. "I really do regret any harm my actions have brought about."

She pinned him with a hard stare. "If that's true, you'll convince your boss to leave us alone."

"All I can do is speak to him again. Try to make him consider another alternative." He wished he could promise more, but even doing that much was a risk.

The tightness around her mouth eased. "Thank you."

"There's no guarantee, though. Mr. Walcott isn't exactly the compromising type." He hesitated at the front entrance, hating the idea that he might never see her again. But with no further excuse to prolong his stay, he tipped his hat. "Good-bye, Oliv . . . Miss Rosetti. I wish you all the best."

Shoving back a huge amount of regret, he let himself out the door and descended the stairs. He truly meant what he'd said. He did hope her home succeeded, yet he was at a loss to determine how he could reconcile that wish with Mr. Walcott's demands.

Engulfed in his unwanted thoughts, Darius barely acknowledged a woman coming up the walkway.

Instead of passing him, she grabbed the sleeve of his jacket. "Is this Bennington Place?" Her voice sounded desperate, and she glanced nervously over her shoulder.

"It is."

"Do you work here?" She wore a floral scarf over her head, covering the lower part of her face.

Something about the woman stirred his protective instincts. "No, I don't. But Miss Rosetti is inside. She can help you." When he went to move away, she tightened her grip on his arm.

"Please. I don't think I can—" She crumpled into a heap at his feet.

Alarm raced through him as he bent over the woman. The scarf fell away and he gasped. Bruises marred her cheek, and her lip was swollen and bloody.

Hefting her into his arms, he rushed up the stairs and opened the door, not even bothering to knock. "We need help here!"

Olivia appeared almost instantly. She gasped when she saw the woman in his arms.

"Where should I put her?" he asked.

"In the parlor."

Thankful he didn't have to carry her up the stairs, Darius laid the woman on the sofa and placed a pillow beneath her head. He took out his handkerchief and gently blotted the blood from her mouth. Her cheek and eye seemed to swell right before his eyes. "She needs ice. And a doctor."

"Right away." Olivia disappeared from the room.

Darius removed the woman's scarf and opened the buttons of her coat, unable to fathom why she would be wearing such a heavy garment in the summer. As he moved the fabric aside, understanding dawned. In all the uproar, he hadn't noticed she was very pregnant.

He returned his attention to her injuries. What had happened to her? Had she fallen? No, it looked like someone had beaten her.

Disgust flooded his system at the thought of anyone harming a woman carrying a precious life within her. Who would be so despicable?

Olivia returned with a basin of water and an ice pack. "Here, hold this against her cheek. Ruth is calling Dr. Henshaw. I told her it was an emergency."

While Darius did as she instructed, Olivia set the bowl down and wrung out a cloth. Gently she dabbed at the rest of the woman's face, working to remove the dried-on blood and clean some of the scrapes.

When the unconscious woman moaned, Olivia pulled away, depositing the cloth back into the basin.

"Where did you find her?" she asked, turning her gaze to Darius at last.

"She came up the walkway as I was leaving. She asked if this was Bennington Place and then collapsed."

Olivia walked around him to the end of the sofa. The woman's large belly protruded so that her dress barely reached her knees. Olivia hesitated a moment before laying her palm on top of her stomach. She frowned, looking off into space for several seconds until the ridges in her forehead eased. "The baby's moving. I hope that means it's okay." She removed the woman's shoes, then gently pulled an afghan over her. "Who could have done this to her? Surely not her husband?"

Darius moved the ice to a different position. "It's possible. Not all men value their wives as they should."

"How incredibly sad." Olivia brushed at her cheek, and he realized she was crying.

Tears for a complete stranger.

Darius couldn't help but wonder how many other people would react to this woman with as much compassion.

When the doorbell rang, Olivia jumped to answer it, wiping the traces of moisture from her face. The poor injured woman didn't need Olivia blubbering all over the place. Nor did Dr. Henshaw.

"Hello, Miss Rosetti."

"Doctor, please come in. The patient is in the parlor."

Dr. Henshaw removed his hat as he rushed into the room, barely pausing at the sight of Darius holding an ice pack to the woman's cheek. "Mr. Reed? You're here again."

"Seems I'm always around in times of emergency." Darius rose, taking the ice with him. As he moved out of the doctor's way, he quickly explained how he'd come upon the woman.

Ruth entered the parlor in time to hear Darius's story and stood beside Olivia while the doctor did an initial examination—listening to the woman's heart, checking her pulse, and lifting her eyelids. Then he moved the stethoscope to her belly, frowning. When the lines around his eyes eased, Olivia breathed a sigh of relief. At least it seemed the baby was unharmed.

"Do you know her name?" Dr. Henshaw rose from his position beside the sofa.

"No. But perhaps you could check her pockets for some identification."

Dr. Henshaw reached over and rifled through the coat but came away empty-handed. "I'll need you all to step out now while I do a more thorough exam."

"Certainly." Olivia headed into the hallway, Darius and Ruth right behind her.

"I have to get ready for an appointment," Ruth said as she closed the parlor doors. "Can I leave you two to handle the situation?"

"Of course," Darius said. "I'll stay as long as Olivia needs me."

"Thank you, Mr. Reed."

Once Ruth had gone upstairs, Olivia paced the hall floor, unsure what to do next. "I feel so helpless."

Darius laid warm hands on her shoulders. "I'm sure Dr. Henshaw will know what to do." He paused, his eyes intent on hers. "Would you like to pray for her?"

She looked up and nodded, the steadying effect of his fingers calming her. "I would."

When he held out a hand, she took it, and the strength of his grip shored up her courage.

He bowed his head. "Lord, please bless this woman and her child and grant them your healing grace. Thank you for bringing her here to this safe place. Please guide Dr. Henshaw to make the right diagnosis and give her the best treatment possible. Amen."

"Amen." Olivia exhaled. "Thank you. That helped more than I imagined."

Darius looked down at their joined hands, then cleared his throat and released her.

Instantly, she missed his warmth.

Dr. Henshaw emerged from the parlor, a grim look on his face. "There's bruising on the woman's torso as well as her neck and face. It appears someone not only beat her but likely kicked her in the abdomen too."

Olivia fought back nausea at the thought. "What can we do for her, Doctor? Does she need a hospital?"

"Her vital signs are normal, other than a slight elevation due to her circumstances. And the baby appears to be fine." He replaced his tools in his bag. "I'd like to wait until she regains consciousness to assess her further, if that's not a problem. There's no need to move her for now."

"That's fine," Olivia said. "Would you like something to drink while you wait?"

"I wouldn't turn down a cup of your coffee, Miss Rosetti." The doctor smiled.

"Coming right up."

She escaped down the hall, glad for a task to keep her occupied. Her relief evaporated, however, when Mr. Reed followed her into the kitchen.

"Are you sure you're all right?" he asked. "You're quite pale."

"I'm fine." She tried to ignore him while she filled a pot with water and got out the tin of coffee.

"I can stay if you think I might be of any help."

His sincere blue gaze did funny things to her pulse as she measured out the grounds. She tried hard to hold on to her anger, yet seeing him tend to the injured woman with such care made it that much harder.

"I'm sure with Dr. Henshaw here, we'll be fine," she said.

A flash of emotion, disappointment perhaps, flitted across his handsome features. "I hope she and the baby will be all right. Would you mind if I telephoned tomorrow to see how she is? I feel somewhat responsible since I was the one who brought her in."

"That would fine." She turned on the flame under the coffeepot, then turned to face him. "Thank you for everything you did for her, Mr. Reed."

"It's Darius, remember. And I only did what anyone else would do."

She shook her head. "Not many people would help a stranger. In fact, some people would purposely go out of their way to avoid them." She paused to study him. "Despite our differences, I do believe you're a good person." Deep down, she sensed this to be true. He'd protected her at the fundraiser, helped with the leaking sink, and hadn't hesitated to come to a defenseless woman's aid. She was certain now that his quest to buy Ruth's house wasn't an act of greed, but something he felt obligated to do for his job.

"Thank you. That means a great deal," he said gruffly. "I'll talk to you tomorrow." He gave a slight nod, then disappeared down the hall.

Olivia stared after him for a long moment, attempting to let her emotions settle before getting back to the task at hand.

"Despite our differences, I do believe you're a good person."

Olivia's words filled him with warmth all the way back to his office. Why such a small compliment meant so much to him he couldn't say. But at least it seemed like she might have started to forgive him for calling the inspector.

He shook his head. Somehow he needed to find a way out of this mess. Convince Walcott that going after the Bennington property wasn't worth the effort. Hopefully the pending re-inspection would buy Darius the time he needed to come up with a viable alternative.

When he reached his office, Mr. Walcott was talking to Kevin in the outer area. "There you are, Reed. I need a word with you."

He held back a sigh. So much for time to prepare. Kevin moved off toward his office while Walcott waited for Darius to open his door.

"What can I do for you, sir?" He set his hat on the coat stand.

Walcott closed the door behind him. "I gather the Bennington Place inspection hasn't yielded the desired results."

Darius sucked in a breath. "Actually, it has. The house needs some substantial repairs to the roof, and unless they can come up with the capital to cover it, they won't pass another inspection." He struggled to keep the guilt from his face.

"That's going to take too long. I've got a better idea." Walcott smirked. "I sent Caldwell to canvass the neighbors in the area to see if he could dig up some dirt on Mrs. Bennington or her operation."

A slow burn of anger flared in Darius's chest. "That's a bit low, don't you think? These women are trying to do something good for the community. They don't deserve this type of treatment."

Walcott stared at him. "Careful. You're breaking one of the cardinal rules of business, Reed. You're making it personal. This is just another property we're trying to acquire."

"You make it sound like they are an anonymous corporation when it's nothing like that." Darius stalked across the room, too agitated to sit.

"Hear me out," Walcott said. "Caldwell came up with some good stuff. One neighbor in particular is very vocal about his dislike of the home and its residents." He leaned across the desk. "Claims that prostitutes are living there."

Darius stiffened. "That's not—"

"If we can get the word out, the public will put up such a stink that the widow will have to leave town. This Simmons character has even got a petition started. He's going around to all the area businesses and residents to get signatures. Says he plans to bring his complaint to the city council in the hopes that they'll shut the home down." He gave a loud laugh. "This guy might do all our work for us."

Unable to muster a response, Darius dragged a hand over his jaw. He knew this would get ugly if his boss had free rein.

"I thought you were going to give me time to do this my way," he said at last.

"I did. In fact, I even offered the inspector an added bonus to make sure he found something wrong. But the whole episode is taking too long and there's still a chance they'll pass the next inspection. Then we'd be back to square one."

Darius sucked in a breath. Did his boss really just admit to bribing a city official?

Walcott pursed his lips as he began to pace. "This is what I want you to do. Interview Simmons and take his statement. Then write up an article and get it into *The Daily Star*. Once this hits the papers and the neighbors learn about the type of people inhabiting that place, there will be a huge outcry."

"That's crazy." Darius flung out his hands. "We don't even know if his claim is true. I've been inside, and I didn't see anyone resembling a prostitute." Tension seized his shoulders. All he could think about was the betrayal Olivia would feel if she found out Darius was still trying to shut her facility down.

"Who cares as long as our ploy works?"

The blatant corruption in that statement snapped something inside Darius. He came around the desk, no longer willing to hide his distaste, and stood eye to eye with his boss. "I care. I'm not going to spread false rumors about someone just for your company's financial gain."

Walcott's nostrils flared. "If you value your job, you will." He lowered his voice to a deadly serious level. "I hear you're marrying Meredith Cheeseman in a few weeks. Do you think your bride will be eager to wed an unemployed nobody? Do you imagine Horace Cheeseman would allow it?"

Darius went still, the fight draining from him as the truth of his boss's statement hit home. Mr. Cheeseman would never allow his daughter to marry Darius if he had no job. His position at Walcott Industries was one of the main reasons Mr. Cheeseman was agreeing to this match. "No, I don't suppose he would."

"Then if you want to keep your job *and* your bride, you know what you have to do." Walcott yanked the door open. "And I suggest you do it soon."

16

The sound of moaning brought Olivia halfway out of sleep, her heart thudding. Was one of the prison inmates sick? Or had Dr. Guest subjected another poor soul to her torments? If so, Olivia could only be glad it wasn't her. This time.

She shifted in the bed, becoming aware of the lavender-scented pillowcase beneath her head. She wasn't in prison. She was safe at Ruth's. Slowly, her heart rate began to return to normal and her muscles relaxed. She must have been dreaming of the reformatory again.

Another loud moan sounded.

Olivia shot up from the mattress and grabbed her robe. This was not a dream. One of the girls could be in labor. She needed to determine who it was and see if the midwife was needed.

In the dark hallway, Olivia encountered Ruth tying the belt on her robe, her gray hair in a long braid over her shoulder.

"I think it's coming from Darla's room." Ruth pointed to the door.

With no name for the stranger, they'd decided to call the battered woman Darla. They both waited outside for some indication to enter. At another, louder moan, Ruth knocked on the door. "Are you all right, dear? Can we come in?"

No answer.

Ruth shook her head and slowly eased the door open. "It's Mrs. Bennington. Are you ill?" She snapped on a lamp.

Under the covers, the woman rocked back and forth, clutching her belly.

Ruth hurried to her side. "Are you having contractions?"

Darla's eyes shot open, terror leaping out. She grabbed Ruth's arm. "Don't . . . let . . . him . . . have . . . my . . . baby." Then her eyes rolled back in her head, and she went limp.

Olivia's hand flew to her mouth. "I'll call Mrs. Dinglemire."

Ruth turned, her expression grim. "Better call Dr. Henshaw as well. I don't think this will be an easy birth."

Ruth's prediction came true with unfortunate accuracy.

Mrs. Dinglemire did one brief examination of the woman and shook her head, silently allowing Dr. Henshaw, who'd arrived at almost the same time, to take over.

"It's in God's hands now," Mrs. Dinglemire said as she descended the stairs.

Olivia went to pay the woman, but she waved her off.

"I can't accept it. I couldn't do anything for that poor woman."

"But you came in the middle of the night," Olivia protested. "We need to pay you for your time."

A sad smile appeared, and Mrs. Dinglemire patted her arm. "Never you mind, dear. I was about to head out on another call anyway. I promised to go there once this situation had been resolved. My services will be of much better use there." She glanced back toward the stairs. "You should go back up in case the doctor needs your help. I can see myself out."

Olivia did as the woman suggested, waiting with Ruth outside the bedroom door while the doctor worked on Darla. A few minutes later, he emerged, looking haggard already.

"Should I call for an ambulance?" Olivia asked.

"There's no time. This baby is coming now. I'll need clean sheets, towels, boiling water, sterilized scissors, and some string. And I'll need one of you to help me with her. We have to rouse her enough so she can push. It's too late at this point for surgery."

A cold chill slid down Olivia's back. "I'll help you."

"Are you sure?" Dr. Henshaw gave her a skeptical look.

She stiffened her spine. "Other than one kind nurse, I didn't have anyone with me when I was in labor. I'd like to be there for her."

Ruth nodded. "I'll get the supplies."

Olivia followed the doctor into the room, which was already overly warm and ripe with body odor. He'd draped the bedsheet over the lower part of Darla's body, exposing her large belly. Purple and blue bruises marred the pale skin on one side.

Dr. Henshaw's jaw muscle ticked. "I hope the baby's all right. For now, the heartbeat is within normal range."

Suddenly, the skin over Darla's stomach grew taut, and a moan came from the weakened woman.

"Go sit with her." Dr. Henshaw moved to the foot of the bed. "Hold her hand. Talk to her and try to get her to wake up more." He pulled a chair over to sit on.

Olivia's legs shook as she went to the head of the bed and shoved the pillows behind Darla to keep her propped up.

Beads of sweat dotted the woman's forehead as she thrashed back and forth. Once the contraction ended, she went limp.

"Come on, honey. You need to help your baby. You can do this." With a corner of the bedsheet, Olivia wiped Darla's face, murmuring encouragement.

Ruth arrived with an armful of items. She set them on the dresser, then went back out, returning moments later with two pots. She set one on the nightstand. "This one is cool water to bathe her face," she told Olivia.

Ruth then set the steaming pot on the dresser. "Just let me know what you need me to do next."

Dr. Henshaw nodded.

Olivia wrung out a cloth and gently wiped the woman's face, careful to avoid the bruises. The coolness had Darla's eyes blinking open.

"It's all right. We're here with you. Dr. Henshaw is going to help you deliver your baby." Olivia prayed that everything would be all right. "What's your name?"

"Mary." The strangled word was so low only Olivia could have heard it.

Mary's face twisted as her whole body tensed.

"Another contraction," Dr. Henshaw said. "I can see the head. You need to push now."

Mary gave a weak attempt, then lay back, panting.

"I know it's hard," Olivia said in a soothing voice. "But your baby will be worth it. Come on, we'll do it together." She put an arm around the woman's shoulders, willing her strength to pass on to Mary.

After another attempt, Mary crumpled.

Olivia moistened the cloth again and ran it over the woman's forehead and neck, hoping to revive her. Her efforts were rewarded when the woman blinked and inhaled sharply.

When the next contraction came, she helped Mary sit up more. Olivia's arms strained under the woman's weight as she labored. "Push, Mary. You're almost there."

Was she? Olivia had no idea. She only knew that she had to give this woman hope.

After several more attempts, Mary panted with exhaustion. Another pain hit and she pushed again.

Concentrating on bathing Mary's face, Olivia was only vaguely aware of the flurry of activity at the end of the bed until a loud cry sounded. She raised her head to see the doctor lifting a red-faced infant onto the sheet Ruth handed him.

"It's a girl," he announced. "Looks to be about six pounds or so. Congratulations."

The relief that spread over his face allowed Olivia to relax. She eased Mary back against the pillows, her own muscles loosening.

The doctor tended to the baby, then handed the sheet-clad bundle to Ruth. Instantly, the child quieted.

Ruth smiled down at the infant as she walked toward the mother. "Would you like to see your baby?"

Mary nodded, barely able to keep her eyes open. As Ruth moved the sheet aside, Mary's whole face softened. "My daughter," she whispered. But the woman didn't seem to have the strength to take the baby. Instead, her eyes rolled back in her head.

Ruth's expression changed from joy to alarm. "Doctor!"

Olivia looked at Mary, only then registering the strange gurgling sounds coming from the woman's throat.

Dr. Henshaw whipped the pillows from behind Mary's head. "Olivia, hold her shoulders. I need to—"

Olivia jerked off the bed, knocking the basin of water to the floor. The air whooshed from her lungs, her heart thumping a loud beat in her ears. "I'm sorry, I can't."

Then she turned and bolted from the room.

Several hours later, Olivia sat on the back step, staring out at the sunbathed yard. How could the day be so calm, the birds so cheery, when inside a tragedy had barely been averted?

They'd confronted life and death before the sun had even risen.

Dr. Henshaw had managed to bring Mary around and, after cleaning her up and giving her a shot of some kind, said she should recover. Ruth had asked if she needed to go to the hospital, but he'd said no. Mary's blood pressure had come back up, and her heart rate seemed steady. Given a few weeks of bed rest, she should be back to normal. He'd given Ruth instructions on how to make formula for the baby in case Mary wasn't strong enough to breastfeed right away, and Ruth had promised to pass the information on to Mrs. Neale.

All of this Ruth had relayed to Olivia when she'd found her in the office, working on the books in an attempt to take her mind off the whole affair, especially the sight of that precious baby, who reminded Olivia far too much of her own infant son. Though Ruth tried to convince Olivia to join her for a bite of breakfast, Olivia had declined, knowing she wouldn't be able to keep anything down.

Soon after, she'd come out to the yard, seeking fresh air and the solace of prayer. Yet nothing could banish the horrible memories that haunted her. Mary's labor had brought back unrelenting flashbacks of the day Olivia had delivered her own child. The bleak beige walls. The bare lightbulb above the bed. The hard metal handrails she'd clutched during her contractions. Only the compassion of one nurse made the experience at all bearable. The woman had kindly wrapped the baby in the blanket Olivia had knitted before she handed Matteo to her.

Even then, Olivia hadn't understood that she wouldn't be allowed to keep her son. Holding Matteo in her arms for that brief time had been the most joyous moment of her life. Until Mrs. Linder arrived to tell her that she was taking him away.

Tears dripped down Olivia's cheeks. *Oh, Matteo. Where are you now? Are you being well cared for? Loved unconditionally? Will your new family ever tell you about me?*

For the first time since they'd opened Bennington Place, real doubts set in to plague her.

What if she couldn't handle being around newborns? What if she had an emotional breakdown every time a woman went into labor or whenever difficulties arose during childbirth? How would that help anyone?

With no easy answers to be found, she got up and crossed the lawn to the rosebushes that lined the property. She fingered the silky petals and vibrant leaves and focused on the healing power of nature. Inhaling deeply, she allowed the soothing floral scent to fill her, forcing away grotesque images of blood and sweat. And instruments of torture.

Here, in Ruth's garden, there existed only sunshine, lush greenery, and the welcoming stone birdbath where the sparrows played.

Here, she'd found sanctuary from the harshness of the world. A roof over her head, a soft mattress to lie on, and food to fill her belly. Here, no matter what the other residents went through, Olivia would be safe and protected. No monsters would find her.

Perhaps if she told herself this often enough, she could really start to believe it.

The wind lifted the ends of her hair, making the tresses dance freely around her shoulders. She plucked a delicate pink blossom and held it to her nose, inhaling its gentle scent, then raised her face to the sky.

Lord, if you want me to continue ministering to these women, I'll need your help. Please allow me to conquer my fears by putting my complete trust in you.

17

Darius waited on the doorstep of Bennington Place, a spray of daisies from his mother's garden in one hand. What kind of offering did a person bring for a battered pregnant woman? Daisies, the most cheerful of flowers, seemed the best option.

He'd told Olivia that he would call to see how the woman was doing, but he'd decided to come by in person to see for himself. As much as he tried to deny it, the real truth was that he wanted to see Olivia again and was afraid that if he telephoned first, she'd refuse his request.

When the door opened, he readied his best smile. But it wasn't Olivia who answered.

A young, freckle-faced girl, obviously quite pregnant, stood with the door only half-open. "Yes?"

"Good morning. Is Miss Rosetti in?"

The girl eyed his flowers, then looked up at him. "I remember you. You were here when the pipe burst."

Ah yes. The girl who'd reported the leak. Margaret, was it?

"That's right. I'm Darius Reed. I came to see how the injured woman is doing. I helped bring her in yesterday."

Somewhat reluctantly, it seemed, the girl stood back to let him enter.

"Margaret, who was at the—oh. Hello, Mr. Reed." Mrs. Bennington appeared in the corridor. Her tone, though not exactly friendly, wasn't as cold as it usually was when she addressed him.

"Good morning, Mrs. Bennington. I came to see how the woman who arrived yesterday is doing." He glanced down the hall, hoping to catch sight of Olivia.

"We've had a rough night of it, but she's stable for now." Ruth turned to the girl. "Margaret, do you know where Olivia is? I thought she'd be in the office, but it's empty."

"She's out in the yard. Has been for a while." With a shrug, the girl returned to the parlor.

Ruth let out a sigh, then turned her attention to Darius. "Mary, the woman you brought in, went into labor in the middle of the night. She gave birth to a little girl, though we almost lost the mother soon afterward. I think the situation affected Olivia more than she expected." She studied him. "You might be just the distraction Olivia needs. If you go out through the kitchen, you'll find her in the backyard."

The importance of her trusting him with Olivia wasn't lost on Darius. He held out the posy of daisies. "Would you give these to Mary for me?"

Her brows rose as she accepted the flowers. "I thought they were for Olivia."

"No, ma'am. But it's a nice idea. I should have thought of it."

"This is thoughtful enough. So is your coming here. You didn't have to do that."

"I didn't sleep very well last night thinking about what that poor woman had been through."

Ruth's features softened. "It's possible I've misjudged you, Mr. Reed. You seem to be a decent person, even though you still want my house."

He laughed. "A high compliment indeed."

"Try to get Olivia to come inside and eat something. She's been brooding for hours now."

"I'll do my best."

Darius walked through the kitchen, past a wary cook, and out the back door. When he paused on the small stoop to scan the yard, his breath caught at the sight before him. Olivia stood with her back to him, her dark hair loose and flowing to her waist. There was an ethereal quality about her that beckoned to him. Yet all he could do was stare as she bent to smell the roses that lined the fence. It was a scene that an artist would love to paint—the sunshine haloing her head, the soft breeze ruffling her dress, the sea of colorful blooms surrounding her.

Breathtaking. Sacred even.

Shaking off his reaction, he descended the steps and crossed the lawn, hating to disturb the peaceful scene.

"Good morning, Olivia."

She whirled around, eyes wide. "Darius. What are you doing here?"

Not the most welcoming greeting. "I wanted to see how our patient is doing. Mrs. Bennington told me she had the baby."

Olivia nodded. "For a while, we thought Mary wasn't going to make it." She twisted a rose between her fingers, scattering petals onto the lawn.

"You stayed with her during the birth, I understand."

"Yes. I didn't want her to be alone."

"That took a lot of courage." He couldn't begin to fathom how she'd endured it, but maybe women had more stamina for the birthing process. He remembered when Sofia was born, how relieved he'd been when the doctor had asked him to leave the delivery room. He hadn't done well witnessing Selene's pain and trusted she'd be better off in the hands of the professionals. Now, after hearing Olivia's story, he felt like a coward.

"I wasn't brave." She shook her head. "When Mary took a bad turn, I ran out." Her troubled eyes met his. "It made me wonder if I'm strong enough to do this."

The wind blew her hair around her face, several strands brushing his jacket.

"From what I've seen, I'd say you're plenty strong," he said softly. "You're a remarkable woman, Olivia Rosetti." The temptation to touch her, to pull her close and kiss her, almost proved too strong. Before he did something foolish—something he couldn't take back—he moved away. "Why don't we go up and see how Mary's doing? I wouldn't mind seeing the baby."

Her brown eyes widened. "Really?"

"Nothing like new life to renew your faith in the world."

"And in God."

"True."

She smiled, a slow lifting of her lips. "All right, then. Let's go."

Olivia's legs still weren't steady as she climbed the stairs beside Darius. After that breath-stealing moment when she thought he might reach out and touch her, when her heart had practically bounced from her chest, she wasn't entirely sure what she was doing.

As they neared Mary's room, Dr. Henshaw emerged, concern shadowing his features.

"How's she doing?" Olivia asked.

"Not well, I'm afraid. She's not picking up like I hoped. I've decided to bring her to the hospital and get another opinion on her condition."

"What about the baby?" Olivia glanced toward the door. Who would care for the infant if her mother was so ill?

The doctor scratched the beginning of stubble on his chin. "I'd prefer to keep her here since Mary isn't capable of looking after her right now. Plus, the child will be less likely to pick up any illnesses."

Ruth came out of the room, the baby in her arms.

Tension snapped along Olivia's shoulders. If Darius wasn't here, she'd have run to her room. Anything to avoid the reminder of her loss.

Dr. Henshaw turned to Ruth. "Did you have any luck?"

"I'm afraid not."

"Luck with what?" Darius asked.

The doctor sighed. "I'm trying to get information for the birth certificate. Mary won't name the father, or even give her own surname."

"She did say she wants to call the baby Abigail." Ruth smiled down at the sleeping infant.

"That's something at least. If you'll excuse me, I'll arrange for Mary's transportation to the hospital." The doctor headed toward the staircase.

"I guess that means she's not up for a visitor?" Darius asked.

"Not now. She's drifted off again." Ruth held out the baby. "But you could hold little Abigail if you'd like."

Olivia stepped back, almost tripping in her haste. Her stomach churned as she tried not to look at the child.

Surprisingly, Darius didn't hesitate to gather the baby against his chest. A soft smile hovered on his lips as he stared down at her. "She's beautiful. With all that dark hair, she reminds me of my Sofia when she was born."

Ruth looked over at Olivia. "You haven't held the baby yet, Olivia. Would you like a turn?"

She shook her head. How could she comfort a baby when she'd been denied that luxury with her own son? It wouldn't be fair to Matteo.

But before she realized it, Darius had placed the bundle on her shoulder. "Here you go. There's nothing to it."

The air stalled in her lungs as the baby snuggled into her neck and the smell of talcum powder surrounded her. Instinctively, her arm came up to clasp the child. The baby sighed, her tiny chest rising and falling at a slightly faster rate than Olivia's. As warmth seeped through her body, Olivia's heart expanded with a fierce protectiveness she'd only felt once before. She squeezed her eyes shut, tears forming despite her best intentions, and rubbed a soothing hand over the baby's back. Maybe it wouldn't be wrong to care for another child. Maybe she'd be making up for not being able to do the same for Matteo.

"Olivia, are you all right?" Ruth's voice seemed to come from a distance.

She opened her eyes. "I'm fine."

Darius and Ruth both stared at her with concerned expressions.

"You're crying." Darius stated the fact in an incredulous tone.

The wetness of her cheeks proved his words, but she smiled. "I am. Because she's so precious."

"Yes, she is." Ruth patted Olivia's arm. "If you wouldn't mind taking her for a while, I have a few things to take care of."

"I'd be happy to." Where moments ago she'd been terrified to hold the baby, Olivia now didn't want to release her. "I'll take her downstairs. Will she be hungry soon?"

"Another hour or two. But she may need changing. There are diapers in Mary's room on the dresser." Ruth smiled. "Thank you for stopping by with the flowers, Mr. Reed. Mary did manage to see them before she fell asleep again."

"I'm glad. And I'll be praying for her recovery."

"That's the best thing we can do for her right now."

Olivia headed toward the stairs. "There's a rocking chair in the parlor. Would you like to join me there?" she asked Darius.

He pulled out his pocket watch and frowned. "I'd love to, but I'm afraid I have to get back to the office for a meeting. Could I come by again in a day or two and see how they're both doing?"

Olivia nodded. "I'd like that."

And this time she truly meant it.

18

What am I doing?

Darius pressed his fingers against his temples, attempting to ease the headache brewing. He tried to concentrate on the staff meeting going on, but Mr. Walcott's words were failing to sink in.

The more time Darius spent around Olivia, the more his heart became engaged. And with his wedding to Meredith in a few weeks, that wasn't fair to anyone.

Meredith and her family had settled on August ninth as the date for the nuptials, though it still seemed rather rushed to Darius. He tried to ignore the gut feeling that something was wrong about the situation. A society girl like Meredith should be holding out for a more lavish wedding, especially since she would be the first daughter to marry. Yet if Meredith was content, shouldn't he be too?

In addition to obsessing about his wedding, Darius's thoughts were consumed with baby Abigail and her very ill mother. The ambulance had been pulling up to the house as he'd left the other day, and a renewed anger had burned through him at the thought of the monster who had hurt that poor woman.

For the first time, he truly understood what Olivia meant by women needing a place where they felt safe. And he knew now that he couldn't be responsible for taking that haven away from them.

When the meeting ended, the employees started filing out of the conference room. Darius rose and gathered his files.

Mr. Walcott stopped in the doorway. "By the way, Reed, since you didn't bother to follow up on it, I submitted an article to *The Daily Star* about Bennington Place. Should come out tomorrow. I'm hoping for front-page exposure."

Darius went still. He couldn't believe Walcott had gone ahead without any input from him. Yet after the man's admission to bribing the inspector, why should Darius be surprised? "What exactly is this article going to say?"

"You'll have to wait and find out like everyone else." With a final disapproving glance, Walcott walked out.

The air left Darius's lungs in a whoosh. The only thing he could do now was hopefully warn Ruth and Olivia before they saw it. However, when he returned to his office, he found Kevin waiting for him.

"Could I speak to you for a minute, sir?"

Darius closed the door. "Sure. What about?"

From the wary look on the man's face, Darius didn't think it was a business matter. Unless he was here to apologize for helping Walcott gather ammunition against the maternity home.

"It's about Mere—Miss Cheeseman."

Dark suspicion curled through Darius. He tossed the files onto his desk. "My fiancée? What about her?"

Kevin paced to the windows and back. "Look, I didn't know if I should say anything, but I figured you have the right to know."

"Know what? That you're in love with her?"

"Me?" He shook his head. "No, sir."

"Come on, Kevin. I saw you mooning over her that day in your office."

Anger flashed in his eyes. "The only reason I was flirting with her was to try and disprove the rumors I've been hearing. For your sake, I'd hoped they weren't true."

Darius slowly sat down. "You're not making any sense."

Kevin ran his fingers through his hair, then blew out a breath. "A guy I know is good friends with Meredith's former boyfriend."

Darius stiffened. Meredith had been seeing someone named Jerry last fall, but it had been over for some time—or so she claimed. "What's he got to do with anything?"

Kevin sat down across from him. "According to my source, they recently attempted to reconcile after a lot of pleading on Meredith's part. But not long after, Jerry took off for parts unknown."

"I still don't see what that has to do with me." Darius's gut roiled. He wanted to demand that Kevin quit spreading gossip. But another part of him, the one that had felt something was off with Meredith, needed to hear the rest of the story.

"Rumor has it she's pregnant, and when she told Jerry, he wanted no part of it. She begged him to marry her, but he refused. The next thing she knew, he'd left town."

A wave of nausea hit hard. That must have been right around the time Meredith had started pursuing Darius, making it clear she was more than interested in a relationship.

Kevin shook his head. "Seems she's desperate for someone to marry her. That's why I was flirting, to see if she'd respond. If she really loved you, she wouldn't have given me the time of day. But if she needed a backup plan . . ."

Darius groaned. Meredith had fallen right into Kevin's trap. She'd flirted back, eating up the besotted look on Kevin's face. Still . . .

"That was weeks ago. Why are you coming to me now?"

Kevin shrugged. "Walcott just told me you're getting married soon. That's when I knew I had to tell you before it was too late."

Darius scrubbed a hand over his eyes. What an idiot he'd been. Meredith was using him to save her reputation. Did she intend to pass off the baby as his once they were married? "This might be nothing more than vicious gossip."

"It's possible. But I wanted to give you a chance to find out for certain before she drags you to the altar." Kevin rose. "I'm really sorry. I hope you know I'm only looking out for you."

Darius rubbed the back of his neck. "Yeah, I do."

Kevin paused at the door. "What will you do if it's true?"

Darius frowned. He honestly didn't know. Could he go along with Meredith's charade if it meant obtaining a mother for Sofia? If he broke off his engagement, Mr. Cheeseman could cancel his account with Walcott Industries, the way Mr. Peterson had ended up doing. That was a prospect Darius couldn't think about. Because if both their biggest clients quit, Walcott Industries would be in serious trouble.

"I guess I'll have to cross that bridge when I come to it."

After a short stroll through the Cheesemans' neighborhood, Darius led Meredith to a nearby park bench. He'd gone to her house right after work and asked her to take a walk, not wanting her family to accidentally overhear their conversation. He needed privacy to confront her about what he'd learned, and the park seemed the best option.

She sat on the bench and smiled. "This was a nice surprise, darling. Although as I told you, I'm very busy with the wedding plans. For you, though, I can always make time." She laughed and tucked a strand of hair behind her ear.

Darius tried to force his lips into a smile but couldn't manage it. "I wanted to speak to you about something important." His insides tightened into a hard knot. How did he even begin this conversation? One question could ruin the day for them both.

"I hope you haven't changed your mind about the date," she said. "Reverend Hill is doing us a favor by squeezing us in on such short notice."

"It's not about the date." He reached deep for a sense of calm. "I want to ask you a question, and I'd like an honest answer."

The brightness faded from her features. "What is it?"

He needed to be blunt. If he danced around the issue, she might have time to cover up. "Meredith, are you pregnant?"

Right away, her eyes filled with tears, and her bottom lip began to quiver. She stared at him for a second, then dropped her face into her hands. Audible sobs emerged from between her fingers, and her shoulders quaked with the force of her weeping.

Disappointment crashed through him, twisting into anger. So it was true. Meredith had gotten herself in trouble and was using him to fix her problem.

"What was your plan?" he said, bitterness lacing his voice. "Pretend the child was mine and claim the baby was premature when it was born months early?"

She raised a tearstained face to look at him. The breeze blew her hair across her eyes. "I'm sorry, Darius. I was going to tell you right after the wedding. I swear."

"A little late then, don't you think?"

"I didn't want you to—" She broke down and sobbed harder.

"Admit it, Meredith. You needed a husband and anyone would've done."

"You're wrong. I care about you a great deal. Plus, you already have a daughter, so I knew you'd be a good father." She rifled through her purse for a handkerchief. "We can still be a family, Darius. The four of us. There's nothing to stop us from going through with the wedding." Hope brightened her eyes.

Needing to move, he got to his feet and paced the grass. Would he have felt differently if he'd been in love with Meredith? He didn't know. The fact remained that although he was fond of her and had hoped to build a life with her, he couldn't marry a woman who would try and pass off another man's child as his. Even if she'd been honest from the beginning, he doubted he could have gone along with her plan.

He turned to face her and shook his head. "I'm afraid I can't condone that type of deception."

Her features crumpled. "What am I going to do now? My parents will disown me. Where will I go?"

"Your parents don't know?" He figured they must have been aware of her situation since they'd agreed to such a quick wedding.

"You know my father. How could I tell him?" She wiped her cheeks again and got to her feet. "Darius, please. I'll do anything if you marry me. We could even get a divorce later, if that's what you want."

"A divorce?" He scowled. "Wouldn't that be just as disgraceful?"

"Not really. Divorce is becoming more common these days. My family could accept a failed marriage but not an unwed pregnant daughter." She reached over to grip his arm. "Just think of what this could mean for Sofia. Think of everything we could give her. A nice home. Beautiful clothes. Private schools."

He tugged free from her grasp. She certainly knew how to tempt him where he was the most vulnerable. He rubbed the back of his neck. Could he compromise his principles for Sofia's sake? To secure the type of future he'd envisioned for her?

His thoughts turned to Mr. Walcott and his underhanded schemes to obtain the Bennington property. Schemes he expected Darius to go along with for the promise of job security and a raise. Now Meredith dangled this reward in front of him if only he'd go along with her ruse.

Were his lofty morals worth losing his job and a coveted life of security for Sofia?

At that moment, the image of Olivia Rosetti rose in his mind. Olivia, weeping over an injured woman she didn't even know, then crying tears of joy for a baby born under terrible circumstances. Olivia was living her faith, helping the unfortunate, just as Jesus mandated His followers to do. She would never compromise her morals for any type of personal gain.

How could he do any less?

Slowly, he turned back to his red-eyed fiancée. "I'm afraid the answer has to be no, Meredith. I'm sorry, but I can't marry you."

19

Seated in a rocking chair the next morning, Olivia cradled the sleeping Abigail in her arms. Mrs. Dinglemire had left a few minutes earlier, after coming to check on the newborn. The midwife had weighed Abigail and rechecked her vital signs, then used the opportunity to give all the women in the home a lesson on bathing and caring for an infant. Promising to return the next day, Mrs. Dinglemire had stopped to see Mrs. Neale on her way out to discuss the formula recipe they'd been using.

All in all, the midwife had seemed pleased with the baby's progress, which gave Olivia an immense feeling of satisfaction.

Little Abigail squirmed in her arms and sighed. The warmth of the tiny body against Olivia's chest acted like a sedative, allowing her muscles to relax and her soul to sing. Never had she felt more at peace, more certain of what she needed to do. She would take care of this precious girl until her mother regained her strength. Then she and Ruth would help Mary determine her future, hopefully one that didn't include the man who'd beaten her. Baby Abigail did not need a father like that. She deserved someone loving and kind, someone who would lay down his life for her.

Olivia's thoughts instantly turned to Darius, and a smile teased her lips. He'd been so thoughtful, coming to visit Mary, bringing her flowers, and gushing over little Abigail. Darius Reed would never harm a woman or child. She knew this in the very marrow of her bones.

And he'd promised to come back and check on the baby one day soon. Flutters swirled in Olivia's stomach just thinking about it.

Stop it, Olivia. You're being ridiculous.

Fantasizing about Darius was a futile endeavor since she'd vowed never to trust a man with her heart again. Besides, if he ever learned the horror of her past, he'd want nothing to do with her.

And soon he would have no further reason to visit Bennington Place, once his boss accepted the fact that the property was not for sale. Disappointment stole her breath at the thought of never seeing Darius again. Never witnessing that engaging grin or being able to stare into those mesmerizing blue eyes.

Surely it couldn't hurt to enjoy the pleasure of his company while it lasted.

Angry shouts from outside the house drew Olivia from her daydreams. What was going on now? Was Mr. Simmons harassing some poor woman again?

Carefully, she rose from the rocker, shifted the sleeping baby to one arm, and walked over to the window. She moved the lace curtain aside and was stunned to see a large group of people— mostly men but a few women too—gathered on the sidewalk across the street. They held up placards and waved their fists in the direction of the house, shouting unintelligible words.

What on earth was happening? It looked like a riot could break out at any moment.

She let the curtain fall back, the slow burn of anger creeping through her system. This had to stop. They needed to do something to keep Mr. Simmons from riling up the neighbors this way or the negativity he spewed would deter women from coming to them for help.

No, he could not be allowed to continue his attack on their facility unchallenged. Perhaps Ruth could obtain some legal advice as to what their options might be.

Olivia laid the baby in a bassinet, then went to look for Ruth. Moments later, she found her at the dining room table, a newspaper spread out in front of her. From her grim expression, Olivia wondered if she'd heard the commotion outside.

"Mr. Simmons is at it again," Olivia said. "But this time he has a whole group of people with him. They're carrying signs and everything."

Ruth shook her head. "I know exactly what's got them aggravated. Look at this." She pointed to the front page of the newspaper. A photo of the maternity home sat above the fold and underneath was a picture of a scowling Mr. Simmons.

"What's this? Did you do another interview for the paper?" Olivia asked.

"Not me." Ruth's mouth was hard. "It's Mr. Simmons. He's been saying that we're nothing more than a cover for a brothel. That the women living here are all pregnant streetwalkers."

Olivia gasped. Why would he say that? Then she remembered him harassing Cherise when she first arrived.

Ruth pointed to a line in the article. "He's started a petition against us, aiming to have the home closed down. Says he's going to present it to the mayor at the next city council meeting."

Olivia's shaking legs forced her to sink onto one of the chairs. "Oh no. What do we do now?"

"To start with, I'm going to call my lawyer and see what legal recourse we have, if any." Ruth folded the newspaper and rose. "I had intended to go to the hospital this morning to visit Mary, but I don't fancy confronting that crowd. Maybe by this afternoon things will have quieted down."

"I hope you're right."

Ruth paused in the doorway. "I think we should have a house meeting after dinner. The women deserve to know what's happening—for their own safety if nothing else. Together we'll come up with a plan on how to handle this little setback."

Olivia only prayed that this *setback* was temporary and that the protestors wouldn't succeed in running them out of the city.

Later that day, however, instead of the interest waning as Ruth had hoped, it seemed that even more protesters had shown up, this time lining the sidewalk in front of Bennington Place and blocking the front gate. Ruth moved away from the parlor window, determined not to let those hooligans get the best of her temper. Cooler heads must prevail. It was only a matter of time until this all blew over, and if it didn't, they still had some options, according to her lawyer.

Unfortunately, the roof repairman was due to arrive soon, and Ruth wasn't sure if he would be willing to go through the unruly crowd to gain access to the house. If he decided her business wasn't worth the effort and canceled their agreement, Ruth would be hard-pressed to find another contractor who could come before their next scheduled inspection.

She sighed. "Lord, why are they making this so difficult? We only want to help people. Is that such a terrible thing?"

"Now who's the one despairing?" Olivia's voice preceded her into the room.

"Oh no. Did I say that out loud?" Ruth shook her head.

"You did."

"Don't mind me. Just a moment of weakness." She crossed the carpet. "I think I'd better call my lawyer again. If we can't get this crowd to disperse, I'm afraid they'll scare off the roofer."

Olivia's brows crashed together. "We can't allow that."

"Let's hope my legal firm can pull a few strings and get someone over here to help." Ruth had just started down the hall when a loud crash broke the silence, followed by the sound of breaking glass.

"What on earth?" Ruth rushed back into the parlor and stared. A brick sat in the middle of the rug, surrounded by debris. The front window was shattered, with only one jagged shard remaining.

Olivia stood with a hand pressed to her cheek. The sunlight glittered off tiny glass fragments in her hair. When she moved her hand away, a slash of red marked her skin.

"Oh, my dear. You're hurt." Ruth moved toward her, but the almost feral look on Olivia's face stopped her.

A string of Italian words erupted, matching the fire in her eyes as she strode out of the parlor.

Ruth's heart jerked at the sound of the front door opening. Surely she wouldn't confront the protesters. "Olivia, wait. Don't go out there. It's not safe."

By the time Ruth reached the front step, however, Olivia had marched down to the gate.

"How dare you!" she shouted. "You have no right to damage our property."

The people shook their cardboard signs, waving them higher in the air, yelling insults.

"Whores aren't welcome here."

"We don't want your filth in our neighborhood."

"Go back to the gutter where you belong."

Ruth gasped as a slew of eggs, tomatoes, and other rotten projectiles came hurtling over the gate.

Olivia raised her arms against the barrage. "You're all a bunch of hypocrites," she shouted. "Leave us alone. We've done nothing to you."

In response, the crowd's volume intensified.

Alarm filled Ruth's chest. Things were quickly getting out of hand. "Olivia, come back inside and we'll call the police."

But the girl ignored her.

Another volley of items flew over the fence, splattering the grass and the walkway. Ruth tried to shield herself from the onslaught, but something rank slid down her face and landed on her blouse. She brushed the slime from her cheek, blinking to clear her vision. Why had the crowd suddenly grown quiet? The eerie silence contained a nervous energy that seemed to pulse in the air.

To her horror, she spied Olivia's crumpled form on the ground in front of her.

"Olivia!" Fighting a rush of panic that thrummed in her ears, she hurried to the girl's side. All color had drained from Olivia's face, leaving it as gray as the rock that had struck her. Blood flowed freely from a large gash above her temple.

Ruth fumbled in her pocket for a handkerchief. "Someone call an ambulance," she cried as she pressed the material against the wound. "This girl needs help. Now!"

20

Darius drove slowly down the street toward Bennington Place. What was going on here? So many people lined the road and sidewalk that he couldn't get past. Not willing to chance hitting a pedestrian, his only choice was to pull over and walk the rest of the way.

After he parked the car, he headed toward the melee, elbowing his way through the crowd, many of whom carried placards. An undercurrent of subdued energy buzzed around him, but it wasn't until he read the degrading slurs on their signs that his stomach began to churn. This was Walcott's doing. He'd stirred up this nest of vipers with that dreaded newspaper article. Darius had hoped to reach Olivia to warn her in person before she saw it. But with all the uproar over Meredith and a minor crisis at the office this morning, he hadn't been able to get away as early as he'd wanted. Now the best he could do was ensure that Olivia and the others were all right.

"Stand back, please," Darius said, then waited while some people moved away from the gate.

"Are you the doctor?" One woman peered anxiously at him. "We didn't mean to hurt her. We only wanted to scare them."

A cold chill slid down his back. "Hurt who?"

But the woman ducked her head and backed away.

Dear God, please don't let it be—

Darius entered the gate, closing it behind him with a clang. He turned to see Mrs. Bennington kneeling on the ground, holding a blood-soaked cloth against Olivia's temple. His limbs went cold, and spots danced in front of his eyes. This couldn't be happening again. Not another person he cared about injured by hate-induced violence.

He gulped in a lungful of air, willing his vision to clear as he strode over. "What happened?" he rasped.

"Oh, Mr. Reed. Thank goodness." Relief slid over Mrs. Bennington's face. "Help me get Olivia inside."

Darius bent to lift the cloth, revealing a gaping wound that made his stomach churn anew. "We need to get her to a hospital. My car is down the street. I'll take her."

Before the older woman could protest, he slipped his arms beneath Olivia's limp form, gathered her against his chest, and rose on unsteady legs. "Call the authorities, Mrs. Bennington. We can't let these thugs get away with this type of violence. They must be held accountable."

He stalked off toward the car, silently daring anyone to try and stop him.

Darius paced the waiting room at Toronto General Hospital. How long would it take for someone to come out and let him know how Olivia was doing? She hadn't regained consciousness during the ride here, and Darius had found it almost impossible to concentrate on driving. In hindsight, perhaps he should have waited until someone could come with him. But at the time, his only thought had been to get Olivia help as fast as possible.

He'd parked as close to the emergency entrance as he could and carried her in, shouting for a doctor. The nurse on duty had glared at him as though he'd totally overreacted.

Then they'd whisked Olivia away, not allowing him to go with her, and he'd been forced to wait for what seemed like hours.

All the while, a dark anger had stewed in his system. Olivia had been injured because that vile article had stirred up hatred in the community, a direct result of his boss's lust for the Bennington property. Why hadn't Darius been firmer when he told Walcott it was a bad idea? Could he have done something more to prevent this catastrophe?

Unable to wait another minute, Darius approached the desk again. "Can someone please find out about Miss Rosetti for me?"

The heavyset nurse looked up with a frown, then huffed out a breath. "Give me a minute." Slowly she finished writing figures on a chart, then rose and went down the hall.

What seemed like an eternity later, she finally returned. "Miss Rosetti's wound has been stitched. The doctor fears she may have a concussion and is holding her overnight for observation. They'll be transferring her to a ward shortly."

Holding her overnight? Darius had not expected that. "Is she awake?"

"No, she's sleeping now."

He reined in his emotions long enough to summon a smile. "May I go back and see for myself? Just a quick look. I promise I won't stay long."

The nurse rolled her eyes. "You have five minutes. Bed number ten."

"Thank you, ma'am." The fact that he'd been pestering the woman for hours might have worked in his favor.

He headed back before she could change her mind. When he reached bed number ten, he peered around the curtained partition. Olivia lay there, her eyes closed, her dark hair spilling over the bedsheets. A white gauze bandage covered the right side of her head, and an angry red scrape marred one cheek. Under the harsh lights, her skin appeared almost translucent, and for the first time he realized how young she must be. She barely looked more than twenty. He grabbed a nearby chair and moved it beside the bed, then sat down and lifted one of her hands, stroking the soft skin with his thumb.

His chest constricted as he gazed at her. He'd never seen her so still. She was always bustling here or there, eager to be of service.

Lord, please let her be all right. She doesn't deserve this conflict. All she's trying to do is help women in trouble.

He brought her hand to his lips, then rested it against his cheek. "You're going to be all right, Olivia. You have to be. Those women need you." The urge to hold her, to protect her from further harm, became almost impossible to fight. But propriety held him in check, and he settled for watching her in silence. He would stay until the nurse or security came to throw him out.

Minutes later, however, Olivia's lids fluttered, and she slowly opened her eyes. Wincing, she pulled her hand free and strained to sit up.

"Take it easy," he said. "You've had a bad blow to the head."

"Darius?"

"I'm right here. You're in the hospital."

Her gaze darted from the bedside tray to the curtained partition. She jerked upright and plucked at the sheet covering her.

"Olivia, no." He reached for her hand again. "You need to lie back and rest."

Just then a different nurse entered the cramped area. She was a short woman, wearing a full-length white apron and cap, and had a stethoscope draped around her neck.

Olivia stiffened, the look of fear increasing. Her whole body shook as she shrank back in the bed.

"It's only the nurse," he said in his most soothing tone, one he used for Sofia after a nightmare. "She's here to check on you."

Olivia turned and buried her face in his shoulder. "Don't let her hurt me."

Why would she think the woman would hurt her? Perhaps her injury had made her confused. He put an arm around her and murmured soothing words, hating to see her in such distress.

The nurse came forward. "There's nothing to worry about, dear. I just need to check your vital signs."

But Olivia continued to shrink away.

The woman speared Darius with a suspicious stare. "Are you responsible for this?"

"Of course not!" Heat flooded his chest. "I would never hurt a woman."

"What happened, then? Who gave her that wound?"

Darius debated how much to reveal but decided on the truth. "She was defending her home from protestors when she got hit with a rock."

The nurse recoiled in surprise. "What were they protesting?"

"I guess you haven't seen the paper. They were opposing the new maternity home in the neighborhood."

She glanced at Olivia, who still cowered against him. "This woman lives at a maternity home? There's no indication on her chart that she's expecting."

Darius shook his head. "Olivia helps run the facility. She's committed her life to helping women in crisis." A fierce pride laced his words, and he tightened his grip around her.

The nurse's demeanor softened. "It's a brave thing you're doing, Miss Rosetti. I'm sorry you got injured."

Whether it was the woman's words or the extra gentleness to her tone Darius wasn't sure, but Olivia slowly raised her head.

"Can I go home?" she whispered.

The nurse scanned the paper on her clipboard, then looked up. "If you have someone to watch over you for the next twenty-four hours, I'll see what I can do to get you released. But the doctor will have the final say."

"I'm sure the women at the home will help," Darius said.

"All right, but you'll need to impress upon them to follow the doctor's instructions to the letter."

"I will, ma'am."

She turned her attention to Olivia. "If you'll allow me to check your stitches and take your vital signs, I'll go find the doctor."

Olivia moved slightly away from Darius. "No needles?"

"No. I'll give you medication that you can take orally."

Only then did Olivia appear to relax. "All right."

Darius rose. "I'll wait outside while—"

"No." Olivia's fearful brown gaze flew to him. "Please stay."

His heart twisted in his chest. How could he refuse such a plea? He turned to the nurse. "Is that all right?"

"As long as you don't get in my way, I've no objection."

He nodded. "I'll be right here, then." He stood by the footrail where Olivia could see him.

What had her so spooked about the hospital? She seemed terrified of the nurse, yet she was fine with Dr. Henshaw. Was it the building or the profession? More and more things about Olivia Rosetti puzzled him.

The nurse took Olivia's temperature, listened to her heart rate, which was likely sky-high given her fear, and then checked her head wound.

"The doctor did a nice job on those stitches," she announced as she re-bound the area. "If you're lucky, the scar will barely show."

Olivia remained silent.

"Any headache? Blurred vision?"

"No."

"What about dizziness, nausea, or vomiting?"

"I don't think so."

"Your temperature is normal, which is a good sign. If you develop any hint of a fever, call your doctor right away."

"I will."

The nurse stepped back. "I'll go and see about your release now."

Only once the woman left did Darius realize that Olivia's eyes had been trained on him the whole time. What had her so traumatized?

———◆———

178

Olivia gulped in a lungful of fresh air, thankful to get away from the horrible antiseptic smells that she would forever associate with the Mercer clinic.

Darius helped her into his car, and she sat back with a sigh of relief, not even caring that her clothes were covered in dried blood and smelled like rotten produce. Darius had a fair bit of blood on him as well, likely from carrying her.

She couldn't believe he'd gone out of his way, waiting at the hospital all that time and then doing his best to calm her fears. It was more than she could comprehend.

"Thank you for staying with me," she said once he'd started the car. She stared straight ahead, unable to look at him. What must he think of her strange reaction?

"I was glad I could be there." He turned onto another street and beeped the horn at a slow-moving vehicle in front of him. "If it's not too personal, may I ask why the nurse frightened you so much?"

She swallowed. How could she ever explain? She'd never told anyone about the horrors she'd experienced while at the Mercer. Dr. Henshaw had guessed some of what had happened, but she doubted even he would believe the full story. She certainly wasn't going to explain it to Darius. "I . . . had a bad experience with a woman doctor recently. It's made me extremely wary of medical people."

"I see," he said slowly. "But you don't seem nervous around Dr. Henshaw. Is that because he's a friend?"

"I was nervous of him too at first, but he's earned my trust. Still, if he ever came near me with a needle or some medical instrument, I can't predict how I'd react." She attempted a weak smile.

Darius glanced sideways at her, a troubled expression on his face. "I'm sorry you've had so much suffering, Olivia. And I hate what those protestors did. They should be arrested for their disgusting behavior."

"Yes, they should." But would that stop all the forces against them? Olivia doubted it. "It's strange," she said. "I thought the hardest part would be opening the home in the first place. I never imagined the community would turn against us." She winced as a ray of sun hit her eyes. "I can't believe Mr. Simmons went to the paper and that they printed his venomous words. They never even bothered to check our side of the story."

When Darius remained silent, Olivia glanced over at him. A nerve pulsed in his jaw.

"I'm afraid it wasn't Mr. Simmons behind the article," he said at last, "although he was more than willing to give his testimony." His knuckles whitened around the steering wheel. "It was my boss who initiated the piece. He's still bent on shutting your home down so Mrs. Bennington will sell."

With the throbbing in her temples, it took a moment for the full implication of his words to sink in. "Did you have anything to do with it?" she asked quietly.

"No. Mr. Walcott came to me with the idea for the article, but when I didn't act on it, he had one of my colleagues take over the assignment."

She released a soft breath. "I'm glad it wasn't you. But that must have put you in a difficult position."

"Unfortunately, it did." His features darkened. "But I intend to speak to my boss on Monday and let him know that I won't be party to such underhanded tactics. Bennington Place is a worthy endeavor. He has no right to interfere with it." He gave her a long look, a mixture of admiration and regret. A look that seemed laced with promise.

The tension in her muscles began to ease. Perhaps as a result of all this uproar, Bennington Place had gained a new supporter. One who might make all the difference in keeping their home open.

She only prayed that the damage done so far hadn't already been too great.

21

"I'm taking Sofia out for a while," Darius said to his mother as they finished up the dishes. "We'll be back in time for dinner."

Darius had gone to his morning class at the university and come home to have lunch with his family. Saturday afternoons were usually reserved for time alone with Sofia, but today the urgency to see Olivia and make sure she was all right left him feeling edgy and restless. So he'd decided that he and Sofia would make a quick stop at Bennington Place before heading to the park.

"Watch she doesn't get overheated. It's a hot one today."

"I will, Mamá." He kissed her cheek. "Is there anything you need while we're out?"

"If you pass the butcher, I need some lamb for tomorrow's stew."

"Sure thing." He peered into the living room to find Sofia sitting on his father's lap, the beloved princess storybook open before her.

Darius's stomach dropped at the sight of it. Did canceling his wedding to Meredith mean his daughter's dreams would never come true?

Perhaps he was being unreasonable rejecting the marriage. Yet his parents didn't think so. Mamá made no bones about the fact that she didn't approve of Meredith and was ecstatic that he'd called off the wedding.

He ran a hand over his eyes. *Lord, I pray I haven't made the worst mistake of my life. And that I haven't been unnecessarily harsh in judging Meredith. Please help her and her family come to terms with the situation in the best way possible.*

Taking a breath, Darius entered the room. "Come on, Sofia. Time to go."

She jumped up with a smile. "We'll finish the story later, Pappoú."

"You have fun," his father said. "See you at dinner."

Fifteen minutes later, as Darius parked the car, he was glad to note that only a few protestors lingered on the sidewalk across from the maternity home. Of course, Mr. Simmons was leading the way.

"What are we doing here, Daddy?" Sofia hopped along the sidewalk, attempting to avoid the cracks.

"We're visiting a friend for a few minutes before we go to the park."

"They live in a big house." Her eyes widened. "They must have a big family."

How did he begin to explain a maternity home to a four-year-old?

"This is like a boardinghouse." Darius led her up to the front door and knocked. "The ladies pay rent to live here." He didn't know if that was true, whether any monetary compensation was involved, but it was the best explanation he could think of.

The front door opened. This time Darius recognized the girl on the other side. "Good afternoon, Margaret," he said. "This is my daughter, Sofia. We've come to see how Miss Rosetti is doing today. Is she up for visitors?"

Margaret opened the door wider. "She's resting in the parlor. Come in."

Darius steered Sofia into the room, pausing for a moment.

What would Olivia think of him bringing his daughter here? He hoped she wouldn't think it too forward of him.

"A baby!" Sofia's squeal was loud enough to wake the neighbors.

From where she was seated in the rocking chair with little Abigail, Olivia's head flew up. "Well, hello," she said with a smile. "And who might you be?"

"I'm Sofia." The girl bounced over to the chair. "Is this your baby?"

"Sofia," Darius growled. "Mind your manners. This is Miss Rosetti. Olivia, this is my daughter."

"What a lovely surprise. It's nice to meet you, Sofia." Olivia's eyes twinkled. "This is Abigail. But no, she's not my baby. I'm looking after her right now because her mother is sick."

Sofia peered at Olivia. "Are you sick too?" she asked, pointing to the white gauze on Olivia's head.

"No. I just hurt my head. That's all."

"Did you cry?"

Olivia's lips twitched. "I did. A little."

"That's all right." Sofia patted her arm. "I cry when I fall down too."

Laughing, Olivia rose with the baby in her arms. "I have to give this little one a bottle. If your daddy says it's all right, would you like to help me?"

Sofia's brown eyes lit up. "Can I, Daddy?"

Darius glanced at Olivia, who winked at him. His pulse shot up like mercury in a thermometer, then he reminded himself that the gesture was for Sofia's benefit, not his. "As long as you do exactly what Miss Rosetti says."

Sofia clapped her hands, her dark ringlets bouncing.

"Maybe you could help your daddy hold the baby while I prepare the bottle." Olivia gave him a questioning look.

"I think we'd like that." He took a seat on the sofa, and Olivia handed him the bundle. Sofia jumped up beside him. "Be careful," he said. "Babies can get hurt easily."

"Like puppies?"

Darius chuckled. They'd had the same discussion when their neighbor's dog had had puppies and she'd wanted to hold one.

"That's right. Remember how you had to hold the puppy very gently? That's how you have to treat a baby too."

Sofia nodded, her features solemn. "I can do that."

Olivia smiled at her. "You're doing wonderfully, Sofia. I'll be right back."

Half an hour later, when Abigail had been fed and diapered, Olivia laid her in the bassinet. Olivia had been so good with Sofia, allowing her to hold the bottle and feel like she was really feeding the baby.

But once Abigail had drifted off to sleep, Darius knew his daughter would soon grow restless and wear out her welcome. The fact that he wanted to stay was another reason he had to leave. "Well, we'd best be off to the park."

"Thank you for coming to visit." Olivia bent down in front of Sofia. "I enjoyed your company."

Sofia reached out to touch Olivia's cheek. "You're very pretty. Do you have any children?"

Darius flinched at his daughter's boldness.

Olivia went very still, then slowly rose. "No, honey. I don't."

"You'd make a very good mommy."

Raw anguish flashed over Olivia's features, but then she smiled. "Thank you. I hope you have a nice time at the park."

Darius hesitated. He wanted a moment alone with Olivia before they left. "Sofia, go wait by the front door. I'll be right there."

"Yes, Daddy."

As soon as she left the room, Darius lowered his voice. "I'm sorry for Sofia's questions."

"Don't be. She's just curious." Yet a hint of sorrow clouded Olivia's eyes.

"How is your head today?"

"Still tender, but I'm feeling much better."

"Did you have any of the symptoms the nurse mentioned?"

"No, Dr. Reed. I'm fine." Her lips twisted into a teasing smile.

When he narrowed his gaze at her, she sighed. "I'm just a little tired. Otherwise I'd come to the park with you."

Darius stared into her eyes, which appeared more amber than brown today with the afternoon sun on her face, and found it hard to look away. Finally, he cleared his throat. "How is Mary? Have you heard anything more?"

"She's about the same. Dr. Henshaw is going to check on her later today and let us know how long she'll be in the hospital." Olivia shrugged. "I know this sounds awful, but I hope she stays a few more days. I'm enjoying looking after Abigail." A delicate blush bloomed in her cheeks.

"You're doing an excellent job. Just be careful you don't get too attached."

Her brow furrowed. "That's what Ruth has been telling me. But I can't help it. Abigail stole my heart from the moment you placed her in my arms."

His gaze fell to Olivia's full lips, and the urge to kiss her buzzed as strong as an electric current inside him. He shoved his hands into his pockets to keep from touching her.

Remember, you just recently broke your engagement to another woman. Keep your priorities straight, Reed.

Olivia leaned closer. "Sofia is precious. You're doing a wonderful job yourself."

Her face was so close that his heart started to hammer in his chest.

He leaned forward and—

"Daddy! I'm waiting."

His breath escaped in a loud exhale. "Coming, sweetheart."

Saved from temptation by a four-year-old.

Olivia waved good-bye from the front porch, thankful that only a handful of protestors remained across the street. Sofia slipped her hand into her father's as they exited the gate, looking up at him with evident adoration in her bright eyes. He, in turn, smiled down at the child and tugged one of her curls.

Olivia's heart gave a slow roll in her chest as the truth became apparent. Not only was she becoming more and more attracted to Darius, she might have just fallen in love with his daughter.

Such a darling girl. How tragic that her mother hadn't lived to raise her and that Darius had lost his wife so young. The unfairness of life continued to be a concept that eluded Olivia's logic.

Why, God? Why did a woman who had a devoted husband and daughter have to die, leaving a child motherless? And why did I, who wanted nothing more than to be a mother, have my child taken from me?

"I don't know if I'll ever understand," she whispered. "I suppose that's why they say God's ways are above man's ways."

Her longing gaze strayed once more to Darius as he walked away, while the harsh memory of her father's rebuke chased the silly fantasies from her mind.

"Olivia will never marry now, Rosina. No man is going to want damaged goods."

The sting of her father's statement was as raw as the day he'd uttered it, yet she couldn't dispute the truth in his words. She needed to remember that and to keep her heart's unrealistic yearnings in check. There would be no romance for her, no words of love or undying devotion. Those were reserved for upright women worthy of such declarations, women untainted by sin and shame.

With a deep inhale of fresh air, she went back inside the house. The roofer should be here any minute. After the fiasco with the angry mob yesterday, he'd kindly agreed to come back today instead. Olivia only hoped the repairs would be finished quickly. The girls and baby Abigail did not need the banging of hammers to disrupt their peace for too long.

She checked on the baby before going in search of Ruth. Now

that Olivia's headache had subsided to a dull throb, she was ready to offer her services again with whatever task Ruth needed done.

When Olivia entered the office, however, she came to an abrupt halt.

Ruth sat at the desk, telephone receiver at her ear, tears streaming from her eyes. "Thank you for letting us know, Doctor. If we can be of any assistance . . ." She paused. "Yes, of course. Good-bye."

Olivia's stomach clenched. "Ruth, what is it?"

Ruth took out a handkerchief and wiped her face. "That was Dr. Henshaw. Mary passed away a few hours ago. She never regained consciousness."

Olivia's hand flew to her mouth, her throat constricting. "I thought she was on the mend."

"I did too. Dr. Henshaw suspects she suffered internal damage as a result of the beating, which was aggravated by giving birth so soon afterward. Her body just couldn't take it."

On shaky limbs, Olivia moved across to one of the chairs. "Poor little Abigail." Another child left motherless. Tears blurred Olivia's vision while guilt ate at her. She'd selfishly enjoyed the time alone with Abigail, not fully considering how Mary might be suffering in the meantime. "What do we do now?"

"Nothing for the moment. Dr. Henshaw said he'd be in touch soon. He's going to request a coroner's report to determine the actual cause of death. He'll also see if he can learn Mary's identity and find out if any relatives might be looking for her. In the meantime, he asked that we continue to look after the baby until further arrangements can be made."

Arrangements? What sort of arrangements? Surely the authorities wouldn't consider giving the child to her father, should they learn his identity. A man who would beat his wife did not deserve to raise a child.

And letting that innocent girl go to a foster home was no better an option. That baby deserved someone who could give her the love and the stability she deserved.

Olivia's thoughts flew to Matteo, and a familiar ache spread through her chest. She would not let anyone take another child from her. Not when she already loved Abigail as though she'd given birth to her herself.

She rose, determination stiffening her spine. Before any such *arrangements* could be made, Olivia would find a way to ensure Abigail stayed with her.

22

On Monday morning, Darius burst into Mr. Walcott's office without knocking. The time for reckoning had arrived, and Darius was more than happy to be the one to provide it.

He came to a halt in front of Walcott's desk, where a curl of cigar smoke hovered in the air. "I hope you're happy with the damage you've caused," Darius snapped. "That newspaper article was so inflammatory it got an innocent woman seriously injured." Just remembering Olivia's wound sent his pent-up anger spewing forth like an uncorked bottle of champagne. "Miss Rosetti could have been killed by those fanatics."

Walcott lowered his coffee cup. "Good morning to you too," he said wryly.

Darius ignored the warning tone. "This harassment has to stop. I looked the other way when I found out you'd bribed the inspector, but inciting violence against vulnerable women is un-acceptable. I want to know how you intend to fix the situation."

"Fix it? This public outcry is exactly what I was hoping for. With this kind of turmoil, the maternity home will soon have to shut down."

Darius clenched his fists. "Did you not hear me? Miss Rosetti ended up in the hospital when someone threw a rock at her. It took seventeen stitches to close the gash on her head."

Walcott frowned. "I never intended for anyone to get hurt."

"Well, she did. What if she'd been carrying an infant? Or if the rock had hit her temple? Someone could have died. Are you really willing to live with that on the slim chance of obtaining the property? Because I can pretty much guarantee that Ruth Bennington would rather sell to the devil himself than let you have her home." Darius's chest heaved with the labor of his breathing.

Walcott slowly rose from his chair. "It's becoming apparent that your loyalties have shifted, Reed. And that does not bode well for your future here."

Recognizing the not-so-subtle threat, Darius took a moment to center himself. "I don't think loyalty is the issue. It's a matter of common decency. And this time *you're* the one breaking a cardinal rule of business, sir. The Bennington property has become far too personal for you, and I believe it's clouding your judgment."

Walcott crossed his arms over his chest.

"We made a proposal," Darius continued, "and the customer turned it down. If it were any other property, you'd have moved on by now." He narrowed his eyes. "What is it about this place that matters so much to you?"

Walcott let out a low growl and turned away. "That's none of your concern."

"It is if it's causing you to make bad decisions."

Walcott's head whipped around, his features flushed. "In case you've forgotten, I'm in charge here. You're getting dangerously close to crossing a line you can't come back from." He strode around the desk to stand inches from Darius. "I'd suggest you cool down and think carefully about your future."

A ripple of alarm raced down Darius's spine. "What does that mean?"

Walcott tilted his head. "I heard you called off your engagement to Meredith Cheeseman."

"What does that have to do with anything?"

"It affects one of our top clients." Walcott scowled. "What if Horace Cheeseman pulls his account because of this and finds someone else to manage his properties? You've already cost us the Peterson contract. We can't afford to lose Cheeseman as well."

With effort, Darius held on to his temper. How had Walcott turned this back on him? "Mr. Cheeseman is a professional. I'm sure he's able to keep his personal life separate from business matters."

"We can't take that for granted." Walcott jabbed a finger at him. "I'm leaving on a business trip in a few hours. While I'm gone, you need to smooth things over with Cheeseman. Arrange a meeting. Better yet, take him out for dinner and drinks on our dime."

Darius's shoulders tightened. He would not stoop to bribery to appease the man. "I'll call Mr. Cheeseman and make sure everything is satisfactory."

"Do whatever is necessary to make sure he's happy. And get your priorities straight, once and for all. This is the last chance you'll get, Reed." On that ominous note, Walcott pointed to the door.

With no other option except to quit his job on the spot—an action too rash to make in the heat of anger—Darius blew out a breath and left the office. The encounter had left a decidedly unpleasant taste in his mouth.

But Walcott was right about one thing.

Darius needed to decide where his priorities lay and determine whether or not to continue on his current career path.

By midday, Darius had scheduled a meeting with Mr. Cheeseman and had lined up two potential properties to view. Both locations would be ideal sites for Walcott Towers, if only his boss would take off his blinders and consider a different option. Darius hoped when Mr. Walcott returned from his trip, he might have gained a new perspective and be willing to forget about Bennington Place.

Unable to stop thinking about Olivia, Darius decided to use his lunch hour to go and see how she was doing and make sure that the protestors hadn't returned. If they had, he would find a way to disperse them.

Ten minutes later, he parked across the street from the house, relieved to note that no demonstrators were visible at the moment. Ruth's calling the authorities must've had a lot to do with that.

A ladder leaned against the exterior of Ruth's house, and the sound of hammering indicated that a repairman was likely at work. Hopefully the company he'd recommended had given the women a good price. A twinge of guilt flared. He wondered if the repairs were even necessary or if they were invented by the inspector to satisfy Walcott. Unfortunately, there was nothing Darius could do about it now, so he consoled himself with the fact that at least they would be spared any potential leaks in the attic.

As he entered the gate, Darius paused to admire the majesty of the residence, with its tall gables, redbrick exterior, and shuttered windows. The ivy climbing the sides of the house added to its charm, softening its lines and giving the place a welcoming air. It would be a travesty to destroy such a beautiful home solely to satisfy Mr. Walcott's desire for an office tower.

He knocked on the door. Moments later, Olivia appeared with Abigail in her arms.

His cheery greeting died on his lips at the tragic look that haunted her features. "Good afternoon, Olivia. Is this a bad time?"

Her lips lifted in a hint of a smile. "It's fine. Come in."

He stepped inside, noting she wore a hat that matched her navy skirt and that a baby carriage took up most of the entryway.

"I was just about to take Abigail for a walk. Would you care to join me, or are you here to see Ruth?"

"I'd love a walk if you don't mind the company. Allow me to lift the carriage down."

"That would be helpful. Thank you."

Soon they were headed down the sidewalk. He waited for Olivia to begin the conversation, but today she seemed unusually subdued.

At last, she released a long breath and glanced over at him. "We received some bad news after you left the other day."

"Oh?" His muscles tensed. Had his boss tried some new trick to discredit the home?

"Dr. Henshaw telephoned to say that Mary passed away that morning." Her voice quavered.

Immediate visions of the woman's battered face leapt to mind. The way she'd grasped his arm before collapsing at his feet. Darius ground his back teeth together. Whoever had beaten Mary was responsible for her death as surely as if they'd plunged a knife into her. "That's terrible. I'm so sorry."

The first birth that had occurred at the maternity home had ended in a mother's demise. Olivia and Ruth certainly didn't deserve this added strife.

"I feel so bad for Abigail. Left all alone without a mother's love." Olivia lifted tear-filled eyes shimmering with sorrow.

He laid a hand on the carriage handle to stop it, then gently pulled her against his chest, the need to offer comfort too strong to ignore. Her breath hitched, and her frame trembled before she relaxed against him. Her warmth, combined with the beat of her heart beneath his, sent streaks of electricity through his system. After several seconds, she released a breath and tilted her head to look up at him, her expressive brown eyes filled with longing.

When his gaze fell to her full lips, heat seared across his chest. This courageous woman, who cared for others so deeply, so selflessly, had no one to lean on to give her strength. His head dipped toward her. She needed—no, deserved— someone to comfort her.

Someone to love her.

Love? He froze, every muscle tensing. Where had that thought come from?

Surely he couldn't be in love with her. This woman, though highly admirable, was not at all right for him and Sofia. The controversial mission Olivia was committed to would never give his daughter the respectability she needed. His thoughts flew to the angry mob protesting the maternity home, throwing rotting food and rocks, their hatred too reminiscent of the crowds that had killed Selene.

And because of that, Darius had no business holding Olivia in his arms.

With an apologetic smile, he reluctantly stepped away from her and resumed walking.

Olivia's pulse wouldn't stop racing. For a moment, while Darius held her, she thought he'd been about to kiss her. Her whole being had yearned for the touch of his lips on hers, to feel loved once more, even if only for a few minutes.

But he'd stiffened suddenly and pulled away. Now he walked beside her with his hands clasped behind him, as though resisting the temptation to touch her again.

She pressed her lips together. *Foolish daydreams, Olivia.* He was just being kind, offering her comfort as a friend would do.

She steered the carriage around the corner and continued on in silence, trying to forget being sheltered in his arms.

Finally, he turned to her. "Does the doctor know the cause of Mary's death? Was it the beating or complications from childbirth?"

"He's not sure. He's ordered a coroner's report to find out."

"I can't help feeling somewhat responsible. Perhaps I should have brought her straight to the hospital." Lines etched his forehead.

"No, you did the right thing. If she had needed the hospital, Dr. Henshaw would have insisted she go."

He gave her a warm look. "Thank you for saying that. I only wish I could have done more for her."

"Me too."

A couple walked toward them on the sidewalk. The man tipped his hat as they passed, and the woman smiled. It occurred to Olivia that she and Darius must seem like a young couple taking their child for an outing.

If only they knew the truth.

"How is Mrs. Bennington holding up?" Darius asked.

Olivia let out a small sigh. "She's heartbroken, of course. It's devastating to have one of the first women we tried to help perish that way. It goes against everything we're trying to do."

Darius gave her a pensive look. "I've often wondered why she chose to start a venture like this at her age."

Olivia gripped the handle of the carriage tighter. "Ever since her husband's death, she'd been floundering with no real direction to her days. I think she was looking for something to give her purpose."

"What about you, Olivia? How did you get involved?"

Her foot caught the edge of a stone and she almost stumbled. Panicked thoughts pinged around in her head. What story had she and Ruth told everyone at the gala? Something about Olivia being at a low point in her life. Oh, why couldn't she remember?

What would Darius say if she revealed the ugly truth? That she'd been in jail and given birth to an illegitimate child? She shuddered, picturing the disgust on his face if she did. No, she could not allow that to happen.

She licked her lips and attempted a nonchalant shrug. "I'm sure I told you. Ruth took me in when I was in need of a job and homeless." Her throat cinched closed until she swallowed hard against the lump forming there. "I was grateful for her help and more than happy to join her endeavor." Olivia could barely breathe. Would he accept her rather sketchy explanation? She could feel the weight of his stare on her face. Heat crawled up her neck into her cheeks.

"I'm sorry you've endured such difficulties," he said at last. "It sounds like God brought you and Ruth together right at a time when you needed each other."

"That's true. Ruth has helped me turn my misfortune into something positive. There's no greater gift than that."

They walked on in silence, and when he didn't pursue the topic any further, she allowed her shoulders to relax. "You never really said why you came by. I assume it wasn't to take a walk with us." The clicking of her heels on the sidewalk seemed overly loud on the quiet street.

He shifted slightly away from her. "I wanted to make sure the protestors weren't still harassing you." He hesitated. "And I wanted to see how you were doing, of course."

Warm tingles spread through her chest. Had he really come just to find out how she was? "As you can see, I'm much better." She touched a finger to the smaller bandage at her hairline. "The stitches are beginning to feel itchy, which is a sign of healing, according to Dr. Henshaw."

"That's a good thing, then." He cast a quick sideways glance at her. "Is Dr. Henshaw treating you now?"

"Unofficially." She gave a self-conscious laugh. "When he heard about my accident, he insisted on seeing the injury for himself. He agreed that the physician did an excellent job with the stitches. Most of the scar will be hidden by my hair." She smiled, yet Darius did not smile in return.

Instead, he frowned, staring straight ahead. "Are you . . . that is . . ." He pressed his lips into a tight line as though to keep from blurting something out.

"Am I what?"

"Are you interested in Dr. Henshaw?"

"You mean romantically?"

He shrugged one shoulder, his complexion reddening.

"Heavens no. What gave you that idea?"

He turned the full force of his blue eyes on her. "Surely you must've noticed the man has feelings for you?"

"Dr. Henshaw?" Olivia slowed to a halt.

"It's not so hard to believe. I've seen the way he looks at you."

She gripped the carriage handle tighter. "I'm sure you're mistaken. He's always acted in a professional manner."

"So you wouldn't go out with him if he asked?"

Olivia's pulse skittered. Why did Darius seem so interested in her answer? "I don't think that would be prudent."

A storm of emotion rose in his eyes. "Olivia, I—"

Just then Abigail let out a squawk, apparently protesting the fact that the carriage had stopped moving.

Olivia tore her gaze from his. "We'd better head back before she gets fussy."

He blinked. "Right. I have to get back to work as well."

Relieved, yet a little disappointed, she swung the carriage into motion and marched forward at a fast clip. Whatever he'd been about to say, it was probably wiser to avoid the whole conversation.

For both their sakes.

23

After bidding Darius good-bye, Olivia parked the carriage by the porch and lifted the baby out, still oddly flustered by their conversation. For the sake of her sanity, she needed to put the man out of her mind. Because too much time around Darius Reed made her heart long for what it could never have.

As she headed up the stairs, the clang of the gate echoed behind her. Olivia turned to see the midwife barreling up the walkway.

"Hello, Mrs. Dinglemire. Did someone call you?"

"Yes indeed." The stout woman huffed as she passed Olivia on the stairs. "I believe Miss Margaret's time is upon us."

"Already?" Nerves jumped in Olivia's stomach at the sudden recollection of Mary's struggles. Margaret must be so scared after learning the other woman's fate.

She entered the house behind the midwife, the baby on her shoulder.

"Don't worry about me, Miss Rosetti. I know the way."

Abigail let out a frustrated cry that echoed through the hall. The poor love was obviously hungry. Olivia had kept her out too long, thanks to Darius Reed and his charms. She headed back to the kitchen, where Mrs. Neale had several large pots steaming on the stove.

The cook looked up with a smile. "Does this wee girl need a bottle?"

"She does indeed. If you're busy, I can heat it up myself."

"Nonsense. I'll have it ready in two shakes of a lamb's tail. You go and relax in the parlor. I'll bring it in to you."

"Thank you, Mrs. Neale." Olivia took the baby into the front room and sat with her in the rocker. The motion would soothe her until the bottle was ready.

Ruth poked her head into the room. "I'll be upstairs with Mrs. Dinglemire. I want to be close by in case she needs assistance."

Olivia nodded. "If you need me, just call. Abigail will be ready for her nap after she eats." But she secretly hoped that her help wouldn't be needed. The memories of Mary's struggles were still too fresh in her mind.

"I will. I also want to reassure the other women and make certain they know everything is under control."

"Good idea. And please tell Margaret I'll be praying for her."

Minutes later, Mrs. Neale arrived with the warmed bottle, and Olivia gave in to the pleasure of feeding the little darling. She cherished these quiet moments. Providing Abigail with nourishment, love, and security gave Olivia a great sense of peace. Even waking with her in the middle of the night was no hardship, for it was in those rare moments of tranquility that Olivia felt certain Abigail was a gift from God. A consolation of sorts for the loss of her son. Not that anything could ever make up for that.

Olivia looked forward to hearing from Dr. Henshaw as to whether or not they'd found any of Mary's relatives. If no one came forward to claim the baby, she would tell him that Abigail could remain at Bennington Place until Olivia could determine what steps were required to make the girl legally hers.

Her heart thumped harder at the thought, and she pressed a kiss to the baby's soft head. She believed Abigail had come to her for a reason. Olivia had lost her son, and this baby had lost her mamma. What more perfect pairing could there be?

After she laid Abigail in the bassinet for her nap, she retrieved the dry diapers from the clothesline and brought them in to the parlor to fold.

When the doorbell rang, she frowned. That wouldn't be Darius again, would it?

She opened the door and found a tall, slender woman on the porch. Something about her seemed oddly familiar. It took a moment, but the memory came rushing back with startling clarity. It was Mrs. Linder, the woman from the Children's Aid Society. The one who'd taken Matteo from her. What was she doing here?

Her heart gave a painful lurch, then just as quickly, a shocking idea occurred to her. Was Mrs. Linder here to tell her that no one wanted to adopt her son and that they were returning him to her?

She swallowed hard and reminded herself to breathe. "Mrs. Linder. What can I do for you?"

The woman's gaze snapped to her face. "I'm sorry. Do I know you?"

Oh. Obviously, she wasn't here to see her. "Um, I'm Olivia Rosetti. We met at Toronto General Hospital." She paused. "You took my son to the Infants' Home."

Recognition, then something resembling compassion, entered her eyes. "I remember you now. How are you doing, Miss Rosetti?"

"I'm well, thank you."

"May I come in? I'm here to speak to the directress about an orphaned baby residing here."

Olivia stiffened. What did she want with Abigail? Dr. Henshaw was still trying to find Mary's relatives, someone capable of taking the child. Why would he have contacted Children's Aid already?

Pushing her fears aside, Olivia summoned her most professional posture. "Mrs. Bennington is occupied at the moment." She smiled, not allowing herself to be intimidated by the woman. In fact, Olivia would need Mrs. Linder on her side so that if the time came to adopt Abigail, she'd hopefully have an ally. "I am the co-directress of Bennington Place. You can speak with me."

The woman's brows shot skyward under the neatly curled row of bangs. "You're in charge?"

"Mrs. Bennington and I run the home together. Please, won't you come in?"

She thought of bringing the woman back to the office but decided it would be best to stay close to Abigail in case she woke. She led Mrs. Linder to the parlor, and they each took an armchair by the fireplace.

Mrs. Linder placed her satchel on the ground, then removed a notebook and pencil. She crossed her legs at the ankles and smoothed her green linen skirt over her knees. "I understand that a woman recently gave birth here and unfortunately passed away a few days later."

"That's right. How did you learn about this?"

"Dr. Mark Henshaw called our office to report an orphaned infant. Apparently he's still attempting to learn the identity of the father and whether the woman had any relatives willing to raise the baby. I decided to come and make the preliminary assessment today since I had another visit in the area."

Olivia fought to retain her composure, the woman's official demeanor bringing back a host of unpleasant memories: Olivia begging to hold her son a little longer; Mrs. Linder ignoring her pleas and leaving with Matteo, a cotton blanket over the precious face that Olivia would never see again. She drew in a shaky breath. "What would you like to know?"

"Do you have any information on the birth mother?"

"All we know is that her name is Mary. Before she came to us, someone had beaten her. We called Dr. Henshaw, who treated her here. In the middle of the night, Mary went into labor. We summoned the midwife, but she deemed the situation too precarious and let Dr. Henshaw handle the birth."

"I see." The woman made some notations on the paper.

"After the midwife left to help another patient, Mrs. Bennington and I assisted with the delivery."

"So, Mary initially survived and the baby was born healthy?"

"Thankfully, yes. Little Abigail is doing well."

"Abigail?" She frowned. "Who gave the child that name?"

"Her mother. That's the only thing she told Mrs. Bennington before she took a turn for the worse."

"Mary never told you her last name or anything about the baby's father?"

"No. The only thing she said was to not let *him* have the baby. We never found out who she meant, but we assumed it was the man who'd beaten her."

"I see." Mrs. Linder scribbled some more words on the page, then set the notebook aside. "I'd like to see the baby now, if I may. Is she upstairs?"

Olivia's heart quivered. What if the woman tried to take Abigail away? Olivia would have no real recourse if she did. But wouldn't there have to be something more official? Paperwork or some type of records? "She's right over here, napping." Olivia rose and walked toward the bassinet. "She'll likely sleep for another hour or so."

Mrs. Linder went over and looked into the bed. A tender expression softened her features. "She's beautiful. It appears she's been well taken care of."

"I've been doing my best."

"You've been caring for her?"

Olivia nodded. "Primarily, yes."

Mrs. Linder's brow creased. "I must caution you, Miss Rosetti, not to get too attached. One way or another, this child will soon be leaving your care, either to go with a relative or to the Infants' Home."

Olivia stiffened. She hadn't had any intention of getting into the matter of adoption this soon, but it seemed her hand had been forced. "Tell me, Mrs. Linder, what if we knew someone willing to adopt the baby? Could a stay at the Infants' Home be avoided?"

"It's possible, but the couple in question would have to go

through the proper channels. They would have to register with Children's Aid and pass all the criteria to be eligible for adoption."

Olivia's spirits sank. She had no idea there would be so much involved. "What sort of criteria is required?"

"Well, we would start by interviewing both the husband and wife to make sure they had the appropriate qualities for parenthood. We'd learn about the husband's profession and how much income he earns, and we'd investigate the potential home to make sure it was an appropriate setting in which to raise a child."

The blood seemed to drain from Olivia's head, leaving her slightly dizzy. "That sounds like a complicated process." She hesitated. "I don't suppose there would ever be a case where an . . . unmarried person could adopt a child?"

Mrs. Linder shook her head, her eyes shining with sympathy. "Highly unlikely. Unless the person was one of Mary's relatives—a sister, perhaps. That might be the only exception. I'm afraid we don't allow single people to adopt."

Just like that, Olivia's dreams came crashing to the ground like a kite that had lost the wind and landed in a heap. Why had she even asked the question? If she hadn't, she'd still have a thread of hope to cling to.

Seemingly unaware of Olivia's turmoil, Mrs. Linder crossed the room to retrieve her notebook and satchel. She drew out a card and handed it to Olivia. "Here's my number. I'll be in touch once I hear back from Dr. Henshaw. Then we can make arrangements to bring the baby to her new home."

Darius stalked down the sidewalk toward his office building, the soles of his shoes smacking the cement with each step. How had he let his conversation with Olivia get so off track? He hadn't intended to bring up Dr. Henshaw and his obvious feelings for Olivia. Doing so had made her uncomfortable. He'd seen it in the way she'd gone from making pleasant conversation to being guarded and practically racing the carriage back to the house.

To make matters worse, his unexpected hug had confused her. He could tell by the flash of uncertainty that had crossed her features when he let her go.

It was clear he needed to get his thoughts and emotions under control. And until he could do that, it would be best if he avoided Bennington Place altogether. He shoved his hat more firmly on his head and increased his pace.

"Darius."

He came to a halt outside the entrance to his office building and looked around.

"Over here." The whispered words sounded frantic.

Meredith stood just beyond the lobby door, mostly hidden by one of the large potted trees that flanked the building entrance. What was she doing here? If she'd come to try to convince him to change his mind about marrying her, she was wasting her time.

"Meredith, why are you hiding behind that tree?"

"Shh. Keep your voice down." She ducked back. "I don't want anyone to see me. Meet me at the coffee shop across the street. I need to speak to you."

He frowned, then looked at his watch. He had a bit of time before the scheduled meeting with her father. "Fine. I'll get us a table."

With a grunt, he set off to the café across the street. This day was not going the way he'd planned at all.

Five minutes later, Darius took a sip of strong coffee and drummed his fingers on the somewhat sticky tabletop that the waitress had wiped haphazardly with a rag. What was keeping Meredith? And what could she possibly want? He was meeting with Horace Cheeseman in less than an hour. Was it a coincidence that the man's daughter had waylaid him now?

A waitress passed by, leaving the scent of apples and cinnamon in her wake. The bell jangled on the door as more patrons entered.

"Sorry. I had to wait until the coast was clear." Meredith slipped into the booth across from him. "Thank you for agreeing to meet me." Her features were pinched, and shadows hugged her eyes.

"What do you want, Meredith? I don't have much time."

"I know you're meeting with Daddy today. That's why I had to see you. I need your help."

He peered more closely at her. Clad in a brown dress and plain hat, she looked different today, more subdued somehow. He imagined her world had been turned upside down if she'd told her family the reason Darius had ended their engagement. The possibility existed that she'd lied, made up some excuse blaming him for their parting. He hoped she hadn't done so, because if she had, he would be forced to tell Mr. Cheeseman the truth in order to uphold both his and Walcott Industries' good reputation.

"I haven't changed my mind about marrying you, Meredith." He needed to establish that fact right away.

Her gaze slid to the cup of coffee he'd ordered for her. "I figured as much."

"Then what help do you need? If you expect me to lie to your father—"

"That's not it. I need you to get Daddy to change his mind about something."

Wariness crept through his system. "About what?"

She bit her lip, her eyes darting to the next booth, as though assessing whether anyone was listening. She leaned closer. "I told Mama and Daddy about . . . my situation. I had no choice, really. They would have found out soon enough."

"How did they take the news?" Though her deception still stung, Darius wasn't made of stone. He could appreciate the difficult position she was in.

"Not well." Her generous mouth, today bare of any color, turned down at the corners. "Daddy is furious with Jerry for shirking his responsibility. He's determined to hunt him down and force him to face the consequences."

"As well he should." Yet Meredith didn't seem pleased with the notion. "That's good news, isn't it? I assume you still have feelings for him if you . . ."

"It doesn't matter. Even if Daddy finds Jerry, he won't marry me. He's made that perfectly clear. Which is why I was so desperate to find someone else." She let out a sigh. "I owe you an apology for that, by the way. It was unforgivably selfish of me."

A measure of guilt convicted him, and he lifted one shoulder in a half shrug. "You're not the only one who was selfish," he admitted. "I had my own reasons for wanting to marry you. Being part of the Cheeseman family would have been beneficial for Sofia and me."

The clatter of dishes being cleared from the next table competed with the hum of conversation.

"Thank you for saying that." Meredith stirred her coffee, not looking at him. "I knew you weren't madly in love with me, so I wondered why you went along with the rushed wedding so easily."

His muscles relaxed somewhat. At least she wasn't bent on revenge or trying to pin the pregnancy on him. "So what is it you need me to talk your father out of?"

Moisture welled in her blue eyes. "He's sending me to stay with relatives in Saskatchewan until the baby is born."

From her agonized expression, she clearly felt it was a fate worse than death.

"Isn't that a good thing? It would spare you from the gossipmongers around here."

She shook her head. "I could never survive there. His cousin lives on a farm in the middle of nowhere. It's a three-hour car ride to the nearest town. And they expect me to help out with chores until the baby comes." She reached across to grasp his hand, her eyes pleading with him. "You have to convince Daddy this is a terrible idea."

Darius stared at her. How would he accomplish that? It wasn't as if he had an alternate solution. . . .

Or did he?

Slowly, an idea dawned, and he straightened on the bench seat. "Meredith, I have the perfect place for you." He lowered his voice. "It's a maternity home here in the city run by two women who have made it their mission to help others in your situation."

"A maternity home?"

"Yes." He became more enthused with the idea. Ruth and Olivia would welcome her with open arms. And Meredith would love the grand old house much better than a rustic farm on the prairies. It was the ideal solution. "Bennington Place is beautiful. They have a midwife and a doctor on staff. They'll help you decide what's best for you and for the baby when it arrives."

Indecision played over her features, but then she shook her head. "Daddy won't agree. And frankly, I don't think I'd feel comfortable either."

He squeezed her fingers. "I assure you, the women are very discreet."

She bit her lip and looked out the window at the steady stream of pedestrians passing by.

"What if I suggest it to your father and see how he reacts?"

"You could try, but I doubt it will do much good." She rose abruptly. "This was probably a bad idea. I doubt anyone can change Daddy's mind. Not even you." Tears glistened in her eyes. "I really must go."

He jumped up, fished a bill from his pocket to leave beside his barely touched cup, and ran out after her. But by the time he reached the sidewalk, she'd vanished. And if he didn't want to miss his meeting with Mr. Cheeseman, he had no time to go looking for her.

He blew out a breath. *Lord, please watch over Meredith and help her make the best decision for her and her child.*

24

Ruth closed Margaret's door with a soft click, then made her way down the carpeted corridor to the main staircase. As per Mrs. Dinglemire's request, Ruth was checking on Margaret and her new son every few hours until the midwife could return later that day. Thankfully, Margaret was resting comfortably, with her baby beside her in a bassinet. Though he'd arrived several weeks early according to the original due date, the babe seemed healthy enough, weighing just over seven pounds. Mrs. Dinglemire pronounced him fit, claiming that Margaret's doctor had likely made an error in the due date.

Not that it mattered, as long as mother and child were doing well. Unlike poor Mary.

As Ruth descended the stairs, her lips formed an automatic prayer for Margaret and her son as well as for little Abigail. But the prayer brought to mind another worry. Something was definitely wrong with Olivia. Since yesterday, she'd been distracted, barely even acknowledging the birth of Margaret's son. The two girls had grown quite close these last few weeks, or so she'd thought, and Ruth had expected Olivia to be very involved with Margaret's delivery. But she hadn't even gone in to see the new baby yet.

Ruth looked into the parlor, surprised to find only Cherise and

Patricia seated on the sofa. Patricia was continuing her attempts to teach Cherise how to knit a blanket. Ruth had to admire how Cherise had adapted to her new environment, wearing more conservative clothing and forgoing her usual cosmetics. She was extremely respectful of the house rules, and she'd taken to Patricia like a sister, though two women more dissimilar would be hard to find.

"Has anyone seen Olivia?" Ruth asked.

Patricia looked up. "Not since breakfast."

"She wasn't herself this morning," Cherise said. "Ever since that woman came by yesterday, Olivia's been *de mauvaise humeur*."

"Translation, please." Patricia set the wool on her lap.

"She's been unhappy. Moody."

"Yes, I noticed that too."

Ruth frowned. "What woman came by yesterday?"

"I don't know, but she left her card." Patricia pointed to the coffee table.

Ruth snatched it up. *Mrs. Jane Linder, Toronto Children's Aid Society.* Her stomach sank. "Oh dear. This might have something to do with Abigail. No wonder Olivia's unhappy." She put the card in her skirt pocket. "Mrs. Linder is the lady who will be coming to speak to you girls soon about your options for your babies' futures."

Cherise's thin brows puckered. "I do not need to talk to anyone. I know I am keeping my *bébé*." Her dark eyes flashed. "She will not take it away."

Ruth sensed the girl's fear and softened her voice. "Mrs. Linder only wants to make sure you girls can provide for an infant without a husband or any extended family to help out. As old-fashioned as that sounds, it's hard for a woman on her own to work and care for a child." She paused. "In fact, that's something Olivia and I are considering, whether to expand our home to include babysitting for infants while the mothers work." She squared her shoulders. "But that's a discussion for another time. Right now, I must talk to Mrs. Neale and then find Olivia—"

The doorbell rang.

"That's probably Mrs. Dinglemire here to check on Margaret." Ruth hurried to the front door so the woman wouldn't ring a second time. With two sleeping babies, the bell now seemed overly loud.

But it wasn't Mrs. Dinglemire. Instead, Reverend Dixon stood on the porch, wearing his clerical collar as he did for official visits. Yet his brow was furrowed, his usual cheerful demeanor notably absent.

"Reverend, this is a surprise. Do come in."

"Thank you, Mrs. Bennington." The pastor stepped inside and removed his hat.

"What brings you by?"

Giggles erupted from the parlor, followed by the murmur of conversation.

Reverend Dixon glanced at the doorway. "Might we speak in private?"

From his somber expression, Ruth doubted it could be good news. She suppressed a sigh. It was going to be one of those days. "Certainly. Come back to my office." She looked into the parlor again. "Ladies, if Mrs. Dinglemire arrives, please let her in. I'll be in my office if anyone needs me."

As she took her chair behind the desk and waited for the minister to choose a seat, she steeled herself for whatever he had to say.

"I've been meaning to come by and see how things are going with this new endeavor of yours," he said.

The thread of skepticism in his voice put Ruth on alert. She didn't get the sense that he was here to offer his assistance.

"Things are going well so far." She wouldn't mention that they were severely short of funds, or that the first woman to give birth at Bennington Place had died, or that her co-directress might have become too attached to an orphaned baby. "We have five women in residence and two infants, as of yesterday." She forced a smile. "As word of our facility spreads, I'm sure we'll be able to help many more women."

A slight breeze blew in from the open window, ruffling some papers on the desk.

"As you know," Reverend Dixon said, "I have recommended your home to a couple of women."

"Yes, and we're most grateful for your support."

"However, some disturbing information has come to my attention. . . ." He trailed off, his gaze faltering.

"If you're referring to that nasty article in the newspaper—which has no basis in reality, I might add—then you're worrying for nothing."

"It's not just the article." His bushy brows dipped together. "One of our parishioners has been collecting signatures on a petition to have Bennington Place closed down. He says that he's personally seen several . . . ah, questionable women come into the house."

Ruth ground her teeth together. It had to be Mr. Simmons. What did that troublemaker do, sit and watch their house all day with a spyglass? She huffed out a breath. "Our mission is to help women in trouble, Reverend. That doesn't mean we get to judge whether or not they are worthy of assistance. These are exactly the people who need our compassion and caring the most."

"I understand that, but—"

"Do you turn people away from the church if they don't meet your standards?"

"Well, no, but—"

"Then why should we?" She leaned over the desk. "We don't interrogate our residents. If they choose to confide their circumstances to us, then we listen and treat each case individually, with the respect and compassion they deserve. As long as a woman agrees to follow our house rules, we don't turn anyone away."

"I see your point," he conceded. "However, I also understand the concerns of the people in this neighborhood. They fear that Bennington Place is attracting undesirable types. The mothers of young children are worried for their youngsters' safety. And the businesses on the next block worry that potential customers might be put off as well."

Ruth closed her eyes briefly. It seemed no argument would sway the man. "What is it you want me to do, Reverend?"

The man's pale eyes met hers. "I've been asked by our parish council, some of whom are city aldermen, to respectfully request that you consider moving your maternity home to the outskirts of the city, somewhere less densely populated. It would be better for everyone involved."

Anger flared in Ruth's chest. "Do they think I can just pick up my house and move it wherever I wish?"

"Of course not, but you could sell this house and buy another in a more appropriate area. Or you could keep the house and lease a more suitable property for the maternity home."

"You make it sound like a trip to the market to choose a cut of beef. It's not that simple. This is my family home, and I don't wish to move anywhere else. Besides, we need the visibility this location affords."

A beam of light from the window illuminated the large silver cross around his neck. He rubbed his chin in a thoughtful manner, appearing to search for another argument to persuade her.

Ruth tilted her head. "You were so supportive of our goal at the outset, Reverend. What happened to change your mind?"

He let out a sigh. "It's complicated, Mrs. Bennington."

"Really?" She folded her arms. "Then why don't you explain it to me."

The man shifted his considerable weight on the chair. "Several of my more affluent parishioners have threatened to switch parishes if I don't do my utmost to gain your cooperation. I'm sure you realize what this could mean for St. Olaf's if our major financial backing was eliminated." He gave her a pointed look.

"Oh, I understand very well, Reverend. Though you don't seem the least bit concerned about losing *my* financial backing."

A flush invaded his cheeks, but he remained silent.

Though she railed against the withdrawal of his support, she could understand his predicament. One couldn't escape the influence of the almighty dollar, even in the Lord's house. She sighed. "Tell these concerned parishioners that I will take their opinions under consideration. That should get you off the hook for a while."

"So you'll think about relocating, then?" His face brightened.

"I'll think about it. That's all I can promise at the moment."

Selling her family home was out of the question; however, she supposed she could look into the idea of a rental property. She and Olivia could work through the numbers to see if it would be economically feasible. Perhaps if she rented out some rooms in her home to boarders, the income could offset the expense of a new maternity home. She made another note to talk to her financial advisor at the bank.

Reverend Dixon rose and gave a bow. "Thank you for hearing me out, Mrs. Bennington. You've been more than fair. I can show myself out. No need to trouble yourself."

"Good day, Reverend. See you on Sunday."

As soon as the door fell closed behind him, Ruth let out a frustrated breath, barely resisting the urge to throw her paperweight across the room. Could people not see the good work she and Olivia were trying to do? Honestly, some of her fellow parishioners were so narrow-minded it made her wonder if they wore their hats two sizes too small. She had a good mind to parade all the expectant mothers down the church aisle to the front pew just to give the old codgers something more to complain about.

But as much as the idea gave her a rush of satisfaction, it did nothing to solve her immediate problem. For that she would need a lot of prayer and a large dose of divine inspiration.

25

Olivia pushed the baby carriage up the street toward home, keeping a steady pace so as not to wake little Abigail.

The sun shone brightly overhead, glinting off the leaves of the elm trees that lined the street. She'd hoped the fresh air would give her a new perspective, but with too many unwelcome thoughts running through her head, the walk hadn't really helped. Even though Olivia realized her obsession over Abigail wasn't healthy, she couldn't stop trying to devise a way to raise the child herself. Yet unless a potential husband materialized out of thin air, one willing to adopt an orphan, she could see no other options.

The other problem on her mind was her friend Joannie. Being so caught up with Abigail's care, Olivia had postponed a scheduled visit to the reformatory, but when she called to speak with Joannie, her request was denied. Though Olivia remembered that telephone privileges were as unpredictable as the matron's mood swings, an undercurrent of worry nagged her. Surely Joannie hadn't suffered the same fate as Mabel. Would anyone tell her if she had? Olivia breathed a prayer for her friend's safety and vowed to keep better tabs on Joannie once things settled down with Abigail.

As the house came into view, Olivia slowed her steps, recognizing the car parked at the curb and the man who stepped out of it. A ridiculous thrill shot through her system, a thrill that only intensified when Darius caught sight of her and smiled. For the moment, she did her best to set her problems aside and give him a genuine smile in return.

"Olivia. Good afternoon." He came toward her.

"Hello, Darius. What brings you by?"

"There's something I'd like to speak to you about." He peered into the carriage. "But I also wanted to see how Princess Abigail is doing." He laughed as the girl, now wide awake, grasped his finger. "Looks like she's doing well indeed."

Princess Abigail. Olivia bit her lip. If only she could adopt the child, Abigail could truly become Olivia's little princess. She blinked hard and swallowed.

"Everything's all right, isn't it?" Concern darkened his blue eyes.

"Of course." Olivia steered the carriage through the gate and up to the front stairs, then lifted the baby out.

Darius watched her with a worried expression. He clearly did not believe her claim.

She sighed, her shoulders sagging. "Everyone warned me not to get too attached to Abigail, and they were right. I don't know how I'm going to let her go." She turned and started up the steps before her emotions got the better of her.

Darius followed her inside. "It will be hard, I'm sure. There's something very special about this girl."

Very special indeed. Olivia walked into the parlor and laid Abigail in the bassinet, then loosened the ribbons under the baby's chin, the strings now slightly damp with drool. Two precious blue eyes stared back at her. "I foolishly thought I could raise her myself, but the lady from Children's Aid told me that wasn't possible."

Darius moved closer. "It's brave of you to even consider such an idea. I know from personal experience how difficult being a single parent can be." His brows drew together as he looked at her.

"But you're still so young, Olivia. Don't you want to get married and have children of your own someday?"

Her stomach twisted into a hard knot. How had they gotten onto such a personal topic? "I stopped thinking about marriage after my fiancé was killed overseas."

Darius placed a warm hand on her arm. "I'm so sorry. I didn't realize you'd lost someone in this horrible war."

Tears pricked her eyes. Losing Rory was nothing compared to the chasm of grief in her soul over losing her son. She drew in an unsteady breath. Dwelling on her misfortunes wouldn't solve anything.

"Still, you're attractive and kind and obviously good with children," Darius said in a soothing voice. "You'll find someone else, I'm sure." He smiled, likely thinking he was being encouraging and not realizing that every word was a barb to her heart.

She set her jaw and focused on undoing the tiny buttons of Abigail's cardigan. "I'm not looking for a husband. I'd be content just raising this girl and helping other women. That would be more than enough for me."

Before he could say anything further, Patricia and Cherise entered the room.

"Olivia, there you are," Patricia said, her gaze bouncing to Darius. "We wondered where you'd gone."

"I took the baby for a walk. You should get out too, now that the protestors are gone."

"Perhaps we'll go after dinner when it's cooler. Right now, Patricia is going to help me some more with my knitting." Cherise pulled the wool from a basket. "Ruth was looking for you earlier. And Margaret is a little hurt that you haven't been up to see the baby."

"Oh." Olivia's chest tightened with a pang of guilt. She hadn't been sure she could muster the enthusiasm Margaret deserved over her bundle of joy. Nor was she sure she could hide the jealousy that consumed her. Margaret was getting to keep her son while Olivia had not, and now she would likely lose Abigail too. But that wasn't Margaret's fault. "I'll go up and see her shortly."

A throat cleared. She turned to see Darius still standing by the bassinet. "About that matter I wanted to discuss . . ."

"Oh, of course." She'd almost forgotten his reason for coming by. "We can talk in the office." She turned to the women now engrossed with their knitting. "Will you keep an eye on Abigail for me? I won't be long."

"Take as much time as you need." Cherise winked.

Heat climbed up her neck. "Shall we?" She gestured to the doorway and quickly escaped into the hall.

Darius followed Olivia into the office, where she smoothed her floral dress as she took a seat behind the desk. She seemed flustered, preoccupied, not quite herself. Maybe not the best time to ask a favor.

"Is this something to do with Mr. Walcott?" she asked.

"No, this problem is of a more personal nature." Darius sat on one of the vacant chairs, suddenly unsure how to begin. "I wanted to talk to you about a friend of mine who could use your help."

After his meeting with Mr. Cheeseman yesterday, when the man refused to consider anything other than Meredith's going to Saskatchewan, Darius wasn't even sure Bennington Place was an option. However, since Meredith obviously found the idea of living on a farm so abhorrent, he wanted to offer her a better solution. Despite how she'd deceived him, he hated seeing her in such distress.

A shuttered look came over Olivia's face. "I take it this friend is a woman?"

He flinched at the way she stressed the word *friend*. "Yes. Her name is Meredith." He hesitated, knowing full disclosure was necessary, but suddenly realizing how bad it would sound. "Up until a week ago, she was my fiancée."

"Fiancée?" The papers Olivia had been sorting slipped from her fingers. "You never said you were engaged."

He held back a groan. It must seem like he'd been deliberately hiding it from her. But that hadn't been his intention. There'd just never seemed to be the right moment to bring it up.

And why is that? Why didn't you want her to know you were getting married?

"The whole engagement came about quite suddenly," he said. "And ended just as quickly."

She gawked at him, as though unable to process what he was saying.

"It's been over two years since my wife died, and my family had been after me to start dating again. When Meredith pursued me with such eagerness, I . . . well, I suppose I got lazy." He shrugged. "I should have suspected something was amiss when she suggested an extremely quick wedding. It wasn't until I learned from a co-worker that she was expecting a child—" He stopped, realizing what she must think, and his cheeks grew hot. "Another man's child," he added hastily, "that I realized she was using me to cover her mistake."

"That must have been difficult to hear." Everything about Olivia's posture remained rigid as she shuffled the papers back into a tidy pile.

"It wasn't as hard as I thought. Which made me realize my feelings for her weren't what they should be." His gaze fell to the desk. "I couldn't continue the relationship since she wasn't the role model I want for Sofia." He clenched one hand into a fist, then slowly released it. "However, ending our engagement left Meredith in a difficult position. Her father wants to send her to live with relatives on a farm out west, but she doesn't want to go. All I could think of was how Bennington Place might be the perfect solution for her."

"I see." Olivia's expression remained unchanged, showing little or no emotion, yet the fact that she wouldn't meet his eyes troubled him.

"Meredith's upset and confused," he went on. "I was wondering if you'd be willing to talk to her? Make her see that Bennington Place could be her best option?" He held his breath, pleading with his eyes.

She seemed to consider his words for a moment, then nodded. "I'll do whatever I can to help." Though her words were polite, an aloofness in her voice told him she was relishing the task as much as a visit to the dentist.

What a mess. The last thing he wanted was to put Olivia in an uncomfortable position, yet he felt an obligation to help Meredith. "Thank you. I really hope you'll be able to get through to her better than I could."

"Will you arrange the details of when and where we'll meet?"

"I'll set something up. Maybe you could meet in a nearby coffee shop." He doubted Meredith would want to be seen coming here.

"That would be fine."

His breath whooshed out of his lungs as he rose. "Thanks again. I appreciate this more than you know."

"No thanks are necessary. After all, that's what we're here for."

He'd achieved his goal, yet as he left, he couldn't help but regret the coolness in her demeanor as she bid him good-bye.

The next afternoon, Olivia stirred a spoon of sugar into her tea as she waited in Marty's Diner for the mysterious Meredith to arrive. It was a good time of day to meet. Not too many patrons remained after the lunch rush, but there was enough activity that they wouldn't be conspicuous.

Darius had telephoned that morning to say that Meredith would see her today and that he hoped Olivia could convince her of Bennington Place's merits since she was scheduled to leave for Saskatchewan in two days.

Olivia still couldn't believe Darius had been engaged for much of—if not all—the time she'd known him, and though she tried to set her resentment aside, she was having a hard time feeling sorry for the girl. If Olivia had been given the option of staying with a relative out west, she would have jumped at the chance. Anywhere would have been better than the wretched Mercer Reformatory.

Yet, Meredith's circumstances were entirely different. Olivia couldn't help but wonder what had led to her getting pregnant by one man, then chasing Darius until he proposed. Had the father of her child been a dishonorable type who'd shirked his responsibility, leaving Meredith looking for a decent man to help raise her child?

She took a sip of tea, forcing back the hurt that continued to surface every time she thought about Darius hiding his engagement. If she'd known from the start that he was spoken for, she never would have read more into his interest in Bennington Place. Never would have allowed herself to fantasize that he could possibly care for her.

Even so, she couldn't quell her morbid curiosity. What would his former fiancée look like? He'd said she would recognize Meredith by her blond hair and the brightly colored dresses she usually wore. She sounded like the very opposite of Olivia—a fact that irritated her more than she cared to admit. Why did the idea that he'd almost married this woman leave a gaping hole in her chest?

At the jangle of the bell, Olivia looked up. A young woman entered, wearing a plain beige dress with a black collar and cuffs. A small straw hat sat atop her blond hair, which was pulled back in a severe fashion. Surely this couldn't be Meredith.

The woman's wary blue eyes scanned the restaurant until they landed on Olivia. Then she grew still, a flash of recognition stealing over her features.

Olivia's muscles tightened. This must be her after all. She took in a slow breath, her resolve firming. This woman was in trouble and needed Olivia's help. She deserved compassion, not idle speculation and jealousy.

Olivia pasted on a bright smile as the woman approached.

"You must be Miss Rosetti," Meredith said.

"Yes, but please call me Olivia."

"I'm Meredith." She darted a nervous glance around the half-filled diner before sliding into the booth.

On closer inspection, Olivia had to admit the woman was very attractive, with blue eyes and lovely porcelain skin. Just like the china doll Olivia had cherished as a child.

"I wasn't sure if you'd want coffee, so I asked for a glass of water," Olivia said.

"Water is fine, thank you." Meredith slid the glass closer. "I don't really know why I came except that I promised Darius I would talk to you."

Olivia paused. How could she broach the delicate subject without offending her? "Darius said you might be interested in some information about Bennington Place."

Meredith's delicate brows rose. "I'm not sure it will be suitable, but I agreed to hear you out."

Olivia did her best to ignore the strangeness of the situation and remain objective. "My friend Ruth Bennington and I started the home to give women who find themselves in trouble a safe place to go. A place where they would be treated with compassion and respect. Our goal is to give them as much assistance as possible in making the best choices for themselves and their children."

"That sounds like an admirable goal." Meredith bit her lip. "The problem is the location. It's too close to home. If any of my parents' friends or associates ever found out I was there . . ." She trailed off. When she lifted the water glass to her mouth, her hands shook noticeably.

"You wouldn't have to go out very often. We have everything you'd need within the residence's walls. A doctor and midwife come out to give the girls monthly checkups, or weekly ones as the due date approaches."

Meredith's eyes widened, fear evident within their depths.

"Have you seen a doctor yet?" Olivia asked gently.

"Just once to confirm my suspicions." A rosy hue invaded Meredith's cheeks.

"Please don't be embarrassed. I'm not here to pass judgment."

Tears welled in the woman's eyes, magnifying a flash of anger. "You couldn't possibly understand how I feel. My family wants to send me away like I'm nothing more than a common criminal."

Unbidden images of the Mercer's iron-barred cells flashed to mind.

"Oh, I understand, believe me." Olivia held the other woman's gaze until understanding dawned.

Meredith raised a hand to her lips. "You've been in my situation?"

Olivia hesitated. If she told Meredith her story, it might help her make a decision. But what if she relayed the information to Darius? He would never look at Olivia the same way again. Yet how could she allow her own insecurities to overshadow this girl's problem? She drew in a breath and nodded. "About two years ago, I found myself with a similar problem. My fiancé had already left for the war, and when my family learned of my condition, they disowned me completely." She closed her eyes until the wave of pain subsided. "I gave birth in the hospital alone. My baby was taken away to be adopted."

Meredith's mouth gaped open. "That's terrible."

"Since then, I've made it my mission to help women facing similar circumstances and give them the opportunity to choose what to do for their child, because my choice was taken away." Her insides trembled. She'd only told her story to a few people, ones she suspected could benefit from her tale. Even fewer knew of her incarceration.

"You're very brave," Meredith said. "I don't know if I could do the same."

"As I've discovered, you never know what you're capable of

until faced with an impossible situation." Olivia smiled, hoping to ease the girl's fears.

But Meredith didn't smile in return, focusing instead on shredding a paper napkin into strips. "I'm not proud of the way I've handled things. The way I treated Darius . . ." She glanced up at Olivia. "I can't believe he's still trying to help me after what I did."

"It doesn't surprise me," she said quietly. "Darius is an honorable man." *As well as decent and kind, and a loving father.* She took a sip of her now-cold tea to ease her dry throat. "You're more than welcome to come and stay with us, Meredith."

The girl hesitated. "I don't know."

"If you'd like to see the house and meet the other residents, I can arrange—"

"Meredith Cheeseman? Is that you?" A shrill voice boomed through the diner as a rather large woman approached their table.

The color drained from Meredith's face. Her mouth opened but no sound emerged.

"Why, it is you!" The woman stopped beside her. "I almost didn't recognize you in that plain outfit. You're usually so stylish." She gave a hearty laugh that jiggled her second chin. "Whatever are you doing on this side of town?"

"Mrs. Dollard. How nice to see you." Meredith gave a weak smile, her cheeks flaming red. "May I introduce Miss Rosetti?"

"Nice to meet you, Mrs. Dollard." Olivia nodded in the woman's direction. "We're in the middle of a business discussion, but you're welcome to join us if you'd like."

Meredith's nostrils flared.

"Oh, heavens no," the woman said. "Don't let me interrupt. I just came in to get my husband his favorite smoked meat. Marty's has the best in town." She tugged the bodice of her dress where the buttons appeared stretched to their limit. "Well, give my best to your dear mother and tell her I look forward to our next bridge night."

"I will." Meredith gave a slight wave.

As soon as the woman left, Meredith's eyes closed, and she pressed a hand to her mouth. Seconds later, she opened her eyes again and exhaled. "You see what I mean? It's not safe here. Even in this neighborhood, there are people who recognize me. I'm afraid this isn't going to work." She shot up from her seat, taking her purse with her.

"Meredith, wait. Let me look into—"

"Thank you for your time, Olivia. But I'll have to come up with another solution." Without another word, she rushed down the aisle and out the front door.

Olivia's heart sank as she sagged back against her seat. How was she going to tell Darius that she'd failed him? And what was Meredith going to do now?

26

Darius drummed his fingers on the desk as he stared out his office door. Mr. Walcott was due back from his business trip today and would expect a renewed commitment to Walcott Industries. If Darius continued to oppose his boss's wishes, he might be out of a job by the day's end.

A mug of cold coffee sat on his blotter, the only thing he'd had in his stomach all day. The uncertainty of his job was wreaking havoc on his system. Mr. Walcott had taken a chance and hired Darius during a time of economic upheaval. And now with the war on, the unemployment rate remained high. Not a favorable time to be out of work.

The other matter weighing on him was Meredith's situation. She was meeting with Olivia today, but would she agree to go to Bennington Place? In his gut, Darius felt that would be her best option.

He rose from his chair and looked out the window to the busy street below. When had his life become so complicated? A few months ago, his only problem had been trying to shield Sofia from his father's Greek influence. Now he had Mr. Walcott breathing down his neck, his career hinging on his ability to coerce a widow into selling her home. His former fiancée, the woman he'd hoped would be a good mother to Sofia, had deceived him and was now drowning in her own unfortunate circumstances. And somewhere along the way, he'd fallen for an Italian beauty who ran a maternity home for unwed mothers. A woman all wrong for him and his daughter in so many ways.

Darius scrubbed a hand over his bleary eyes. This was not how he'd imagined his life turning out. Not at all. When he'd married Selene, his future had stretched before him with unbridled optimism—until violence had robbed him of that dream. Yet he'd survived, for Sofia's sake. Then, just when he thought he had his future back on track, life had thrown him another curve that sent him reeling. And no matter how much he tossed and turned at night, trying to find solutions to appease everyone, all he ended up with was bags under his eyes in the morning.

A knock sounded on his door.

Darius suppressed a groan. Time to face the music. But instead of Walcott, he found Meredith standing there.

She came in and closed the door behind her. Anxiety seemed to roll off her in waves, and Darius could only surmise the talk with Olivia hadn't gone well.

"Did you meet with Miss Rosetti?" he asked.

"Yes, but it was a waste of time." She paced to one side of the room and stared at the artwork on the wall, rubbing her hands up and down her arms.

"Why is that?"

Meredith shrugged. "The place sounded fine, but while I was talking with Olivia, a friend of my mother's came into the diner and recognized me. There's nowhere I can go in the city that's safe." She came back to face him, her expression earnest. "I appreciate what you were trying to do, Darius, sending me to talk to someone who's lived through my situation. But it doesn't change the fact—"

"Wait." Darius frowned. "What do you mean someone who's lived through your situation?"

Meredith sighed. "You don't have to cover for her anymore.

Olivia told me how her family disowned her and how her baby was taken away. I can see why she's so determined to help people like me." She fumbled in her bag for something. "I admire her for turning her life around. I just wish I could be that brave."

Darius sat down hard on his chair, clenching the armrest in an iron grip, the cold chill of truth sliding down his spine. It all made sudden sense. Perfect, horrible sense.

Olivia had given birth to a child out of wedlock.

And she hadn't said a word to him about it.

"Are you telling me you didn't know?" Meredith had taken a seat and was leaning forward to stare at him.

"No, I didn't. I figured she had a reason for wanting to run a place like that. Maybe a friend or cousin had gotten in trouble. But she never said anything about her own child." Not even when he'd asked her point-blank about her motives for becoming involved with Bennington Place.

"Well, I don't suppose it's something she goes around telling everyone."

Maybe not, but he thought they were friends. He ran a hand over his eyes, trying to corral his jumbled emotions.

"Oh, now it's starting to make sense." Meredith gave a humorless laugh and shook her head. "You have feelings for her. That's why this is hitting you so hard."

He met Meredith's gaze. "I guess the joke is on me."

Her features softened somewhat. "Olivia seems like a nice person. Doesn't she deserve the chance to explain?"

With no ready answer, he rose and walked to the window. He wouldn't discuss this with Meredith. Wouldn't let her see how his heart was being shredded into pieces alongside the image of the woman he thought he loved. "So, does this mean you're going to abide by your father's wishes and go to Saskatchewan?"

"Not if I can help it. Hearing Olivia's story made me realize I could find another maternity home in a city far enough away that no one will know me."

"Like where?" A deep weariness invaded his body as he turned back to her.

"Maybe Ottawa. Who knows, I might even like it there and stay after . . ." Her brows crashed down and she rose abruptly. "Anyway, that's really why I came to see you. To thank you . . . and to say good-bye."

He walked around the desk. "Will you tell your parents?"

"Not right away. Daddy would only try to stop me. But once I'm settled somewhere, I'll let them know."

He laid his hand on her shoulder. "Promise me you'll find a reputable place. And that you'll let me know you're all right."

"I will."

"Do you think you'll keep the baby?" he asked softly.

A flash of pain rose in her eyes, and then she shook her head. "I don't think I'd make a very good mother. My baby deserves a real family. Not one that would forever resent it or consider it a liability, the way my parents would."

Darius's throat thickened. He couldn't imagine anyone thinking of Sofia as a liability. Or as anything less than a perfect child of God. "Take care of yourself, Meredith."

"I'll do my best." She flashed him one of her old smiles, then walked out the door.

Darius waited until he heard the ding of the elevator doors before returning to his desk.

A thousand emotions flowed through him at once, twisting his insides until he dropped his head into his hands with a defeated groan. Olivia had lied to him the entire time he'd known her. The paragon of virtue whom he'd compared Meredith to had fallen off her pedestal with a resounding crash. Had he really been prepared to quit his job over her?

Because honestly, if he hadn't gotten swept away by his admiration for Olivia and what she was trying to do at Bennington Place, he would've tried a lot harder to get Ruth to sell—might have even been on board with all of Walcott's schemes. Which didn't say a lot about his character, except to prove that he was no paragon of virtue himself.

Olivia had made him want to be a better man. She'd made him take a hard look at himself and his ambition, and he'd found himself lacking. But now it seemed it had all been a sham.

Darius pushed up from his seat, grabbed his coffee cup, and headed toward the staff room. Anything to stop the torturous thoughts raging through his skull.

As he passed the elevator, the doors opened.

Mr. Walcott stepped out, a rumpled suit jacket over one arm. "Reed. Perfect timing. I need to talk to you."

Darius came to a halt. Maybe the timing *was* perfect. "Let me get a coffee, and I'll be right there."

"Grab me one too."

A few minutes later, Darius entered Walcott's office with two cups in hand. He set one in front of his boss and took a seat.

"How was your trip?" he asked, more to be polite than because he had any real interest.

"Fruitful." Walcott riffled through his briefcase on the credenza behind his desk. "I met with several investors in Vancouver who are looking to acquire properties here, and I'm confident they'll choose Walcott Industries to help them do so."

"That's good news." Darius took a long drink and grimaced. How long had this coffee been sitting in the pot?

Walcott threw some papers down and pulled out his chair. "I trust you've had time to reevaluate your priorities while I was away."

Something about Walcott's wary expression made Darius uncomfortable. But at this particular moment, with his emotions in such a state of upheaval, he wasn't prepared to do anything as final as quit his job. To put his family in jeopardy over some misplaced loyalty would be foolhardy at best. No, for now he would have to make the best of things. "I have, sir."

"And what conclusions did you come up with?"

"I am committed to my career at Walcott Industries. However, I do have one stipulation."

"What would that be?"

"I consider myself an ethical person, sir, and I wish to uphold my reputation as such, even in the business place." He paused. "If that's going to be a problem for you, then I would respectfully request time to look for alternate employment."

Walcott studied him across the desk. "Unfortunately, ethics and business do not always mix well. As you found out with Elliott Peterson."

Darius's stomach fell. It was true. His impulsive words to Peterson at the gala had cost the company one of their most lucrative clients.

Walcott pointed a pen at him. "I do, however, value your contribution to our company. You're smart, capable, and have a way with people. I'd be a fool to let you go."

"That's good to hear."

"I'd already decided to remove you from the Bennington project since it seems to cause you such angst. In the future, I can get other employees to handle any . . . ethically sensitive situations that might arise."

Darius swallowed. "That sounds like a reasonable compromise. I appreciate your understanding."

"To be fair, you did have a point about my being a little too close to the Bennington situation for my own good." Walcott's brow crinkled as he struck a match, held it to his cigar, then blew out the flame. "Long before there were businesses in that area, Henry Bennington's father cheated my grandfather out of that land. It's been a sore spot in our family history for years, and I vowed to one day get that property back. Restore the family legacy." He blew out a ring of smoke. "Closest I've come is buying the property next door."

"The empty lot?"

"That's the one. I knocked down the house that was there.

Wasn't worth saving anyway. And I've been biding my time, wait-ing for the Bennington property to go on the market." Ash formed on the end of the cigar. "I want to build Walcott Towers in honor of my grandfather. To right the wrong done to him."

"I see," Darius said slowly. "That does explain a lot. Though I doubt Mrs. Bennington has any idea about the history of her late husband's land."

"Maybe not." Walcott set the cigar in the ashtray with a loud exhale. "I have to admit a bit of the fight has gone out of me lately. I've decided that if the city council votes for the maternity home to stay open, I'll cut my losses. Sell the lot and build my tower elsewhere. But if the council orders the home to close, I'll take that as a sign to continue."

Darius took in a hopeful breath. At least it seemed like his boss might now be willing to consider other possibilities. "Sir, I took the liberty of lining up some potential sites I think might work for Walcott Towers."

His boss rolled his chair back, an unreadable expression on his face. "I guess it wouldn't hurt to have an alternate plan in place." He glanced at the calendar on the wall. "With everything I have to catch up on around here, I won't have time for a while. Why don't we meet in the next few days?"

"Sounds good." Darius exhaled slowly, almost afraid to believe the battle was over. Because despite his disillusionment with Ol-ivia, he still supported the good work of the maternity home.

Walcott nodded. "I'm glad we cleared the air, son. From now on, we know where we stand. The company can only benefit from that."

"I'll do my best to make sure of it, sir."

Darius pushed to his feet, his determination solidifying. He'd also do his best to help Walcott stay on the straight and narrow, whenever possible.

Maybe that way this partnership could work for the both of them.

27

"This little girl is doing just fine." Dr. Henshaw removed his stethoscope and returned it to his medical bag. "All thanks to you, Olivia. You've done a marvelous job with her."

His admiring regard sent warmth surging into her cheeks. She tried not to think about Darius's claim that the doctor might have romantic feelings for her. "It's no hardship," she said. "I'd do anything to make sure she's healthy and happy."

The baby lay in one of the cribs in the nursery where Dr. Henshaw had been examining her. She waved her little fist in the air and kicked her legs. Olivia pressed her lips together to keep her emotions in check. How much more time would she have with this precious girl? To hold her, rock her, and sing her to sleep with long-remembered lullabies?

"Olivia?" Dr. Henshaw's voice sounded near her ear. "You haven't seemed yourself lately. Is there anything I can do?"

She gripped the crib railing. Of course she hadn't been herself. Caring for Abigail these past weeks had brought back painful memories of having her own child taken from her. Now she was faced with losing another baby. It was only through God's grace that she was clinging to any semblance of sanity at all.

The doctor gently turned her to face him. "Ruth tells me you've been spending every waking moment with the baby, to the exclusion of the other residents—even shirking your work duties. She's worried about your emotional state," he said quietly, "and how giving up Abigail will affect you."

Raw grief scraped the back of her throat. "Why did you have to call Children's Aid? Why couldn't you have left matters alone? Then Abigail could have stayed with me." Her voice broke, and her whole body began to shake. The tears she'd been valiantly trying to suppress burst forth in a torrent.

The doctor's arms came around her, and she wept against his chest, reluctantly accepting the comfort he offered. When she was finally able to collect herself, she stepped away from him.

"I'm so sorry, Olivia." He handed her a handkerchief, regret blooming in his eyes. "I know it might seem unfeeling, but I did what I'm required to. Though I hate that it's causing you such pain."

"It's not fair." She sniffed and wiped her eyes. "I could give Abigail a good home with all the love she would ever need. She wouldn't be lacking for anything."

"Except a father," he said. "And maybe brothers and sisters." His earnest hazel eyes met hers. "Don't you think she deserves that?"

Her thoughts flew back to her family's crowded apartment over the store. Yes, her brothers were annoying and obnoxious at times, but together they'd created many wonderful memories, ones she wouldn't trade for anything. "I suppose you're right."

"And if you were honest, you'd admit this wouldn't be the ideal place to raise a child."

Her shoulders slumped. She didn't want to hear the truth in his words. "I don't know if I have the strength to go through this again." She reached over to straighten the baby's blanket. "Can you think of any possible way for me to keep her?"

Dr. Henshaw glanced at the baby cooing contentedly, then his gaze grew serious. "If I had no other obligations, I'd consider marrying you so you could adopt Abigail, but right now that's not an option." He gave a rueful shrug. "I don't know if Ruth told you, but I've been raising my younger brother ever since our parents died."

"She did mention that. I'm so sorry about your parents." Why had she never bothered to ask about his personal life? He seemed so polished, so confident. Yet he'd experienced tragedy too.

"Thank you. Unfortunately, my brother's been having a hard time coping, and it wouldn't be fair to add any more upheaval to his life."

"Of course not. It's kind of you to even suggest it, Dr. Henshaw, but I could never let you do that."

He smiled, his eyes crinkling around the edges. "Don't you think it's time you called me Mark? At least in private? I think of you as a friend, not merely a patient or colleague."

She gave a small laugh. "Very well. Thank you, Mark."

"I'll continue to ask God to provide Abigail with a good home," he said. "I have to believe that no matter what happens, it will be in her best interest."

"I pray you're right." She looked down at the tiny being, so helpless and vulnerable. "I'd do anything to protect her. Anything to have the privilege of being her mother."

"I know you would." Mark snapped his bag closed. "It's not much, but I'll do what I can to stall Mrs. Linder and give you a little more time before you have to say good-bye."

A lump of emotion lodged in her throat, and all she could do was nod.

Mark paused to pat her shoulder before he let himself out of the nursery.

Unable to sleep, Darius sat in his mother's dark kitchen, his head in his hands. A ribbon of moonlight shone from the window over the sink, providing the only illumination in the room. He'd come down from his overly warm bedroom, but the change in scenery had done nothing to ease the torturous thoughts plaguing him. Thoughts of Olivia and her shocking past.

He still couldn't fathom that she'd been pregnant and had a child. And been disowned by her family because of it. Her fiancé, presumably the child's father, had gone off to war and been killed. How utterly pathetic was he that a stab of jealousy pierced him every time he thought about this phantom person? This man whom Olivia had loved enough to conceive a child with? Was she still in love with him? Still grieving his memory?

Which brought up another even more unsettling question. What, if anything, did she feel for Darius?

Not that he should even care about that right now, because he couldn't get past his anger at her hiding such an enormous secret from him. Which he realized was totally hypocritical since he had kept his engagement from her.

Once again, his thoughts circled back around in a never-ending loop.

Frustration, disillusionment, and self-recrimination balled up into one hot tangle in his chest. He folded his arms on the table, laid his head down, and let the tears fall.

Lord, I have become a selfish, judgmental person and a poor excuse for a Christian. Even though I don't deserve it, I'm asking for your grace. Help me rise above my pettiness and my own flaws and find a way to forgive Olivia.

The light over the sink blinked on.

"Darius. Why do you sit in the dark?" His father's voice echoed in the room.

Darius swiped a hand across his damp face. "Couldn't sleep."

"So you lay on the kitchen table?" His father's dark hair stood on end, while his favorite striped bathrobe hung open over an undershirt and pajama pants.

"I just put my head down for a minute." Darius pushed up from the chair. "What are you doing up at this hour?"

Papá shrugged. "A little indigestion. I drink some milk and

it will go away." He opened the icebox. "You want a glass? It can help you sleep too."

Darius hesitated. How long had it been since he and his father had shared a simple drink? Too long. "Sure. It couldn't hurt."

Minutes later, they sat together at the table, sipping the milk.

After Papá drained the glass and set it down with a *thunk*, he looked over at Darius. "Your mother worries about you. She thinks you have problems you're not telling us about."

Darius resisted the immediate urge to deny the claim and considered the benefit of confession instead. Who better to tell than his father? At the very least, he'd get an honest, albeit blunt, opinion. "It's true. I do have a few problems weighing on me."

"Is this about that girl you were going to marry? Because Mamá says she wasn't good for you. That you don't love her like a husband should."

His mother's astuteness never ceased to amaze him. "She's right. But it's not about Meredith."

"Then what is wrong?"

Darius drew in a breath. "I . . . I've recently met another woman. One I thought to be kind, generous, and self-sacrificing. But today I found out that she's been hiding an unsavory past. And I don't know what to do about it." He stared at the tablecloth, unable to bear the pity in his father's eyes. "I know I should forgive her. But there's something lodged here"—he pressed a hand to his chest—"that can't let it go."

He waited for his father's words of admonition, citing the Lord's teachings on forgiveness.

Instead, a warm hand landed on Darius's back. "Everyone does things they regret at one time or another. I'm sure you have too."

"More times than I care to admit."

"And the people you hurt, they have forgiven you, yes?"

He thought about the many times Selene had excused him for not being the best husband. For putting his career above her. "Yes."

"Did they do it right away? The moment you hurt them?"

"Not always. Sometimes Selene would make me suffer for a day or two before she forgave me."

His father chuckled. "That is the way with all wives, I think. Your mamá does the same to me."

Darius straightened on his chair. "You think I'll be able to get past this in time? Is that what you're saying?"

One thick brow rose. "Time is the gift God has given us. It gives us perspective. Allows our emotions to settle and tempers to cool." He pointed at Darius. "Give yourself this gift. In a few days, you might feel very different."

"What if I don't? What if I can't accept it?"

"Then perhaps she's not the woman for you." Papá squeezed his shoulder. "You are a good man, my son. I know you will do the right thing. For the woman and for you."

The warmth in his father's voice made Darius's throat close up. "Maybe once I find out why she kept these secrets, I'll understand better."

"That sounds like a good place to start." Papá nodded. "And you should keep praying. Pray for God to take away the anger and the hurt. To give you understanding and wisdom."

Darius looked down at his father's forearms resting on the table. Strong, muscular arms covered by dark hair, tapering down to thick fingers with the perpetual hint of black around his nail beds. Those hands represented good, honest labor. Hard work for the money he earned. Why had Darius ever been ashamed of them?

"The milk has done its job." Papá patted his stomach as he pushed the chair away from the table, the metal legs scraping the linoleum. "Good night, Darius. I hope you sleep better now." He headed toward the door.

"Papá, wait a minute. I owe you an apology."

"Me? What for?"

Darius slowly rose. "I was wrong to deny our Greek heritage. I should be proud of it. We have nothing to be ashamed of."

His father studied him, nodding. "I know it's terrible, what happened to Selene and her parents. No one deserves to die like that." He swallowed hard before continuing. "But it's good that you finally see it's not the answer to hide who you are. You can be Canadian, but at the root of it all, you're Greek."

Darius considered his words. "I still want to send Sofia to a Canadian school, but I promise she'll take Greek classes on the weekend."

His father nodded again, a gleam of approval in his eyes. "You are a good son, Darius. *Theós na se evlogeí.*"

Darius's chest tightened as he pulled his father into a hug. "God bless you too, Papá. And thanks for the talk."

28

Olivia awoke the next day filled with new determination. If she had any hope of keeping Abigail, desperate measures needed to be taken. Mark's words yesterday had inadvertently given her an idea, a potential way to be able to adopt the girl, and though it seemed farfetched, she had to at least try.

She carried Abigail downstairs and moved the bassinet from the parlor to the dining room, intending to have a quick bite to eat before putting her plan into action.

The main floor was oddly quiet at this early hour. Only Mrs. Neale seemed to be up and about, with a big pot of porridge ready on the stove. Olivia took her breakfast into the deserted dining room and sat, enjoying the solitude.

She was just finishing her coffee when the doorbell rang. Trepidation beat in her throat, and she prayed it wasn't Mrs. Linder to take Abigail. Olivia would never be ready for that.

Instead, Mark Henshaw stood on the front porch, looking freshly groomed in a tweed jacket, his brown hair neatly combed. "Good morning, Olivia. May I come in?" He gave her an uncertain smile.

The coffee in her stomach churned. What would bring him by again so soon? "Certainly. Come into the dining room." She led him inside and sat down. Even though it was summer, a morning chill hovered in this room where the sun never reached to warm it. "Would you like some coffee?"

"No, thank you. I can't stay long." Mark took a seat across from her. "I wanted to talk to you before my shift at the hospital." The somber tone of his voice told Olivia this would not be good news. "I heard from Jane Linder late yesterday. I had to report that we had no new information about Mary. No one has come forward to say they are looking for her, and we haven't been able to identify any relatives. Which means . . ."

Olivia's spirits sank. "They'll be coming for Abigail soon."

"Likely today or tomorrow, depending on how long the paperwork takes." He gave a sympathetic shrug. "I'm sorry I couldn't stall her longer."

She shook her head. "It's not your fault. I knew this would happen sooner or later."

Several sets of feet thumped down the stairs, accompanied by a chorus of female chatter. At almost the same time, Abigail gave a loud squawk.

"I'd best be getting to the hospital," Mark said as he rose.

Olivia stood as well and lifted the baby from the bassinet. "Thank you for coming by. I appreciate you letting me know."

"You're welcome. I'll see you later in the week for the residents' checkups, if not before." He gave her a quick smile, then moved into the corridor, greeting Patricia, Nancy, and Cherise as he went.

Olivia escorted him out and stood on the porch, wishing she could appreciate the beautiful day that was dawning. But a storm might as well be brewing, because by all accounts, Mrs. Linder could show up at any moment to take Abigail. On a sigh, Olivia closed her eyes and kissed the baby's soft head, firming her determination to find a solution.

If she had any chance at all of keeping this sweet girl, she needed to put her plan into motion now.

———— ❖ ————

Darius had considered going over to confront Olivia before coming into the office that morning but had just as quickly rejected the idea. As his father had said last night, Darius needed time to process everything before he saw her again. Time to have his emotions under control in order to be more objective. Perhaps in a day or two, he'd feel able to do just that.

Yet as the morning waned, he found he wasn't able to concentrate on work, his mind continually drifting from Olivia to Meredith. In the end, praying for them both was the only thing that eased his worries.

When someone knocked on his door, he actually welcomed the interruption from the thoughts that kept circling in his brain. "Come in."

The door opened hesitantly, and Olivia stepped inside. "Hello, Darius."

A thousand emotions surged through his chest all at once, making it difficult to breathe. He jerked to his feet. "Olivia. What are you doing here?"

"I need to talk to you—if you have a few minutes." She was wearing a dress he'd never seen before. It was blue with yellow and white flowers, paired with a yellow cardigan to match. She looked even prettier today if possible, her hair neatly rolled in the latest style, her lips painted a pale shade of pink. Was this for him, or was she on her way somewhere else?

"I'm free for the moment. Have a seat." He glanced into the outer work area, where his office mates strained to catch a glimpse of what was going on, then firmly closed his door before resuming his seat.

He wasn't prepared for this meeting. Hadn't determined what he'd say when he saw her again. Now he'd be forced to act purely on instinct. "What can I do for you?" he asked in a level voice.

"I . . . I'm not sure how to begin." Olivia seemed anxious, clutching her handbag and biting her bottom lip.

Alarm snaked through his system. "Is something wrong?"

"Yes. I mean, no. That is . . ." She pressed her lips together, then huffed out a loud breath. "I have a proposition to make."

He schooled his features to keep his surprise from showing. Was this something to do with the property? Or could it be more personal? His conflicting emotions waged a battle within him, but he squared his shoulders. She'd done him a favor by talking to Meredith. He could at least hear her out. "What sort of proposition would that be?"

"A type of merger, you might say." She leaned forward on her chair. "I know you were recently planning to marry Meredith. I was wondering if—" she drew in a breath—"if you'd consider marrying me instead."

Darius simply stared, certain he hadn't heard her right. Had she just asked him to marry her?

"You said you need a mother for Sofia," she rushed on, "and I need a husband in order to adopt Abigail. It would be an advantageous match for both of us. I promise to be a good mother to your daughter and do my best to be a good wife to you as well." Her brown eyes swam with a mixture of hope and what looked like terror.

Terror that he would say yes or that he'd turn her down?

Darius dragged a hand over his jaw, then got to his feet and walked unsteadily to the window, his heart beating too loudly in his chest. For a few seconds, he simply stared out at the buildings in the distance.

How did he begin to process this? If she'd asked him before he'd learned about her past, his answer might have been very different. But now, all he could think about was her lack of faith in him. Everything he knew about her had been thrown into question, leaving him confused and unsure if he could trust himself. More importantly, he had Sofia's best interest to consider.

When at last he turned to face her, he kept his expression as neutral as possible. "Do you remember why I wouldn't marry Meredith? Because she'd deceived me about her pregnancy?" He pinned her with a hard stare. "It turns out you haven't exactly been honest with me either."

The blood drained from her cheeks, and she closed her eyes. "Meredith told you," she said flatly.

"She assumed I already knew." He paced behind his chair, tension twisting his insides. "I don't understand, Olivia. After all the conversations we've had, why did you never tell me you'd had a child? That you were once one of those women in trouble, which was your real reason for opening Bennington Place?" Despite his best effort, hurt and anger laced his voice.

When she opened her eyes, misery swirled in her gaze. "I . . . I was ashamed. Afraid I'd lose your respect. And your friendship."

"You must have told some people. Like Ruth." He stiffened. "And probably the doctor. Why was I so different?" He hated the petulant tone to his voice but couldn't seem to prevent it.

Olivia stared at her lap. "Ruth knows my story, or most of it. As for Dr. Henshaw, he figured out a large part of it on his own after he treated me when I was ill. But I never told him or Ruth the full extent of what I went through. I've never told anyone that." Her lips quivered as she got to her feet, looking ready to bolt.

He moved toward her, needing more answers before he let her go. "Your fiancé, the one who died in the war. Was he the father of your child?"

She nodded. "He'd already left for duty when I found out I was expecting."

Tension seized his muscles. What type of cad made love to his fiancée and then left her to face the consequences of their actions while he went off to war? Darius couldn't imagine how hard it must have been for Olivia to break the news to her parents. "Meredith said your family disowned you. Did you have the baby in a maternity home?"

"No." A stricken expression crossed her face. "I didn't have that option because . . ." She bit her lip. "Because my father had me arrested."

"Arrested?" Disbelief roiled in his gut. "What on earth for?"

Her gaze remained fused to the floor. "There's a little-known law where a woman can be charged with being incorrigible if she's pregnant, unmarried, and under twenty-one. The authorities had no choice but to incarcerate me."

"He had you put in jail?" Darius's mouth fell open before he clamped his jaw shut. He must look like a fish the way his mouth kept gaping open.

Olivia nodded. "I was sent to the Mercer Reformatory for Women."

Darius scrubbed a hand over his eyes. How could a father treat a daughter so cruelly? Nothing could make him betray Sofia that way—ever.

"Did you give birth in jail, then?"

"No. When I went into labor, they took me to the hospital." She wrapped her arms around her middle. "I got to hold my son for about five minutes before the woman from Children's Aid took him away." Moisture glinted in her eyes, and she blinked hard several times.

His own throat grew tight just thinking about it. How could anyone be so heartless to a young mother? No wonder Olivia wanted to provide a safe haven for women. To allow them the option of keeping their child if they chose to.

If only she'd been given that chance.

His shoulders sagged as the anger seeped out of him. This woman had endured so much heartache. It was no wonder she wanted to keep Abigail after losing her son that way.

Slowly he came around the desk. "I feel terrible for everything you've gone through, Olivia. I see now why it would be hard to share such a painful story."

"Thank you." She still wouldn't look at him directly.

"I also understand why you want to keep Abigail. I wish . . ." He shook his head. What did he wish? He had no clue at this moment, except that he wished he could erase her pain.

When Olivia raised her head, the raw anguish on her face sent a spasm through his chest.

"It's all right, Darius. I had no right to come here and burden you with my problems. The truth is . . ." Tears swam in her eyes, highlighting the amber flecks in their depths. "I don't deserve to be a mother or a wife. I don't know what I was thinking." Her voice broke on a sob, and she rushed to the door, flung it open, and dashed out.

"Olivia, wait!" He ran after her, but she was already halfway across the outer office.

She bypassed the elevator and raced through the doorway to the stairs.

Darius came to a halt, conscious of the stares of everyone in the office. He couldn't let Olivia leave in such a distraught state. He had to catch her, make her understand . . .

Darius made eye contact with the receptionist. "If anyone asks, I'll be back shortly."

Then he charged down the stairs, taking them two at a time. By the time he reached the main level, however, there was no sign of her. He ran out onto the sidewalk and craned his neck in both directions, but to no avail. She was gone. Swallowed up in the sea of pedestrians.

His stomach sank to the tips of his shoes. He could go after her. Catch up with her at the maternity home and . . . and do what? He certainly wasn't ready to propose marriage, so really what was the point in prolonging the misery? He let out a defeated breath as he slowly made his way back inside.

His father was right. The only thing that would help him now was time. Time to process all that he'd learned today and allow God to work on his heart. Hopefully then, the Lord would make it clear what Darius needed to do next.

29

The next day, Olivia sat with Abigail in the rocker. The child grew heavy in her arms, and Olivia knew she should lay her down for a proper nap. However, she couldn't bear to let her go, even for half an hour. It was only a matter of time before Jane Linder showed up to take her, and Olivia wanted to cherish every last moment with the girl. She looked down at Abigail's sweet face, so relaxed in slumber.

If only God would grant her a miracle, a way to spare her the anguish to come.

She'd foolishly thought that marrying Darius would be that miracle. How could she have been so blind, imagining she could propose to him and he'd simply accept? Even if he had agreed, she couldn't have married him without disclosing her past. She realized that now.

But her desperation to hold on to Abigail had clouded her judgment, making her oblivious to everything but her own selfish desires. And that might be her worst crime of all.

She'd deluded herself into believing she could be a good mother—not only to Abigail, but to Sofia too. In reality, Darius had every reason not to want her around his daughter. He'd said Meredith would make a poor role model. If so, then Olivia would be ten times worse.

A sigh escaped. *Lord, forgive me for trying to take matters into my own hands. You know what's best for Abigail and for me. Help me to accept your will for the both of us.*

Three sharp knocks sounded on the front door. Olivia's eyes flew open, and her heart began to thump heavily in her chest. Slowly, she rose with the baby and headed to the door.

Mark Henshaw stood on the porch, looking very serious. "Good morning, Olivia. Mrs. Linder is here to pick up Abigail."

Olivia looked past him to the walkway, where Mrs. Linder stood holding a briefcase.

Her lungs refused to inflate, and she clutched the baby tighter. "Please come in."

"Hello, Miss Rosetti." Mrs. Linder sailed by her into the parlor, looking very efficient in her cream-colored suit. "Is Mrs. Bennington at home? I'll need her signature on some paperwork." She set her case on the coffee table.

"She's upstairs," Olivia said in a voice she barely recognized as her own. "I'll get her. I have to change Abigail anyway and pack her bag."

"Fine. I'll wait down here."

Olivia took as much time as she dared, changing the baby's clothes and gathering her few belongings. With shaking fingers, she folded the delicate items and placed them one by one into a small satchel. Her eyes burned. How empty this room would be without Abigail. No more soft cooing from the bed, no more midnight feedings or cuddles in the night.

She picked up the now-content girl, kissed her head, and breathed in the soothing scent of talc and baby soap one more time. Giving up this baby seemed almost harder than losing her own son, probably because Olivia had spent so much time with her.

Lord, I don't know how I'm going to let her go. Please grant me the strength to face this terrible day.

Then, on a deep inhale, she grabbed the satchel and went to find Ruth. She'd need her friend's support to get through this.

If that were even possible.

Ruth was just coming out of her bedroom when Olivia reached the door. She looked bright and alert, her gray hair fashioned in curls around her face. "Good morning, Olivia."

Olivia couldn't manage a smile or a greeting. "Mrs. Linder is here for Abigail. She needs your signature on some paperwork."

Immediately Ruth's features softened, and she put an arm around Olivia. "Oh, my dear. I'm sorry. I know how much you will miss that child."

Olivia's chin quivered. Unable to say a word, she turned and headed down the stairs. She set the satchel at the door and followed Ruth into the parlor. Several sheets of paper lay beside Mrs. Linder's briefcase on the coffee table, along with a pen.

"Do you need me to sign anything?" Olivia managed.

Mrs. Linder looked up. "No. Mrs. Bennington and the doctor's signatures will suffice."

"I'll wait with Abigail in the hall, then."

She couldn't stand to watch them sign away the little girl's life, condemning her to a foster home and a lengthy adoption process. All Olivia could do was pray that a caring couple would claim her soon and that Abigail would grow up knowing she was loved.

Even if she never remembered the woman who'd nurtured her the first few weeks of her precious life. The woman who loved her so very much.

Tears gathered in Olivia's eyes, and though she blinked hard, several broke free to trail down her cheeks. She closed her eyes and pressed her lips to the baby's face. The girl began to stir, opening her eyes and staring right at Olivia, as though she understood exactly what was happening.

"Be good, little one. I know they'll find you the best parents possible. And I'll be praying for you every day. I'll never forget you. I promise." She hugged the girl until she squirmed in protest.

"We'll do our best to make sure she gets a good home, Miss Rosetti. I can assure you of that much."

She looked up to see Mrs. Linder watching her with sympathetic eyes. The woman waited a few seconds, then held out her arms.

Olivia froze as horrible memories of the exact moment she'd lost Matteo flooded her senses. This time, however, the woman wasn't snatching the child from her arms. This time she waited for Olivia's surrender.

Conscious of Ruth and Mark watching her, Olivia forced her wooden feet forward. She kissed Abigail's cheek one last time, then reluctantly, achingly, handed her over.

She pressed a hand to her mouth to contain the sob building inside her. Her legs shook as she moved backward, away from them, and the air in her lungs thinned, causing a cascade of tiny spots to dance before her eyes. She couldn't bear to watch Mrs. Linder leave with Abigail. Nor could she endure the sorrowful expressions on Ruth's and Mark's faces. She wasn't ready to accept their attempts to console her—not when the roar of grief had just begun.

With a strangled cry, Olivia whirled around and raced upstairs to the sanctuary of her room. There, she crumpled to the hardwood floor and let sorrow have its way.

30

Olivia lay on top of her bed, staring at the swirls in the ceiling plaster above her. Her limbs felt like lead, so heavy that she wouldn't be able to move them if she tried. Her eyes burned from hours of constant weeping, and her lips were parched from lack of moisture, as though every ounce of water had been drained from her body.

She glanced over at the window, attempting to ascertain if it were day or night. The days blurred together now, since she slept almost around the clock with no concept of the passage of time. What did it matter? She had no reason to get up, no reason to leave her room. Ruth could manage the home without her, and the girls didn't need her. They had all the resources they required. In fact, since no one needed her, perhaps if she just kept sleeping, eventually she wouldn't awaken at all.

Two sharp knocks sounded. "Olivia? Are you up?"

Olivia winced. Ruth's voice was loud enough to rouse a coma patient.

She kept her eyes closed and ignored her. Hopefully, she'd assume she was sleeping and go away.

"Olivia, you have a visitor."

She frowned, irritation mounting. Ruth had probably demanded Dr. Henshaw come to try and coax her from her self-imposed exile. But it wouldn't work. She had no intention of seeing anyone.

The door creaked open.

Olivia steeled herself for Ruth's inspection. As she'd done every day, Ruth would come in, hover for a few minutes, murmur a prayer, then let herself out again. A tiny part of Olivia felt bad ignoring her friend that way. But she couldn't summon the energy to convince Ruth that she wanted to be left alone.

The bed sagged under the weight of someone sitting down.

Olivia held her breath. This was something new. And unwelcome.

A hand touched her leg.

She tensed. What if it wasn't Ruth? What if she'd sent someone else in?

Olivia opened her eyes, her muscles loosening the moment she recognized her friend.

"Good." Ruth peered at her. "You're awake."

Olivia scowled. "I want to be alone."

"Well, that's too bad. Because it's time to return to the land of the living, and I'm not taking no for an answer, young lady."

Heat surged through Olivia's chest. She swallowed to force her emotions back down. She would not fall for Ruth's attempt to goad her into an outburst of temper.

"You have a visitor downstairs. Darius Reed has been by almost every day. I think you should get up and see him."

"I don't want to talk to anyone." She flipped onto her side, putting her back to Ruth.

"We also have a new resident who'd like to meet you. Her name is Monica. She's about four months along in her pregnancy, I believe, and settling in nicely so far. I've told her all about you."

"Well, you shouldn't have. I have nothing to say. Nothing to give. Nothing left but . . ." She bit her lip.

"But what, pain?"

Amazingly, the burn of tears built behind Olivia's eyes. She'd thought her insides too barren and dry to cry anymore, but apparently she was wrong.

"Olivia, I want you to listen to me." Ruth's voice had become gentle. "What you've been through is more than any one person should have to bear in two lifetimes. If I could take away your pain or bear the brunt of it myself, I would gladly do so." She sniffed. "But life goes on, whether you want it to or not. Right now, you probably think it's preferable to shut yourself off and exist in a state of numbness. I did that quite successfully for a very long time. The problem, however, is that you're not really living."

A warm hand landed on Olivia's shoulder. She stiffened, but Ruth didn't remove it.

"You have so much love inside you, but you're afraid to share it. I've watched you with the women here, the way you hold yourself back from really connecting with them. Holding yourself in reserve, waiting for the pain to arrive."

Every muscle in Olivia's body became taut. She did not want to hear this. Did not need to listen.

"With Abigail, though, the real Olivia emerged. I saw how much you loved that baby, saw your incredible tenderness and devotion. You showered her with such love that it almost became an obsession. Yet deep down you knew it couldn't last. That she wasn't yours to keep."

Tremors rippled through Olivia's body. She held herself tight, hardly daring to breathe, lest the dam inside her break.

Ruth rubbed a hand down Olivia's back. "Remember the joy you felt when you held Abigail? That's how life is meant to be lived. You can hide from love and live an empty, joyless existence, or you can open your arms wide and embrace it.

"Does it mean you'll never have heartache? Unfortunately, no. Everyone experiences loss and grief. I lost my son and daughter-in-law, then my husband, and, in another way, my grandson too. And yes, I wallowed in that state of numbness for longer than I care to admit, wishing for death. But then God brought you into my life. You made me remember how good it felt to care about people again."

Spasms wracked Olivia's chest as tears slowly slid down her face onto the pillow. "I can't do it. I can't take any more pain."

Warm arms surrounded her as Ruth pulled her close, rocking her like she was an infant herself. "The heart has an amazing ability to heal, my dear. If you'll only let it."

Olivia buried her face in the woman's shoulder, clutching Ruth's arm as though anchoring herself to the room, to the world.

"There, there," Ruth murmured against Olivia's hair. "I'm here to help you through this if you'll let me. And God is with you as well. He will sustain you in your sorrow and grant your heart peace. I promise you."

As her tears subsided at last, Olivia absorbed the shelter of Ruth's embrace, allowing her soothing words to sink deep into her marrow. She'd never had a grandmother, not one she could remember, but in this moment, she had an idea what having one would feel like.

Olivia raised her damp face to see Ruth wiping her own eyes.

"I'm sorry I let you down," Olivia whispered. "I thought I'd be strong enough to handle being around mothers and their babies. But I don't know if I am."

Ruth shook her head. "You did not let me down. It's only natural to go through a period of adjustment. The next babies who come along will be easier. You won't expect to keep every one of them."

Olivia's lips twitched as she dried her eyes. "That probably wouldn't be wise."

"Nor very practical." Ruth helped her sit up. "Now, I'm going to prepare you a nice hot bath and bring you up a sandwich and some tea. And maybe tomorrow you'll feel like joining us in the dining room." She kissed Olivia's cheek, then moved off the bed.

"Ruth?"

"Yes, dear?"

"Would you ask Darius to come back tomorrow? I might be up to seeing him then."

"Certainly."

"And Ruth?"

"Yes?"

"Thank you."

Ruth pressed her lips together, sorrow and relief reflecting in her eyes. She nodded once, then slipped out the door.

Darius wasn't sure what to expect when he arrived at Bennington Place the following afternoon. It had been five days since Ruth Bennington had called to give him the news that Abigail had been taken from the home and to ask that he come by the house in an effort to coax Olivia from her room. And so, every day he'd gone over, and every day Ruth had sadly shaken her head. Olivia refused to leave her room, seeing no one, barely eating or drinking. Darius had been beside himself with worry, yet all he could do was pray that Ruth could get through the wall of Olivia's grief. To his great relief, yesterday Ruth told him that Olivia might be ready to see him.

Now he had to figure out what to say to her. Olivia was suffering, and he had no idea how to ease her pain, especially when he felt a measure of guilt about the whole situation.

"I know you were recently planning to marry Meredith. I was wondering . . . if you'd consider marrying me instead."

Rather than hearing her out, he'd been consumed with making her pay for the hurt she'd inflicted on him. Not one of his finest moments.

This morning, as he was getting ready to leave, however, he'd had the brilliant idea to bring Sofia along. From experience, he knew that a child's exuberance could do wonders to cheer a person, and Sofia had been asking when she could go back to see Miss Olivia. Perhaps having his daughter there would ease the tension between him and Olivia as well. He'd already prepared Sofia for the fact that baby Abigail had gone to a new home, and he prayed the girl wouldn't bring up the subject in front of Olivia.

As they reached the gate to Bennington Place, he looked down at Sofia, who clutched a folded piece of paper in her fingers, apparently a drawing she'd made for Olivia. "Remember, Mouse, Miss Olivia might be a bit sad today, so we won't mention baby Abigail, right?" It couldn't hurt to remind her one more time.

"I remember, Daddy. That's why I made her a picture." Sofia smiled, a dimple winking in one cheek.

"That was very thoughtful."

"Is that why you brought her flowers?" She pointed to the colorful bouquet of carnations and daisies in his hand.

"That's right. Most ladies like getting flowers."

He went up to the door and knocked, a habit he'd started so the bell wouldn't wake the babies.

Ruth opened the door. "Darius. It's good to see you again." Somehow over the last few days, they'd moved to a first name relationship. "And who is this darling girl?"

He smiled. "This is my daughter, Sofia. Sofia, this is Mrs. Bennington, the owner of this residence."

"Hello," Sofia said. "I like your house. It's pretty."

"Why, thank you." Ruth's eyes gleamed as she gazed down at Sofia.

Once again, his daughter had instantly won someone's heart. How he envied that skill.

"We're here to see Miss Olivia. I have a picture for her." Sofia waved the folded page in front of her.

"I'm sure she'll love it. Won't you come in?" Ruth moved aside as they entered. "I believe Olivia's in the backyard. If you'd like to go out, you can get there through the kitchen."

"I know the way, thank you." Darius took Sofia's hand and led her down the corridor.

They walked through the kitchen, which smelled of freshly

baked bread and cinnamon. Mrs. Neale stood at the counter, her fists buried in a batch of dough. When she looked over, she gave him a subtle nod. The weight of everyone's expectations suddenly seemed as heavy as the iron skillet on the stovetop. He only hoped he wouldn't let them down.

Opening the back door, he led Sofia out to the lawn, where he spotted Olivia immediately. She was seated on a bench at the far end of the yard, surrounded by greenery and blooming flowers. Even at a distance, he could sense the aura of sadness enveloping her.

Sofia tugged her hand free and raced across the grass, waving the paper. "Miss Olivia! Miss Olivia! I brought you a picture." She came to a halt in front of her.

Olivia smiled as she took the offering. "Hi, Sofia. Did you draw this?"

"Yes. To help you feel better."

Darius came to stand beside the bench. "Hello, Olivia. I hope you don't mind my bringing Sofia. She was dying to come back and see you."

Olivia raised her gaze to his, and his chest tightened. Her beautiful brown eyes seemed hollow, and the light that usually glowed within them was missing.

"I don't mind. It's good to see you both." Her words fell flat, no emotion behind them.

"Open your picture, Miss Olivia." Sofia bounced from one foot to the other.

Olivia wrestled the paper against the breeze that threatened to tear it from her grasp, then stared at the crude stick figures, her expression unreadable.

Darius almost groaned.

Sofia had drawn a woman, presumably Olivia, judging by the long dark hair, with a baby in her arms. At the top of the page, another figure that looked like an angel spread its wings above them.

"That's you and baby Abigail. Oh!" Sofia's hand flew to her mouth. "I'm not supposed to talk about her. But I wanted you to have a picture so you could remember her."

Darius winced. Why hadn't he asked to see the drawing before she showed it to Olivia?

"It's beautiful." Olivia's voice was strained. "And who is this?" She pointed to the angelic figure.

"That's my mommy. She's in heaven now. Daddy says she watches over me. So I asked her to watch over you and Abigail too."

Darius's throat slammed shut. His beautiful girl, with a heart the size of a western prairie, had meant well. He knelt beside her, his hand on her shoulder. "That's a lovely thought, Mouse. I'm sure all God's angels will watch over them." He darted a glance at Olivia.

Her eyes remained focused on the picture while tears streamed down her face. His spirits plummeted to the dampness of the grass seeping through his pant leg. Ruth had asked him to help Olivia feel better, not to reduce her to tears again.

Olivia refolded the page. "Thank you, Sofia. I'll put this up in my bedroom so I can see it every day."

His daughter beamed at her, then darted off across the lawn, calling over her shoulder, "You need some swings in this yard for when all the babies grow up."

Darius rolled his eyes and dropped to the bench beside her. "I'm sorry, Olivia. I thought bringing Sofia might cheer you up. I didn't expect this."

She wiped the back of her hand across her wet face. "Please don't apologize. This is the sweetest thing anyone's done for me. I love it." A genuine smile emerged, and her eyes brightened.

"Oh, I almost forgot." He handed her the flowers. "These are for you too."

"You didn't have to do that." She buried her face in the blooms, inhaling deeply.

"It was the least I could do, especially after I bungled your marriage proposal." He gave a tentative smile, hoping to discover how she felt about the whole situation. "Am I forgiven?"

She raised her head with a sigh. "There's nothing to forgive. I was the one in the wrong. I don't know what I was thinking."

"Totally understandable, given the situation." He squinted against the sun's glare to watch Sofia, who was doing twirls on the lawn that made her dress billow out. "How would you feel about coming for a walk with Sofia and me to the park nearby?"

She hesitated for the briefest of seconds, then nodded. "I believe a walk might do me some good."

31

The fresh air and exercise certainly helped lift Olivia's spirits, as did the precious girl who chattered the whole way to the park. Sofia's innocent exuberance was just the distraction Olivia needed from thinking about infants and bottles and diapers. Perhaps, if she were lucky, some of the girl's joy would rub off on her too.

While Sofia alternated between walking beside her and darting ahead to get a better view of the park, Darius matched his pace to Olivia's. He was so thoughtful to bring his daughter and a bouquet of flowers to cheer her up. And to laugh off her crazy marriage proposal.

She could see in hindsight that losing Matteo had made her cling even harder to Abigail. And now that she was aware of this tendency, she could hopefully avoid it in the future. Somehow she'd have to find a way to cope with being around babies and not getting swept away by grief—or by the desire to adopt all the ones destined for the Infants' Home.

They turned into the park, following the winding path to an open area where a swing set and slide came into view.

"Daddy! Can you push me on the swing?" Sofia's childish delight rang out.

"Coming." Darius ran over to join her at the equipment.

Olivia found a bench where she could watch Sofia and the other children playing, absorbing their heartwarming laughter into her battered soul. A soft breeze lifted pieces of her hair off her neck, and above her in the canopy of trees, the birds warbled their songs. All of it eased the ache in her heart just a little.

After a while, Darius came to join her, and they sat enjoying the scene in comfortable silence, until Olivia's guilt would no longer allow her to remain silent. She glanced over at his profile as he kept a keen eye on his daughter. Such a considerate man, one who deserved an honest conversation to clear the air.

"I owe you an apology," she said softly. "First, for that terrible marriage proposal. I had no right to impose on you that way. It was selfish and thoughtless."

"Olivia, I really—"

"No, please let me get this out. It's been weighing on me for days." She shifted on the bench, tucking her skirt around her knees so the breeze wouldn't lift it. "The bigger apology I owe you is for not telling you about my past." She couldn't look at him, staring instead at the children running around on the grass. "I didn't purposely set out to deceive you. I hope you can believe me."

"I do," he said in a quiet voice. "Once I set aside my pride, I realized you had every right to keep that part of your life private."

She plucked a piece of grass and twirled it between her fingers. "I was afraid," she murmured. "Afraid that once you knew, you'd reject me like almost everyone else in my life has."

He grimaced. "And I reacted just as you feared. I feel terrible about that." He shook his head. "For someone who claims to be a Christian, I sometimes fall far short of the ideal."

Olivia bit her lip. She wanted to tell him that it was a natural reaction and that she forgave him, but the lump in her throat made speaking impossible. He wasn't the only one who'd fallen short.

Just then Sofia called out, "Daddy, look. I'm swinging by myself."

He looked over and waved. "That's wonderful, Mouse. Keep pumping your legs."

"Look, Miss Olivia. I can almost touch the trees."

Shielding her eyes with one hand, Olivia waved too. Then she turned to Darius again. "I wanted to ask you about Meredith. Did she go out west after all?"

"No, she didn't." His brows dipped down. "At least I don't think so. She said she wanted to find a maternity home in another city, perhaps in Ottawa. I haven't heard from her yet, though she promised to contact me once she was settled."

A pair of squirrels chased each other up a nearby tree trunk. Olivia enjoyed their antics for a moment, pausing to say a quick prayer for Meredith. "I hope she finds a place that suits her."

"So do I." Darius looked at her fully for the first time. "Meredith's plight made me truly appreciate the good work you and Ruth are doing at Bennington Place."

"That means a lot. Especially since I know in the beginning you considered it a nuisance."

"It shames me to think of my judgmental attitude." He brushed at some grass on his pant leg. "I'm only thankful my boss has removed me from 'the Bennington project,' as he calls it, so it won't be such a source of conflict anymore."

"I'm glad too." Some of the tension in Olivia's shoulders eased. At least she wouldn't have to worry that she and Darius were on opposite sides of the issue. "I suppose all we can do is trust in God's will for the home and its residents." Olivia gave him a long look. "Losing Abigail has made me see that I need to loosen my grip on the things in my life. The more I try to hold on to them, the more they slip away." She shrugged. "A lesson I'm unfortunately learning the hard way."

Darius shifted closer. The wind lifted the clean scent of his soap to her. "I'm sorry you've had to suffer this way again, Olivia. I can't begin to imagine the pain you've been through." He laid his hand over hers.

The heat from his palm seeped through her, wrapping her in a cocoon of warmth. Her heart rate kicked up as she raised her eyes to his. "Then you don't think I'm a terrible person?"

He stared at her with such intensity that her lungs forgot to take in air.

"What I think," he said slowly, "is that you are the most amazing person I've ever met. Generous and kind, compassionate and forgiving. I'm honored just to know you."

Before she could react, he lowered his mouth to hers. Her whole world seemed to come to a halt, narrowing down to the feel of his lips on hers. They were warm and gentle, tasting of coffee and something sweet, like maple syrup. How many times had she dreamt of this moment? Longed for it? Never believing it could happen.

When his arm came around her, drawing her closer, every nerve ending came alive , infusing her with energy. Warmth radiated through her body, and her heart thudded loudly in her chest as she kissed him back, drinking him in like a thirsty plant soaking up water. She'd forgotten how much she'd missed this connection with another person. The warmth, the security, the sense of belonging.

Someone tugged on her sleeve. "Why are you kissing my daddy?"

Darius jerked back.

A rush of heat enveloped Olivia's face as she looked down at Sofia. "I . . . I was . . . thanking him for the flowers and for being so kind to me."

Sofia stared at her, her brow crinkled. She pushed aside some strands of dark hair that had escaped her braid. "Do I get a kiss too for my picture?"

At the stunned look on Darius's face, Olivia stifled a laugh. "Of course, sweetie. I can't believe I forgot that earlier." She held out her arms, and the girl lunged onto her lap. Then Olivia kissed the girl's flushed cheek. "Thank you for coming today and for your lovely picture."

"You're welcome." Sofia threw her arms around Olivia's neck and squeezed, almost cutting off her air.

But Olivia didn't mind. She clasped Sofia tight against her chest, relishing the feel of her and the way she smelled of fresh air and sunshine. For the moment, her heart was full of this wonderful child and her amazing father.

It turned out Ruth was right about one thing. Olivia could cower in her room and hide from love, or she could simply open her arms and receive it.

Surely the risk would be worth it in the end.

Darius practically floated all the way back to the maternity home.

He had kissed Olivia in the middle of a public park. And she had kissed him right back. When their lips met, a thousand sensations had flooded his system. Not since Selene had he felt so alive, so filled with emotion that he could barely think, only feel.

He glanced at Olivia as they walked, and she smiled shyly, the color rising in her cheeks. He grinned back, his chest expanding as though his heart had grown too big to be contained. They had taken an important step forward in their relationship, but what exactly did that mean for them now?

"Daddy, who's that?" Sofia tugged on his hand.

He looked ahead on the sidewalk. A man moved away from the maternity home gate and started toward them. He had dark hair, cut fairly short, and was dressed in a black shirt and pants. Odd for the warmth of the summer day.

"I don't know, sweetheart."

As he got closer, Darius noticed the white clergy collar. A minister of some sort? Perhaps someone who worked with Bennington Place to help troubled women in the parish?

Beside him, Olivia went still and gasped. "Sal? Is that you?"

The man broke into a run, a grin blooming on his face. "Livvy!"

She threw herself at him, and he picked her up, swinging her around. Then she buried her face in his neck.

He set her feet on the ground but kept his arms around her, his eyes closed. Tears seeped out from under thick lashes. "*Grazie a dio.* I found you at last."

Olivia's shoulders shook, and she clung to him awhile longer, until she finally moved away. "What are you doing here?"

"I wanted to see you and make sure you were all right. I've been so worried." He pulled her close again.

Darius kept a hand on Sofia's shoulder and stepped back a few paces as unsettled emotions churned through him. Who was this man?

At last, Olivia turned around, seeming to remember he and Sofia were there. Her eyes were damp, but her happy smile had brought the sparkle back to them. "This is my brother Salvatore. Sal, this is a good friend, Darius Reed, and his daughter, Sofia."

Her brother. The tension loosened in his neck. Of course, the family resemblance was now blatantly obvious. It struck Darius then how much this must mean to Olivia, to have one of her family members reach out to her this way. "Good to meet you, Reverend." He stepped forward to shake the man's hand.

"Please, just call me Sal." He bent down. "Hello, Sofia. That's a beautiful name."

"Hello." Her brown eyes settled on his collar. "Are you a priest?"

"Yes, I am. You're very observant."

"I'm smart. My pappoú tells me that."

Sal and Olivia laughed out loud, the sound so refreshing to Darius's ears. *Thank you, Lord, for bringing some extra happiness to Olivia today.*

"Can you come in for coffee?" Olivia asked her brother.

"Sure. I have some time to spare. And I want to hear all about you. The good and the bad."

She linked her arm through her brother's. "There's been a lot of bad. So let's start with the good." They headed up the sidewalk.

When they reached the gate, Darius held Sofia back. "I think we'll head home and let you two catch up."

Sal turned to shake his hand again. "It was good to meet you, Darius. If you're ever at St. Michael's for Mass, make sure to find me."

Darius nodded. "I will." He looked over at Olivia, reluctant to leave her but happy she was reconnecting with her brother. "Thanks for coming to the park with us."

"Thank you for the visit." Olivia smiled, hesitating a little as though not sure whether to hug him or shake his hand. Instead, she turned her attention to Sofia. "And thank you again for my beautiful picture."

"Did it make you happy?" Sofia asked.

"Very much." She bent and hugged his daughter. "I hope to see you again soon."

"Me too. Bye-bye." Sofia waved, then hopped down the sidewalk.

So many words hovered on Darius's lips, but with Sal looking on, he didn't have the nerve to say them. Instead, he gave her a long look, then turned and followed his daughter to the car.

One day soon, he hoped he'd have the chance to tell Olivia all the things on his heart.

32

Seated on the sofa in the parlor, Olivia watched Sal quietly sip his coffee, while her own cup remained untouched on the table before her. Her nerves were far too jumpy to tolerate an infusion of caffeine. She could hardly believe her brother was here in Ruth's house, sitting beside her. Stretching her fingers out, she laid her hand on his sleeve as though to convince herself he was real. With sisterly pride, she took in his neatly trimmed dark hair, crisp black shirt, and starched clergy collar. Her brother was no longer a boy but a grown man. How long had it been since she was in the same room with him? Since they'd shared even a cup of coffee together?

He smiled. "You look good, Liv. Are you keeping well?" His brown eyes searched hers.

"I'm doing fine." *Mostly.* "How about you? How is life as a priest?"

"Challenging." He laughed, revealing his even white teeth.

So handsome, her brother. All the girls in the neighborhood had been devastated when he'd left for the seminary. Yet Sal had known from the time he became an altar boy at the age of ten that he was destined for the priesthood.

"But it's a rewarding life as well." He set down his cup, his expression suddenly serious. "I saw you at my ordination, Liv."

"I thought so, but I wasn't sure." Olivia offered him a plate of biscuits, which he declined. "I didn't want to ruin your special day, but I had to see you, even if from afar."

"I felt terrible that I didn't acknowledge you. Like I was betraying my own sister." Lines marred his forehead, his dark eyes anxious.

"It's all right. With Papà there, you couldn't risk causing a scene in front of everyone." She smiled. "I'm just glad you're here now. I've missed you so much." Her throat cinched closed. She would *not* cry any more tears today.

"It took me a while to get Mamma to admit why you went away, and when I found out what Papà had done . . ." His jaw clenched. "I've never been so angry with anyone."

Relief spilled through her, so incredibly thankful that her brother didn't despise her as she'd feared. "I know," she said softly. "I'm trying hard to forgive him for what he put me through, but it's not easy."

Sal shifted to face her, his expression solemn. "What about the baby? What happened to him?"

She drew in a breath, steeling herself against the pain that caught her unaware at times. "Children's Aid took him. I imagine some couple has adopted him by now." She swallowed hard. "I can't believe Matteo's over a year old already. I only pray he has parents who will give him the love he deserves." Her voice broke.

Sal reached for her hand and squeezed. "Oh, Liv. That must have been so hard."

"Harder than anything I've ever had to do. Even harder than saying good-bye to Rory."

He let out a sigh. "I heard what happened to him too. Such a shame the way things turned out."

Shame didn't begin to describe the situation. "I have to believe that God has a reason for everything," she said. "And that one day it will all make sense."

Sal nodded and squeezed her fingers again. "I've been praying for you and your son every day since I found out. And I want you to know that no matter what Papà says, I will never disown you." His brown eyes grew damp. "I love you, Liv. You're my sister, and I will always be here for you."

She reached over to wrap him in a hug. This boy—now man— who'd shared her childhood and was now an ordained servant of God. "I love you too, Sal. Just knowing you're on my side makes all the difference."

He cleared his throat and looked around the room. She tried to picture the house as he was seeing it. The rich carpet, the fancy furnishings. What would he think of all this luxury?

"Are you happy here?" he asked, his eyes searching hers.

"I am, Sal." Despite her heartache over Abigail, it was true. "Ruth has been so kind, and helping these women makes me feel useful. Like something good has come from my ordeal."

He nodded. "Serving others is a good step toward healing. I'm proud of you, Liv."

"Thank you." Her lips trembled. "It's been a long time since anyone said that to me."

He gave her another quick hug, then got to his feet. "I should get back to the rectory now."

Reluctantly, she rose as well. "I wish you could stay longer, but I'm so happy you came." She managed a faint smile. "When you see Mamma, tell her I'm all right and that I love her."

"I will."

In the front entry, Sal paused. "Who was that Darius fellow you were with? Is he a suitor?"

Her cheeks burned at the memory of the kiss they'd shared. "I'm not sure. Right now, he's a good friend."

"Friends are important."

"Especially ones who know your mistakes and accept you anyway."

His expression turned grave, his brows scrunching together.

"I'd be neglecting my duty if I didn't ask you this." He looked her in the eye. "Have you been to confession, Olivia?"

If anyone other than Sal had asked her that question, she'd have unleashed her Italian temper. But she knew her brother's heart, knew he was genuinely concerned for the state of her soul. "Yes, Sal, I have." She didn't tell him how unpleasant the experience had been and that she hadn't been back to their church because she no longer felt welcome there.

"Remember, Liv, God loves you no matter what. I hope you believe that, because you deserve to find happiness in your life."

"Thank you, Sal. And who knows, maybe I'll come to hear you say Mass one Sunday." She winked at him.

"I'd like that." With a laugh, he bent to kiss her forehead. "I hope to see you again soon."

After Olivia had walked him down the sidewalk, she returned to the house and let out a sigh. "Thank you, Lord, for your gifts today," she whispered. "It was just what I needed."

She touched her lips with a smile, the memory of Darius's kiss spreading warmth all the way to her core. And for the first time in a very long while, Olivia dared to believe that her shattered heart might survive after all.

The next morning, Darius walked into the kitchen, filled with the delicious scent of bacon and freshly brewed coffee, and grabbed his mother in a bear hug. "Good morning, Mamá. Isn't it a beautiful day?"

"Darius, you squeeze me like a lemon." She batted him with a dish towel, but her eyes danced with delight. "Why are you so happy today?"

Because I kissed Olivia. And she kissed me back.

"Do I need a reason?" He tossed her a grin.

She narrowed her eyes at him. "You have a new girlfriend?"

He ducked his head into the icebox and took out the orange

juice. "Just because I'm in a good mood doesn't mean I have a girlfriend." But his pulse scrambled at the image of Olivia's warm brown eyes and full lips.

"Sofia says you were kissing a lady in the park yesterday."

He choked on a swallow of juice, and liquid spilled down his chin. He grabbed a cloth from the sink to wipe his face, and when he turned around, his mother was watching him, one hand on her hip.

"Sofia needs to learn when to keep quiet," he muttered.

"Sofia's papá shouldn't kiss strange women in front of her." Scowling, she waved a spatula at him.

Warmth bled into his cheeks. "I didn't intend to. It just sort of happened."

"Who is this woman?" She went back to the stove, where eggs and bacon sizzled in the pan.

"Her name is Olivia." He wiped the counter, trying to act nonchalant. "She helps women at a local maternity home."

"Is she Greek?"

"She's Italian. She comes from an immigrant family like ours."

Mamá pursed her lips. "She sounds . . . all right."

His lips twitched. That was high praise coming from his mother.

"Are you going to marry this Olivia?"

"I don't know, Mamá. We were just friends until yesterday. Then things changed and we haven't had a chance to talk about it."

Mamá flipped the eggs and peered over her shoulder at him. "You bring this Olivia to dinner one day soon."

"Yes, ma'am."

The telephone rang, and Darius rushed to answer it. Anything to escape his mother's scrutiny.

"Can I speak to Darius Reed, please?" a deep voice said.

"This is he."

"Darius, this is Horace Cheeseman."

Chills of foreboding raced along Darius's spine. He glanced at the clock on the wall. Why would Mr. Cheeseman be phoning him at home on a Saturday? At seven forty-five in the morning?

"I'm sorry to bother you, but I have some bad news about Meredith." The man's voice cracked.

"What is it?" Maybe Mr. Cheeseman was just learning that Meredith hadn't gone out west after all. That she'd found somewhere else to spend her confinement.

"My daughter is dead."

The blunt words struck Darius like a blow to the chest. He sank onto a chair, his mind spinning. That wasn't possible. The man had to be mistaken. "I don't understand. She told me she was going to a maternity home in Ottawa. How could she be dead?"

"She didn't go to a maternity home." Mr. Cheeseman sounded gritty, as though he'd swallowed sandpaper. "She went to some back-alley quack and paid him to take care of her problem. But she developed a serious infection and ended up in the hospital, too afraid to call her mother or me. At least that's what the nurse at the hospital told us when she called with the news."

Darius raked a hand through his hair. "I . . . I don't know what to say. I can't believe this. . . ." His throat seized up. Meredith was gone? Lovely, vivacious Meredith . . .

"Since you cared for my daughter once, I felt you should know."

"I'm so incredibly sorry for your loss, sir."

"The funeral will be on Wednesday morning at St. Cornelius Church. Eleven o'clock."

"I'll be there, sir. If there's anything I can do—"

The connection cut out, leaving nothing but silence buzzing in Darius's ear, along with the sinking sensation that he may have somehow played an unwitting part in Meredith's demise.

Olivia tried not to let the fact that she hadn't heard from Darius since their kiss in the park disturb her. He took classes on Saturday, she remembered. And Sunday was spent with his family, going to church, and then having Sunday dinner. But by noon on Monday, while she helped Mrs. Neale make sandwiches, Olivia couldn't help but wonder if he regretted his impulsive action and was now too embarrassed to call her.

Margaret entered the kitchen with her son on her shoulder. "I think we'll have to call Mrs. Dinglemire soon," she announced. "Cherise has been complaining about a sore back. That's how my labor started."

Momentary anxiety hit Olivia at the thought of another baby coming, but she forced herself to breathe. She would have to get used to this happening on a frequent basis and not panic every time. She cut the last sandwich and placed it on a plate. "Thanks for telling me. We'll be sure to keep a close eye on her."

Margaret bounced the baby, who had started to squirm.

Olivia took a closer look at Margaret, noticing the fatigue around her eyes. "Why don't I take Calvin for a bit while you get some rest?" She wiped her hands on her apron.

Margaret's eyes widened. "Are you sure?"

"Positive." She held out her arms. "I'm feeling a lot better now. I can handle a baby again."

Margaret still seemed uncertain as she handed over the red-faced bundle. "I think he needs a diaper change."

"I can do that. You go take a bath or a nap. If he gets hungry, I'll come and find you."

Relief flooded Margaret's features. "Thanks. I could use a nap. I didn't get much sleep last night."

"Go on then. We'll save some sandwiches for you."

Two hours went by in a flash. Tending to the baby kept Olivia occupied, with no time to dwell on Darius. She tried to sit with Cherise in order to keep an eye on her, but the girl wanted no part of her company, preferring to be alone with her discomfort. So instead Olivia rocked little Calvin in the nursery. She had just decided that it was near his feeding time when a groan sounded from the next room, followed by a string of French words that Olivia didn't understand.

She took the baby into the next bedroom. Whether Cherise wanted company or not, she was getting it.

The girl was bent over the bed, one hand at the small of her back.

"*Bonjour*, Cherise. Looks like you're having contractions. Remember to breathe through the pain."

Cherise glared over her shoulder. "How can I breathe when it feels like a knife is stabbing me in the back?"

"I know it's hard, but it does help." Olivia could recall the discomfort of her contractions in vivid detail and had blessed the nurse for helping her manage the pain. "I'll call Mrs. Dinglemire and be right back."

"Wait." Cherise huffed. "Promise me something, Olivia."

"Of course. What is it?"

"Promise you won't let that woman near my bébé."

Cherise didn't need to elaborate. Olivia knew exactly whom she meant. She walked over and laid a hand on Cherise's shoulder. "I promise no one will take your child. Mrs. Dinglemire and Dr. Henshaw both know your wishes, as do Ruth and I." She shifted Calvin in her arms. "Keep breathing. I think your little one might be making his or her grand entrance very soon."

Olivia's prediction proved correct. A beautiful little girl was born just after midnight. Olivia cried tears of joy along with Cherise at the first sight of her. Cherise named her baby Angelique, and indeed the infant looked like an angel.

Olivia helped Mrs. Dinglemire get the pair cleaned up and settled. By the time they finished, it was one o'clock in the morning. The midwife then shooed everyone out of the room.

Bone-tired herself, Olivia was all too happy to leave Cherise in the midwife's capable hands and flop into bed with no worries to hinder her rest. For the first time since Abigail had left, Olivia believed she would truly sleep well.

As her eyes drifted closed, her gaze fell on the picture Sofia had drawn for her, and she floated off to sleep with a smile on her face.

33

On the morning of Meredith's funeral, Darius trudged downstairs to the kitchen, certain he would need a cup of strong coffee to get him through this day. But no enticing aroma met his nose.

He pushed through the swinging door and stopped short. Mamá was dressed in her going-out clothes, a small hat perched on top of her hair.

"Mamá? Are you going somewhere?"

"I have to take Helena to the emergency department. I'm going next door to wait with her for the taxi."

"What happened?"

"She fell down the basement stairs. Her arm might be broken." Mamá snapped her handbag closed. "I'll do my best to be back in time for you to go to the funeral."

Darius held back a sigh. Already this day wasn't going his way. But his mother couldn't refuse to help her friend, a recent widow who was having trouble coping with life alone.

"You go on," Darius told her. "And don't worry about Sofia. I'm sure I can find someone to watch her for an hour."

Mamá tugged on her gloves. "You can always take Sofia to the church with you if you must."

True. Sofia knew how to behave in church, having attended

the Greek Orthodox service every Sunday since babyhood. But he didn't want to expose her to this tragedy if he could help it. With her curious mind, she would likely ask all sorts of uncomfortable questions that the Cheesemans didn't need to hear on this terrible day.

Once it was late enough that people would be up, Darius took out his list of usual babysitters and began calling. Half an hour later, he hung up the telephone with a loud exhale. Every possible person he could think of was busy. Granted, it was last minute, but surely someone was available. He even thought of asking his father to come home to watch her, but he knew Papá would only take Sofia back to the garage while he worked, and that was not a good solution.

Guilt churned in his stomach. He needed to attend this service, needed to make peace with God and with himself for his part in what happened to Meredith. If he hadn't been so judgmental, if he'd married her as promised, she and her baby would still be alive.

He dragged a hand over his jaw. The only other option he could think of was Olivia. Before he could change his mind, he dialed Ruth Bennington's number. As he waited, he realized he should have called Olivia sooner to let her know about Meredith, but he hadn't been thinking straight, still attempting to come to grips with the tragedy.

"Darius. It's good to hear from you." Olivia sounded cheerful, if not a bit wary.

A new tug of guilt hit him. He hadn't talked to her since their kiss in the park. What must she think of him? But he had no time to worry about that now.

"Hello, Olivia. I have some unfortunate news to tell you and a favor to ask."

"Oh?"

He hated the trepidation in her voice. But could he blame her for being distrustful? He sighed. "I don't know how to say this. . . ." He paused. "Meredith passed away on Saturday."

Silence pulsed over the line.

"No." Her whisper was barely audible. "What happened?"

Darius looked around the kitchen to make sure Sofia wasn't within earshot. "She went to some back-alley doctor to take care of her . . . situation and developed a terrible infection. She never recovered."

"Oh, Darius. I'm so sorry." He could hear the tears in her voice.

His throat constricted. Somehow, her sorrow made the tragedy even harder to bear. "I want to attend the funeral this morning, but my mother had a bit of an emergency come up. I was wondering if I could impose on you to watch Sofia for an hour or two?"

A beat of silence passed, then, "Of course. I'd be happy to."

"Thank you." His shoulders sagged. "I'll be over soon."

While Olivia waited for Darius to arrive, she paced the parlor floor, battling to control her grief at the loss of such a lovely young woman as well as her anger at the unnecessary waste of a life. She kept picturing Meredith on the day she'd met her, the pretty but nervous girl who had so much ahead of her. What had made her seek such a dangerous solution to her problem instead of finding another maternity home like she'd intended?

If only Olivia had been able to convince Meredith to come to Bennington Place. At least then she and her child would still be alive.

Olivia blinked back her tears, determined to be in control when Darius and Sofia arrived. The little girl didn't need to know anything about this. And Olivia needed to be strong for Darius. She could only imagine how he must be feeling. After all, he'd been planning to marry the woman not that long ago.

When she heard Darius's car pull up, Olivia went to greet them at the curb. As he got out, she wasn't prepared for the haggard lines hugging his face or the hollowness shadowing his eyes. Going on instinct, she stepped up to wrap him in a hug. His arms came around her, and a shudder of emotion rumbled through his chest.

"It's all my fault," he murmured. "I should have done more for her. I should have tried harder. . . ."

Olivia leaned back to look at him. "You can't blame yourself for her actions, Darius. If she was so determined, you couldn't have stopped her."

Tears swam in his eyes, and he drew in a ragged breath. "I keep telling myself that, but I can't stop feeling guilty."

A tug on her arm had Olivia looking down.

"My daddy is sad, Miss Olivia." Sofia wore a tiny frown.

Olivia bent down beside her on the sidewalk. "I know, sweetie. Maybe we can make him a picture to cheer him up."

That got a smile and a nod.

"I have to go now or I'll miss the service," Darius said. He laid a hand on Sofia's head. "Be good for Miss Olivia, Mouse. I'll be back in a few hours." He looked at Olivia. "Thank you again for doing this."

"No trouble at all." She forced a bright tone to her voice. "Sofia and I will have fun together." She hoped for a smile from him, but his features remained grim as he nodded and headed back to the car.

Watching him drive away, Olivia had never felt so torn. Darius shouldn't have to do this alone. He deserved to have someone by his side to help him face this terrible day. But as she and Sofia entered the house, she comforted herself with the fact that she *was* doing something to help him by watching his daughter.

After settling the girl at the dining room table with paper and a pencil, Olivia opened the morning paper that sat in the middle of the table. She turned to the obituaries to find the information on Meredith's funeral. The church wasn't that far away. Two streetcar stops at most. Her mind whirled until she came to a bold decision. She might not be able to attend the service, but she and Sofia could be waiting for Darius afterward. Seeing two friendly faces might be just what he needed after such a sorrowful morning.

She folded the newspaper and set it down with a decisive slap. "Sofia, honey, how would you like to take a streetcar ride?"

Once the funeral was over, Darius numbly followed the large congregation out of the church, eager to be free of the cloying scent of lilies that permeated the space. Once outside, he inhaled the fresh air, doing his best to ignore the flower-laden casket being loaded into the hearse. The cemetery where Meredith would be buried was on the other side of town, in a plot owned by Horace's family.

The story the Cheesemans were telling anyone who asked was that Meredith had gone to visit some cousins in Ottawa, and, while there, she contracted a deadly virus.

Only a select few knew the gut-wrenching truth.

A fact that only increased the guilt churning inside him.

If he'd agreed to marry Meredith as he'd intended, she would still be alive. Her child would still be alive. Instead, he'd worn his moral superiority like a righteous cloak and dismissed her plight as a personal affront. Why hadn't he been more understanding and compassionate, tried harder to help her? Now, instead of celebrating their daughter's wedding, the Cheesemans were burying their eldest child.

Darius's tears had flowed freely during the service, especially during the eulogies given by her parents and younger sister. And now, as he descended the church steps, grief ate a hole in his chest.

I'm sorry I failed you, Meredith. You didn't deserve my anger or my judgment.

When he reached the grassy area below, a hand clapped him on the back.

"Such a shame about the girl," Mr. Walcott said. "I'm sure this must have come as quite a shock."

Darius had forgotten his boss planned to attend the funeral.

It made sense since he and Horace Cheeseman went back a long way, which was how they'd acquired Mr. Cheeseman's business in the first place.

"Shock doesn't begin to describe it," Darius said quietly. "I still can't believe someone so young and full of life could be gone so fast."

Walcott nodded grimly. "I'm heading back to the office, but don't come in if you're not feeling up to it."

"Thanks. I appreciate that."

"If you'll excuse me, I need to pay my respects." Walcott headed over to where the Cheesemans were accepting condolences.

Darius stiffened, bracing for the task that he would have to do as well.

Once Mr. Walcott had spoken with the couple and had headed off, Darius knew he couldn't delay any longer. With dread roiling his stomach, he approached Meredith's parents. Sissy leaned on her mother's arm, weeping quietly. A soft breeze toyed with the dark fabric of the family's mourning attire. The black netting of Mrs. Cheeseman's hat barely concealed the grief hugging her features.

"I'm so very sorry for your loss," he said. "Meredith was . . ." His mind went blank as Mrs. Cheeseman stared daggers at him. "Meredith will be greatly missed."

His condolences sounded feeble even to his own ears, yet what could he possibly say to ease their pain?

Mr. Cheeseman took him by the arm and stepped out of the fray, seemingly to give them a bit of privacy.

"Thank you for coming, Darius." Deep grooves were etched in Horace Cheeseman's face. He appeared to have aged a decade in a matter of weeks.

"I feel terrible, sir. If I hadn't ended our engagement, things might have turned out so differently."

Horace let out a tortured breath. "I understand why you did. I likely would've done the same thing were I in your shoes."

Darius's throat swelled with emotion, and he could only nod. At least Horace didn't blame him. If only he could grant himself the same absolution.

The crowd around him pressed in to greet the family, forcing Darius aside. He shoved his hands in his pockets and moved out of the way, not sure what to do next. There would be a reception at the family's residence, but he couldn't bring himself to go back there, to remember Meredith so young and vibrant on the night he'd proposed. Instead, he headed blindly across the church property, not even sure where he'd parked his car.

When he looked up, he blinked. Then blinked again. Olivia stood on the sidewalk, holding Sofia by the hand. When Olivia gave him a tentative wave, he couldn't respond. Couldn't make sense of her presence here.

Then a sudden, irrational fear gripped him. Was something wrong with Sofia? Or had Mamá called Olivia with some bad news? He'd left Mrs. Bennington's telephone number on the kitchen table for his mother so she wouldn't worry when she returned. A thousand thoughts raced through his mind as he forced his feet into motion.

Sofia's big smile eased some of his panic. "Hi, Daddy. We came to cheer you up."

He swallowed and gave Olivia an inquiring look. "Is everything all right?"

"Everything's fine. We thought you could use some friendly faces when you came out of the service." Her brown eyes, wide and luminous, shimmered with sympathy and possibly something deeper.

Sofia waved a piece of paper at him. "I made you a drawing, Daddy. Like I did for Miss Olivia." She held it out to him. "You can open it later."

"Thank you, Mouse." He attempted to smile but couldn't quite manage it.

Olivia glanced at the crowd behind him and frowned. "Do

you have to go to the cemetery or the reception? I should have considered that."

"No. I don't think I could bear going back to their house right now. And Mr. Walcott doesn't expect me in the office either."

"Well then, if you have no plans, I thought we could take Sofia down to the harbor to look at the boats." Olivia smiled up at him, and the horrible grip of sorrow that held his lungs in a chokehold released long enough for him to take a full breath.

"I'd like that," he said. He inhaled again, deeper this time. "I'd like that very much."

As he led them down the sidewalk toward his car, he realized that he'd never been more grateful to see anyone, and he thanked God for sending this angel to his rescue.

34

Olivia leaned her head back against the front seat of Darius's Ford, the warmth of the sun spilling through the window making her drowsy. They'd spent a lovely afternoon eating hot dogs by the water, watching the big boats come and go, and skipping stones over the lake. The long walk had tuckered Sofia out, and she was fast asleep in the back seat as they pulled up in front of the maternity home.

"Thank you again for watching Sofia today." Darius turned off the engine. "I really didn't want to bring her to that funeral."

"I understand. It's not the place for a child."

Darius gave her a sideways look. "I'm sure she must have asked you a hundred questions."

"She did, but don't worry. I managed to deflect most of them."

His mouth twitched. "And thank you for this afternoon. It was exactly what I needed."

She smiled, glad to see the easing of the haggardness from his features. "You've done so much for me. I'm only happy I could return the favor."

"Olivia." On a sigh, he leaned closer.

She held her breath for a moment, thinking he might kiss her, but he nodded toward Sofia in the back seat.

"There's so much I want to say, but now's not the time. Could

I . . ." He hesitated. "Would you go to dinner with me one night soon?"

Her breathing hitched in her chest. Was he asking her on a date?

Her head told her it was foolish to even consider such a thing, but her heart leapt at the chance to spend more time with him. She was tired of fighting her feelings. Tired of denying herself. She drew in a breath and nodded. "I'd like that."

The lines in his forehead eased. "All right then. I'll make arrangements and call you."

He got out of the car and came around to open her door, then helped her out, holding her hand a minute longer than necessary. Nerves danced in her stomach, and when she looked into those captivating blue eyes, she couldn't seem to look away.

She cleared her throat. "Um, I should tell you that Sofia invited me to her birthday party, but if that would be too awkward, I can give her an excuse why I can't make it."

"No, I'd love for you to come. As long as you think you can handle a Greek celebration." His eyes glimmered with a hint of his usual teasing.

"Should I be nervous?"

"I'm not sure what Italian parties are like, but ours are boisterous affairs. Loud singing is usually involved, and sometimes dishes get broken. On purpose."

"Oh." She blinked. "You might need to give me a lesson in Greek culture before then."

He laughed out loud. "I could tell you more, but I wouldn't want to scare you off."

She grew serious, mesmerized by the way his thumb caressed her palm. "If my past hasn't scared you away, I think I can handle some singing and a few broken dishes."

He gave her a long look that ignited her pulse, then slowly brought his mouth to hers. Her heart fluttered in her chest, her body heating from the delicious warmth of his lips and the strength of his arms around her.

"Aha! I knew I was right about you people." A hostile male voice broke through the bliss of their embrace. "Nothing but brazen hussies living in that so-called 'maternity home.'"

Olivia jerked out of Darius's arms, horrified to see Mr. Simmons standing on the road, scowling at them.

Heat flooded her face. They'd been kissing in broad daylight on a public walkway. How could she have been so careless?

Darius stiffened and moved in front of her as though to shield her. "It was a simple kiss good-bye, sir. But I apologize if we offended you in any way."

"Darn right, I'm offended. Luckily, I won't have to worry about this happening much longer. The streetwalkers will be gone soon enough." He spat on the road and turned back toward his house.

What did he mean by that?

Darius turned back to Olivia, his brows drawn together. "Forgive me. I should have been more careful of your reputation."

She shook her head and met his troubled gaze. "Mr. Simmons is always spouting off. I've learned to ignore him for the most part." Her lips tipped up. "Besides, it was worth it." In fact, she half hoped he'd repeat the offense.

His nostrils flared, and a smile stretched his lips. "I'd better leave before I'm tempted to do it again." He dropped a kiss on her cheek, then headed back to the car. "I'll see you soon, Olivia Rosetti."

On Saturday night, Olivia paced the floor of her bedroom, waiting for Darius to arrive, and prayed the nerves in her stomach would subside. Would she even know how to act on a date? All she and Rory used to do was share a soda at the local diner. This outing with Darius would be a completely new experience for her.

She stopped in front of the mirror to once again check her appearance. On Ruth's insistence, she'd gone shopping for a new dress and had chosen a rose-colored chiffon with short sleeves and tiny covered buttons down the front. As per the current style, the dress sported a thin belt at the waist, but it was the gauzy overlay on the bodice that made the dress seem so elegant. She'd also bought new high-heeled pumps and a matching hat. Overall, the purchases might be a bit extravagant for one dinner, but she hadn't been shopping in ages. Ruth had insisted on providing Olivia with a small salary, and with little else to spend her money on, she didn't feel too guilty for splurging.

When the doorbell rang several minutes later, she hurried down the stairs to answer it.

Darius stood on the porch, a box of chocolates and a bouquet of pink roses in his arms. "Good evening." He came in and handed her the gifts. "These are for you."

"Thank you." Olivia's hands trembled as she accepted the offerings. "You didn't have to do that." She smiled, taking a better look at him in the entryway lighting.

He wore a blue suit, white shirt, and striped tie. His hair was slicked back off his forehead, making his eyes appear even bluer. And when they trained on her with such focused intensity, her pulse skipped up two notches.

"You look beautiful," he said in a husky voice.

"Thank you." She bent to inhale the heady scent of the roses. Did he know they were her favorite?

Two heads poked out from the parlor. Monica, the newest resident, and Patricia, who was due in a few weeks, watched them with wide eyes.

"My, don't you two look fancy," Monica said with a wink.

Olivia's face grew warm. "Darius, this is Monica and Patricia."

"Nice to meet you, ladies." He gave a bow, his lips twitching.

Olivia handed the flowers and candy to Patricia. "Could you take care of these for me? And help yourselves to a chocolate." Then, before the women could comment further, Olivia turned back to Darius. "Shall we?"

"By all means."

"Don't keep her out too late," Monica called. "Mrs. Bennington is a stickler for curfews."

"Ignore them." Olivia closed the front door to block out their giggles.

Grinning, Darius escorted her to his car and helped her inside, then started the engine and pulled away from the curb.

Several blocks later, Olivia shifted on the seat, searching for a topic of conversation. They'd always had things to talk about before, but now that they were on an actual date, her lips seemed glued shut.

"I made reservations at a Greek restaurant," Darius said as he steered the car around a corner. "I thought you might like an introduction to our cuisine before Sofia's party." He hesitated. "But if that doesn't appeal to you, we can go somewhere else."

"No, that sounds perfect. I'd love to try something new."

He smiled, his features relaxing.

"Actually, I haven't been to very many restaurants," she told him. "My mother always insisted that her cooking was better than anywhere else."

Darius laughed. "My mother feels the same way. She has yet to eat in a restaurant."

The tension in Olivia's stomach eased a fraction. They did have a lot in common, simply by virtue of their families being from Europe. She couldn't help stealing sidelong glances at his strong profile and remembering his amazing kisses. Would he try again tonight? The very idea made her pulse climb. Not since Rory had taken her to a school dance had she been this nervous.

Twenty minutes later, they pulled up across from a restaurant called Mikos. The neighborhood had a European feel, the shops and eateries reminding her of the area where her parents lived.

Soon they were seated at a table for two by the front window, near a charming brick hearth. Tall pillars with carved vines flanked several large Greek statues draped in flowing togas. A display of wine bottles and grapes held a prominent place near the hostess's desk.

"It's beautiful," she said as Darius opened the menu.

"A little exaggerated, but it gives the atmosphere of Greece."

"Have you ever been there?"

"Sadly, I haven't. My parents never had enough money to take us all back to their homeland. I have three older siblings, so it would have been expensive."

"I didn't know you had siblings."

"A brother and two sisters, all much older than me and all living in different parts of Canada with families of their own. We get together about once a year." He shrugged. "I wish we could see each other more often, but since we're so far apart, it isn't really feasible."

The waiter arrived then with a large jug. After he poured two glasses of water, he pulled out a pad of paper and a pencil and said something in Greek.

Olivia stared at the foreign words on the menu and realized there was no English to be found. "Would you mind ordering for me?" she whispered.

"Oh, I should have realized. I could translate for you."

"That's all right. I trust you to pick something tasty. Not too spicy, though."

He laughed, then spoke in fluent Greek to the waiter, while the man scribbled down their orders.

Olivia tried not to stare at Darius, but her eyes were drawn to him like a magnet. Every time she was around him, she grew more impressed. The way he handled himself with quiet confidence yet no trace of arrogance. The gentle way he treated his daughter. Even his grief over Meredith's death showed how decent and caring he was.

"Is something the matter?" He watched her, a hint of amusement in his eyes, after the waiter had headed off to the kitchen.

She dropped her gaze to the tablecloth, her cheeks heating. "I was just admiring . . . your tie." She almost groaned. How inane did that sound? Her ears now felt on fire.

He chuckled, as though knowing she hadn't said what she'd

really been thinking. "Thank you. Sofia picked it out for me. She has very good taste."

The waiter returned with a basket of some type of flatbread, which he set in the middle of the table.

Olivia had never been more relieved for an interruption. She plucked a piece from under the cloth and set it on her plate, praying to get her emotions under control before she humiliated herself and ruined the evening.

Darius gazed at Olivia's flushed face and wished he knew what she was thinking. Was this all a bit too much for her? Should he have taken her somewhere less blatantly romantic?

Well, it was too late to second-guess his decision now. He'd have to make the best of the situation.

He tried hard to calm his nerves as he watched her. She looked so incredibly beautiful in the candlelight. He couldn't believe she'd agreed to this outing.

He forced his gaze to his plate. Tonight, he would concentrate on getting to know her better, and hopefully coax her into opening up a bit more about herself. And he wouldn't make the same mistake he had with Meredith. He would offer no criticism or judgment of the events that had changed her life.

"What did you order for us, or is it a surprise?" Her teasing question brought him out of his thoughts.

"No surprise." He smiled, relieved at a turn in the conversation. "I ordered us roast lamb with rice and grilled vegetables. Lamb is a Greek specialty."

"It sounds wonderful. Mrs. Neale does an admirable job cooking for us, but I find her dishes a bit bland. Maybe because I'm used to my mother adding loads of garlic and spices."

"This meal definitely won't be bland." He winked, then took a sip of his water as he mulled ways to bring up the topics he hoped to discuss.

Soft music played in the background. Muted conversation and the occasional burst of laughter sounded from the other guests in a room across the way.

"If it's not too painful," Olivia said softly, "would you tell me about your late wife?"

His hand stilled on his glass. "What would you like to know?" It was a subject he usually avoided at all costs, unless Sofia asked about her mother.

Another couple entered the restaurant, and the hostess seated them several tables away, enough to ensure their privacy, which suited Darius.

"How did you meet? How long were you married?" Olivia gave a tiny shrug.

Maybe it would be cathartic to talk about Selene. Perhaps it was time to test the scab over the wound. "Selene and I grew up on the same street. Our parents were best friends. It became understood that we would marry one day, and when I finished school and got my first job, I proposed. We were married that summer and moved into her parents' house."

"Was Selene Greek as well?"

"Yes. Her family came over around the same time as my parents. We had so much in common, which was the bond that strengthened our relationship. When we learned Selene was expecting, we became our own little family."

Olivia bit her lip. "I wish I'd had the chance to share that with Rory. I wrote to him, of course, but I don't know if he ever received my letters."

He frowned. "Didn't he write back?"

"He might have, but by that time I was in the reformatory. After I was released, I found out that my father had destroyed all his letters."

His chest constricted at the sorrow on her face. "You must have loved him very much."

She raised troubled eyes to his. "At the time, I did. I was so very young, and my father didn't approve of Rory because he wasn't Italian, which made him all the more enticing." She set the bread down on her plate. "We got engaged right before he enlisted, and then I made that one terrible mistake, giving in to him the night before he left."

From her frown, Darius deduced she blamed herself more than Rory.

"I don't wish to speak ill of the dead," he said slowly, "but an honorable man wouldn't have made such a demand, knowing he would be leaving you to bear the possible consequences of his actions."

She nodded. "I went through a great deal of anger thinking about that—not to mention fury with my father for his actions." She straightened her shoulders. "However, I came to realize that living with that type of resentment only harms me and doesn't change anything."

He covered her hand with his. "I don't know if I've told you this, but I admire you greatly for your courage to turn your life into something positive."

She shook her head. "Please don't make me out to be anyone special. I'm only doing what I can to move forward. With God's help, I've found that giving back to others is allowing me to heal." She gave a sad smile. "Well, except for losing Abigail, but that was another lesson."

The desire to comfort her became a physical ache. He wanted to protect her and make sure no harm ever came to her again. "I wish I hadn't reacted so badly when you suggested we marry. I might have spared you one heartache."

Tiny lines appeared between her brows. "Darius, we've been over this. I had no right to put you in such a terrible position."

His gaze faltered. He'd been so judgmental of her and of Meredith. Yet who was he to judge anyone when he was so clearly imperfect himself?

The defeat on Darius's face was almost more than Olivia could stand. Didn't he realize what a kind and caring person he was? That any woman or child would be proud to have him as a husband and father?

The waiter arrived then with their meals. He set the steaming plates down in front of them with a flourish.

Olivia inhaled the savory aroma of meat and spices, and her stomach growled. "This looks delicious."

The waiter said something in Greek, which Darius answered, then he left them alone.

After several minutes of eating, Olivia gained the courage to ask the question weighing on her mind. "You never said how Selene died," she said softly. "Was it an accident?"

His features hardened, and a nerve pulsed in his jaw. "No, it was a deliberate act. Selene and her parents were killed simply because they were Greek. A group of rioters set their store on fire. They were trapped in the back, and the firefighters were too late to save them."

She gasped. "How horrible." She couldn't imagine losing someone that way. How did one go on after such a senseless act of violence?

"The only consolation was that Sofia wasn't with them that day. Sometimes Selene took her to the store."

"Thank God." She blinked hard and took a swallow of water. "You must have been devastated."

"I was. I could barely function for almost a year. And for a long time after that, I tried to shield Sofia from every part of her heritage, determined that she would never suffer such hatred because she was Greek." He set down his knife. "That's part of the reason why I wanted to marry Meredith—to give Sofia a Canadian stepmother as well as the security associated with the Cheeseman name. I'm ashamed at how petty that sounds now."

She studied him for several seconds. Part of her was relieved that he hadn't been madly in love with Meredith and that he'd agreed to marry her for more practical reasons.

"I can understand how you felt," she said. "For a while, I was embarrassed about my heritage too, ashamed that my father was so hostile toward Rory simply because he wasn't Italian. Yet Rory wasn't as accepting of my culture as I would have liked, and if we had ended up together after the war, I don't know if our relationship would have survived." She'd never told that to anyone, barely acknowledging it to herself.

"That's brave to admit."

She gave a small shrug. "I've had a lot of time to think about our relationship and to view things in a more realistic light."

He looked as though he wanted to say something more, but instead he picked up a small dessert menu. "This conversation has gotten far too serious. Would you like some dessert? Baklava is a famous Greek delicacy."

She sat back with a sigh. "I'd love to, but I don't think I could eat another bite."

"That's all right. When you come to Sofia's birthday, you can try my mother's." He grinned. "I may be biased, but I think hers is the best."

Olivia laughed. "I'll remember that."

Darius motioned for the waiter, spoke to him in Greek, and the man returned with the bill. After Darius paid it, he looked over at her. "How would you feel about an after-dinner stroll?" he asked. "There's a pretty park nearby where we could walk off our meal."

She nodded, mesmerized by the glow the candlelight cast over his cheekbones. "I'd like that very much."

Only a short car ride away, Riverdale Park was just as pretty as Darius had described. In the early evening, with the sun just beginning its descent, a golden aura surrounded the tops of the trees, spreading down to the paths that wound through the grassy areas. Several families were finishing up picnics on the rolling lawns, while some adults played ball with the children. The path ahead was crowded with several couples who'd apparently had the same idea for an after-dinner stroll.

Olivia breathed in the smells of fresh air and newly mown grass and released a contented sigh. "It's lovely," she said. "Like an oasis of greenery within the city."

"That's a perfect description," Darius said. "There's even a full-fledged zoo at one end of the park. I've taken Sofia a couple of times. Her favorite is the elephant." He chuckled.

"Are you serious? There's an elephant?"

"There is. Along with lions, monkeys, and alligators." Darius reached for her hand. "Come on, I want to show you a spot I love."

As they increased their pace slightly, he kept her hand tucked in his. He led her down a path away from the main park, where Olivia thought she heard the gentle gurgle of water.

"That's the Don River ahead," Darius said as he guided her over to what looked like a bridge. "Sounds like the water's moving fairly quick tonight."

He tugged her forward, but she hesitated. "I don't really like heights."

"It's not that bad, I promise. Besides, you can hold on to me if it makes you feel better." He grinned, then gave her a brazen wink.

Her stomach gave a slow roll as she followed him, and she was not sure if it was due to the wink or the height.

When they reached the middle of the bridge, he stopped at the railing. "You don't have to look down. Just look out. The view is magnificent."

He was right. Ahead of them, the river stretched as far as she could see, winding its way through the lush valley.

Darius's arm came around her shoulder, and heat from his body enveloped her.

She held her breath, fresh nerves leaping in her stomach.

"Sometimes we fail to appreciate the simple things in life," he said softly. "A stroll through the park. The view from a bridge. A pretty girl to share the evening with." His free hand came up to caress her cheek, his expression serious. "You are so amazing, Olivia. Beautiful inside and out. I'm not sure how it happened, but I think I might be falling in love with you."

Her heart gave a hard thump in her chest, and she blinked, not sure how to respond to his sudden declaration.

"Now that I've come to this realization," he said, "I have no idea what to do about it. Except maybe this." His lips came down on hers, brushing them gently at first, and when she didn't object, he pulled her more firmly against him to deepen the kiss.

Olivia held on to him as the world around her fell away, narrowing down to the sensations coursing through her system. His mouth, firm yet gentle, giving and taking. The warmth of his fingers on her face. The scent of his cologne surrounding them.

She tightened her arms around him and surrendered to the pure pleasure coursing through her.

After a couple of minutes, he pulled back to look at her, his expression dazed. "Wow," he breathed. "I don't think I've ever felt anything quite like that."

The air fairly pulsed with the electricity winding through them, binding them together.

Her heart still thumped too fast in her chest. "Neither have I," she whispered. "And to be honest, it scares me to death."

Olivia's admission thrilled him and at the same time stirred his protective instincts. He tucked her against his chest, keeping his arms around her. "It scares me too. I guess all we can do is entrust our relationship to God."

She nodded. "Sounds like a good place to start."

He bent to give her another kiss, this one more chaste. "Shall we head back to the car?" he asked reluctantly. "It will be getting dark soon."

"I suppose so." When she smiled at him, he had to use all his willpower not to kiss her again or they might never get off the bridge.

The walk back to the car and the drive home passed in a golden haze of bliss. With Olivia at his side, he felt he could take on the entire world. The more he learned about her, the more she surprised him with the depths of her courage and intelligence, her compassion and caring.

When they reached the maternity home, he parked the car and came around to help her out, then walked her to the door, wishing the night didn't have to end.

On the doorstep, she turned to him, her brown eyes glowing under the porch light. "Thank you for tonight, Darius. I had a wonderful time."

"My pleasure." He wanted to ask if he could come over tomorrow, or the next day, not sure how long he could go without seeing her. Instead, he said, "I'll pick you up for Sofia's party next Saturday. Unless I can think of another excuse to see you before then." He gave her a slow grin.

"Do you need an excuse?" She peered up at him through her lashes.

"Actually, I have a very good one," he said huskily. Then he captured her mouth in another lingering kiss that left his brain buzzing. "Good night, Olivia."

"Good night." She opened the door and went in, then turned around to wave.

Walking backward down the flagstones, he gave her a salute, then almost crashed into the gate. With a self-conscious laugh, he let himself out and got into his car.

No doubt about it, he was in way over his head here. But with this powerful feeling of euphoria rushing through his system, making him feel more alive than ever, he wouldn't change a thing.

35

Olivia hummed as she dusted the furniture in the office. It had been two days since her date with Darius, and she was having a hard time keeping the smile from her face every time she remembered being held in his arms. Arms that made her feel safe and protected, sheltered from reality. And those wonderful kisses—the kind that drugged a girl's senses and almost made her forget her own name.

Fortunately, she trusted Darius not to take things too far, unlike Rory, who had used her fear of losing him to compromise her morals. Darius knew what Olivia had been through and had seen the dire consequences—not only with Olivia, but with Meredith as well. Plus, he'd been married before, so he understood the sacredness of a physical union. She had no doubt that he would never put her in that position.

"I believe that's the fourth time you've dusted that row of books." Ruth's amused voice came from the door of the office.

Olivia startled and turned to face her, heat climbing into her cheeks. "Sorry. I guess I was daydreaming."

Ruth took a seat at the desk. "I don't have to ask what—or should I say whom—you were dreaming about."

That same smile bloomed on Olivia's face again.

"I take it your date was a success?" Ruth pulled out a pencil and opened the ledger.

A tug of guilt pinched Olivia's conscience. She hadn't seen Ruth much since Saturday. The poor woman always seemed to be working or attending meetings in town. Olivia had been too wrapped up first in her grief over Abigail and then in her romantic haze to pay attention to her friend.

"The date went very well. But I want to hear what's going on with you. What are all these mysterious outings you've been going to?"

Ruth rubbed the bridge of her nose. "I've been meeting with my solicitor."

"Your solicitor?" Olivia set the duster on the desktop. "Is there a problem I should know about?"

"I suppose I might as well tell you." Ruth laid down her pen and removed her glasses, her gaze steady. "I'm having him rewrite my will. I've decided to leave the house and the property to you."

Olivia grasped the arm of the chair. "What?"

"It makes sense, Olivia. I'll be gone from this earth long before you, and when I am, I want you to be able to continue our work here with no legal impediments. Bennington Place will be yours."

Olivia's hand went to her throat. "I don't know what to say." She couldn't begin to understand Ruth's generosity. "What about your grandson? Shouldn't the house pass to him?"

"I haven't left Thomas out completely. He'll get whatever is left. Besides, he's already inherited the balance of my son and daughter-in-law's estate. And, sadly, my grandson has no sentimental attachment to me or this house." She sighed and squared her shoulders. "Anyway, I've put the matter in the Lord's hands and in my lawyer's. That's the best I can do for now." Ruth gave a rather forced smile. "Let's change the subject, shall we? I've been thinking we should do something fun for the ladies this weekend. Something a little out of the ordinary. Maybe we'll have a game night or play some music and sing songs. Something to bring a little merriment into our lives."

"That's a marvelous idea." Olivia clapped her hands together. "We could make a cake or bake cookies. And have punch. I'll ask Mrs. Neale if she has any good recipes."

"Excellent. We'll make it very festive."

"Can we do it on Friday, since I have plans for Saturday?" Olivia asked.

"Another date?" Ruth's brow rose.

Heat infused Olivia's cheeks. "Actually, I've been invited to Sofia's fifth birthday party. Which reminds me, I have to go shopping for a gift. Maybe I could pick up some decorations while I'm out."

Ruth nodded, the lines around her eyes easing. Yet their usual sparkle was missing. "This is exactly what we need around here. Everyone can forget their problems and have a little fun for a change."

Olivia hated to ruin the moment, but from her friend's down-hearted demeanor, she had to ask. "Is anything else bothering you, Ruth?"

Ruth let out a long breath. "The city council meetings resume in a few weeks' time. Our alderman contacted me to say that Mr. Simmons will be presenting his petition against Bennington Place at the first fall meeting. I've heard he has close to five hundred signatures."

Olivia flew to her feet. "That man is such a nuisance." She paced to the bookcase and back. "We have to be there to counteract his petition. If only some of the women would come too and testify about the benefits the home provides. But I don't think any of them would agree to do that."

"What about you, Olivia?"

"Me?"

"Your passion for the cause inspired me. Perhaps if you told the council what made you want to open a maternity home, it would help to sway the vote."

Olivia's legs began to shake. She could never get up before a panel of council members and share her shameful tale. To do so would destroy any chance she ever had at regaining her respectability. "I don't think so, Ruth. I'm sorry."

Ruth regarded her with a faint air of disappointment. "It's all right. We'll have others to plead our case. I'm sure it will be enough."

Olivia hated that she wasn't brave enough to do what Ruth asked. But the mere thought of it made her stomach churn and her palms sweat.

The telephone on the desk rang. Ruth answered it, then handed the receiver to Olivia. "It's for you. Someone named Joannie."

A flood of guilt rushed through Olivia. Despite her good intentions, she'd never gone back to visit her friend. What must Joannie think of her?

Ruth slipped out of the room, giving Olivia some privacy. After a moment to collect herself, she spoke into the receiver. "Joannie, how are you? I'm sorry I had to cancel my last visit."

"That's all right. I know it can't be easy coming back here. Besides, I have great news."

Olivia's tense muscles loosened. Joannie had never sounded so cheerful. "What is it?"

"I'm getting out of this hellhole early. Next week, to be exact." Her excitement was palpable even over the phone.

"That's wonderful," Olivia said. "Are you still planning to stay with me for a while until you get a job?" Her mind raced with the preparations she'd have to make for Joannie's arrival.

The silence on the line gave Olivia her first niggle of worry.

"Actually, that's why I'm calling. I've made other plans. I hope you don't mind."

Something in her tone had warning bells ringing in Olivia's head. "Of course not. I'm happy you have somewhere to go. Did your family come around after all?" She prayed that was the case.

"Not exactly."

"Then where are you going?"

A long pause ensued. Olivia's fingers tightened on the receiver.

"Jimmy came to see me. He said he misses me like crazy and asked me to move in with him. He's got a place in a rooming house near the garage where he works. And once I find a job, we'll be able to get a better place."

Oh, Joannie. Olivia pressed a hand to her forehead. This was the last thing her friend needed. A sure way to sabotage her fresh start. "Are you sure that's a good idea? You could do anything you choose with your life. You could go back to school—"

"I don't want to go to school. I want to marry Jimmy, and as soon as we have enough money saved, that's what we're going to do." A pause. "I thought you'd be happy for me."

Olivia winced at the hurt in Joannie's voice, but how could she act pleased when the girl was about to make a terrible mistake? She inhaled and tried to quell her misgivings. "As long as you're happy, then I am too. Promise me you'll keep in touch?"

"I promise."

"Do you want me to be there when you're released?"

"No, Jimmy's coming to get me. He's got a surprise planned."

Olivia's stomach twisted tighter than the phone cord. She could only imagine what that would entail. "Be careful, Joannie. You don't want to end up in the same situation a second time."

"That's not gonna happen. I know better now."

Olivia bit back additional words of caution, not wanting to alienate the girl altogether. "All right. Well, you'll have to come for a visit once you're settled."

"I will. Look, I gotta run now. Take care and wish me luck."

The connection ended before Olivia could even say good-bye. Slowly, she hung up the receiver, an unsettled feeling swirling inside her. Would she ever hear from Joannie again? She let out a long sigh, then bowed her head.

Lord, please watch over Joannie and protect her from any further harm.

———— ❖ ————

Later that afternoon, Olivia stepped out of Woolworth's Department Store onto the sidewalk. Despite her success in finding a perfect gift for Sofia, her mind kept drifting back to her conversation with Joannie. She hated that her friend was returning to the same circumstances that had caused all her problems in the first place. But there was nothing Olivia could do to help the situation, except pray for her friend.

Olivia waited for the next streetcar, paid her fare, and sat with her parcels on her lap. As the streets passed by, her thoughts turned to her family. Her visit with Sal had resurrected a deep longing to reconnect with her parents. Sal had said her mother missed her. And she desperately missed Mamma. Why should her father dictate that they couldn't see each other? If he wanted nothing to do with her, so be it. But she had every right to see her mother. At the very least, she had a right to patronize Rosetti's Market, and if she happened to run into Mamma there, well, he couldn't stop that.

Olivia checked her watch. It was still early enough in the afternoon to squeeze in a trip to the store. Before she could change her mind, she got ready to disembark and catch the next bus going north.

Thirty minutes later, she walked slowly down the street toward the store, enjoying the late-August sunshine. This time, Olivia paused to drink in the sights and smells of her old neighborhood. Mrs. Egan changing the mannequin in the window of her dress shop; old Mr. Franco sweeping the sidewalk in front of the barber shop; the enticing aroma of garlic and onions drifting down from the open windows above the stores. Each brought back cherished memories of her childhood.

When she reached Rosetti's, she slowed to a stop and eyed the women who stood by the sidewalk bins, fingering the nectarines and peaches. Olivia didn't recognize them, but it didn't mean they wouldn't know her. With a determined lift of her chin, she walked past them into the store. Inside, she inhaled the familiar scent of fresh produce before scanning the area for her mother. She hoped to catch her alone, to talk to her without Papà's hawkish eyes watching them.

Luck was on her side. She found her mother in the last aisle, mopping up a broken jar of pickles. She wore a black skirt, a red apron, and a kerchief tied around her hair.

"Ciao, Mamma." A bubble of warmth surged through Olivia's chest.

Her mother's head snapped up. "Olivia." The initial delight on her face faded as quickly as it had appeared. She set the mop aside and turned to glance over her shoulder.

Olivia moved closer, the warped wooden boards creaking beneath her feet, and clasped her mother in a hug. "I came to let you know I'm all right." She closed her eyes, breathing in the scent of oregano and garlic. "I'm sorry I haven't been in touch."

Mamma hugged her back. "I've missed you, *cara*. You look better." She held Olivia at arm's length. "You gained some weight."

"A little. I'm almost back to normal."

"Salvatore says you work with troubled women. Are you happy there?" Little creases marred Mamma's forehead between her small dark eyes.

"Yes, Mamma." She forced any sad thoughts away. Now was not the time to remember her sorrows. "How is everyone? Have you heard from Tony?"

"*Sì*, he writes often. He is doing as well as he can in a war."

"I pray for him every night," Olivia whispered. "And for all of you too."

"*Grazie, cara*. I worry so much for you." Tears sprang to Mamma's eyes.

Olivia pulled her close in another warm hug. Though Olivia was not considered tall, her mother came only to her chin. "I love you, Mamma. And despite everything, I love Papà too. I'm trying hard to forgive him for what he did, for making me lose my son. But it will take some time."

"I understand." She wiped tears from her cheeks. "I have to get back to work. Thank you for coming."

"I'll try to visit more often." Olivia smiled, kissed her mother's cheek, then headed toward the door. For a brief second, she considered trying to talk to her father but quickly dismissed the idea, not wanting to ruin this small moment of victory.

Her gaze drifted behind the counter where the opening to the staircase was visible, and for a moment she allowed herself to imagine living upstairs again. But with a start, she realized she didn't belong in that apartment anymore. Like her barren bedroom, stripped of everything that mattered to her, she no longer fit there. She'd changed too much to go back.

The bell jangled as a woman came in.

Olivia recognized Mrs. Ceruti, one of her neighbors. Genuine pleasure flooded her system, along with a rush of memories. Louisa Ceruti had been Olivia's best friend through school, and this woman had once been as close as a second mother. Smiling, Olivia approached her. "Mrs. Ceruti, it's good to see you."

A flash of recognition registered on the woman's face, but immediately her features froze. She lifted her chin and, without so much as a word, turned up the aisle.

Olivia sucked in a breath. A slap to the face couldn't have hurt more. Perhaps she should let the snub go, but remnants of her old temper rose hot in her chest. How could the woman dismiss Olivia as though she didn't exist?

"Mrs. Ceruti, how is Louisa doing?" she called up the aisle.

The woman pivoted, her brows raised. "Louisa is fine. She's married to a doctor, and they're expecting their first baby." Her nose couldn't get much higher.

Heat flared in Olivia's gut. *She knew.* Somehow Mrs. Ceruti knew and now deemed Olivia beneath her. Despite every urge to duck her head and run, some dark force twisted inside Olivia, spurring her on. "You must tell Louisa hello for me."

Mrs. Ceruti's nose wrinkled. "She would want nothing to do with the likes of you. Frankly, I can't believe you have the nerve to show up here and disgrace your parents this way."

Her voice had grown loud enough to create a stir in the store. People stopped what they were doing to gawk in their direction.

Olivia looked up and met the scowling countenance of her father. Customers turned, looks of disdain on their faces. Snatches of whispers made their way to her.

"Isn't that the daughter? The one who . . ."

"Such a shame how she turned out. . . ."

"After all they've done for her . . ."

Each hateful comment pricked at her skin, tearing at her composure. She thought her pregnancy had been kept secret, but obviously her family hadn't bothered to hide her disgrace after all.

"How dare you judge me?" Olivia's limbs shook as she glared around the motley group. "I seem to remember all of you attending the same church as our family. A church that preaches compassion and forgiveness. Not hate and condemnation." Her glare moved from Mrs. Ceruti to her father. "I may be far from perfect, but I have come to know God's grace and have experienced His forgiveness. So from where I stand, I'm closer to a Christian than any of you can claim to be." Her chin quivered, and before she could make more of a spectacle of herself, she whirled around and rushed out the door.

Olivia stormed down the street, outrage buzzing through her body like static on the radio. Angry tears blurred her vision, but she refused to let a single drop fall. Several blocks later, the rage drained away, leaving her limp and shaky. She looked around for a bus stop and found one nearby. Thankful for the bench there, she sank onto it.

With the adrenaline rush gone, a cold dose of reality began to sink in. The tiny seed of hope she'd reaped with her mother's acceptance—hope that one day she might regain her place in the community—shriveled and died inside her.

More than anything, Olivia craved respectability, and she'd foolishly believed that if she worked hard enough and repented long enough, she could achieve it once more. What a naïve fantasy. It was clear to her now that she would never be respectable again.

The bus arrived, and she hauled herself onto it, claiming the first vacant seat. As the vehicle lurched forward, Olivia's gaze fell to the Woolworth's bag on her lap, and her thoughts inevitably turned to Sofia and Darius. If she continued to be part of their lives, would her disgrace taint them as well?

Of course it would.

Her throat closed up, swallowing a cry of despair. Darius deserved a righteous woman, one he could be proud of. Not one who'd been jailed for immorality and given birth out of wedlock. He and Sofia certainly didn't deserve to pay the price for her sins. To be ostracized because of her.

"I think I'm falling in love with you."

Oh, Darius. I'm sorry. Tears slid down Olivia's cheek and dripped onto her arm. She couldn't break her promise to attend Sofia's birthday, so she would go. But after that, she would have to find the strength to distance herself from Darius and his precious girl and allow them to be free to find someone more suitable for their lives.

No matter how it would tear her heart out in the process.

36

On Saturday afternoon, Darius glanced over at Olivia seated beside him in the car. Looking lovely in a pretty green dress, she sat primly, her back barely touching the seat behind her, with a wrapped present and a plain white box on her lap.

He could only imagine the nerves that were racing through her at this moment. If he were meeting her parents, he'd feel exactly the same.

"Please try to relax, Olivia. My parents may be loud, but they're harmless."

She turned wide brown eyes on him. "I'm afraid this might give them the wrong idea. That we're more than just friends."

"That's because we *are* more than just friends." He longed to hold her hand, but her fingers remained in a death grip around the parcels.

She looked like she wanted to say something more. Instead, she pressed her lips together.

He decided to let it go. Once they arrived and her nerves settled, she'd see that she'd been worried for nothing.

Soon he pulled up in front of his parents' house and turned off the engine. He came around to help Olivia out. She stared at the house, a frown marring her forehead.

"Don't worry," he said. "Sofia will be the center of attention. You may notice that her grandparents tend to spoil her."

Olivia gave a strained smile. "All children should be spoiled on their birthdays. It's only right."

Darius resisted the urge to hug her, conscious that people might be looking out the window. Hopefully, before the day was over, he could sneak in a few private kisses. It gave him a thrill just thinking about it.

He led the way in the front door, hoping to shield Olivia from his relatives for a moment and give her time to adjust. Sure enough though, his mother and two of his aunts came rushing forward.

"There he is. Darius is back."

"Where is this mysterious woman?"

Darius cringed but pasted on a smile, tucking Olivia's arm under his. "Mamá, everyone, this is Olivia Rosetti."

He began the introductions, rattling off the names of his relatives and neighbors, certain by her bemused look that she wouldn't remember one of them.

Then a beaming Sofia burst through the crowd. She wore a homemade paper crown on top of her dark curls and her favorite pink dress. "Miss Olivia! You came! Is that a present for me?"

"Sofia," he warned. "What did I say about asking for presents?"

"I forgot." She eyed the gaily colored package with guilty, puppy-dog eyes.

Olivia set her parcels on a table and held out her arms. "Happy birthday, sweetheart."

Sofia ran to hug her.

Then Olivia whispered something in Sofia's ear that caused his daughter's face to light up.

"It's for me?" she asked.

"Well, you're the only birthday girl here, right?"

Olivia handed her the package, then rose and picked up the other box. "This is for you, Mrs. Reed. I know you've made a lot of wonderful food, but I wanted to contribute something. It's a batch of cookies I made this morning."

His mother accepted the package with a smile. "That's so nice. You didn't have to bring anything." She looped her arm around Olivia's waist. "Come to the kitchen where we women can talk."

"Wait a minute, Mamá." Darius followed. "Give Olivia time to get used to everyone."

But his mother just waved a hand of dismissal.

Olivia looked over one shoulder, a hint of panic in her eyes.

"I'll be right outside the door if you need me," he said before the swinging doors swallowed her up.

"Daddy." Sofia tugged on his sleeve. "When can I open my present?"

He released a breath and turned his attention to his daughter. "When Olivia and your grandmother come back out." He glanced at the door and bent to look her in the eye. "Or . . . you could take the present into the kitchen and ask Miss Olivia if you can open it."

Maybe Sofia would provide enough of a distraction to save Olivia from his mother's interrogation.

She went to skip off, but Darius put a hand on her shoulder.

"And make sure Grandma's being nice to her, Mouse."

Sofia giggled. "You're funny, Daddy. Yiayiá is always nice to company." She pushed through the door into the kitchen.

Darius turned to see his father grinning at him.

"That is one pretty lady you have there, son." Papá waggled his thick brows.

Heat ran up Darius's neck. "Thanks, Papá. But she's so much more than that."

"Ah, I understand. It's a fortunate man who finds a woman with heart, intelligence, and beauty. One would do well to keep a treasure like that."

Darius quirked a brow. "I intend to. I just have to convince her that we belong together."

"Once you work your charm, she will come willingly." His father bellowed out a laugh and clapped him on the shoulder.

Darius eyed the kitchen door. How long should he give his mother alone with Olivia before he went to her rescue?

Olivia followed Mrs. Reed into a homey kitchen. The woman set Olivia's box on the table, which was already laden with platters, pots, and jugs. The room wasn't terribly large, but it was filled with exotic scents that reminded Olivia of her mother's kitchen at home. A window over the sink let in the warm breeze, bringing with it the sound of children's laughter.

"One minute while I check my sauce." Mrs. Reed busied herself with a large pot on the stove. She was plump in stature, and her dark hair was styled in tight curls around her face. She reminded Olivia very much of her own mother.

"Miss Olivia." Sofia burst into the room, carrying the present.

Olivia smiled on a wave of relief. "Yes, Sofia?"

"My daddy said to ask you if I could open this now." Her eyes brimmed with hope.

Olivia glanced toward Mrs. Reed, who had paused her stirring. "If your grandmother says it's all right, it's fine with me."

Mrs. Reed wiped her hands on her striped apron. "Just this one present and then you go outside with the others."

"Thank you, Yiayiá." Sofia set the parcel on a chair and began to tear into the wrapping. Soon ribbon and paper were scattered everywhere as the girl plucked the stuffed elephant out of the box. Olivia had found it in Woolworth's toy department. It was gray with a large pink bow around its neck.

"An elephant!" Sofia shrieked, hugging it to her chest. "I love elephants."

"Your daddy may have mentioned that." Olivia laughed, delighted with the girl's response.

Sofia threw her arms around Olivia's waist and squeezed.

"Thank you, Miss Olivia. I love it." She pulled away to examine the treasure more closely. "I'm going to name her Penelope."

"That's a lovely name."

Mrs. Reed pointed with her wooden spoon. "Sofia, pick up the paper and take it to the trash."

"Yes, Yiayiá." She tucked the elephant under one arm, scooped up the debris, then skipped out the door.

"She's a delightful child," Olivia said. "So happy and well-mannered."

Mrs. Reed gave a snort. "You haven't seen her when she's having a tantrum."

"True." Olivia chuckled. "Can I do anything to help?" She needed something to occupy her hands and keep her nerves at bay.

"No, no. You are a guest. You sit and I get you some lemonade."

Seeing no escape, Olivia pulled out a chair and sat down. Seconds later, Darius's mother placed a large glass in front of her. "You have a very nice home, Mrs. Reed."

"Thank you. We are comfortable here." She opened the oven door, murmured something in Greek, then closed it again.

Olivia took a sip of her drink, savoring the burst of flavor on her tongue. "This is delicious." What could she talk to this woman about? Maybe she could get her talking about the rest of her family. "Darius tells me you have three other children."

Mrs. Reed's features brightened. "Yes. I have another wonderful son and two daughters. And eleven grandchildren."

"My, that's a large family."

"It's nothing compared to back home. In Greece, most families have more than six children each." She took a container from the icebox and set it on the counter. "But I think my family will be giving me many more grandchildren yet." She fixed her dark eyes on Olivia. "I know my Darius wants brothers and sisters for Sofia." She huffed out a long sigh. "If only God hadn't taken his Selene."

Olivia squirmed on her seat. "I was very sorry to hear of his tragedy." What else could she say? Olivia was out of her element with no idea of this family's dynamics.

"How about you, Olivia? You have a big family?"

"I have three brothers. One is away at war."

"Oh, your poor mother. I was fortunate that none of my boys had to go." She made the sign of the cross. "Like Darius, my Nicolas has a family to look after."

Olivia nodded. "My brother Leo lives at home and works in my parents' store. And the youngest one, Salvatore, just became a priest."

"Ahh." The woman's face softened. "It's always nice to have a priest in the family."

"We're very proud of him." Olivia let her gaze dart to the door, wishing someone would come in and provide a distraction. How long could she skirt all the topics that could force her to lie to this nice woman?

"And you, Olivia? You want a big family someday?" Mrs. Reed stared right at her.

Olivia swallowed hard and set her glass on the table. "I love children," she said slowly, "and I will accept whatever family God sees fit to give me."

Mrs. Reed pursed her lips. "A wise answer. Only God knows our future."

The door opened, and Darius poked his head in. "How's it going in here?"

Olivia shot to her feet, relief flooding her system like a drug. "Fine. I offered to help, but your mother wouldn't let me."

He smiled, coming farther into the room. "Of course not. You're a guest." He held out a hand to her. "I hope you don't mind, Mamá, but I'm going to steal Olivia away now."

"We had a nice talk. You send your aunts in now to help."

"Yes, Mamá." Grinning, Darius led Olivia out a side door and headed toward the rear of the house.

Olivia breathed in the fresh air, allowing her tense muscles to relax for the first time since arriving at the Reeds' home. With her hand securely tucked in Darius's, she took a moment to savor the confidence he exuded and the heady sense of safety she felt in his presence.

When he turned and sent her a wink, her heart hiccupped in her chest.

It was becoming more and more difficult to resist his charms, and she found her resolve to distance herself wavering.

The backyard was long and narrow, with a vegetable garden occupying most of the left-hand side. Blossoming vines covered the rear fence, and the right side of the yard was taken up with long tables, gaily decorated with balloons. Guests milled about the lawn, talking and laughing, and the smell of roasting meat drifted through the air.

Darius nodded to the others but continued to the far corner of the garden.

There, she was surprised to see a secluded nook with a wooden bench and a covered trellis that afforded them a degree of privacy.

Darius tugged her down beside him, keeping her hand in his. "I hope my mother didn't interrogate you too much."

"No, she was fine."

"Are you sure? You seem a little . . . overwhelmed." His blue eyes radiated concern.

"This is a lot to take in," she admitted. She'd pictured a relatively intimate family celebration, but there had to be more than forty people here.

"Thank you for putting up with it. And thank you for Sofia's gift. She adores it."

A blush heated her cheeks. "I'm glad she likes it."

"She likes you more. And I must say I agree with her." He grinned, then leaned forward and pressed his lips softly to hers.

A thrill shot right through her, sending tingles dancing up her spine. When his hand came up to cup her face, every argument why she couldn't be with him flew from her mind. She started to kiss him back, but the sudden realization of what she was doing dawned on her, and she quickly pulled away.

"Your family is right over there," she said.

"No one can see us. Besides, I've wanted to do that all day."

He bent toward her again, but she laid a hand on his chest.

"Behave yourself," she whispered.

A loud clanging sounded. "The food is ready," a voice called out. "Everyone to the tables."

Darius groaned. "Saved by the dinner bell."

Her relief bubbled out in a laugh as they got up to join the rest of the group.

"To be continued later," he said in a husky voice, sending another parade of chills up her spine.

For the rest of the celebration, however, they were never alone, which was probably for the best. Olivia sat by one of Darius's many aunts, who regaled her with stories of Darius as a boy for the majority of the delicious meal. Olivia managed to deflect most of his aunt's questions with vague answers and was relieved when all the attention turned to the birthday girl. Sofia beamed as she cut her cake and opened her gifts. When dusk fell and the singing and dancing started, Olivia rose to find the bathroom.

Darius was waiting in the hall when she came out. "I'm sensing you might be ready to leave."

Shouts of "*Opa!*" echoed from outside.

She nodded. "If you don't mind."

"Not at all. Just let me tell my parents."

She bit her lip, her manners warring with her nerves. "I should say good-bye to everyone. . . ."

"I would advise against that, or they'll hold you hostage until you dance with all the uncles." He laughed. "Don't worry. I'll tell

313

them good-bye for you. Believe me, I know how much energy our family requires. You have to get used to us in small doses."

He was right. Even with a fairly large Italian family, Olivia had never experienced a gathering like this.

Sofia ran up. "I have to use the bathroom." Her battered crown slipped over one eye, and she pushed it up.

Darius put a hand on the girl's shoulder. "Say good-night to Miss Olivia first. She's going home now. I'll be right back with the car keys." He strode away.

Sofia's nose scrunched. "You're leaving already? It's not even my bedtime yet."

"I know, honey." Olivia bent down. "But I have to get up early tomorrow. Thank you for inviting me to your special day." She hugged the girl, who squeezed her neck hard with slightly sticky fingers. Olivia tried desperately not to think that she might never see her again.

"Thank you for my elephant," Sofia said solemnly.

"You're very welcome."

The girl leaned closer to Olivia's ear. "You know what I wished for when I blew out my candles? I wished you could be my mommy."

"Oh, sweetie." A hard lump rose in Olivia's throat. What she wouldn't give to be this precious girl's mother. To have the privilege of loving her and helping to raise her. If only she could be worthy of that honor. Not trusting her voice, she gave a forced smile and patted Sofia's shoulder.

Thankfully, Darius returned then. He kissed his daughter, promising to be back before she went to bed.

As he escorted Olivia out to the car, her chaotic emotions churned inside her, leaving her more torn than ever before.

37

"'m sorry if tonight was too much for you," Darius said quietly a few minutes later as they drove down the darkened streets.

Olivia glanced over at him. "You don't need to apologize. Your family is very . . . charming."

"Charming but overbearing." One brow quirked up. "I should have known that such a big gathering might be too much for a first meeting."

She let out a sigh. "I did have second thoughts about coming, but I didn't want to disappoint Sofia."

"Well, thank you. You made her day."

"It was worth it, then." She focused on the streetlights ahead, but she couldn't get Sofia's wish out of her mind. The girl was already thinking of her as a potential mother figure. It wasn't fair to let this go any further. But how did she go about removing herself from their lives when her heart railed at the very thought?

Suddenly, Darius swerved into an empty parking lot. He stopped under a lamppost and turned off the engine.

"All right. I can't stand it anymore. I need to know what's bothering you. You haven't been yourself all night, and I'm sensing it's more than just meeting my family."

She gripped her purse tighter. It was utterly unfair how the

man could see right through her. She'd had no intention of starting such a serious conversation tonight, but now that he'd brought
it up, perhaps it was for the best. "You're right," she said. "There
has been something weighing on me."

"Did my mother do something to upset you?"

"Not really. It was a combination of things that made me come
to a realization." She met his eyes. "One I don't think you're going
to like."

He shifted on the seat, a wary expression on his face. "What
is it?"

Her heart squeezed, and she focused on the top button of his
shirt. *Lord, give me the courage to say what I must.* "For your sake
and Sofia's," she said slowly, "I think it's best to end our relationship."

His nostrils flared. "What did my mother say—?"

"It wasn't her." Olivia paused to choose her words carefully.
"I realize now that I haven't been fair, leading you to believe we
might have a future together. I can't be the wife you need or a
good mother for Sofia."

His brows slammed together. "That's not true."

"Yes, it is. For several reasons." She released a slow breath. "I
went back to my parents' store this week. At first, Mamma hugged
me, and it was almost like old times. But then one of our neighbors came in, and she wouldn't even look at me. She said I was a
disgrace to my parents. All the other customers were whispering
about me. It was terrible."

"Olivia . . ." He reached for her, but she shook her head.

"No, please let me finish."

He lowered his hand to his lap.

"I know now that no matter how hard I try, I'll never be respectable in most people's eyes. I'm forever branded by the mistakes of my past."

He huffed out a breath. "I don't care about that."

The air inside the car seemed overly warm. Olivia rolled down
her window a few inches before continuing. "Today your mother

was talking about big families—"she swallowed hard—"and how you want more children. That's when I truly realized I wasn't being fair to you."

He reached for her hand. "I'm not sure I understand, but whatever the issue, I'm sure we can resolve it."

The temptation to simply agree and rest in the warmth of his nearness tugged at her. But she needed to get the whole sordid story out in the open—now, before she changed her mind. "Let's walk a little. There are some things I haven't told you that you have a right to know."

Darius tried not to panic as they got out of the car and started down a deserted stretch of Danforth Avenue. They walked in silence for several minutes while Olivia seemed to wrestle with how to begin. Judging from the worry lines between her brows, whatever she was about to tell him was most likely unpleasant. He braced himself for what was to come, determined that nothing she said would shake his love for her or his certainty that they were meant to be together.

"While I was at the reformatory," she said at last, "I was treated . . . badly."

The hairs on the back of his neck rose. Was she abused by the guards? Or someone in authority? "You can tell me about it, Olivia, no matter how terrible it might be."

She gave him a grateful look, then turned to stare at the road. A truck rumbled by, expelling exhaust from a tailpipe. Once it passed, the street became still again.

"There was a woman doctor there," she said. "Those of us who were expecting babies were required to undergo weekly exams, at which time the doctor performed various . . . procedures on us."

Under a streetlight, he watched the color drain from her face. Alarmed, he guided her to a bench at a bus stop and sat beside her. "What sort of procedures?"

Lines bracketed her mouth. "Surgical procedures. Injections. Burning chemical treatments. I don't even know everything that was done, only that the pain was intolerable." She closed her eyes, her lashes standing out against the pallor of her skin.

Darius put his arm around her and drew her close, absorbing the tremors that passed through her. "I can't imagine the terror you must have felt."

She nodded. "Twice afterward I was left alone in a basement cell for over a week with no relief from the pain, not even an aspirin, and very little food."

His eyes smarted as he tightened his arm around her. How could anyone treat another human being so cruelly? And the perpetrator was a doctor, no less. Someone who was supposed to protect and heal. "All this happened while you were pregnant?"

She nodded again. "I thought I would miscarry from everything I'd been through, but somehow I didn't." Tears slid down her cheeks.

He wanted to weep for her suffering. Instead, he offered her a handkerchief. "I'm so sorry, Olivia. I can hardly believe you came out alive."

"A few times, I thought I was going to die. I actually prayed that I would. But then I realized that if I did, my baby would die too. So I had no choice but to endure it." A shudder went through her. "For a few minutes after Matteo was born, every bit of suffering seemed worth it—just to hold my baby at last." A hint of a smile trembled on her lips. "But then he was taken from me without my consent, and suddenly nothing mattered anymore." She blew her nose and moved away from his shoulder. "I've never told anyone what happened to me in there, not even Dr. Henshaw. I'm telling you now because . . ." She drew in a ragged breath. "I don't think I'll be able to have any more children as a result of what was done to me." She raised her eyes to his. "You have the right to know that."

Her words hit him like a fist to the gut. He ran a hand over his jaw, attempting to sort through his emotions before he spoke.

This was far too important to say the wrong thing. "I appreciate the courage it took to tell me this," he said carefully. "But if you think it's made me reconsider my feelings for you, it's done just the opposite. I admire you even more."

Olivia shook her head. Fat tears leaked from the corners of her eyes. "You deserve a wife who's not broken. One who can give you more children. Brothers and sisters for Sofia."

He took her hand in his, trying to calm his frantic heartbeat and think logically.

He recalled her near hysteria at the hospital after her head injury, and it all made so much sense now. Her fear was real, something that could never be trivialized, and he struggled to find the right words to convey his thoughts. "There are other ways to have children, Olivia. Ones we can explore together."

She'd wanted to adopt Abigail, but would she even consider adoption again after losing her too?

The streetlight above them flickered twice, then the yellow glow steadied. Another car passed them with a *whoosh*, creating a gust of air that swirled the dust on the road.

"I realize that." Olivia let out a sigh. "But I won't let you sacrifice yourself on my account."

"What if I don't consider it a sacrifice?" Frustration curled through his chest.

She shook her head. "I'm just trying to save us both the inevitable pain." Abruptly, she got up from the bench and began walking in the direction of the car.

"Olivia, wait." He rushed after her and matched his stride to hers. "We can't leave it this way."

She kept going as though she hadn't heard, slowing only when she reached the car. Then she yanked open the door and got in.

He raked a hand through his hair. What could he say to convince her that it didn't matter to him? Instinctively, he knew that because her wounds ran so deep, no matter what he said right now, she wouldn't believe him.

Slowly, he got in the driver's side and closed the door. He sat in silence for a few seconds, gripping the steering wheel but not starting the engine. At last, he forced his shoulders to relax and turned to look at her. Her back was ramrod straight as she stared out the window.

"Thank you for trusting me with your story," he said quietly. "But it doesn't change anything for me. I'm not giving up; however, I will respect your wishes. For now." His chest ached at the thought of backing away from her, even temporarily. Now that Olivia had reawakened his heart, he couldn't imagine not having her in his life.

But if she felt that strongly, what could he do to change her mind?

For the present, all he could do was trust that God would work things out for their mutual good.

He drove the rest of the way back to Bennington Place in miserable silence, then parked the car and got out.

Olivia had already stepped onto the sidewalk. "You don't need to walk me to the door." Her eyes appeared hollow. Haunted. This decision was costing her as well. That thought brought him no real consolation.

"Good night, Darius." Still not looking directly at him, she opened the gate and went through, closing the door with a solid *clang*.

Darius leaned against the car, his shoulders sagging, and watched her climb the stairs to the front door. He would wait until she was safely inside and try not to think about how differently he'd planned the end of this evening.

A loud shriek pierced the night air.

Darius sprang away from the car. In two strides, he was inside the gate. "Olivia, are you okay?"

A shadow moved on the porch, and a tall, stout man stepped forward, his gaze focused on Olivia. "Well, hello. Aren't you a pretty thing?"

Darius bounded up the steps to her side, adrenaline flooding his system. Even though it was barely nine o'clock, a man skulking about at this hour did not seem right. "What do you want?" He placed a protective arm around Olivia's shoulder.

"I'm here for Jenny." Beneath the porch light, the man's features were visible. He had a round face, a blunt nose, and piercing eyes. The distinct odor of stale liquor wafted toward them.

Under Darius's arm, Olivia stiffened. "Men aren't allowed here without prior authorization," she said in a clipped tone.

The man scowled. "You can't keep me from seeing my wife."

His wife? Why would a man's wife come to a maternity home?

Olivia pulled herself up tall. "Unless Jenny wants to see you, you're not welcome here. You may telephone the directress in the morning and discuss the matter with her."

Veins stood out in the man's neck, and his face turned a mottled shade of crimson.

Darius moved between Olivia and the stranger in case things got out of hand. "If I were you, I'd take the lady's advice. There's no need to disturb the women and children inside." He kept a steely eye on the man.

At last, the fellow stepped back. "I'll go for now. But you've not heard the last from me." With a final glare, he stomped down the stairs.

Darius remained on the porch beside Olivia until the man was through the gate and out of sight. Then he turned to study her. "Are you all right?"

"Yes, he just startled me is all." She let out a breath and shivered.

It took all his willpower to resist pulling her closer, but he'd promised to respect her wishes, and he would keep that promise. Reluctantly, he put some space between them. "I'll wait until you're inside before I leave. Make sure all the doors and windows are locked in case he decides to return."

Her brown eyes met his. "I will." She hesitated. "Thank you,

Darius. You'll never know how sorry I am . . . about everything." Sorrow flashed over her lovely face.

"I am too." He reached out a hand toward her, the longing to touch her nearly slaying him, but at the last second, he shoved his hands into his pockets. "I can't imagine my life without you in it, Olivia. And I'm definitely not ready to give up hope yet."

She gave him a sad smile. "Good-bye, Darius."

He waited until she went inside and he heard the lock click into place, then he turned and walked slowly away.

Only as he climbed into his car did he realize that she'd said good-bye and not good night.

39

Olivia squeezed her eyes shut at the sound of Darius's car pulling away, then waited with her back against the door until her heart rate slowed to near normal. Once she had herself under control, she opened her eyes. The house sat in shrouded darkness, with only the faint glow from the porch light illuminating the hall. The downstairs seemed quiet, but just to be certain, Olivia glanced into the parlor. It appeared everyone had already retired for the evening.

She sighed as she started up the staircase, mustering all her strength just to lift her feet. She couldn't think about Darius right now, or the fact that she would never see him again. If she did, her last thread of control might snap, sending her into another abyss of despair. After losing Abigail, she'd promised herself that she would never become so consumed by darkness again. And though she craved nothing more than to crawl into her bed and sleep for the next two days, she owed it to Ruth and Jenny to warn them about the strange man's unwelcome visit. If he returned unexpectedly, they needed to be prepared.

She headed to Ruth's room at the far end of the house and gave three sharp raps on her door.

"Come in."

Olivia opened the door. Ruth sat in an armchair with her Bible open on her lap.

"Oh good. You're still awake. I didn't want to disturb you."

"You're home earlier than I expected." Ruth took off her reading glasses to study Olivia. "From the look on your face, I don't think you have good news."

"I need to tell you what just happened." Olivia walked in and took a seat on the ottoman. "When I got back a few minutes ago, a man was waiting on the porch. He claimed to be Jenny's husband."

Ruth went still. "Oh dear. I was afraid something like that might happen." She closed the Bible on a soft exhale. "We had our suspicions when Jenny first arrived, but recently she confided that she left an abusive husband, who is also a heavy drinker, because she was worried that his violence would escalate and harm the baby."

A chill slid down Olivia's spine. Thank goodness Darius had been with her. "I told the man he'd have to call and talk to you if he wanted authorization to visit. He wasn't happy, but he finally left. I thought you and Jenny should know."

"I'm glad he didn't give you too much trouble, but you're right. Jenny needs to be told." Ruth got up from the chair. "Let's do it together, with as little fuss as possible. Then, once the three of us come up with a strategy to deal with him, we'll tell the others in the morning. No need to disturb everyone in the house at this hour."

"I agree," Olivia said as she rose. "Besides, I doubt he'd have the audacity to come back again tonight."

At least she fervently hoped not.

The next day, Olivia rose just after dawn and went downstairs. Between the heartache over ending her relationship with Darius and worrying about Jenny, Olivia had suffered another restless night. The talk with Jenny had been unsettling at best. Olivia hated causing the girl such distress and only hoped she wouldn't become even more withdrawn now. They would have to keep a close eye on her in the days to come and assure her that she was safe, that she wasn't alone.

Olivia found Ruth eating breakfast in the sunroom instead of the usual dining room. The space was filled with bright light that bathed Ruth's head with a golden glow.

"Good morning." Olivia managed a weak smile as she entered.

Ruth raised her head from the newspaper. "You're up extra early. In all the excitement last night, I forgot to ask how your evening was."

Olivia walked over to the table and poured herself a cup of coffee. "It was . . . festive. Sofia enjoyed her birthday very much."

Ruth narrowed her eyes. "How was it meeting the Reed clan?"

"Interesting. They're certainly a lively bunch."

"Is that all?" Ruth's brows rose as she lowered her cup. "I would think meeting the man's family for the first time would be a rather momentous occasion."

A cloud moved over the sun, momentarily blocking its bright rays.

Olivia wished she could share some amusing stories with Ruth; however, there was no point in trying to pretend everything was all right. "The party was lovely, but on the way home, I . . . ended our relationship."

Ruth's mouth fell open. "Why would you do that when you're obviously crazy about him?"

Olivia resisted the urge to flee from Ruth's sharp gaze. But she would have to give her some type of explanation. She'd only persist until she did. "I'd already decided that I couldn't continue seeing Darius, but I didn't want to disappoint Sofia, so I waited until the party was over."

Ruth shook her head. "I don't understand. I thought things were going so well. What changed?"

Olivia glanced to the open doorway to make sure no one else

was around. "I ran into an old neighbor a few days ago, and she refused to speak to me. I realized then that no matter how hard I try, my past will always haunt me. And I can't let my mistakes harm Darius and Sofia."

"Oh, my dear." Ruth leaned forward. "I'm sorry that happened, but you mustn't let one unfortunate incident ruin your future."

"It's not only that." Olivia sighed. "Mrs. Reed told me that Darius wants a big family like the rest of his siblings have. And I can't give him that." Avoiding Ruth's probing gaze, she chose a scone from a basket on the table.

"Why not? I assumed you'd want more children of your own one day."

A band of pain seared across Olivia's chest. "I don't think I can have any more children, Ruth. I hadn't really considered that when he asked me on a date. But it became clear last night that it wouldn't be fair to lead him on."

Olivia waited for the expected words of sympathy, but Ruth remained thoughtful as she stirred her coffee.

At last she looked up. "Why do you think you can't have more children? Did a doctor tell you this?"

"Not in so many words." Olivia spread a napkin on her lap. "But I know in my heart it's true."

Ruth leaned forward, compassion evident in her soft gaze. "My dear, until you get a proper exam, it's nothing more than speculation. I understand that you're scared, but for the sake of your future, shouldn't you try to find out the truth?"

Olivia shifted her gaze to the lace tablecloth. Her friend couldn't begin to understand what she'd been through because she'd never told her. She raised her eyes. "I can't, Ruth. Horrific things were done to me in the reformatory by the doctor there. Things I have a hard time even speaking about." Her hands began to shake. "That's why I was so afraid of Dr. Henshaw at first. And why I can't tell my story at the city council meeting." She closed her eyes and focused on regulating her breathing.

Ruth squeezed her arm. "I'm sorry you had such a bad experience."

Olivia didn't dare look up, knowing the sympathy shining in her friend's eyes would be her undoing.

"If having your own children is out of the question, there are other ways to have a family," Ruth said gently. "Did you discuss that with Darius?"

"We skirted the issue, but I told him I wouldn't let him sacrifice his future for me. He deserves someone less broken, someone who won't bring shame to his family." She jutted out her chin, pushing the hard ball of emotion down deep. There was no point in discussing the matter any further. "Now, can we please change the subject before the girls come down?"

Ruth's mouth opened, then she clamped it shut. After several seconds of silence, she inclined her head. "Very well. We'll table this conversation for now, but I intend to continue it again another time." Though her tone was no-nonsense, she gave Olivia's arm another gentle squeeze.

Olivia pressed her lips together. As far as she was concerned, there was nothing more to say. Ruth would eventually have to accept that Olivia had made her decision and that nothing would make her change her mind.

The morning after Sofia's party, Darius left home just after sunup. Too restless to sleep and too edgy to linger over his morning coffee, he'd rinsed out his cup and glanced at the clock on the wall.

Sofia would sleep in this morning after staying up so late last night. He would likely be back before she even stirred. Setting his jaw, Darius set out for the one place he hoped to find solace.

Thankfully, St. George's church doors were already open for the day. Removing his hat, Darius entered and took a seat halfway up the long aisle. A hushed stillness enveloped the sanctuary, where everything lay ready for the services later that morning. Darius worked hard to quiet his mind and simply breathe in the soothing scent of candles and lemon furniture polish before lowering himself to the kneeler.

Lord, my spirit is heavy today. Heavy with the burden of Olivia's suffering. I'm here to pray for her and ask that you ease her pain. Help her to realize that she is worthy not only of your love but also the love of others in her life. Remind her that she doesn't have to shut herself off from the world or deny herself the comfort of people who care about her. She deserves a husband and family . . . even if it's not with me.

He bowed his head over his clasped hands, fighting the sting of tears. He could barely comprehend the physical tortures she had endured, much less the emotional pain of having her son taken from her.

"For a few minutes after Matteo was born, every bit of suffering seemed worth it—just to hold my baby at last. But then he was taken from me without my consent, and suddenly nothing mattered anymore."

In addition to that devastating loss, Olivia might not be able to have any more children. Darius didn't know how she even managed to carry on. And now she was denying herself the family she so richly deserved.

Sure, he'd be thrilled to have more children, but if Sofia was the only child he was blessed with, he would be content with that. And if he could have Olivia as his wife, he'd consider himself the luckiest man ever.

"But your will not mine be done, Lord," he whispered. "If I'm not the man who can make Olivia happy, then let me accept that. The only thing that matters is her peace and happiness, and if I can help in any way, please show me how. Amen."

He knelt there for several more minutes until a measure of calm settled in his soul. The peace that only prayer could bring. Now that he'd taken his problems to the Lord, he felt certain an answer would be forthcoming.

What that answer would look like, he had no idea. But he trusted God's plan implicitly.

Outside on the steps of the church, Darius breathed in the crisp air and listened for the faint peal of bells in the distance. He'd always loved hearing St. Michael's bells, even as a child.

As he made his way to the car, his thoughts turned to Olivia's brother. Didn't he say he worked at the cathedral?

Darius stopped dead, his mind whirling. One of the things that continued to haunt Olivia was the loss of her son. Would knowing what had become of him ease her pain in any way? Darius had resigned himself to the fact that there was nothing he could do to fix the situation. But now, as the bells rang out over the city, a new thought dawned. If anyone might be able to help, it was Salvatore Rosetti. A trusted clergyman and family member.

At the very least, it was worth a try.

Before he could change his mind, Darius turned on his heel and headed toward St. Michael's, hoping he wasn't about to make a very big mistake.

Ruth looked around the sunroom at the expectant faces watching her. Calling a meeting on a Sunday morning was out of the ordinary, and an atmosphere of uncertainty permeated the room.

The last time they'd been all together here had been for an evening of fun. Everyone had laughed and sang and drank punch, enjoying the festivities and managing to set aside any thoughts regarding the future of Bennington Place.

But now, as much as Ruth hated to be the bearer of bad news, the residents deserved to be warned. After speaking with Jenny last night and getting her permission to tell the others a bit of her story, Ruth was ready.

"Good morning, ladies. I won't take too much of your time, but a situation has arisen that we feel you should be aware of."

A murmur went around the room. Cherise and Margaret

each held their babies. Jenny sat somewhat removed from the group, as though her mere presence might taint the rest. Olivia, Monica, Patricia, and Nancy filled out the circle of chairs near the windows. Outside, dark clouds still blocked the sun, casting a gloomy pall over the gathering.

"Is it the finances again?" Cherise asked. "Because the girls and I have been talking and we don't mind contributing something toward our keep."

"That's very generous of you, Cherise. We will discuss business in a minute, but this is a more personal issue. One that concerns our safety."

"Are the protestors back? I didn't hear any commotion out there." Margaret patted little Calvin's back protectively.

"It's not the protestors." Ruth glanced over at Jenny, who stared at the floor. "Jenny's husband has found out where she's staying. He showed up here last night, and although Olivia managed to get him to leave, he made it clear he'd be back."

An uneasy silence followed as the women exchanged worried looks.

"Why the concern? Is he dangerous?" Patricia gave Jenny a pointed stare.

Jenny only shrugged, her gaze darting back to the floor.

"He's been known to be violent." Ruth didn't wish to say anything more. She'd promised Jenny to reveal only what was absolutely necessary, but the women needed to be aware that the man wasn't to be trifled with. Ruth cleared her throat. "So I'm asking all of you to be extra diligent. Make sure the doors and windows on the main floor are locked at all times. If you hear anyone outside, please alert either myself or Olivia, or simply call the police."

"I'm sorry to put you in this position," Jenny whispered. "But I had nowhere else to go. I was afraid he'd hurt the baby." She laid a protective hand over the swell of her stomach, tears rolling silently down her face.

Olivia went to put an arm around Jenny's shoulders. "It's not your fault. That's why we're here, why Bennington Place exists. To provide a safe place for women who need it." She looked around at the other residents. "We all need to stick together to protect one another."

"Olivia's right. Can we count on all of you?" Ruth raised her brows and looked around the room.

"Yes, ma'am."

"Of course."

"We'll do whatever it takes."

"Excellent." Ruth gave an approving nod. "Now, to discuss other matters. You mentioned finances, Cherise. Happily, we've had a few sizable donations come in, which should be enough to cover our roof repairs. However, the reality remains that we're barely meeting our day-to-day expenses."

"I think it's only fair to pay a modest fee for room and board, especially if we're working," Nancy offered.

"Thank you, ladies. Though I wish it wasn't necessary, your suggestion of some type of payment would be greatly appreciated. A small contribution would go a long way to offset our expenses." Ruth rose from her seat to walk behind the chairs. "The other issue looming over our heads is the upcoming city council meeting."

As much as she disliked bringing up the topic, she knew the girls had been worried about the possibility of having to close the home. They deserved full transparency about the matter.

"I'm fairly confident that the council will see the pettiness of Mr. Simmons's petition and allow us to continue our operation here. However, I would be remiss if I didn't mention that we may have to close. In that event, I plan to find another location for Bennington Place. I have an agent scouting potential sites outside the city limits."

"That could take months. Where would we go in the meantime?" Monica asked.

Ruth held back a sigh, hating the fear on the girls' faces. "I'm not sure, but we will figure something out. I promise."

Several of the girls frowned, and murmurs went around the room.

Cherise got to her feet. "I, for one, will follow wherever you and Olivia go, if you'll allow me. At least until I can earn enough to move out."

"I appreciate your loyalty, Cherise." Ruth smiled, still amazed by the woman's complete turnaround from streetwalker to church-goer and staunch supporter of all the women at Bennington Place. "You're welcome to stay as long as we have the room."

"Well, I don't want to move out of the city." Margaret's lip wobbled. "It will be too hard to commute to my job, especially if the streetcar doesn't go that far."

"I agree." Monica sighed. "I just hope it doesn't come down to that."

Nancy and Patricia both nodded, grim looks on their faces.

Ruth looked at each resident in turn. "I understand if the uncertainty is too much for you and you wish to find different accommodations. Just know you're all part of our family and will always be welcome." Ruth cleared her throat. "In the meantime, I ask for your prayers to help us discern the Lord's will for Bennington Place. And on that note, for those of you who wish to attend church with us this morning, we should be on our way."

As the women trailed somberly from the room, Olivia came over to give Ruth a warm hug. "I know that was difficult. But I'm sure everything will work out."

Ruth squeezed Olivia's hand. "I pray you're right, my dear, because right now the odds certainly seem stacked against us."

40

Darius sat in the back pew of St. Michael's, biding his time until the morning Mass was over. It wasn't so different from his own church, except they spoke Latin instead of Greek. When he'd realized a service was in progress, he slipped in the rear door, hoping to see if Salvatore was present. From the back of the cathedral, Darius peered at the robed men near the altar, fairly certain that the taller of the priests was indeed Salvatore Rosetti.

At the end of the Mass, after most of the people had filed out, Darius walked down the aisle toward Sal, who stood in his flowing vestments, talking to a parishioner. When the woman moved on, the priest looked up and caught sight of Darius.

"Hello," he said with a surprised smile. "Mr. Reed, isn't it?"

"That's right, but please call me Darius."

"It's nice to see you. Is Olivia with you?"

"No, she's not. I was hoping to talk to you, if you have a few minutes."

A slightly puzzled expression came over the man's face, but he nodded. "I have some time now. Follow me."

His heart beating a tad too fast, Darius trailed the priest through a side door into a hallway that led to some offices. Sal entered one of them and gestured for Darius to take a seat.

The room was dark and somber. A bookcase of religious materials lined one wall, while several framed pictures of saints adorned the other. Darius sat down and waited while Sal got comfortable behind the desk.

"What can I do for you, Darius? I presume this has something to do with my sister." Though Sal's smile was friendly enough, his expression remained somewhat guarded. Maybe he could sense Darius's trepidation.

"It does, yes." Darius shifted on the creaky chair, suddenly unsure of his right to be here. "There's something I need your help with." He inhaled and let out a breath. "I believe it would bring Olivia some peace of mind to know what became of her son. He's likely been adopted by now, but if we could only find out how he's doing . . ." Darius trailed off, the man's frown not inspiring much confidence.

"From what I understand," Sal said, "adoption records are sealed. The agency doesn't usually give out that type of information to anyone."

"I know they won't talk to me, but I was hoping that with your connection to the child and with the weight of your profession in your favor, you might be able to get some news about him." He leaned forward. "I'm certain it would mean the world to Olivia to know that her son is with a good family."

Sal sat back in his chair, studying Darius. "Did my sister ask you to come here?"

"No, she didn't."

"Then may I ask what your intention is in doing this?" The priest's eyes narrowed.

Darius swallowed, the collar of his shirt suddenly too tight. The Spanish Inquisition couldn't have been much worse than this. "I simply want to help her heal from the pain of her past, if that's at all possible."

"I sense there's more to it than that. Something more personal, perhaps?" One dark brow rose.

The man was astute, Darius would give him that. "I care very deeply for Olivia. And I know losing her son haunts her. If there's the slightest chance the boy hasn't been adopted . . ." He took a breath. "I'd like to marry Olivia and help her get him back."

Sal's eyes widened. "Marriage? That's a big commitment."

"It is. One I've given a great deal of thought about." Darius squared his shoulders. "I love Olivia very much, but she doesn't think she's worthy of my affection. Nothing I've said seems to make a difference, so I need to do something to prove how serious I am about wanting a life with her."

And he was serious, he realized. He would do everything in his power to convince Olivia that they belonged together and that they'd make a wonderful family, if only she could let go of her fears.

"What if the boy has been adopted?"

"As long as I can ease Olivia's mind in some small way, I'll be happy."

"I see." Sal steepled his fingers together while he appeared to contemplate the situation. "Well," he said at last, "I suppose it couldn't hurt to make an inquiry. All they can do is say no."

A tidal wave of relief crashed through Darius, loosening his tense muscles. "Thank you."

"I'll need more information, though. The approximate date of birth and the hospital where he was born."

"I don't know the exact date, but I believe it was about a year ago at Toronto General Hospital. They could likely give you more accurate information." He gave a small shrug. "I doubt they'd refuse a request from a priest."

"I'll do my best."

"Oh, and there's one more thing." Why not shoot for the moon while he was at it?

"What's that?"

"Olivia recently helped deliver a baby whom she grew very fond of. The girl was taken from Bennington Place to the Infants'

Home a few weeks ago after her mother passed away. The authorities were looking for any relatives who might be willing to take her, but if she hasn't been claimed . . ."

Sal's brows shot up. "You want to adopt her too?"

Darius rubbed his chin. "I might be getting ahead of myself here, but I'd like to have all the facts before I propose to Olivia officially this time." He hadn't really proposed at all, actually. She'd never let him get that far.

Sal waited a beat, then pushed a pen and a pad of paper across the desk. "Write down as much information as you can and a phone number where I can reach you. I can't promise anything, but I'll see what I can do."

Darius grabbed the pen. "Thank you. It means a great deal just to have you try."

He wrote down everything he could think of that might help the priest with his search, then jotted down his work and home telephone numbers. "I won't say anything to Olivia until I hear back from you. I wouldn't want to get her hopes up for nothing."

Sal rose and extended his hand to Darius. "I'm glad my sister has someone to look out for her." The wary expression was gone, replaced by what looked like growing respect.

Darius smiled and shook his hand. "And I'm glad she has a brother willing to do the same."

On the walk home from St. Olaf's Church, Olivia fought to shake the sense of gloom that enveloped her. After yesterday's upsetting events, she found herself clinging hard to her faith for some sense of optimism. Only her belief that the Lord was guiding her steps allowed her to keep going.

Ahead on the sidewalk, Ruth and the other women walked in silence, seemingly preoccupied with their thoughts as well. Jenny had been too shaken up to venture out, while Margaret and Cherise had chosen to stay home with the babies.

As if to mirror their dark moods, the day that had started off with sunshine and clear skies had turned a stormy gray. In addition, a strong wind had picked up, blowing threatening clouds across the sky.

"We'd better increase our pace if we want to beat the rain," Ruth said, pulling the lapels of her light jacket more firmly about her throat. "I wish I'd thought to bring my umbrella."

"It wouldn't do much good in this wind." Monica clamped her hand on her head, fighting to keep her hat from flying off.

They quickened their steps as much as possible with the pregnant women trying to keep up. Monica managed well, while poor Nancy and Patricia lumbered on as best they could. The two girls were due any time now, and Olivia hoped this exercise didn't send either one of them into early labor.

With the threat of a summer storm, perhaps it was best that the other residents had opted to stay home. At the time, though, Olivia had been more than a little discouraged by the women's reaction to the morning's meeting, especially with some of them talking about finding alternate living arrangements.

You're being silly, Olivia chided herself. Bennington Place had been created as a temporary sanctuary for its residents. No one was ever expected to stay indefinitely. Just because Olivia had grown fond of the girls and their babies didn't give her the right to judge their decisions.

Olivia's steps slowed as she came upon the entrance to the park. Unbidden images of Sofia and Darius came rushing to mind with painful clarity. Almost against her will, her gaze traveled down the path to the bench where Darius had kissed her for the first time.

Had it only been yesterday since she'd last seen him? It already felt like months.

She pressed a hand to her chest to soothe the ache there, while her other hand clutched her hat. Fat drops of rain had now started to fall, creating large splotches on the sidewalk. They would soon be drenched if the sky opened up any more.

Across the street, a mother pushed a baby carriage while a young boy ran to keep up with her quick strides. An elderly couple walked behind them, huddled under an umbrella. A little farther up, Mr. Simmons wrestled his trash container onto the porch, then stood glaring at them with his arms crossed.

The rain increased as they approached the house, drenching Olivia's hair and seeping through her clothing. She hustled forward, head down, attempting to avoid the puddles forming on the sidewalk.

The sudden squeal of tires made her head snap up just in time to see a beat-up automobile careen around the corner, swerving from one side of the street to the other. Her heart seized in her chest. What was wrong with the driver?

Across the road, someone screamed, and a child started to wail. The car barely missed the woman with the carriage before it crossed back over, jumped the curb, and barreled toward them on the sidewalk.

"Look out!" Ruth grabbed Olivia and jerked her toward the hedges.

At the last second, the car swerved by them and smashed into a lamppost. Steam poured from under the crumpled hood. The driver slouched over the steering wheel, not moving.

The rain pelted harder, sending beads of water down Olivia's neck. She blinked to clear her vision and followed Ruth over to the car. When they peered in the open window, the distinct odor of liquor wafted out.

Ruth's face became grim. "Olivia, will you call the police? I believe this man is drunk and may need medical attention."

Olivia took a closer look. "I think that's the man who was looking for Jenny last night. He's still wearing the same shirt."

"Perhaps you should let Jenny know, then."

Olivia nodded and headed for the house. Her legs were shaking as she climbed the steps.

The front door opened when she got there, and Margaret and Jenny peered out.

"We heard a loud *bang*," Margaret said. "What happened?"

Olivia went inside and stood dripping on the mat, trying to come to grips with how close they'd just come to a terrible accident. Her teeth began to chatter—whether from shock or the rain she didn't know. "A car smashed into the pole outside. The man appears to be hurt. Could you call the police and an ambulance, please?"

"Right away." Margaret immediately rushed down the hall.

Olivia turned to the other girl. "Jenny, I'm not certain, but it might be your husband."

The color left Jenny's face. With jerky movements, she pulled a coat from the hook on the wall, shoved her arms in, then picked an umbrella from the stand and stepped outside.

Olivia followed her out, the rain pelting her with renewed fury. Already Jenny's skirt was plastered against her legs as she walked out the gate toward the wrecked car.

Olivia glanced across the street, noting with dismay that a small crowd had gathered, huddled under their umbrellas, with Mr. Simmons at the forefront.

Ruth made way for Jenny to look inside the car. Tears filled Jenny's eyes. "That's him." Then she backed away from the vehicle, as though expecting him to jump out and accost her.

Mr. Simmons crossed the road, his brows an angry slash on his forehead. "What the devil is going on here?"

The injured man groaned and began to stir. Then his eyes opened, fastening right on Jenny. "There you are, you ungrateful wench. Look what you made me do." Blood dripped down his face from a gash on his forehead.

Jenny bit her lip, and Ruth put her arm around her.

The sound of a siren broke the eerie silence. A police car headed down the street toward them, its red lights flashing.

Olivia stood with the rain pouring off her, water puddling in her shoes. She didn't know whether to cheer or groan. At least Jenny's husband would no longer be a threat. He'd likely be sentenced and maybe jailed for destroying city property.

However, this was not the type of attention the maternity home needed right now. And with the neighbors having a front-row seat to the whole debacle, it would only add more fuel to Mr. Simmons's campaign against them.

Just in time for the September council meeting.

41

livia sat on the bench in the backyard of Bennington Place and watched the sun rise over the trees. Shielding herself from the crisp morning air, she wrapped her cardigan more firmly around her middle, attempting to soak in the garden's serenity.

It had been over week since the car accident, and to Olivia's utter astonishment, Jenny had insisted on going with her husband to the hospital. Then, two days ago, she'd returned for her things, saying that she was moving back in with her husband. She said he'd learned his lesson and had promised to give up drinking. Ruth had tried to convince her that change wouldn't come so easily, but to no avail. Jenny had bid them a tearful farewell and taken her leave.

A brisk wind blew up, stirring the grass at Olivia's feet. She shivered. It was as if turning the calendar to September had created a distinct change in the weather. Now the evenings and mornings were decidedly cooler, and the first hint of color tinted the trees.

It also meant that the Toronto City Council would soon resume. Olivia glanced at her notebook and pencil on the bench beside her. She'd been trying to write something about the necessity of keeping Bennington Place open but hadn't come up with more than a few disjointed sentences.

Some of the residents said they would stand up and offer testimony if Olivia did as well. How could she refuse when she wanted the other women to speak up?

Now one of her worst nightmares was coming true. She'd almost rather go through another round of torture at the reformatory than stand before the city council and expose her disgrace to the whole world. But she could see no other way around it.

She pushed away the ball of dread in her chest and read the few sentences she'd written so far. If only she could summon a bit of her initial passion for the maternity home. But lately, between missing Darius and worrying about Jenny, she'd lost some of her zeal for their mission. Somehow, some way, she needed to get it back.

Olivia looked up to see Cherise crossing the lawn toward her, clutching her cardigan about her.

"*Bonjour*, Olivia."

"Good morning, Cherise. You're up early."

"Angelique woke me at dawn, but she's sleeping again." Cherise took a seat beside her on the bench. "I came to tell you that I've decided to speak at the council meeting. You and Ruth have changed my life. And I would like to do something to show my gratitude."

With the abundance of caregivers for Angelique, Cherise had begun working a few hours a week in a nearby restaurant, determined never to go back to her previous profession, so she could be a good role model for her daughter.

Olivia leaned over to hug her. "Thank you, Cherise. Your testimony will help tremendously, I'm sure."

"I hope so." Cherise frowned. "Have you heard from Margaret since she left?"

"Yes. She said she's going to do her best to be at the meeting."

"*Bon*. That is good." Tears welled in Cherise's eyes, belying her words.

A similar wave of sadness tugged at Olivia. Margaret and Calvin had left Bennington Place a week ago. With the threat of the home's possible closure, Margaret had reached out to her older sister, and the two had reconciled. When her sister invited Margaret to move in with her, she had gratefully accepted. Olivia was happy for her, yet she still grieved the loss of her friend.

"I miss Margaret too," she said. "But this is what's supposed to happen. Our goal, after all, is to help you move on with your lives." Margaret and little Calvin were, in fact, Bennington Place's first real success story. They should be grateful for that.

Cherise gave Olivia a curious stare. "You are very sad lately, *mon amie*. You must have faith that everything will work out for the best. For the home . . . and for you."

"I'm trying hard to believe that." She managed a smile for the girl's sake. Yet she feared the underlying pain from all the losses in her life might never go away.

Cherise rose and smoothed her skirt. "I must get back before Angelique wakes again."

"I'll come with you. It's getting chilly." She was making no headway with her speech anyway. Perhaps a change of location would help.

Back in her room, Olivia sank onto her bed and stared at the ceiling. She couldn't seem to escape the black cloud of depression that continued to hold her hostage. Ever since she'd ended her relationship with Darius, nothing but disappointment had followed. Margaret and Jenny had moved out of Bennington Place, their absence leaving a gaping hole in the household. Patricia and Nancy had both recently given birth, which only served to remind Olivia once again how she would never have children of her own. How many times would she force a smile to her lips as she watched the women happily moving on with their lives, while she remained trapped by her own unchangeable circumstances?

Her gaze fell to the hand-drawn picture on her wall, and a spasm of grief shuddered through her. She missed Darius and

Sofia more than she thought possible, the ache inside her almost as deep as the one reserved for Matteo. Several days ago, at an extremely low point, Olivia had nearly broken down and called Darius. But then she'd remembered the reasons why she'd left him in the first place and replaced the receiver before making the call.

With a heavy sigh, Olivia forced her uncooperative limbs up from the bed, removed the drawing from the wall, and carefully folded it in half. From the top shelf of her closet, she took down her bag of mementos and carried it to the bed. This was torture, she knew, yet she couldn't seem to help herself. Loosening the drawstring, she reached inside to touch the softness of Matteo's baby blanket. She brought the wool to her cheek, inhaling deeply, desperate for a trace of her son's scent. He'd only worn the blanket for a few minutes, but Olivia held fast to the belief that the wool still contained his smell. Yet even that, like his memory, was fading.

If only she knew once and for all what had happened to her son, perhaps she could find peace. Had Matteo been adopted by doting parents? Or was he still in a foster home somewhere in the city? Despite her litany of prayers, those troubling questions continued to haunt her.

She let out a shaky breath and placed the blanket and Sofia's picture into the bag, a decision firming in her mind. One way or another, she had to try and find out something—anything—about Matteo's situation. If she never tried, she would always regret it, always wonder whether she could have done something to get him back. Because until she had some idea what had become of him, until she knew that he was better off without her, she doubted she would ever fully heal from the pain of losing him.

The next morning, Olivia's heart thudded in her chest as she stepped through the doors of the Children's Aid Society. Would the people here take pity on her? Or would they send her away empty-handed once again?

Please, Lord, please let me learn something that will finally give me peace about my son.

Twisting her hands together, Olivia headed over to a woman at the reception desk and forced a cheery smile. "Good afternoon. My name is Olivia Rosetti. I'd like to speak to Mrs. Linder, please."

The woman looked up. "Do you have an appointment?"

"No, but I'm with the Bennington Place Maternity Home. I just need a few minutes of her time." Perhaps it was cheating to make it seem like she was here on business, but if it got her in the door, she couldn't feel too bad about it.

"Wait here and I'll see if she can fit you in."

Several minutes later, Mrs. Linder appeared. She wore her hair in a fashionable roll, and her dark blue suit gave her a very professional air. "Hello, Miss Rosetti. This is a surprise. What brings you to our office?"

"I'd like to discuss something with you if you have the time."

"You're in luck. My next appointment isn't for twenty minutes."

She led the way to a small, crowded room and offered Olivia a seat.

"First of all," Mrs. Linder said as she sat down, "I want to compliment you on the work you and Mrs. Bennington are doing. I've always hoped that a maternity home of your caliber would open in the city." Her face softened. "I only wish you'd had the opportunity to stay at such a place yourself."

Olivia drew in a breath, making a note to ask Mrs. Linder if she would consider speaking on their behalf at the city council meeting. But not today. Today she had only one focus. "Thank you. However, it was my experience at the reformatory that led to us opening Bennington Place, so at least some good has come from it. Which brings me to the reason I'm here."

"I assume this has something to do with one of your residents?" The woman smiled and folded her hands on the desktop.

"Actually, no." Olivia lifted her chin, grasping her handbag in a death grip. "I need to know what became of my son after he was taken from me."

Mrs. Linder winced, then quickly schooled her features. "I'm sorry. I wish I could—"

"I realize adoption records are private," Olivia cut in. "I only want to know whether Matteo is still in the system or if he's been placed with a good family." Tears pushed at the corners of her eyes. "Maybe then I can put the matter to rest once and for all." She fumbled in her bag for a handkerchief. She'd promised herself she wouldn't break down in front of the woman, but that was proving far more difficult than she'd anticipated.

Mrs. Linder gazed at her with compassion. "I do regret how events transpired with your son, Miss Rosetti. And off the record, I do not condone the way Mercer Reformatory treats the women in their care." She hesitated, then sighed. "Let me see if I can at least find out whether your son has been adopted."

Olivia sagged with relief. "Thank you."

"What was the date of your son's birth?"

"June sixth, 1940."

"Give me a moment to check with one of the clerks." She rose and left the room.

Olivia closed her eyes and focused on regulating her breathing. Mrs. Linder had reacted better than she'd dared hope. Perhaps she really did regret the manner in which she'd had to take Matteo from her.

Too restless to remain seated, Olivia got up to walk around the cramped area. For such an important organization, they sure seemed to lack space. A calendar and a round clock were the only adornments on the walls, except for a framed certificate citing Mrs. Linder's academic achievements.

Finally, the woman returned, a frown creasing her brow. She sat down and placed a manila folder on the desk. "I need to ask you a question, Miss Rosetti, and I'd like an honest answer."

Olivia's heart thumped hard. Mrs. Linder seemed annoyed.

What could have happened to change her demeanor? "Of course. What is it?"

"Did you recently send someone—a relative, it seems—to inquire about your son on your behalf?"

The hairs on Olivia's neck rose. "No, I didn't. Why?"

"Last week, a priest from St. Michael's came in to inquire about him. Even though he was a clergyman and claimed to be a relative, Martha refused to give him any information."

Olivia's hand flew to the collar of her blouse. "That must have been my brother. But why would he do that without telling me?"

"Perhaps he knew the odds weren't good and didn't want to get your hopes up."

Olivia's eyes blurred with fresh tears. Dear Sal. It would be just like him to want to do this for her.

"Well, he didn't get far, which is a good testament to Martha's dedication to our clients' privacy." Mrs. Linder paused, still frowning slightly. "Technically speaking, I am bending the rules here. I hope I can count on your discretion."

Olivia dashed the moisture from her eyes. "Certainly. We value your role at Bennington Place too much to jeopardize our relationship."

"All right then." The woman opened the folder, pulled on a pair of eyeglasses, and scanned the paperwork inside. "It looks like your son stayed at the Infants' Home for about a week before being placed with a foster family, a nice Italian couple, who intend to adopt him."

"Intend to? You mean he's not adopted yet?" A bud of hope came alive in Olivia's chest, quickening her pulse.

"Not yet. But only because there's a two-year mandatory waiting period before the adoption can be finalized. The family has had him for over a year now and is raising him as their son. The official document is really just a formality."

Olivia's throat tightened. She pressed her fingers to her trembling lips. "So there's no hope that I could ever . . ." She swallowed. "Even if I were to marry?"

Mrs. Linder's eyes filled with sympathy. "I'm sorry, but I really don't see that happening. Besides, you have to consider what's best for the child. These are the only parents he's known. To rip him away after this long would be cruel."

"But I'm his mother." Olivia twisted the handkerchief between her fingers, not caring that she sounded like a petulant child. "Doesn't that count for anything?"

"Legally, I'm afraid not." The woman patted Olivia's arm. "This couple passed the rigorous approval process with flying colors and are very grateful to have him." Mrs. Linder closed the folder. "All our follow-up visits have been excellent as well. I hope knowing that your son is healthy and has a loving home will go a long way toward easing your mind." She gave a soft smile and stood, signaling the meeting was at an end.

Olivia blew her nose and rose with as much dignity as she could muster. "Thank you. It does help to know that." She hesitated at the door, still unable to concede defeat. "If anything changes with my son, would you let me know and possibly give me a chance to get him back?"

Mrs. Linder shook her head sadly. "I don't think that's wise. I can almost guarantee the family won't change their mind."

The last thread of hope stretched and broke. Olivia's shoulders sagged under the weight of knowing that she had truly lost her son and there was nothing she could do about it.

Unable to say another word, she simply nodded and made her escape before her tears could fall in earnest.

42

"Y ou look like a worn-out dollar bill." Mr. Walcott stood in the open doorway of Darius's office, his arms crossed.

"Didn't get much sleep last night," Darius muttered.

"Me neither." He entered the office and perched on the edge of Darius's desk. "I know you're officially off the Bennington case, but I assume you've heard about the city council meeting scheduled for the sixteenth of this month? The neighbors will be presenting their petition to have the home closed."

Knots tightened in Darius's neck. "I just heard they'd set the date." He rubbed the back of his neck, trying to loosen the tension. He'd already had disappointing news this morning. Salvatore had called earlier to tell him that his visit to the Children's Aid Society had been unsuccessful. He wasn't able to get any information on either Matteo or Abigail, effectively destroying Darius's hope to give Olivia good news.

"Caldwell is out sick," Walcott continued. "And the other staff members are tied up on important projects. You're the only one who seems to be at loose ends."

Darius couldn't deny the statement. With the loss of the Peterson contract and Mr. Cheeseman still in mourning, Darius's major accounts were presently inactive. Sure, he'd been doing the basics—collecting the rents, arranging for repairs that were needed, and finding new tenants for any vacant building space. But over the past weeks, he'd lost his initiative to drum up new business. In short, he wasn't doing much except the bare minimum to earn his paycheck these days.

Walcott leaned toward him. "I want you to round up more people who oppose the home and who'd be willing to testify at that meeting. Preferably local businessmen since their word will carry more weight."

Was he serious? Darius had been very clear about not wanting to take action against the maternity home. Yet could he refuse a direct order? His gut clenched as the answer became clear.

Darius pushed up from the desk. "I'm afraid I can't do that."

"Why not? There's nothing intrinsically immoral about canvassing support."

Darius walked to the window and stared out. "I happen to think Bennington Place is an excellent facility. And I also know how much that house means to Ruth Bennington. I'm not going to help anyone take it away from her."

At the unnerving silence behind him, Darius turned to face his boss.

"It's that pretty partner of hers, isn't it?" Walcott sneered. "I saw you talking to her at the fundraiser, and if memory serves, it was because of her that you burned our bridges with Elliott Peterson." He stood up, his eyes narrowing. "I can't believe you'd risk your career over a skirt."

"My feelings for Miss Rosetti are irrelevant. I've made my position clear. I don't feel right about trying to manipulate a widow out of her home."

Walcott's mouth twisted into a grim line. "If you refuse to do this, then you leave me no choice but to terminate your position."

Darius stared at the man he'd once considered a mentor. "That's all our association means to you? One disagreement and I'm out?" A twist of disappointment tightened his chest. He'd thought their relationship stronger than that. One based on trust and mutual respect.

Apparently he was wrong.

"It's more than a simple disagreement, Darius. I thought you were a team player, someone I could count on to get the deals done. But if you're going to always let ethics get in the way, you're in the wrong business, my friend." He pointed a finger at him. "Think long and hard about this. You have until tomorrow to start canvassing those neighbors."

Darius let the waves of hurt and anger roll over him. He'd expected this confrontation would happen at some point, but it still irked him that Mr. Walcott couldn't see past his own greed to recognize the inappropriateness of his actions. "I don't need more time to think about it," he said. "Consider this my official resignation. I'll have a letter on your desk first thing tomorrow."

Walcott blinked, then his expression turned thunderous. "I never took you for a fool, Reed. Seems I was wrong about you after all." Then he strode out of the office and slammed the door so hard that the frosted glass rattled.

On a loud exhale, Darius sat down and dropped his head into his hands. Had he just thrown away his whole future? He had Sofia and his parents to think about. And without a stable source of income, he'd have nothing to offer Olivia. No way of passing the requirements to adopt Abigail, if that ever became a possibility.

I need your help, Lord. I've made a mess of everything. Please show me a way to make things right.

Walking into St. James Park, Olivia marveled at the hidden beauty tucked away in this corner of the city. A sea of multi-colored flowers flanked the walkways that led to a central stone fountain and a gazebo in the distance. Huge trees that were just beginning to change color provided shade for multiple seating areas. Olivia scanned the park for her brother. More than likely she'd beat him here since she was early for their meeting.

She found an empty bench and sat gingerly on the edge, her purse on her lap. She'd donned her best dress and hat, wanting to make sure she looked respectable when in a priest's company. She'd thought it better to meet out in the open, rather than in a restaurant or at the rectory, where her presence might cause too many questions.

The autumn sun warmed her shoulders as she waited, yet it did nothing to settle her nerves at having to confront Sal. He'd seemed puzzled when she asked him to meet her here, but she'd explained that she had something she wanted to discuss face-to-face.

"Livvy." Sal's booming voice reached her before she saw him approaching.

"Hello, Sal." She hesitated, not sure of the protocol of greeting a priest who happened to be her sibling.

But he lifted her into a warm hug, easing her nerves. "It's good to see you. You look lovely."

"Thank you."

He wasn't wearing his clerical collar today, which made their meeting less conspicuous, allowing her to relax.

"So, what's on your mind?" Sal asked. "Is this about your visit to the store? Mamma told me how Mrs. Ceruti caused a scene."

Olivia squared her shoulders. "No. It's about *your* visit to the Children's Aid office."

A pained expression crossed his face, and he regarded her with guilt-ridden eyes. "How did you find out about that?"

"One of the caseworkers told me when I went to try and find out some information about Matteo. Apparently we had the same idea." She tilted her head. "But why would you go without telling me?"

A beat of silence followed. "It wasn't my idea," he said at last. Two lines formed between his brows. "Darius Reed came to see me. He asked me to make the inquiry, thinking I'd have a better chance at getting an answer. He wanted you to have peace of mind about your son's well-being."

Her heart kick-started at the mere mention of Darius's name. *He* was behind this? After everything she'd done to push him away, he was still trying to help?

"It was a waste of time, though," Sal said. "The lady wouldn't tell me anything. I'm sorry."

She nodded. "I know."

"How about you? Did you have any luck?"

Olivia hesitated, remembering Mrs. Linder's words about keeping the matter confidential. "Only that Matteo's with a good family. They couldn't tell me much more than that."

They sat in silence for several moments, watching people pass by on the sidewalk.

"Did it help, Liv?" he finally asked.

She took in a breath and slowly released it. "It still hurts a lot. I doubt that will ever change. But knowing he's in a loving home is some consolation, at least."

He laid a hand on her arm. "I'm glad. And I hope you're not angry with me."

"No. You were only trying to help." She frowned. "I just can't understand why Darius did this."

Sal's lips twitched into a smile. "I think it's pretty obvious. The man's in love with you."

Heat scorched Olivia's cheeks, and she swallowed against the sudden rush of emotion. How could he still love her after everything he knew about her?

"He seems like a decent guy, Liv. Is there some reason you won't marry him?"

She stared at him. "He told you he wanted to marry me?"

"He did. He also said you didn't believe you deserved to be loved."

A shaft of pain spiked through her chest, radiating down to her toes. She bit her lip and stared out at the happy people coming and going through the park. "It's not about me," she finally said. "Darius deserves someone better. I'd only bring shame to his family."

Sal remained silent for several minutes. "Do you remember one of Mamma's favorite verses? 'As far as the east is from the west, so far has he removed our transgressions from us.' God wouldn't want you to remain a prisoner of your shame, Olivia. You are His beloved child, forgiven and redeemed. Be brave enough to claim the happiness He has in store for you."

Her throat tightened as Sal's words found their mark. He made it sound so easy. "Do you really think I'm worthy of Darius and his daughter?"

"Of course I do. But what really matters is how Darius feels." His voice gentled. "If he knows everything about you and loves you anyway, isn't that your answer?"

Tears burned her eyes. It was true. Darius knew all her short-comings, every one of her flaws, and despite the seemingly insur-mountable obstacles to their relationship, he still held out hope. He'd even tried to find Matteo for her when he had nothing to gain by it. His love was evident in his words and deeds, but could she really accept it? Was that what God wanted her to do?

She drew in a ragged breath. "Thank you, Sal. Your support means a lot to me."

"That's what big brothers are for." He pulled her into a hug. "And don't worry about Mamma and Papà. They'll come around eventually."

She heaved a great sigh. "From your lips to God's ears."

With a somewhat lighter heart, she bid her brother good-bye and began the walk home. Sal had given her a lot to think about. Could she really cast off her mantle of shame and accept that she was worthy of love? If she believed the residents of Bennington Place deserved happiness, couldn't she allow herself the same grace?

Perhaps once the council meeting was over and the fate of Bennington Place had been decided, she could figure out whether she was truly brave enough to take her brother's advice and face Darius again.

43

On the morning of September sixteenth, Olivia held Ruth's arm as they climbed the stairs to city hall. Nerves rioted through Olivia's stomach, and she prayed she could hold on to her composure during her planned speech. Only the assurance that God was with her gave her the courage to do this at all.

They entered the building and followed the signs that led to the council chambers. Olivia tried not to let the official atmosphere overwhelm her as she stepped inside the impressive assembly room. A raised platform dominated the front area with three throne-like seats. Below the platform were tables and chairs, presumably for the council members. The rest of the room was filled with public seating, along with an upper viewing gallery overhead. Many people had already filled the room, a fact that made butterflies take flight in Olivia's stomach.

Sensing her trepidation, Ruth patted her arm. "Don't let any of this worry you, my dear. Remember, we have God's army on our side."

"I'm trying my best." Olivia managed a weak smile, if only to reassure her friend.

They found seats close to the wooden railing that separated the council area from the public and sat down. Olivia scanned the room, hoping to catch sight of any friendly faces. Cherise and Patricia hadn't been ready to come with them but had promised they would arrive in time to give their statements.

From across the aisle, Margaret waved at them. Olivia smiled and waved back, one layer of tension receding. At least someone other than Ruth would clap after she spoke.

On the far side of the room, Mr. Simmons stood in conversation with several men in suits, likely the business owners from their neighborhood. Ruth's lawyer had explained that when the time came, Mr. Simmons would speak first, then others would be allowed to present opposing opinions.

Olivia turned in her seat, discreetly searching the far corners of the room. Would Darius or his boss be here? It would make sense that Mr. Walcott would wish to attend, if only to learn the fate of the maternity home firsthand. She'd thought Darius might as well. Yet there was no sign of the handsome face that haunted her dreams. She released a soft breath, disappointment leaking from her pores. Perhaps it was just as well. She would need a clear head with no unnecessary distractions while giving her short speech.

Soon the room was called to order as Mayor Conboy and the council members filed in to take their seats.

Olivia found it hard to concentrate on the initial portion of the meeting as it droned on in formal language, but she perked up immediately when the floor opened to concerns from the public. Mr. Simmons came forward to present his signed petition of five hundred and sixty-two signatures and gave a heated speech about the undesirable facility that had opened across the street from him. After he finished, he invited several local businessmen to speak.

"This maternity home is a disgrace." Mr. Weiss, a butcher, peered over his glasses at the councilors. "How can I expect to keep my customers with those type of women invading our neighborhood?"

A parade of other businessmen followed, each pronouncing their distaste for Bennington Place and how it was bringing down their property value. Then a few women got up to speak, citing the danger to their children.

"Why, just a few weeks ago," one lady said, "a drunken man almost ran my baby carriage down before he crashed into a lamp-post. Turns out he was related to one of the women in the maternity home. We can't have derelicts ruining our neighborhood."

Olivia cringed but did her best to block out their negative words and focus on her own speech.

Finally, the chairman asked for anyone who wished to speak in favor of the maternity home. Ruth squeezed Olivia's hand and rose. The impressive woman held her head high as she crossed to a microphone stand.

"Good morning, Your Worship, esteemed council members. My name is Ruth Bennington, and I am a co-founder of the Bennington Place Maternity Home. We are a small private facility that can house up to twelve women and infants. We employ a doctor from Toronto General Hospital and an accredited midwife to attend to our residents. For the most part, we exist quietly and peacefully. Other than the unfortunate car accident, the only interruption to our community was a recent riot incited by an inflammatory newspaper article. These rabble-rousers, led by our neighbor Mr. Simmons, not only caused damage to my property but injured my partner, Miss Rosetti, which resulted in seventeen stitches to her head."

A murmur went through the crowd behind them. Olivia couldn't tell whether the tone was sympathetic or not.

Ruth cleared her throat. "Some of you may wonder why a woman of my years would decide to open a maternity home."

Olivia's muscles tightened as she moved to the edge of her chair. Ruth was about to take a huge risk, putting her good name and reputation on the line. How would these people handle her confession?

"Fifty-four years ago," Ruth said slowly, "I was pregnant and unmarried. With no resources at my disposal, I was shipped off to a distant relative, where I gave birth to a daughter whom I gave up for adoption. Yet I was one of the lucky ones who managed to go on and make an excellent life for myself, mostly due to my dear late husband, Henry." She paused. "When I met Miss Rosetti last spring, she shared her own story with me and spoke of her desire to open a maternity home. It struck a chord deep inside me, and I knew this was the path God wanted me to follow." Ruth glanced over at Olivia. "At this time, I invite Miss Rosetti to come forward and give her own testimony."

Quiet shrouded the council chambers as Olivia rose on unsteady legs to approach the microphone. Her palms were clammy, and perspiration dampened her dress. When she unfolded the piece of paper containing the words she had written, her hands shook hard enough to rattle the sheet.

Dear Lord, give me the courage to see this through.

"Thank you, Ruth," she said. "My name is Olivia Rosetti, and I am the other co-founder of Bennington Place." She stared straight ahead at the wall above the mayor's chair. If she made eye contact with anyone, she might lose her nerve. "This maternity home came into existence as a result of a deeply personal experience. Not long ago, I found myself in trouble with nowhere to turn. My fiancé had already left to join the war when I found out I was expecting." She swallowed. "Upon learning of my condition, my father disowned me and had me sent to the Mercer Reformatory for Women, a place where unspeakable atrocities occur every day. Where women are treated worse than laboratory rats." She wet her dry lips, her hands shaking even harder. "After giving birth, I got to hold my son for only a few minutes before he was taken from me and put up for adoption against my wishes—a fact that haunts me to this day. A mother should have some say about what happens to her child, shouldn't she?" She blinked hard to keep tears from forming. She would not break down in front of these men. Instead, she forced herself to make eye contact with the council members, one by one. "Unwed mothers are not criminals. We are people who have made an unfortunate mistake, but we still deserve compassion and the right to make good decisions for our futures."

Some of the councilors were nodding their heads, while others stared at the tabletop, not looking at her. Olivia heard a few sniffles behind her and someone blowing their nose.

She looked down at her notes and forged on. "My ordeal is what led me to envision a residence such as Bennington Place. We provide shelter for women in crisis, without judgment or condemnation. We help them with their pregnancies and provide options for their futures. All we want is the right to remain open and to be of service to those in need, as God has mandated. I hope you'll allow us to continue our work. Thank you very much for your time."

A weak smattering of applause broke out as Olivia stepped away from the microphone, her heart still thundering in her ears. With a hand to her stomach, she sank back onto her chair.

"Marvelous job." Ruth patted her knee.

Judging from the lack of enthusiasm, Olivia wasn't at all sure. When the buzzing in her brain eased, she focused back on the proceedings. Margaret had come forward and was praising Bennington Place for everything it had done for her and little Calvin. Then Cherise and Patricia each gave a brief account of their experience at the home. As per Ruth's advice, Cherise wisely avoided any mention of her former profession, since it certainly would not aid their cause.

Dr. Henshaw and Mrs. Dinglemire both came forward as well to offer their expert testimony on the value of Bennington Place in the community.

As each person spoke, Olivia studied the eighteen council members. A few of the men nodded and wore sympathetic expressions, while the majority stared with stone-faced countenances. Her stomach twisted. This did not look good at all.

Olivia wished that Mrs. Linder could have been here, since her testimony might have held more weight. But the woman's busy schedule hadn't allowed it.

"Any additional speakers?" the chairman asked after the women had finished.

Olivia glanced nervously over her shoulder. Would any of the other residents come forward?

"Yes, sir. I'd like to say a few words."

Olivia's mouth fell open, her heart jumping into her throat. Tingles shot up her spine at the sight of Darius striding to the front of the room, her brother Sal right behind him.

What on earth were they doing here together?

Darius adjusted his tie as he approached the microphone and cleared his throat. From the corner of his eye, he was aware of Olivia's shocked reaction, but he couldn't dwell on that now.

Judging from the council members' weak response to the women's speeches, he needed to make this the best pitch of his life. One that would sway more than half of the men seated before him to vote against Mr. Simmons's petition.

"Good morning, gentlemen. My name is Darius Reed. Up until recently, I worked for Walcott Industries, a property management firm in the city. I was tasked by my boss to acquire the Bennington property, which meant I found myself inside the maternity home on several occasions. At first, I believed the facility was not only unnecessary, but if it did exist, it should be located on the outskirts of town, away from respectable society."

Murmurs of agreement rose from the audience.

"However, I soon learned how wrong I was. Bennington Place is exactly where it should be, where the people who need help can find it. I happened to be there on the day that a severely battered woman arrived at their doorstep. It was a wonder she made it there at all, but she certainly wouldn't have if the home hadn't been accessible. Sadly, after giving birth, the woman passed away. Yet, if it hadn't been for the quick work of the Bennington Place staff, the baby wouldn't have survived either."

Darius cleared his throat, wishing he could see Olivia's face. Were his words having any effect? The flinty stares of the council members gave him little indication.

"As for the residents of the home," he continued, "they are a true community who work together to help one another, whether it's making clothes, knitting blankets, or caring for the newborns. There is nothing untoward or undesirable about anyone at Bennington Place. As Miss Rosetti stated, they are doing God's work, and I, for one, believe they should be allowed to continue their admirable mission. Thank you."

As Darius turned away from the stand, he glanced over to where Ruth and Olivia were seated.

Olivia held a handkerchief to her cheek. "Thank you," she mouthed with a trembling smile.

He nodded and let out his breath. Had his words hit their mark? He wasn't sure, but it was the best he could do to show Olivia his support. Whether it would make any difference to the council's decision—or to Olivia herself—he had no idea. All he knew was that he had to follow his heart and give credit where credit was due.

Darius took a seat as Sal stepped forward.

"Good morning. I am Reverend Salvatore Rosetti, priest at St. Michael's Cathedral and brother of Olivia Rosetti, whom you've already met." Sal looked at each of the men in front of him in turn. "Please do not negate the testimony I am about to give solely based on my relationship to the home's co-founder. My first and foremost priority is always to God, and the second is to my parishioners and the surrounding community. That is the main reason I come before you today.

"I believe that our city can only benefit from the presence of Bennington Place in our neighborhood. By providing refuge for those in crisis, we are fulfilling our mandate as Christians to help the less fortunate and to act out of love and compassion, not fear or hatred. The founders of Bennington Place are doing just that. Instead of condemning women for their mistakes, they are offering them a hand up, giving the innocent children the best start in life, despite their unfortunate circumstances." He paused, letting his words resonate like a Sunday sermon. "Two of the most powerful mandates Jesus gave us are 'Judge not, that ye not be judged,' and 'Do to others as you would have them do to you.' These are not mere platitudes. These are the cornerstones of our faith, the very foundation of what we are called to do as Christians. This is what my sister and Mrs. Bennington are doing— serving others in their community as Jesus decrees. I challenge all of you here today to do the same."

This time the audience responded with enthusiastic applause. Several people even stood to shake Sal's hand when he passed by.

Darius leaned back in his seat and allowed his muscles to relax. He only prayed that everyone's combined testimonies would be enough to convince the mayor and the council members to allow the maternity home to remain open.

Then, perhaps in some small way, he'd have helped one of Olivia's dreams to come true.

44

O livia had been prepared for the council to defer their decision to a later date, as was their prerogative, so she was both relieved and terrified when they indicated they would vote on the matter today. The members asked for a brief recess to discuss the issue before rendering their decision.

As soon as the council members filed out of the room, Olivia rose and followed the spectators who'd chosen to stretch their legs or go out for a cigarette. Her emotions were still reeling from Darius's and Sal's speeches, and she needed to thank them both for their support.

No matter the outcome, she would be forever grateful for their generosity.

Out in the crowded corridor, her brother's head was visible above the fray, and she immediately went to greet him. "Sal, thank you for speaking on our behalf," she said. "It was so thoughtful of you."

"My pleasure, Liv." He gave her a quick hug. "When Darius suggested it, I knew it was the right thing to do." He smiled down at her. "I'm sorry I can't stay to hear the verdict, but I have to get back to work."

"That's all right. Thanks again for coming. I know your testimony made a big difference." She darted glances around the hallway but couldn't see Darius anywhere. "Do you know where Darius went?"

"He said he needed some air. Why don't you walk me out?"

"Good idea." She looped her arm through her brother's and followed him out the front entrance on slightly shaky legs. The mere thought of seeing Darius again had her heart thudding loudly in her chest.

After Sal wished her good luck and set off toward the cathedral, Olivia stood on the city hall steps and nervously scanned the sidewalk below. Darius was nowhere in sight. A crush of disappointment swept over her. Would he have left before the decision was rendered? Or was he avoiding her? After all the turmoil she'd put him through, she couldn't really blame him.

"Hello, Olivia."

Her heart stuttered at the familiar voice behind her. She slowly turned to find Darius on the steps above her. It had been three weeks or more since she'd last seen him, and she drank in the welcome sight of him, so distinguished in his navy suit, his dark hair blowing around his forehead. When she met his gaze, those unforgettable blue eyes seemed to swallow her whole.

"Darius." Her voice sounded breathless. "I was looking for you."

"I needed some air. And a minute alone to pray." He came down to her level, an unreadable expression shadowing his features.

"Thank you for being here," she said, "and for speaking on our behalf. It was . . . good of you to come." How lame could she sound? She twisted her damp hands together, every thought seeming to drift from her mind like the leaves blowing about the sidewalk below.

"I'm glad I could do something, though I'm not sure it helped much."

"I think it helped a lot." She paused, sifting through her jumbled thoughts. "But did I hear you right? Did you say you no longer work for Walcott Industries?" It couldn't be true. Darius loved his property management job with his office that overlooked downtown.

He lifted one shoulder. "I handed in my resignation about a week ago."

"Not because of me, I hope?"

"Not directly." He squinted against the glare of the sun. "I just couldn't keep working for a company that had no moral compass to guide it."

Olivia's stomach swooped. It *had* been because of her. "I . . . I don't know what to say. I feel terrible."

"It's for the best, really. You and Ruth helped me see that Walcott Industries wasn't a good fit for me." A gust of wind ruffled his hair. "I'll find work somewhere else. This time I hope to follow your example and put my skills to use in helping others in whatever way God chooses."

She shook her head as a slow smile bloomed. "You might be the best man I know, Darius Reed. Well, maybe second to Sal."

He laughed out loud. "I suppose I can't top a priest."

With the crowds still filing past them, he guided her to a less busy area.

"Speaking of Sal . . ." She narrowed her eyes. "I know what you put him up to with the Children's Aid."

He stiffened, his grin fading. "Olivia, I never meant . . . that is . . . I hope you're not angry. I only wanted to bring you some peace of mind."

"I'm not angry." She softened her gaze. "It was kind of you to try."

The lines across his brow eased. "I hoped Sal might have some success, but they wouldn't tell him anything."

"I know. I went to the office myself a week later, and that's how I found out Sal had been there." She smiled. "I didn't have much better luck, except I did learn that Matteo has been placed with a good family."

He let out a breath, tension seeming to leak from his frame. "That's good. I hope it's some consolation at least."

"It is." She bit her lip, hating the stiltedness between them. There was so much she wanted to say, but now wasn't the time or place for such an important conversation.

He stepped closer and laid a warm hand on her arm. "Olivia, I want you to know . . ." He swallowed and hesitated, his Adam's apple bobbing.

The breath stalled in her lungs. His serious expression made her heart squeeze in sudden terror. Was he about to tell her good-bye? After today, they really had no further reason to stay in contact.

The people on the steps began to shuffle toward the door. "Council's back," someone called.

She couldn't let him go. Not yet. She gripped his arm. "I have some things I need to tell you. Could we talk after the meeting is over?"

He gave her a long look and nodded. "I'll look for you afterward. Good luck, Olivia. I'm praying they decide in your favor."

"Thank you. Though I guess it's up to God now." She gave him a tense smile, and as they headed back inside to learn the home's fate, she didn't know what she dreaded more—the council's verdict or figuring out what to say to Darius afterward.

Fresh nerves rioted through Olivia's system as she resumed her seat. When one of the council members, a Mr. Nathan Phillips, rose to declare the decision, she gripped Ruth's hand tightly in hers.

This was it. The make-or-break of their home. If the vote was no, Ruth would do her best to find a new location, Olivia was certain. The fact that she had a real estate agent already scouting potential rentals gave credence to that reality. But the atmosphere of Bennington Place, the everyday fundamentals, would never be the same again. Olivia breathed a silent prayer that she could accept God's will for whatever the future held for them.

Mr. Phillips unfolded a piece of paper and cleared his throat. "The council members have reached a decision. By a vote of ten to eight in favor of the maternity home, Bennington Place will be allowed to continue its operations."

Olivia's hand flew to her mouth. Instant tears sprang to her eyes.

A burst of outrage sounded from the other side of the room, overpowering the few gasps of pleasure.

"Thank you, Mr. Simmons," Alderman Phillips continued, "for bringing your concerns before this council, but we now charge that all opposition to this facility must cease. In the event that any new circumstances arise, you are, of course, free to bring it to the council's attention. Although I caution you that the members will not tolerate your wasting our time on trivialities."

The speaker of the house rose. "I now pronounce the current session of the Toronto City Council to be adjourned."

Ruth gave a cry of elation and leaned over to clasp Olivia in a tight hug. "We did it, my dear. We won."

"I can hardly believe it." Olivia squeezed her back. Her head spun with the sudden release of tension. "I feel like I can finally breathe again."

"You and me both." Ruth laughed out loud, the lines of worry vanishing from her face. "I believe this calls for a celebration. Why don't we get the other girls and go out for a treat? I'd say we've earned it."

Olivia hesitated. "That sounds wonderful, but I need to speak to Darius first. Could I meet you somewhere?"

Ruth got to her feet. "Oh, by all means. That man deserves a huge thank-you, as does your brother. I believe their testimonies went a long way toward swaying the officials." She turned toward the aisle. "We'll be at Marty's Diner if you care to join us. But if not, I'll see you at home." She gave Olivia a bold wink, then moved off.

As the people filed out, Olivia attempted to gain control of her emotions at the thought of the upcoming conversation. "Am I doing the right thing, Lord?" she whispered.

She took in a few deep breaths, allowing Sal's words to repeat in her head. *"God wouldn't want you to remain a prisoner of your shame, Olivia. Be brave enough to claim the happiness He has in store for you."*

A sense of peace washed over her, and with it, her resolution firmed. She would speak the truth, no matter the outcome. That way, nothing would be left unsaid between them.

A few minutes later, Olivia found Darius waiting for her in the corridor. Her heart fluttered in her throat as their eyes met. He looked so strong and protective. Her own personal guardian angel.

The moment she stepped in front of him, he gathered her into a hug.

"Congratulations, Olivia. I'm so happy for you and Ruth."

She drank in his warmth and his familiar clean scent. "Thank you. I still can't quite believe it."

He moved back and frowned at the crowds chattering excitedly around them. "How about we find somewhere a little quieter to talk?"

"I'd like that," she said. "Do you have anywhere in mind?"

"There's a spot not far away that should do." He took her by the hand and led her past the marble columns, out the main entrance, and down the steps. Then he continued along the sidewalk.

Walking quickly, Olivia did her best to calm the nerves jumping in her stomach.

He turned the corner and veered over to a patch of grass, where a lovely crabapple tree created a secluded area. They stepped beneath its welcoming canopy of branches and the rest of the world simply fell away.

Darius leaned his back against the tree trunk and gazed down at her. "I'm so proud of you, Olivia. It took a lot of courage to tell your story in front of all those people."

Pleasure curled through her chest at the admiration in his

gaze. "It was one of the scariest things I've ever done. But it was worth it."

"Yes, it was." He smiled at her, tiny lines creasing his mouth. "So, Miss Rosetti, what is it you wished to talk to me about?"

Now that the moment was here, Olivia's mouth went dry. How did she begin to reveal everything in her heart? Would he welcome her words, or had he become used to life without her? "First, I want to thank you again for coming today. I never imagined you would speak on our behalf."

Darius laughed. "I never imagined that myself."

She hesitated, closing her eyes as a wave of uncertainty crashed over her. Was she really going to bare her soul here on the city hall's side lawn?

"Is there something else?" Darius's gentle prompt made her eyes open.

His tender expression as he searched her face brought a lump to her throat, giving her the reassurance she needed.

"Yes, there is." *Be brave, Olivia. You can do this.* "I've done a lot of soul searching since Sofia's birthday, and something my brother said the other day made me come to a realization." She squared her shoulders, the soles of her shoes shifting on the grass. "He told me that God wouldn't want me to live in shame, and that I should be brave enough to claim the happiness He has in store for me." She paused, the slight fluttering of the leaves overhead seeming to whisper encouragement.

"He's right." Darius placed a finger under her chin and gently brought her gaze to meet his. "You deserve the best in life, Olivia. And I'd do anything in my power to give it to you—if you'd only let me."

She stared into his eyes, so earnest and kind, and swallowed against the rise of tears. "Then I don't suppose you'd reconsider my earlier proposition?" The breeze blew several strands of hair across her face.

"What proposition is that?"

She placed a hand on his sleeve, needing the physical connection between them. "The personal merger I mentioned once before in your office."

Darius's eyes widened. "Olivia Rosetti, are you asking me to marry you?"

She bit her trembling lip and nodded.

Darius's heart jackhammered against his ribs as he stared into Olivia's beautiful face, the face he'd missed more than his next breath. A river of joy spread through him, but he took a moment to hold himself in check. Although he longed to simply blurt out his answer, he owed it to them both to be practical. He needed to take into account the fact that his circumstances had changed and he had no way to provide for her at present. "Before I give you my answer," he said, "there's something I need to tell you."

A flicker of uncertainty bloomed in her eyes. "What is it?"

"Now that I'm unemployed, I've been considering a pretty drastic career change." He pushed away from the tree and took one of her hands in his. "I want to do something to serve my community. Perhaps even help prevent the type of violence and hatred that killed Selene." He paused. "I'm thinking of becoming a police officer. So I need to know if you'd be willing to be a policeman's wife." He held his breath, searching her face. His own mother hadn't taken the news well, making it clear she was not in favor of his decision. Would Olivia feel the same?

Olivia frowned, shadows hugging her features. "I think you've got it wrong," she said slowly. "Would they accept *you* if I was your wife? A woman with a questionable past who's been incarcerated?"

"I hadn't thought of that." He had no idea if that would prevent his acceptance onto the force, but if it did, he had other options in mind. "If not, I could always apply to the fire department instead."

Her lips twitched. "You have it all worked out, I see."

"I do. Either way, I'd be using my life to help others, which is all that matters." An insect flew by his ear, its buzzing matching the hum of nerves inside him as he awaited her answer.

"Both are admirable careers," she said carefully. "And although the thought of you being in danger makes me nervous, I think you would make a fine policeman or fireman." Then her brow furrowed. "What about Sofia, though? Are you sure my background wouldn't be a detriment to her?"

He held her gaze. Never again would he let her feel unworthy. He tightened his grip on her fingers. "Olivia, you are the kindest, bravest, most loyal person I've ever met. Sofia would be lucky to have you in her life."

Moisture welled in her luminous brown eyes. "Really?"

"Really." He brought one hand up to caress her cheek. "I love you very much. I have for quite some time now. Would you do me the great honor of becoming my wife and Sofia's stepmother?"

Tears spilled down her cheeks as she held his gaze. "I love you too, Darius. You have no idea how much. And I promise to be the best wife and mother I can be."

Relief flowed through him like quicksilver. How often had he dreamed of this moment, fearing it might never happen? Yet now by the grace of God, she was finally ready to accept his love. With one hand cupping her face, he lowered his head to kiss her. Her lips were soft and pliant under his. When she reached up to entwine her arms around his neck, heat spread through his system, and his heart seemed to explode in his chest. He wrapped his arms more firmly around her until he felt the answering beat of her heart against his.

Gratitude rose up within him on a prayer. *Thank you, Lord. I promise to take care of her heart every day from now on, for as long as she'll let me.*

On a rush of joy, Olivia returned Darius's embrace, relishing the feel of his solid frame against hers, breathing in the familiar scent of his aftershave. In his arms, she found a place of belonging that she'd never experienced before. She wanted nothing more than to stay there forever. When his lips left hers to trail down her jaw, electricity zinged through her system. She still couldn't believe this wonderful man loved her—despite all her flaws, her tainted past, and her compromised reputation. What had she ever done to deserve someone so compassionate and kind? So loyal and protective?

With a contented sigh, she pulled back to look into his eyes. "You're sure you don't mind having a wife who works at a maternity home?"

His blue eyes darkened. "I know how important Bennington Place is to you. I'd never ask you to give that up. With my mother to help look after Sofia, it shouldn't be a problem."

At the mention of his mother, a niggle of fear surfaced as she recalled the other reason she hadn't felt worthy to be Darius's wife. "What about the fact that I may not be able to have more children?" She searched his eyes, dreading to see regret blooming there. What if he realized he'd made a mistake?

Darius held her face in his hands, his gaze steady. "Every couple that gets married has no idea whether they'll be able to have children or not. But they marry in faith, trusting God's plan for their life. And that's what we will do. We'll take whatever God gives us and be grateful for His gifts."

Her heart expanded with even more love than she'd thought possible. All she could do was nod through her tears as he smiled down at her.

"I did have one possible idea on that subject," he said. "I thought we could put in an application at the Children's Aid Society. If no one has claimed Abigail yet, maybe we'll get lucky enough to adopt her."

More tears bloomed. Her throat constricted, making speech

impossible, so she simply rose up and pressed her lips to his once more.

He caught her against him with a surprised laugh, then quickly claimed her mouth for a much more lingering kiss. She kissed him back greedily, as though a dam had broken inside her, and all the love she'd suppressed for so long now spilled out.

A few minutes later, he released her, his eyes brimming with happiness. "What do you say we go somewhere to celebrate this momentous occasion?"

She beamed up at him, her hands resting on his chest. "We could meet Ruth and the girls at Marty's."

"Hmm." He wrinkled his nose. "Nothing against the ladies, but I was hoping to have you all to myself for a little longer. How about sharing a sundae at the ice cream parlor?"

"That sounds perfect." She laughed, feeling so light and free that she just might float away on a wave of bliss. "And maybe while we're there, we could discuss possible wedding dates. Because I don't want to wait another minute to marry you, Darius Reed."

He picked her up and twirled her around, his laughter blending with hers. "I like the way you think, Miss Rosetti."

Epilogue

Eighteen months later

"I'll send him right in." Despite the exhaustion hugging his face, Dr. Henshaw smiled as he rolled down his shirtsleeves.

"Please do," Olivia said, "but let me break the news."

"Of course." The doctor slipped out of the bedroom door, leaving Olivia alone.

She bit her lip, barely able to contain the roller coaster of emotions racing through her system. She couldn't wait to see her husband's reaction.

Seconds later, the door opened, and Darius's anxious face appeared. "Is it all right to come in?" His hair was standing on end, as though he'd been raking his fingers through it for the last several hours.

Sitting up against the pillows, Olivia couldn't keep the tired smile from blooming. "By all means, my love. Come in . . . and meet your son." She gazed down at the warm bundle in her arms, unable to contain the joy that bubbled up through her like a fountain.

"It's a boy?" A look of awe spread over his features.

"A beautiful, healthy boy." She cradled the little miracle against her chest, utterly humbled by God's goodness.

Darius sank onto the chair beside her, not even bothering to wipe away his tears as he skimmed a finger over the baby's cheek. "I have a son." Wonder filled his words.

Olivia laughed, euphoria rushing through her. Never had she imagined she'd be able to give Darius such a gift, but God, in His perfect wisdom, had proved her wrong. She'd thought that becoming baby Abigail's foster parents a month after they were married would be their happiest moment. Little did she know that God had even bigger blessings in store for them.

Darius leaned over and kissed her soundly. "I love you so much, Olivia. You've made me the happiest man in the world."

"Nowhere near as happy as you've made me."

The baby gave a squawk and squirmed within the blanket. Olivia laughed again. "It looks like this little one won't be content to be overshadowed. He wants to be the center of attention."

"I don't blame him, since he has two older sisters to contend with." Darius grinned at her.

"Well, Mr. Reed, what are we going to call this miracle boy of ours?"

"I did have a name in mind." One brow quirked up. "I was thinking of Constantine. After my grandfather in Greece."

"Constantine. That's a noble-sounding name." She smiled. "I'm proud of you for embracing your heritage."

He shrugged. "He'll likely get a Canadian nickname, which is fine by me."

"Me too." She brushed a kiss over the wisps of her son's downy hair.

"I have another suggestion for a middle name, if you agree." A hint of a smile played through his tender expression.

"Really? What's that?"

"I was thinking of Matteo. After his older brother."

Instant tears flooded her eyes, blurring her vision.

"Since I couldn't get your son back for you," he said huskily, "I figured this was the best way to keep him as part of our family."

"Oh, Darius." She pressed a hand to her mouth. "That's the most beautiful thing you've ever said. How did I ever deserve a husband like you?"

He smiled down at her with such love that it stole her breath.

"I'm the lucky one," he said. "The day God led me to you was the day of my salvation. You woke me from the stupor I'd been living in and challenged me to become a better man. A better person." His gaze moved to the baby. "And together we're going to raise our children to live with the same type of integrity."

A loud knock sounded on the door. Sofia poked her head inside. "Grandma Ruth says to tell you that Abigail is napping now." She pushed the door open and stared. "I want to see the baby. So does Yiayiá."

Darius laughed. "Come in, Mouse. Come and meet your new brother."

Her eyes went wide as she skipped across the room. "I have a brother?"

"You do," Olivia said. "How do you feel about that?"

Sofia hopped up on Darius's knee, peered down at the tiny face, and pursed her lips. "A brother is good. We already have lots of girls. Daddy needs another boy."

Olivia laughed. "You're right. He's very outnumbered at the moment."

"Speaking of numbers, I have a surprise for both of you." Darius's blue eyes danced.

"Is it a puppy?" Sofia demanded.

Olivia almost groaned. She'd been after them for a puppy for a while now, but at least she was no longer asking for an elephant.

"No, Mouse. Remember I told you a puppy would be too much work with two babies to look after?"

"Oh. I forgot." Her face fell. "But Abigail won't be a baby for long. Can we get one then?"

Darius shook his head, barely suppressing a grin. "We'll discuss that when she's older. My surprise is that I've found us a new house. It's big enough for all of us and close to Bennington Place as well." He looked at Olivia. "If you like it, I'll put in a bid."

They'd been living in rather cramped quarters with Darius's parents, and although Olivia tried to be patient, Darius knew how much she wanted her own house. A home near Bennington Place sounded perfect. Close to Ruth, yet near enough to Darius's parents that they could visit anytime they wished. And maybe one day, if her own family came around, a place where they could all gather for the holidays.

"I'm sure it's wonderful. As soon as I'm up and about, I'll be eager to see it."

"Me too." Sofia bounced on her father's lap, her eyes bright.

Unable to stem the happy tears that welled again, Olivia reached out to touch the girl's soft curls, basking in the glow of Darius's warm regard. In the time of her darkest despair, she could never have imagined feeling so loved and protected, the way she felt every time her husband took her in his arms. With Darius, she'd found not only the security and the respectability she craved, but a true haven for her heart. She had no doubt he would cherish it always and do everything in his power to keep it safe.

She smiled into her husband's eyes. "I never believed I could be this happy. Only God could have dreamed up such blessings for me."

Darius gazed down at her. "For all of us."

Then he bent and kissed her again, proving once more that with God's help and a little courage, love would always be worth the risk.

Acknowledgments

This story was both heartbreaking and inspiring to write, and yet Olivia and Darius have become two of my favorite characters (with Sofia totally capturing my heart as well!).

As usual, many people helped bring this story to life:

Thank you to David Long and Jen Veilleux, my editors at Bethany House. Jen, your thoroughness continues to amaze me! You catch so many details, big and small, that I often overlook. And thank you to the entire team at Bethany House who work so hard to make our books shine. I especially love this cover with Olivia at the gate of the maternity home!

I'd also like to thank my agent, Natasha Kern, for all her hard work and dedication.

My sincerest gratitude goes to my amazing critique partner, Sally Bayless, who gives me such great advice and treats my stories with as much care as her own work.

And, as always, thank you to my family for their love and encouragement. Thanks to my husband, Bud, who went with me on two different research trips to Toronto for this story in order to get the feel of Greektown and Little Italy. It was fun exploring with you!

Thank you to my wonderful readers and influencers. I appreciate you all so much, especially those who take the time to let me know how my stories have impacted them. After all, that's the reason we write!

Blessings until the next time,

Susan

To learn more about my books, please check out my website at www.susanannemason.net.

Susan Anne Mason describes her writing style as "romance sprinkled with faith." She loves incorporating inspirational messages of God's unconditional love and forgiveness into her stories. *Irish Meadows*, her first historical romance, won the Fiction from the Heartland contest sponsored by the Mid-American Romance Authors chapter of RWA. Susan lives outside Toronto, Ontario, with her husband and two adult children. She loves red wine and chocolate, and is not partial to snow even though she's Canadian. Learn more about Susan and her books at www.susanannemason. net.

Sign Up for Susan's Newsletter

Keep up to date with Susan's news on book releases and events by signing up for her email list at susanannemason.net.

More from Susan Anne Mason

Determined to keep his family together, Quinten travels to Canada to find his siblings and track down his employer's niece, who ran off with a Canadian soldier. When Quinten rescues her from a bad situation, Julia is compelled to repay him by helping him find his sister—but soon after, she receives devastating news that changes everything.

The Brightest of Dreams
CANADIAN CROSSINGS #3